Stan Lee is an advertising executive and lives in New York City. *Dunn's Conundrum* is his first novel.

'I defy any reader to put it down. . . A tough, funny, quirky, bawdy, suspenseful romp'
John D. MacDonald

'Both an entertainment and a manifesto, *Dunn's Conundrum* is destined to be talked about – partly for its qualities as a thriller, mainly for the brashness with which it portrays the hawks in our midst and the peril to our lives'
Publishers Weekly

'A sly, implausible, yet oddly controlled suspense-comedy debut. . .Lee's cool, playful treatment – smart dialogue, inventively convincing technology, likeably cynical people – makes it all seem sharp and fresh, in an uneven but beguiling no man's land somewhere between *Dr Strangelove* fantasy and dead-on-target Washington reality'
Kirkus Reviews

'Solid entertainment from beginning to end'
Library Journal

Dunn's Conundrum

STAN LEE

SPHERE BOOKS LIMITED
London and Sydney

First published in Great Britain by
Michael Joseph Ltd 1985
Copyright © Stan Lee 1985
Published by Sphere Books Ltd 1986
30–32 Gray's Inn Road, London WC1X 8JL
Reprinted 1986

TRADE
MARK

Set in 10/10½ pt English Times Compugraphic

Printed and bound in Great Britain by
Collins, Glasgow

To
Bernice and Jess
and
Francis Bartlett

I   The Library

Eberhart's Job

Harry Dunn was studying Eberhart's face. Or, anyway, half of Eberhart's face, which was all he could see from where he was sitting. But Eberhart was symmetrical, so it didn't make any difference; you saw one side of Eberhart, you saw them all. Dunn was feeling a botch of emotions: compassion, anger, bafflement, curiosity, even anxiety, which was an odd emotion to be feeling toward the deceased, but Dunn had his reasons.

All the lines of Eberhart's face turned down, leaving a generally negative expression. Was that one of the costs of pessimism? Dunn wondered. The gravity of existence literally pulling those delicate muscles downward, giving them a good daily workout as Eberhart faced life? Or maybe it was simply through the accumulated disappointments of an undiscourageable optimist. He had to admit that he'd never taken the trouble to know Eberhart better. At least the undertaker had left things pretty much as they were, not painting over a lifetime of negativism; Charley's face looked authentic. It seemed to be saying, 'I don't think I'm going to like this.'

Dunn had said the usual words to the widow and now he was sitting on a folding chair a few feet away from the casket, worrying, imagining, trying to get into his playful problem-solving frame of mind, trying to control his anxieties. He didn't lose his grip like this too often, but Eberhart had been a shock. By the time he was getting it all under control, Ives arrived. He could tell because an usher was tapping the few mourners on the shoulder and they were all getting up to leave. As Ives came in, someone closed the double doors behind him.

Ives was wearing a dark suit and a standard blue

television shirt and he went right up to the casket, immediately going into his conversational pose: arms folded, back arched in, head moving up and down or from side to side, depending on his reaction to what he was hearing – in this case, from side to side. He kicked the catafalque.

'You fucking bastard,' he said to Eberhart.

Ives was a design-center American; he was within all tolerances. Medium height, medium weight, not handsome, not ugly, a white Anglo-Saxon Catholic who didn't practice but who had a daughter doing time in an ashram. Ives was only an aide, meaning he had power without a constituency, which was a vaporous kind of power, but he was a big aide, he had the Ear, the President listened to him. Ives cultivated the image of the quiet, hard-working, behind-the-scenes publicity-hater. But he was extraordinarily adept at the use of makeup to compensate for a bad beard and he happened to own a lot of blue shirts and always managed to look impeccable and have words ready on any conceivable issue should a television crew happen along.

'We give a man an important job in government,' Ives said. 'A sensitive, crucial important job. It was probably a lot higher than he ever expected to rise in life. I'll bet his damn mother never expected him to get that high, the son of a bitch. And what do we get for thanks?'

'The worst thing anyone in government or the stock market can do,' Dunn said cooperatively.

'I don't think Eberhart ever cared about people. Otherwise, how could he have done this to us?' Ives sat down three folding chairs away from Dunn, whose 240 pounds were oppressive to some people. 'Has it been made to look like an accident, at least?' Ives said. Ives didn't bother with circumlocutory language; it took too much time.

'They're calling it a ruptured appendix and peritonitis.'

'But, I mean, how can you get away with that? Doesn't anybody check on that stuff? Pathologists? Coroners? I mean, I don't know what I'm talking about, but doesn't somebody check stuff like that out?'

Dunn was starting to feel better. He was in his element now. Problems. 'One of the first contingency plans I had drawn up at the Library was the contingency of Library personnel suicide.'

4

Ives nodded. He wasn't giving satisfaction yet, but at least he gave it his slow nod, which was a nice congenial way of not saying anything.

'It's our doctor. As a matter of fact, it's our widow. She doesn't want to hurt the insurance and pension and she's been told that because of Charley's long service in government, we want her to have what he'd want her to have and so forth and so on. So you can forget about the newspapers; Charley will be buried on page thirty-seven.'

Ives nodded some more. He'd been in government long enough to appreciate competence. The nod slowly sped up and modulated into a shake. 'Did you have any idea he was going to do it?' he said.

'He talked about his problems now and then, but I didn't pay any attention. Everybody bitches. If you've got a job like Charley's, you're going to bitch. I played good listener, but I didn't take it seriously.'

Ives was shaking his head, thumb and fourth finger massaging his eyes at the bridge of his nose. 'It's undermining,' he said. 'I mean, when you think about it, anybody could pull this. It's aberrational. How can you plan for an aberration, for Christ sake?'

'You can't plan for an aberration. You can only plan for cleaning up the mess. You can't tell about people. How can you predict them? They're people. You can predict the actions of ten thousand people. But not one.' Dunn shrugged his shoulders, thinking that the problem with Charley Eberhart was that his job had left him without a single illusion; in Harry Dunn's opinion, the man had OD'd on truth, which was toxic when taken excess.

'What are you going to do now?' Ives said.

'I'm thinking, I'm thinking.'

'The President will want to know who you've picked.'

'I'll tell you the truth, Gene – it's a tough call.'

He'd been running through the names of his staff people compulsively – in the shower, eating, on the pot, driving to the office. In an oddball way, it was the most important job in government.

Eugene Ives took out an expensive, anachronistic cigarette case, lit up with a touch of effeminacy, and blew smoke in Eberhart's direction, one suicide scorning another.

'What about Beebe?' he said.

'My first thought too,' Dunn replied. 'He's good. And he's mean. He's good and mean. He's mean enough to do it. He'd be like Truman. He could drop the Bomb and never lose a night's sleep over it. I thought of Beebe.'

'Yeah, and what did you think of Beebe?'

'Hell, he's even mean enough to like the job.'

Beebe's large, oval face was built for intimidation. He had sheer, unscalable, Everest-like cheekbones and a smile that was on a par with the vermiform appendix or better yet the sneeze – something his nervous system did out of some distant racial memory – or even better, like the gaseous smile of a new baby; it was all muscle and neurons, signifying nothing.

Dunn trusted Beebe more than anyone else in the Library, in spite of the fact that Beebe variously referred to the Library as the Bureau of Bureaus, Big Bureau, Super Bureau, Bureau Squared, the Bureau of Departments, the Department of Bureaus, and so on. It was the epitome of big government, which he loathed with good conservative venom, but over a few Scotches – which he knocked down so swiftly that people rarely ever saw him with glass to lips – he would actually concede that it was a necessary evil.

McDermott Beebe III was a West Point graduate who'd spent ten years in Special Forces in Vietnam; the Pathet Lao had had a price on his head. Now he was in charge of Library security and he was totally reliable, 100 percent committed. Loyal. Trustworthy. Vicious. The one thing about which Harry felt certain was that if anyone tried to physically break into the Library, they would meet up with Siva, the Hindu god of destruction, a.k.a. Mac Beebe III.

It was possible that Beebe had been in the security field too long; security work tended to be bad for one's poetic nature. There weren't too many shades of gray in Beebe's mind. He was righteous, judgmental. You were for or you were against. Sober, Beebe looked like he'd make a mean drunk; drunk, he glided lightly around like a fifth of nitro-glycerin.

6

'I don't think Beebe has a delicate enough temperament for this job,' Dunn said, stealing a look at Ives which was meant to be sly and witty.

Ives was nodding again, very slowly, basic grudging assent. 'I can understand that,' he said. 'I like him because I think he's suicideproof, but I can see your point. But you have to watch out you don't go too far in the other direction. You know who I think could do this? Sort of a surprise choice. Vera.'

'Sure,' Dunn said. 'A definite possible. She's got a lot to recommend her, no getting away from it.' But he was thinking that Ives was way off, which was just as well. Better that they spend a few minutes on it, go through the exercise, consider the considerations.

Vera Bishop had spent years as a photoanalyst in charge of the satellite photos of the Soviet Union, studying it from 160 miles up. Now she had computer access to millions of frames of film covering virtually every square inch of the entire landmass. She undoubtedly knew the Soviet Union better than most Russians. If she were suddenly plopped down in the middle of, say, Dnepropetrovsk, she could take one look around and say, 'Hmm, I think I'll get a loaf of black bread in that shop around the corner.'

A year earlier, the CIA had urgently asked for a reliable means of emergency communication from its agents in the Soviet Union. Vera took a tenth of a second to invent it. They were simply to scrawl the message in the grime on the roof of an automobile and park it away from tall buildings. Within any eighteen-hour period a satellite would pick it up. Even if the car was relatively clean, computer enhancement could bring out the message.

Vera had started out as a chemist and had a Distinguished Service Medal from the U.S. Army for her work on the synthesis of defoliants. She'd gotten into photo-reconnaisance during the Vietnam War, when she began to look at photographs of defoliated areas and regularly picked out details that experienced analysts had missed.

Vera Bishop had a lot of qualities that were perfect for Eberhart's job. She had an encyclopedic mind, a quality that came out of sheer interest in the world, rather than being a genetic aberration. Vera knew the precise geographic location of every missile silo in the Soviet Union. She could also tell you how many days' coal reserve was kept at the steel mills in Magnitogorsk. She knew where every army division was stationed in the Soviet Union, and how many vehicles each had, in quantities and types. She was carrying around the entire battle order of the Soviet Union in her head. But she also knew how long it took for the traffic lights to change in Red Square. She knew countless irrelevancies, *(a)* because they fascinated her, and *(b)* because she expected that eventually something would come up that would make them relevant.

She was also the complete opposite of McDermott Beebe III. Harry Dunn thought of it as a peculiarly feminine attribute, an acceptance of things as they were without the sugar coating that men seemed to require. She could adjust to what she'd have to do and see in Eberhart's job. She'd accept the knowledge in a realistic, unrighteous way, without agonizing over it the way men would. After all, people were people and they did people things. Frailty in others didn't make her anxious. Vera would be clinical about it: a good, objective nurse looking at awful things and making calm, reasoned judgments, all in the best interests not of the patient but of the republic.

The trouble with Vera, as Dunn saw it, was that she tended to get too interested, even from 160 miles up. She told Dunn that she had a few frames of a couple making love in a meadow not far from Kursk. A small thing. It was the way she talked about it, a little signpost to the psyche. She said it must have been a torrid affair, because the satellite was picking them up regularly. Then one day she'd observed a second man in the meadow, pointing at the couple lying on the ground. The angle was all wrong; no amount of computer enhancement could tell her whether the second man had a gun in his hand or not; but her satellite lovers never appeared again.

So even though Vera had made incalculable additions to the Bombing Encyclopedia, Dunn wondered if at bottom she didn't have too much of a tendency to get involved, maybe play God, the all-powerful goddess up on Mount Olympus looking down at the mortals, perhaps drawn to the thought of a preemptive first strike lightning bolt attack on the husband, thus saving the lovers. That kind of thinking was okay at 160 miles of altitude but not in an extreme close-up, which was where Eberhart had functioned. Dunn didn't want God in that job.

What was it Eberhart had? What was it he ran out of? Detachment? The novelist's attitude? Dunn had considered hiring a novelist for the job. They were born undercover agents. Voyeurs, secretly making notes. There wasn't that much difference between the Japanese doing sketches of Governors Island and a novelist spying on some widow lady, looting her psyche while nibbling on her cucumber sandwiches. That's what the job called for, a dedicated and professional voyeur – not a God-player and especially not a killer. Whoever they picked would have to resist the common human trait of kicking the other guy's Achilles' heel at the first opportunity; he would have to be able to resist inflating his own paltry ego with the sheer joy of spotting weakness in others.

Dunn's thoughts were interrupted by a beeping sound. The White House was summoning Ives to a phone and Ives was looking for a place to drop his cigarette. With amazing shortsightedness, the undertaker hadn't provided ashtrays. Ives abruptly shoved the butt past some lilies into a vase and turned off the beeper. Dunn played at one-upmanship; he didn't even wait to see if Ives would rush off to a phone. *Nothing* was this important.

'I'd say Vera is a possibility,' he said.

'Then give her the job,' Ives replied. He didn't mean it; it was his way of asking what was wrong with her.

'I'm not completely at home with it.'

Ives was wandering around the place, hands clasped behind his back. 'Okay, she's out. I guess we don't even have to consider Gardella.'

Dunn said nothing. He had considered Gardella. Gardella was a mad, depressed Italian who was so good at so many things it was hard to decide where to use him. He'd originally started out to be an architect and had a degree. Then he had switched to electronics and eventually become a group head in the design of the MX missile. In dealing with the think tanks that had been in on the strategy aspects of MX, Gardella had revealed a tremendous grasp not only of nuts and bolts but of strategy.

In time, Gardella had also assumed management of the microcam operation. The microcam was a camera so small you could hide it almost anywhere. It was an offshoot of satellite photography, all lens, smaller than a collar button. It didn't have to handle film; it stored images on a chip that was more sensitive to light than any photographic film. The chip would periodically be interrogated by a Library van passing the site where the chip was installed, and everything stored up would be transmitted in four seconds, the only time it was vulnerable to detection. In Washington, D.C., where the density of microcam installations was high, it paid to have a van circulating at random, constantly interrogating all the microcams within range; it was a means by which the Library could see the images and hear the voices in real time, as they were occurring.

When Leo Gardella was asked to plan an installation, he would go into a deep depression until he had figured out how to do it. Besides being an architect, he was an expert photographer. He could figure out from architects' drawings of the target site where to place the microcams to get the desired shots. He knew how to camouflage the little collar buttons. He drew up scenarios for agents to follow in order to be able to gain surreptitious entrance. Leo Gardella was so good at it, it was no longer safe for a politician to have sex in Washington, D.C., except in the missionary position with a woman of his own race to whom he was married, with the paperwork on file.

Gardella was a nice Beebe, a sweetheart, but he was too volatile; he took everything too personally. He was living proof of the importance of sage administration; in the right job he was a genius, in the wrong one he'd be wearing a straitjacket to work.

Dunn was playing it very close to the vest. It was obvious that Ives wasn't going to leave him alone until he'd gotten a decision about Charley Eberhart's replacement. Ives was the executive type right down to his shoelaces. Fast decisions, click click click, done. Whereas Dunn was the staff type, who liked to circle warily around a problem, think through, prepare position papers, factor in all factors.

The problem was that the Library knew everything.

Everything there was to know, the Library knew. It was Harry Dunn's own personal contribution to intelligence: he had succeeded in overturning the age-old intelligence rule of Need to Know and changing it into Need to Know Everything. It was either classically bad intelligence doctrine or else a stunning revolution, which was the way Harry felt about it. Anyone in intelligence work who knew more than the minimum was potentially dangerous. The defection of one such person to the Soviet Union – or, worse yet, to Senator Oliver Garvey's subcommittee – would be catastrophic. Which was why practically nobody in the intelligence community itself knew for sure what the Library's real purpose was. To the others it was known as the Intelligence Library, a mere collection and storage agency.

What did they get for taking such risks, for allowing everyone in the Library to know everything? For the first time in the history of intelligence, all national intelligence data was under one roof where there could be cross-fertilization, feedback, open discussion, interdisciplinary leaps of imagination, all of which was vital for creativity, not to mention across-the-board planning. There was only one security classification in the Library: ALL EYES. Everybody saw everything. For the first time in the history of government, the left hand knew what the right hand was doing. That was Dunn's contribution.

Every one of the twelve Librarians had access to everything: the combined output of CIA, DIA, NSA, and all the other government intelligence agencies. They could see all the films, hear the phone calls and the tapes, read the telegrams, the mail, the trash covers, the agent reports. Even the beeper frequencies were monitored so the Library computer would know that much sooner when important phone calls were about to be made. They had access to the think tanks, the scientists, the military intellectuals. There was even a method, developed by NSA scientists and mathematicians, for interrogating Soviet satellites, so that we knew what they knew, or at least what they thought they knew. It was, as Dunn had argued to the President, the only way America could be prepared for anything. An-nything. But it created a new kind of problem.

Which poor Charley had handled rather well during the almost three years of the Library's existence.

Ives had been flipping through the guestbook. 'Hey, how about Hopkins?' he said suddenly, as though coming up with an inspiration.

Dunn got slowly to his feet, using a hand on each knee to achieve liftoff. He began to pace ponderously before the coffin, as though talking to Eberhart.

'I've been through the list a thousand times,' he said. 'The fact of the matter is they're all terrific people. Highly motivated. Intelligent. Creative. Cross-trained. Specialized abilities. I've got giants working for me. Including Alex Hopkins. He has a Ph.D. in International Political Economics. He's got seven years in at Rand, creating games. Brilliant man. But at this job he'd be grossly incompetent. Alex Hopkins is the most amoral person I've ever known who isn't actually behind bars or at least under indictment. His experience is priceless or he wouldn't even be here. I'm telling you, Hopkins wouldn't know the difference between good and bad, he wouldn't know what was discreet, what was indiscreet, what was blackmailable, what was evil, what was human. Now take Yeager.' ('Hmm,' Ives was saying, still reacting to Hopkins.)

'Yeager's a cool character, which is as it should be for a man in charge of fieldwork. Ex-jet-fighter pilot. Nine years in the CIA, undercover in *Rumania*, for God's sake. Offhand he seems right for the job. But he's fake. He works on his image like a potter. He's forever throwing my name around because he thinks it gives him stature. Totally fake. Dunn and I went here, Dunn and I went there, Dunn said this, I said that. The man seems exclusively concerned with appearances. Reality is something you just naturally bury out of sight, doesn't everybody? How would he react if he had his nose rubbed in it every day? I wouldn't want to take the chance.'

'Okay. Kraus.'

Ives looked as if he was prepared to stay the winter for an answer. But he was still going in the wrong direction. Fine. Harry would gently, imperceptibly lead him by the nose. Dunn paused, waiting for an idea. On the surface,

Kraus looked good. The man had the odd talents that went with being an expert at simulations. Apparently, Emil Kraus could set up any exercise and make it look real to as many people as desired. There was a diabolical quality to his thinking, not unlike that of a paranoid. He was a master at manipulating others.

'Eight more inches of altitude and Kraus could have the job,' Dunn said flatly. 'The fact of the matter is his height disqualifies him.'

Ives's beeper was beeping again, but Dunn went on ignoring it and Ives absently hit it.

'What's the problem?' Ives said. 'Is he too short to see over transoms?'

'He's so short there are some things he'll never see. Shortness in a man is dangerous. Turns him into a giant-killer. But the killing is done with short means, in short, underhanded ways. Kraus has a pronounced tendency to undermine anyone around him. You can almost feel the ground dribbling out from under your feet when you're talking to him. No, it would be a case of putting the little fox in with the big chickens, and I don't know *what* the hell would happen.'

Now Dunn was ticking them off on his fingers. 'Johnny Burnish. Out of the question. He's deputy. Too busy. First to arrive, last to leave. He's got to be psychotic to be keeping the job, much less liking it, which he does by the way. He'd do everything if I let him. Wash the windows, change the typewriter ribbons.' He waved a hand.

'Shanley? He's wonderful on NATO and the Middle East. I think you've seen his scenario for Saudi Arabia. Brilliant wasn't it? But you know as well as I do, Shanley is four years old. What killed Charley, Shanley would find titillating. At first, anyway. Then he'd decide that he himself wasn't such a nut after all. Then he'd become insufferably superior, until I'd have to slip and let him see himself on tape, in which case he'd jump out the window.'

'But maybe before then you could at least get a year out of him,' Ives said, shrugging, reduced to depending on suicides. Ives had turned one of the folding chairs around and was sitting on it backward, fingers holding up his cheeks. 'Maybe somebody like Shanley is right for the job.

Like an idiot, sort of – know what I mean?'

Dunn went right on with his slow pace, dismissing thought entirely. 'Our man has to have a mature sense of proportion. What am I trying to say? Judgment? Feet on the ground? Common sense? I don't know what to call it.'

'How about you, Harry?' Ives said, a slight protective smile on his face. It meant that he could have meant it or not meant it, depending on how Dunn took it.

'One of the main advantages of coming into government at a high level,' Dunn said, not missing a beat in his pacing, 'is that you don't have to take shit jobs like this. Okay, who else? Beatty?'

'Yeah,' Ives said. 'What *about* Beatty? I've got a lot of respect for him. He's terrific on Latin America. He's a born geopolitician.'

'He's also a born-again Christian. The reformed rake-hell who's given himself to Jesus. He'd never get anything done. When you think about the stuff he'd be exposed to, you *know* he'd be on his knees praying to God twenty hours a day. Or he'd start holding revival meetings in the War Room.'

'Heh,' Ives said. Harry had a way of massing the evidence; you didn't stand a chance against him. The problem was beginning to look unnecessarily difficult. It couldn't be this hard, could it?

'Okay, how about Ma Bell?' Ives waited warily to see what objection Harry would come up with this time.

Harry nodded. 'Good thought,' he said. Ma Bell was Mike Barber, a phenomenal programmer, a Beethoven, really, of programmers, who also seemed to know the key facts about everything. Put the two together and you had a masterpiece of a program for red-tagging only those telephone conversations that were of interest to the Library. Otherwise the telephone monitoring operation would have been impossible. Harry pretended to go along for a moment. 'He's invaluable on missile strategy too, by the way.' Harry's voice sank to a whisper. 'O.F.F. was his idea.'

'I didn't know that,' Ives said, also whispering.

'Problem is, Barber is the only human being I've ever met who has no ego. None. No defenses. Nothing to fall

14

back on. Flick him over with your finger. Know what would happen to him if he ever heard his own name taken in vain or, God forbid, was laughed at? The clamshell would come down for a year. Now who's left? Farnsworth?'

'Jesus Christ,' Ives said. 'Listen, we've got to solve this thing. Pick somebody, Harry. So you get less than the ideal. Fine. Otherwise you'll worry this thing around forever. Okay, it's a shit job, so –'

Ives stopped. He had a look of revelation in his eyes. He stood up, still straddling the chair. His arms were out wide and his shoulders were hunched up as though he'd just seen the obvious which had been under their noses all along.

'You forgot about the Garbageman,' Ives said, triumphantly. 'What's-his-name.'

Dunn stopped pacing. He thought a moment. 'If there's one thing I don't like, it's looking stupid.'

The Garbageman was Walter Coolidge, who supervised the trash covers. Coolidge had been trained as an anthropologist with a minor in archaeology. He was a man who could look at anything as though it were 22,000 years old. The clinical cast of mind was feverish alongside Coolidge's; he could walk down Pennsylvannia Avenue and feel as though he were strolling through Pompeii. He was a genius at trash analysis and had single-handedly almost managed to make the field respectable. Dunn had decided on him eight hours earlier.

Ives raised a cautionary finger. 'Wait a minute. Isn't he the one who gets migraines?'

'Yeah.'

'Is that a bad sign, maybe? Know what I'm saying?'

'Don't worry about it. I trust people who get migraines. It shows they're good at repressing stuff and keeping themselves in line.'

'Huh. Never thought of it that way. Oh, well,' Ives slapped Dunn on the back. 'You see, I'm not just a pain in the neck. I help too.'

Dunn was having a damnable time trying to look flustered, but Ives was so pleased with himself it didn't matter. And Ives's beeper was going again. 'I've got to get the hell out of here,' he said. 'Then it's the Garbageman, right?'

'It's ideal. It's gorgeous.'

'Anytime, Harry.' Gene Ives was picking up speed, heading for the door. He gestured at Charley. 'Give that son of a bitch the bum's rush, will you?'

Garbage Is Never Wrong

The Garbageman was cradled in the arms of Vera Bishop, brainless, oblivious. He and Vera had left the Library for lunch and gone to her apartment in Washington, S.W. The code word was 'Chinese.' 'Feel like a little Chinese?' one of them would say on the phone, a phrase that got its meaning from the fact that they'd made love for the first time after having dinner with Harry Dunn and Leo Gardella at a well-known Chinese restaurant. They'd been celebrating the successful placing of a micro-cam in the Russian embassy's conference room.

Vera had twin beds in her bedroom, one with a hard mattress for sleeping, one with a soft one for Chinese. They were lying in the soft one, pressed against each other, kissing, hotting up the ambient temperature, groans escalating, when the phone rang.

'Leave it,' Coolidge said, briefly breaking off a kiss.

'Could be an important person,' she said.

'You're the person that's important,' he said, licking the spiral of her ear. He infiltrated his left arm under her body so he could have a hand on each buttock.

The phone was ringing away.

She pressed against him even closer, growing more insistent, pushing. He gave in to the pressure and rolled over on his back, with Vera on top of him. The ringing stopped. 'Yes,' she said, with a fake sweet soprano. 'Oh, Jake, how are you?'

Coolidge shook his head in short, frantic movements. He even abandoned one buttock long enough to make a cutting motion across his throat with an index finger.

'I don't know, Jake,' she said. 'I really don't keep track of the man. Have you tried that Italian restaurant near the

Hill?' Coolidge's hands were busy caressing cheeks, thighs, shoulders, back. She winked at him. 'Maybe he's at a massage parlor. Have you tried that place on E Street?'

Coolidge could hear the sound of Jake's voice, but he ignored it to suck on her shoulder. Vera was beginning to have trouble keeping her voice from quavering. 'If I see him, tell him there's an anomaly. I won't forget. I'm writing it down. An anomaly. Anything else, Jake?'

Coolidge stopped sucking; his hands were losing interest in flesh, his head fell back on the pillow.

'That's *if* I see him,' she was saying, 'but I can't guarantee it.' Coolidge grabbed the phone away from her. 'Okay, what the hell's going on,' he said to Jake.

'Uh,' Vera said with disgust, and rolled off him.

Jake was apologizing rapidly, abysmally. 'Jesus Christ, I'm sorry, Walter. You know I wouldn't do this if it wasn't important. We've got something here that looks like a genuine anomaly. I think it does; you'd know in a second. I swear to God, Walter, I wouldn't interrupt – er – you if I didn't think it was worth it.'

Coolidge was sitting up in bed, cross-legged.

'Stuff really looks funny, huh?' he said.

'This stuff breaks all the rules, Walter. This garbage stinks out loud.'

'Huh,' Coolidge said. He'd gone from total uninterest to fascination in seconds. But it was going to be hard to get out of bed. 'Okay, I'll be right over.' He put the phone back on its cradle.

'What's an anomaly?' Vera said. She was standing in front of her vanity mirror, wearing only pink pumps and earrings, spraying something on places. Vera was five-four, fairly well shaped, good-looking. And whatever she had was available for duty; Vera's inner conflicts were at the bare minimum for the human condition and her energy was natural, undriven, uncontaminated by neurosis. Vera was a member of the froufrou branch of feminism: not only were women as good as men; they were prettier. Shaving her legs was a cosmetic act, not an ideological one. Vera also understood fashion better than most women: all her clothes fit her, concisely.

Coolidge sat down on the hard bed with a sock in his hand. 'An anomaly is garbage with a point of view,' he said.

'So what?'

'It's rare.'

'Rare garbage,' she said to the wall.

'If I were a bird-watcher, it would be like spotting what I'd thought was an extinct species. Something like that.'

She sat down next to him, smoking a cigarette, one hand on his thigh, 'I mean, how fascinating can a piece of shit be?' she asked. 'Garbage with a point of view. You're turning into a bureaucrat, giving things fancy names. It sounds like extravehicular activity, although that's at least a little sexy.'

'Sexy?' Coolidge was poised to put the sock on his foot. 'What the hell's sexy about extravehicular activity?'

'I don't know, but it sounds, you know, kinky.'

Coolidge dropped his sock. He put his arm around her waist, sniffing her. Perfume. Did it still come from whales with upset stomachs? How had it been discovered? Maybe some innocent fisherman from Gomorrah, out there spearing mackerel; then this mess floats by and he gets horny as hell, probably thinks he's crazy.

'Why don't you take a shower,' he whispered in her ear. 'First hot, then cold.'

'So help me God, if you pick up that sock, we're finished. All over. Okay sweetie?' She was doing really gross things between his thighs.

'You see, it's like this, Vera. There are such things as priorities in life. Oooh. Jake has spotted a yellow-throated warbler with purple eyes and – aaaah – one green feather.'

'But don't you understand *you're* the boss? Jake can wait for you. Jake is a very patient fellow. As a matter of fact, he doesn't assert himself nearly enough. He lets you walk all over him. Lie back, darling.'

'If it was a photograph of a new silo,' he said, 'that would be different. You'd run out of here like a burglar.'

'That's different,' she said. 'A new silo? Oh, honey.'

She stood up and was pacing back and forth fantastically, flesh quivering everywhere. 'A new silo? Oh, come on, Walter. How about my silo? Let's launch a preemptive first strike.'

'See? You're just like the rest. Trash covers aren't important. Trash covers don't belong in the same *century* with satellites.'

'You sound like a housewife complaining about her vacuum cleaner.'

'After all I've explained to you about garbage.'

'Don't put that sock on.'

'But, darling. The country. The republic.'

She ditched her cigarette and squatted on him, pushing him back on the bed. 'Fuck 'em,' she said.

Since the proper expression was 'trash cover', by all rights Coolidge should have been called the Trashman, but that sounded too Ivy League and affected. Garbageman was inevitable. He was lucky it wasn't worse. It was referred to officially as DAP: Discarded and Abandoned Property. It was referred to semiofficially as CRAP: Collected and Reviewed Abandoned Property.

Most of the trash covers were in Washington, D.C., it being the seat of government, but Coolidge had trash covers going all over the world. It all came into his department, located in the basement and sub-basement of the Library's building. After analysis, it was burned to provide heat and light.

The trash covers, as well as all the other activities of the Library, were apart from anything the FBI, the CIA, and the other intelligence bureaus might be doing. The Library received all their data, plus.

With the possible exception of Harry Dunn, who took everything seriously and didn't want to miss any tricks, CRAP wasn't highly regarded as an intelligence tool. It was a minor ancillary service which the other Librarians availed themselves of simply because it was there.

But Coolidge believed that garbage was amazingly pristine data. People weren't subjective about their garbage. They didn't listen, as it were, for the sounds of bugging on the line. Garbage was all innocence and unselfconsciousness. It wasn't cunning, evasive, false. Garbage was frank and open and refreshing. It was confession without the need for Miranda warnings. It was autobiography, self-portraiture, a voluntary strip search.

Better yet, sooner or later everybody got stupid. Stupidity seemed to be a basic part of the human condition. It was almost as though stupidity had survival value and was in the chromosomes of even the most brilliant people. One of these days, Coolidge expected to find a nuclear warhead someone had absently tossed out in the garbage. After all, garbage was the place where the entire GNP ended up sooner or later, the daily mountainous unburdening of that which was used up and that which offended the eye. Out!

In! Into the basement and sub-basement of the Library for tagging and analysis, for conclusions, for action, perhaps, or as an aid in the creation of new contingency plans so the nation would always be ready for anything.

Coolidge had come to associate the smell of garbage with logic, deduction; with the controlled irrational wanderings of his mind on a speculative binge, looking for associations, clues – clues that were as much in his own head as in the garbage. When Coolidge had finished with it, he had stood the computerist's gag on its head: garbage in, data out.

Coolidge had become interested in trash as a teenager, after reading Gustavus Lange's seminal work, *Neolithic Middens*. The book had made him realize that the most important contribution to civilization and knowledge of all but a few of the vast mass of humanity, of the myriads who had ever trod the earth, had been their trash: it was more significant than their lives, their accomplishments, their hopes, dreams, desires.

Gustavus Lange had compiled and synthesized all the techniques archaeologists had developed for the study of ancient trash. For example, he had demonstrated how one broken piece of pottery – a jar, a pot, a flask, its pieces scattered over acres and centuries, buried by nature and the detritus of living – could, when painstakingly reassembled, tie together an entire community, freeze time, produce a snapshot of the past: each and every shard of the jar was a link; every item of garbage adjacent to every shard of the jar was inevitably related in time and place to

21

every other shard of the jar. Thus one broken clay jar, when reassembled, recreated a village, a city, a civilization, at a moment in time. Coolidge was stunned by the possibilities inherent in trash.

After getting his degree in anthropology, Coolidge had gone to the Department of Health, Education and Welfare as a fieldworker, evaluating the effect of poverty programs on the lives of the people they were designed to help. It was an assignment that gave him the opportunity to make observations and collect data for his doctoral thesis, *Inner City Trash*.

His thesis was to have been divided into two parts: One, Methods, and Two, Applications. Methods described the basic categories and characteristics of trash and how inferences could be drawn by using a combination of anthropological, archaeological, and mathematical techniques. When his faculty adviser read Part One, he sent it to a contact in the CIA. The half-finished thesis promptly became *the* book on trash, the standard, and Coolidge, without any intelligence background, ended up working in the newly established Library, simply because he was the best there was at trash analysis. He never did write Part Two.

This was a peculiar job for Coolidge. He'd always thought that the study of society was to be his field; it had even affected his appearance. Coolidge was tall and bony and conservative. He'd never worn jeans or facial hair and he always bought clothes that didn't draw attention to themselves. It was his anthropologist's disguise, since his aim was to blend in with the background, frustrate Heisenberg's uncertainty principle, disturb as little as possible the particular societal phenomenon he was observing, without appearing to be deliberate about it. On the rare occasions when he bought a new jacket or slacks or shirt, he was impatient for them to lose their newness.

Politically he was vaguely to the left. His grandfather had gone to work for the post office during the Great Depression of the thirties and had stayed there for the rest of his life, enjoying the security of being a civil servant; he had given up on life in the capitalist arena.

Coolidge's father, working as an electronics engineer

during the cold war and McCarthy years, had become apolitical, kept a clean nose; his income depended upon his security clearance. It was only when close to retirement that he dared to risk marching on the Pentagon during the Vietnam War. Coolidge therefore had grown up in a household that was free of political cant and stereotypes. Skepticism was the prevailing mood. Minding one's business and getting on with life was the order of the day.

All of which was how, after six years of working his way up the bureaucracy in HEW, Coolidge had suddenly found himself at work for *the* most secret intelligence agency in the government.

Coolidge sped from Vera Bishop, leaving her sprawled on the sleeping bed, smiling and out. The time of Chinese had passed; now it was the trash hour.

Jake Shoemaker had fourteen samples of trash that broke the rules, that constituted an example of what Coolidge had previously only postulated and had never actually encountered professionally: faked garbage. Garbage that contained no data whatsoever, revealed nothing about anybody, and therefore was prima facie proof (in Coolidge's mind) that felonies, nature unknown, were being committed.

Coolidge was standing in one of the trash analysis rooms, contemplating it, trying not to speculate too wildly, each day's trash pickup displayed before him on a large tray covered by a transparent plastic dome. Trays were lined up on long, narrow tables that ran the length of the entire room.

'This trash doesn't know what it is,' Jake said, coming up behind him. 'I've been watching it for two weeks, waiting for something to happen. But nothing's happened. All of a sudden I figured I better get you in on it.'

Shoemaker had a nervous, fast way of talking, which was the way his tall, thin body moved: in fits and starts. 'It isn't a married couple with two and a half kids. It isn't two gay males. It isn't two heteros. It isn't two females, name your type. This trash is Marx Brothers trash. There's no sanity clause.'

Coolidge decided to go along with Jake's game of movie

quotes, since it would break any tension between them. 'Doesn't matter; I'm too old to believe in sanity clause.'

It worked.

'Walter, are you pissed?'

'No, I'm not pissed.'

'I mean, I wouldn't have called if I didn't have a three-bedroom house that seems to have twenty-three adults and half a child living in it.'

'You're off the hook,' Coolidge said, lifting up one of the plastic domes. 'It's fascinating.' He poked around in the garbage with the kind of croupier's stick that all the garbagemen used. 'Where? Who?'

'A private house on Adams Mill Road, N.W. It's listed under the name of Jones. John Jones. Jesus.'

'How long have they lived there?'

'Twenty-eight years.'

'Heh.'

Coolidge was strolling along the table, taking in the garbage.

'I ran a check on the utilities,' Jake said. 'They're using a lot of electricity. They're using a lot of fuel oil. But they are not using water. No water. Zero on the water. I requested a mail cover. It was easy. There's no mail going into that house.'

Coolidge looked from Jake to the garbage. There was third-class junk mail all over the place. He started to lift a dome.

'There aren't any envelopes,' Jake said quickly.

'This garbage is guilty, all right,' Coolidge said. 'No getting away from it. It's so guilty, it's stupid. Now why would anybody be this dumb about it? On the other hand, if they're like everybody else, they probably wouldn't take trash covers too seriously. Just do a superficial job on it. Who requested the cover?'

'Ma Bell. He found out somehow that the phone in this house is the only phone in Washington, D.C., that doesn't have any calls, in or out.'

'Lovely,' Coolidge said.

Jake sat on one of the high stools they had scattered around the long tables. He folded his arms, sitting very stiffly. 'Is there game afoot?' he said to the master.

Coolidge nodded. 'It's afoot, all right. It isn't only that this garbage is fake; it's self-conscious garbage. I feel that very strongly.'

He gazed around at the fourteen plastic domes, thinking that to an outsider he could look like a Roman priest reading entrails. 'Sanitized garbage. Discreet garbage. It's almost as though someone were trying to make a good impression with their garbage. Look at the magazines. *Harper's. Newsweek. Foreign Policy.* Where are the *Playboys* and the *Hustlers* and the *Cosmopolitans*? Improbable. No liquor, no wine, no beer. None. Improbable. The junk mail is totally innocuous. Save the Whales. Fur sales. The college of your choice. No hot causes, no left wing, no right wing. There are four different brands of breakfast cereal. Impossible? No. Three different brands of cigarettes, but only a pack of each kind in – what? – two weeks? Okay, could be visitors. Could be. Baby food jars. A sprinkling, not enough to feed a Bombay Hindu. Could be visitors.'

Coolidge went to the ninth day and poked through the grapefruit halves and carrot tops, half-eaten pickles, chicken bones. He clawed something and held it up on the croupier's stick.

'A pair of children's socks,' he mused. 'They're worn but there are no holes. That means the kid outgrew them. But if the kid was there long enough to outgrow his socks – looks about size six – there ought to be a lot of other stuff to go with a kid who wears size six. What's that, third grade?'

Shoemaker looked over his Trash Reports.

'Nothing,' he said. 'No toys, no clothes, kids' books, drawings, crayons. Zero on the kid.'

Coolidge nodded. 'Improbable plus improbable plus improbable plus improbable. Equals certainty.'

'What do we do?' Jake said.

'We break a few amendments.'

With a few exceptions, like Harry Dunn's office, the Library was using cast-off furniture almost exclusively. The idea was to look neglected and unimportant. Ferd, the Library's legal counsel, was sitting behind a big, beat-up slate-colored metal desk that had spent seventeen years at the Department of Pesticides and another twelve in a warehouse. Ferd was busily scrawling on a legal-sized pad and he looked up at Coolidge over the top of his glasses.

'You guys collecting for a birthday party or something?'

Coolidge's eyes were already starting to glaze over from the professional wallpaper surrounding him, the rows of legal tomes in metal bookcases with dents in them. He'd expected to have trouble with Ferd because a trash cover generally wasn't considered rigorous enough as evidence to justify action.

'Explain it to the man in simple terms,' Coolidge said to Jake, and then wandered around the office, eavesdropping on Ferd's wastebasket, fighting off the annoyance he felt at perpetually not being taken seriously.

Jake presented the evidence, talking fast, exaggerating whenever necessary on the grounds that Ferd wouldn't understand the subtleties.

'Listen,' Ferd replied. 'I don't want to be one of the small army that's always putting you guys down, but can you really make weighty conclusions like this from trash? I mean, I understand one and one makes two, and if you find a nickel bag of heroin in the garbage, there's presumptive evidence of a stupid junkie.'

While Ferd was talking, Coolidge picked up the wastebasket and dumped it out on Ferd's desk.

'Oh, no,' Ferd said, holding his head in his hands.

'Let's see now. *Washington Post* crossword puzzle, normally very simple; you tried to do it in ink and botched it. Nervous about anything, Ferd? Lipstick-stained tissue. Leans toward the magenta. Could that be Lay-Me-Again Lorraine up on eight? Now then. The remains of lunch at your desk. What's this? You ate all the french fries. You usually leave most of them. Ah! Lipstick on a coffee container. You had lunch together. Charming. Empty chewing gum wrappers. One paper cup, triangular. The kind you can't put down. You must have gotten it at the water cooler, which is quite a ways down the hall. Why carry it all the way back? Possibly you wanted to take aspirin but you didn't want anybody to see? Could that mean you were hung over this morning, Ferd? Bank loan application half filled out, then torn up. Maybe it's money worries. That could explain a lot. More chewing gum wrappers. Candy too. After a hangover? Goobers. Nonpareils. American Civil Liberties Union newsletter. Various fund request letters, unopened. That would either be a political change of heart or you're broke. That would explain why you and your friend ate in.'

'Hey, ace.'

'Ah, what's this? An unopened pack of chewing gum with five slices inside. You don't really like chewing gum, do you, Ferd? I guess we'll have to come to the conclusion that you've given up smoking again. Jake, be nice and offer the man a cigarette.'

Jake drew the pack like a six-shooter, with an extra little flip of the wrist to pop a cigarette up. One-hundred-millimeter bore length, caliber eighteen milligrams. Ferd stared at it sticking out of the pack for about three seconds before taking one and holding it to Jake's lighter, which had psychically materialized.

Ferd breathed out a ton of smoke. 'Oh, God.'

'Small point, Walter,' Jake said. He picked up a tiny shard of red. 'The question is what was she doing to break a fingernail? You might as well confess, Ferd. We can check the shade of her nail polish easily enough.'

'Get that crap off my desk,' Ferd said, turning to his typewriter, the cigarette still in his mouth. 'Okay, Sherlock. You're saying that in your professional opinion,' he said, hunting and pecking, 'based on long professional experience in trash covers, that there is a presumption of illegal activity of a threatening nature to the security of the United States based on the unprecedented nature (can I put it that strongly?) of this – uh – rubbish.'

'Trash,' Coolidge said.

'Trash,' Ferd said.

'That's it.'

'I hope so, ace. I mean, the judge may just decide to ask questions, you know. Happens now and then.'

Coolidge nodded desultorily and Ferd yanked the form

out of the typewriter. Coolidge signed it without even reading it.

'Let's go,' Ferd said.

'Do you put Lorraine down on your time sheet?' Jake said to him as they went out of the door.

The court was on the sixth floor of the Justice Department. It was referred to as the FISA court, for Foreign Intelligence Surveillance Act. In the beginning, the court had served only one function: to approve (or disapprove; it never did) electronic surveillance measures in cases of suspected foreign intelligence activity. As time went by, its area gradually expanded, until it now was used to approve a number of counterintelligence activities. Only a few Federal District Court judges served on the FISA bench, and it went into session on demand.

The participants filed into the cavernous room together: Coolidge and Jake, Ferd, the judge, the court recorder. A mean-looking Green Beret without the beret closed the door behind them. The public was never admitted to the FISA court. There wasn't even a defendant's table; all defendants in the FISA court were presumably enemies of the state.

Ferd was talking before Coolidge had even found a chair, talking in that rote lawyer's way, not having to hunt and peck; when it came to talk, Ferd was a touch typist and the court recorder had to scramble to set up and get going, a good paragraph in the red.

'Your Honor, in the case of John Jones, Docket Number 9860, it is the considered opinion of this agency that the premises listed as 3212 Adams Mill Road, N.W., City of Washington, constitute a potential threat to the security of the United States. The attorney general has signed off on this, sir.'

The judge cupped his ear. 'Did you say 4212 Adams Mill Road?' He was small and his body had long since begun its vanishing act. He was seventy-eight years old and had been called out of retirement for the job. To the judge it was literally a lifesaver, and his gratitude toward the agency was boundless.

'No, sir. It's 3212.'

'Oh, okay. Good friend of mine lives at 4212. Wonderful fellow. Couldn't imagine what he'd be doing with you people. Now I know that came out sounding critical, but you know what I mean.'

'Yes, sir,' Ferd said. 'Your Honor, under Federal Statute 236.4 paragraph capital G subparagraph small b, agency requests authorization to surreptitiously enter said premises at agency's convenience. Said entry not to occur more than ninety-six hours from now.'

The judge didn't bother asking about grounds.

'So ordered,' he said, adding a surprisingly vigorous rap of his gavel, and they were all walking toward the courtroom door.

Somehow, a special aura had descended over the operation. It was vaguely like the youngest son going to his first dance. The Garbageman had called for a field operation. And it had been approved. Dunn had been reached at the funeral parlor and had said yes. Yeager had even agreed to allow Coolidge and Shoemaker to go along, although they wouldn't get anywhere near the action, if there was any; the Library intellectuals weren't trained for it.

Four hours after the judge ruled, they were in Yeager's limousine, cruising on the Beltway outside Washington.

Coolidge, seated next to Yeager, was staring out into the night, trying to create innocent theories that would explain the strange garbage. Shoemaker was on one of the jump seats, his long legs stretched out sideways, scuffing the side of the door.

'Tell us how you're going to keep this out of the papers tomorrow,' Shoemaker said.

'Technique,' Yeager said, smiling fatly. Yeager had once been fat and then lost fifty pounds, but his face had stayed fat. 'I don't like to gamble unless it's absolutely necessary. You start with enough troops to do the job right. You get troops to take care of every possible obstacle. Then you walk in.'

Coolidge couldn't help noting some lipsticked cigarettes in the ash-tray. He wasn't sure he believed them; knowing Yeager, they could have been planted.

'It's an odd-shaped lot,' Yeager said. 'Lucky. House is sitting catercorner. The houses on either side face away. A catercorner house tends to be neglected by the next-door neighbors. And there's nothing across the street; it's Rock Creek Park. There are no signs of life in the house. All the omens are good.'

The telephone buzzed. Yeager flipped the receiver up from its cradle under the armrest.

'Yeager.' There were only muted road sounds in the Lincoln as Yeager listened. He hung up.

'One or two complications,' he said. 'Nothing really complicated, but we'll cruise for a couple of minutes while they work it out.' He picked up the intercom mike. 'We'll stay on the Beltway a few more minutes,' he told the driver. 'Did I tell you guys about a restaurant Harry and I discovered the other day?'

'What the hell's going on?' Coolidge said.

'They set off an alarm.'

'Is it still ringing?'

'They cut it in seven seconds. I brought an electrician along.'

'Then why are we still cruising around on the Beltway?' Jake asked.

Yeager closed his eyes.

'Does all this mean we're inside the house?' Coolidge asked.

'No, it does not mean we're inside the house.'

The phone was buzzing again. Yeager said 'Yeager' into it.

'This is where we all end up in jail,' Shoemaker said to Coolidge.

'Watergate all over again. I'm finally getting my chance to read Proust. What do you bet it turns out to be Ellsberg's psychiatrist?'

'We're legal,' Coolidge mumbled.

'Yeah, uh, huh, hmm, okay.' Yeager didn't bother to hang up the phone this time. He looked irritated.

'You geniuses missed two Great Danes,' he said. 'They're barking their goddamn heads off.'

Coolidge and Shoemaker looked at each other and the two of them actually blushed for an awful moment, stung at the thought of such gross incompetence. Then they began to recover, first staring up into their heads, eye-

30

brows knitted, reconsidering, raking over the data, going down the line of plastic-covered trays.

'Did I miss something?' Coolidge said.

'Hell, no.'

Shoemaker got rattled easily and that's when his words tended to pour out with the bare minimum of parts of speech.

'No dog food cans. No Milk Bone boxes. No hair balls. No frayed collars, no leashes, no sprays. Two? Great Danes?'

'Maybe they're only Dobermans,' Yeager said.

Coolidge had his head back, resting comfortably, staring up at the domelight, thinking.

'I don't want to sound dogmatic, but there is no dog coming out of that house,' he said.

'There isn't so much as a canary in there,' Jake said.

'Now wait a minute,' Yeager, the savvy field man, said to the two amateurs. 'The whole point of this operation is that the garbage has been faked, right?'

Shoemaker and Coolidge looked at each other and timed their reponse, giving a simultaneous 'Right.'

'That being the case, they might easily have hidden evidence of dog. Right?'

Shoemaker spoke as though talking to a child: 'But the dogs are supposed to be a deterrent. They're *obviously* not trying to hide them, right?'

'Oh. Yeah. Ha-ha. Right.' Yeager managed to recover quickly. 'You know, I actually had a dart gun brought along in case of dogs. They brought the wrong shells for it.'

'Don't wait,' Coolidge said. 'Move right in. There aren't any dogs in there. It's probably a tape.'

Yeager looked as though he was sorry he'd brought the amateurs along.

Coolidge was making himself comfortable, legs stretched out, head back against the plush cushioning. He sniffed the new-car smell, which Yeager refreshed every four thousand miles with a spray can.

'That place is goddamn fascinating,' Coolidge said.

'There's no sanity clause,' Shoemaker said.

*   *   *

31

Yeager had been brought to the point of retiring from the field, defeated. Which was not only un-American, it was un-Dunn. Yeager hated to quit, but the alarm had been set off eighteen minutes before, and no matter how bad they were, sooner or later someone was going to show up.

His neat little operation, with troops for all eventualities – everything under control, Yeager marching in at the last moment without even breathing hard – had become a total fiasco. Three in the morning. Lights on in both floors of the house. Agents in small groups on the lawn near the sidewalk, waiting for Yeager to command. The loose cannons, Coolidge and Shoemaker, up close to the house, provoking the dogs.

'That's it, we're getting out of here,' he said, as Coolidge strolled back.

'Give me the key,' Coolidge said. 'It's a goddamn loop. The pattern repeats after three minutes. Come on; you can tell Harry I picked your pocket.'

'Walter, don't tempt me.'

Coolidge knew it was completely improper, but he also knew that underneath Yeager's easy friendliness there was a solid case of meanness. Enough of it to want to see what happened if Coolidge were to walk through that front door.

'Come on, come on. Break the rules. That shows leadership. Harry will love you for it.'

Yeager nodded slightly, thinking about it. He smiled slightly. Shrugged slightly. 'We'll see that you get the very best of care, Walter,' he said, handing over the key.

Coolidge went up the flagstone walk as if he was coming to dinner, with Vera waiting inside wearing nothing but caviare paste. He was 99 percent sure. The dogs were going crazy. He could practically hear saliva dripping on parquet flooring. But he stuck the key in the lock, anyway, holding tightly to theory.

'Get away from here or I'll blow your head off,' a voice said.

Coolidge stopped. He briefly flirted with the problem of turning back and facing Yeager. He told himself that had nothing to do with his decision, that he was sticking to fundamentals. He flung the door open.

It was a conventional D.C. colonial. Living room to the right. Dining room to the left. Stairs going up in between. Coolidge strolled into the living room through the din of dogs barking and a man's threatening voice, feeling the pure joy of craftsmanship. There was a body on the living room couch. Slowly he walked up to it. He couldn't say why, but he wasn't in the least surprised when it turned out to be a dummy. It was just another little proof.

Garbage was always right.

Yeager's troops were bustling around taking pictures, searching, making notes. Someone had turned the dogs off: it was a tape recorder in the pantry. The man's voice came from an old Dokorder in the hall closet.

Coolidge was flopped in a big soft chair. Shoemaker was on the ottoman. The red Oriental on the floor was made of cotton, but it was hardly worn. The decor seemed strangely out of date for this part of Washington. The furniture was pre-Danish-modern ten-cent-store chintz.

The male dummy was lying, arms behind his head, in the classic position of television watching, and the TV was on. There was a timer set for on at noon, off at 2 A.M. There were sensors in the dummy, with multicolored wires that ran off to a hole drilled through the Oriental rug into the floor. There was another dummy in the kitchen, leaning over the sink, and two offspring upstairs. Standard family, wired for something.

Yeager came in and sat down heavily at the far end of the couch. He looked at the television set.

'Anything good on?' he said.

'Do you understand this?' Coolidge replied.

'What do you think I am – nuts? This place looks like the Ho Chi Minh Trail: there's sensors all over the place. And Geiger counters. *Everywhere*. There's some pretty high-class data-transmitting equipment in the attic. It's on. Transmitting.'

Coolidge sat there.

'Don't say it,' Yeager said. 'I'll never make cracks about garbage again, so help me. Oops, excuse me, trash. There now, I've eaten my crow like a good boy. I cleaned the plate.'

33

'It isn't enough,' Shoemaker said, gazing off into space, and then the phone rang.

The phone, a model that hadn't been around for a while, was on an imitation-ebony flower stand. According to Ma Bell, it hadn't rung in twenty-eight years.

Even Yeager's jaw dropped. But then he quickly returned to his laid-back mode, groaning to his feet, going over to the phone perturbed at having his rest interrupted, the ex-fat man still moving like a fat man.

Yeager picked it up and listened. He frowned. His eyes seemed to get lost somewhere. His mouth didn't know whether to go up or down; it stayed absolutely horizontal. But Yeager remained Yeager. Whatever conflicts he was feeling resolved themselves into nonchalance. He held the phone out to Coolidge.

'It's for you,' he said.

All Eyes

Harry Dunn was in his private screening room scanning data, cutting across categories, touching all bases, working on his never-ending state-of-the-world report. The screening room was a small theater, its rows of seats raked sharply upward toward the console at the rear, where Harry sat, in control, minding everybody's business.

He was working on his favorite category, which was no category; it was SAMPLE, which sampled the planet, going randomly to all sources. It gave Harry a fast look at the world without going into the details. It also gave him satisfaction, watching his baby at work. He watched, pleased, as the staggering variety of data whipped across the screen. Satellite shots of the missile installation at Chelyabinsk. The lounge of a bordello on K Street. Aerial footage of the new MIG-32 performing aerobatics. Three views of the men's room at Union Station. A three-page CIA analysis of the Soviet SS-22 missile. An appreciation of the morale of the Chinese 57th Army in Mongolia. A map, fifteen minutes old, of the current Soviet missile sub deployments in the Atlantic.

It was endless. And it would always be endless, since the data was monitoring a changing, growing, restless organism: mankind. There was a meeting of the nine *comandantes* of the Sandinista National Directorate in Managua, with running translation. A meeting of the Argus group in Princeton, discussing the feasibility of the new Barbarossa missile concept. A satellite shot of the Kremlin. General Cyrus Munk and his secretary, Master Sergeant Linda Schwartz, making love in a room at the Whitley Hotel. The airport waiting rooms: LAX, LAG, JFK, MIA. The entrance to a KGB safe house on Forty-seventh Street in New York City. A Defense Intelligence Agency memo on Russian missile doctrine. An unauthorized Xerox of a State Department policy position paper. It was marked 'Copy 1 of 1 copy.' It was somebody's oddball way of saying Supersecret. Copy 1 of 1 copy, Dunn mused. A real bureaucrat had thought that one up. And then had gone one step further. The total content of the message was: 'The distribution list for Operation Hypotenuse is hereby revoked.' In other words, from now on there would only be blank sheets of paper with 'Copy 0 of 0 copies' written on top. It would be the perfect secret.

Preposterous, Dunn thought, shaking his head, but the thought applied to many things, it being his currently favorite word. Even though he'd started out as an atomic physicist, Dunn had never lost his sense of wonder at technology. He had a way of looking at technology with the amazed eyes of a caveman. It was still hard for him to believe that radio waves actually flew through the air and somehow came out of the speaker. To be tuned in to the world so thoroughly still struck him as preposterous, to have so much data displayed so comprehensively, so easily, so usably.

It was also preposterous not to have had it sooner, given the technical resources of the 1970s. But there had been no Library; the idea had never even received serious consideration. Not until Dunn had proposed it to the President during the campaign, once the polls showed he was likely to beat the incumbent. He had shocked the then candidate when he told him that not even the director of Central Intelligence – the top man in the intelligence community – knew everything: there were vast areas of data that even the top man was shielded from because of the strictures of Need to Know.

It was actually an incredible gap in the government. Nobody knew everything, which cut off countless possibilities for cross-fertilization. And prevented any kind of sensible control. The President-to-be was a believer in control. If he was to have the responsibility for what his government was going to be doing, then he most definitely wanted to know what it was going to be doing.

These two problems had been going deliberately unsolved, decade after decade. When Dunn got around to setting it all down on paper, it took only off-the-shelf ideas. Creativity was hardly required. Dunn's proposal was that a new, highly secret agency be created; an agency that would be far more secret than, say, the National Security Agency, which up until then had been the most secret of all. In the new agency, All Eyes would be the rule. All members of the agency would have access to all data. But as a security precaution, the number of people would be kept to a total of twelve. Twelve superior, proven analysts. Talented at anticipating problems, proposing new options, plans, strategies, contingencies. Generalists who would be culled from among other governmental agencies and private think tanks, solely on the basis of merit. To keep the number down to twelve, each of the generalists also had to be a specialist in some major area.

There was a television news clip of the Soviet President. Dunn froze the frame for a moment. The Soviet leader didn't seem to have deteriorated since his last public appearance, but that wasn't saying much. The question was who? Who would succeed? How could we be ready with contingency plans? It was a key item on the intelligence agenda. The computer resumed its random survey and the head of the Soviet Union was replaced by Congressman Slocum, a member of the Missile Subcommittee, seated at his desk in the House Office Building. He was smiling and beckoning with his index finger, a tumbler of straight bourbon on the desktop. His secretary, about forty-five and stoutish, moved into frame and sat on his lap. Dunn thought the computer was at times diabolical, sampling just enough of a scene to tease and then cutting away, forcing you to call up the whole sequence so it could show you how comprehensive it was, what goodies it had to offer, stored away on tapes and chips and disks. Slocum was replaced by the Soviet Black Sea Fleet in line astern, and then went to the latest combat readiness report, two hours old, of the Minuteman missiles.

SITE	READY	NOT READY
Ellsworth AFB, SD	99	51
Grand Forks AFB, ND	103	47
Malmstrom AFB, MO	163	37
Minot AFB, ND	129	21
Warren AFB, WY	119	81
Whiteman AFB, MI	78	72

It was really inexcusable. They badgered the hell out of everybody to get the damn missiles and then they could only manage to keep about two-thirds of them on line. Fortunately, the Russians were even worse; they were doing only about 40 percent flyable.

Senator Garvey flashed on the screen, asking questions. It was Garvey's favorite pastime. He was always picking brains, taking all he could, giving nothing in return. He was sitting at his favorite table at Auburn's, pumping his speechwriter, Davey Reed.

Garvey was chairman of the subcommittee that oversaw the Library. Dunn had gone up against him any number of times, dodging and weaving through executive sessions. It wasn't all that difficult; Garvey's questions tended to be like mush. He was obviously suspicious of the Library, didn't believe that it was a mere collecting and collating agency, but was too cautious to make any accusations or even ask provoking questions without knowing what he was talking about.

Which was Garvey's style: tightrope walking. He was a closet liberal from a conservative state. Both the Americans for Democratic Action and the Americans for Conservative Action, polar opposites in outlook, gave him a 50 percent rating on his Senate voting record. Which was one of the reasons Harry Dunn considered him to be dangerous.

Garvey had been so careful with his career that he was virtually unassailable; he was considered to be 'sound,' he was trusted. The other side of the coin was that since he didn't seem to stand for anything in particular, he had no national constituency. It was Dunn's theory that Garvey wanted a shot at the presidency, and was going to use the Library as the means of achieving it. He would try to expose the Library in some way, create a scandal about it, perhaps demonstrate that its efficiency was undemocratic. Go about it in a way that both liberals and conservatives could rally around. The fact that he would be destroying *the* most fruitful intelligence organization the country had ever had would be immaterial. Politicians used what was available, what was exploitable, what would get the public's attention.

Harry wasn't even bitter about it. Bitterness was not a constructive emotion; it was irrelevant to the problem-solving process, Harry simply accepted Senator Garvey as a given, one more contradictory factor in American life, and gave him Computer Importance.

The senator was looking over the top of his glass at his aide, tossing out one question after another. Garvey gave the strong impression of roundness: his cheeks were pudgy and pink and he was short, with a substantial belly, although it didn't stick out like the usual middle-aged paunch; he was round everywhere, it seemed a natural part of his curvature.

'What do you think they're really doing at the Library?' Garvey was saying, flat noncommittal expression on his face, carefully developed blank expression in his eyes, as though not putting any curves on the ball, not prompting his victim in any way, asking only for objectivity. But it was clearly something they had discussed many times.

'It's a rest home for basket cases they don't want drinking in the daytime – or it's the Eyes and Ears of the World.'

Davey Reed was the physical and psychological reciprocal of his boss: thin, medium height, intense, neurotic, fast on the trigger, a chance-taker. There was a lot less ice in his glass.

Auburn's was a political hangout, and Dunn saw a group of congressional aides and congressmen walking by at the edge of the frame. There was a pause until they disappeared.

'They aren't spending a hell of a lot of money,' Garvey said, a flat observational tone, as though he were looking through field glasses at a butterfly and making idle conversation.

'If their input is everybody else's output, they don't have to,' Reed said.

Garvey showed a lot of emotion: his eyes narrowed.

'Importance is usually revealed by budget size,' Garvey said. 'It's invariable. Big budget, important agency. Little budget, they're working on regulations for windmills. What's a guy like Dunn doing in a low-budget agency?'

'I know a guy who knows a guy who knows a guy,' Reed replied. There was an almost perpetual half smile on his face. 'He said he said he said that the director of Central Intelligence said that the President said the Library was the meeting place of historical inevitability and technology.' Reed stopped smiling. 'Does that answer your question?'

But Reed suddenly disappeared and was replaced by the kindly but scowling face of the Russian ambassador, sitting in his conference room, as the computer continued its random sample, tantalizing, titillating, showing, telling, presenting the world as it was, moment by moment, without computer enhancement. The running translation had the ambassador complaining about prices, railing at his aides about how Moscow wouldn't increase his budget. Even the computer seemed bored, and quickly cut away to the Hungarian evening news.

As the idea for the Library was discussed among the President's advisers, more and more enthusiasm had been generated. It suddenly seemed as though the Library was a major opportunity, which past Presidents had been totally ignoring because of the entrenched orthodoxy of the intelligence community. It would give the new President an invaluable tool for dealing with the Russians and with foreign policy in general. It was a way to avoid surprises. It was a means of more accurately determining world realities, and so enabling him to take initiatives where they were most likely to succeed.

Position papers were written and passed around within a select group. The idea of the Library was analysed from every possible point of view. It became apparent that Dunn's concept was too pure. The notion of a mere twelve analysts having access to every bit of intelligence in the country was an ideal, a dream. To turn it into practical application, a supporting organization would be needed. A Beebe, for example, to manage the security of the Library itself, to be the Protector of the Data. There would inevitably be some field operations required which couldn't very well be farmed out to the CIA or FBI, since this would compromise the Library's fundamental secrecy. This meant a Yeager. And other support personnel. There were all those microcams to install, for instance.

The ever-present specter of Richard Nixon brought up the problem of legality. This was solved merely by stretching the meaning of certain clauses in the Foreign Intelligence Surveillance Act, originally passed in 1978 during the Carter administration, which had set up the FISA court system. Fortunately, the drafters of that legislation had used the term 'electronic surveillance' to describe such devices as phone taps. It easily applied also to such devices as microcams. Before too long, the President had appointed three circuit court judges who would sit on the FISA court, thereby guaranteeing cooperation. The Library was thus made legal from top to bottom, with every single microcam and bug having a court order behind it.

And the essence of Dunn's idea remained, which was that twelve, and only twelve, analysts were to be given access to all intelligence data in the nation. (Beebe and Yeager, the operational agents, were not among the twelve.) By doing most of the planning before the election had even taken place, the President had managed to get around *the* major remaining problem: securing the agreement of all the major intelligence agencies to what they would normally have deemed a hare-brained scheme. The President appointed his own loyalists to head CIA, DIA, and NSA, which earned him cooperation that would have been impossible by the middle of his term, when his own appointees would have been largely captured by their own bureaucracies, all with their own new imperatives, loyalties, points of view.

But for Dunn, there remained a fundamental problem: to keep the twelve sane and loyal, and loyal to the right ideas, the right people. He was worrying about that as he watched the world flung past his eyes – a psychiatrist's office in Washington, a homosexual pickup point, the map of a nuclear war game being conducted in the Pentagon, a long shot of the *Washington Post* newsroom, a shot of the Chinese nuclear testing site in Lop Nor – when the computer landed on the worst footage he'd seen in the three years of the Library's existence. He'd already looked at it a dozen times.

There'd been a break-in. The Reference Room had been violated. It was inconceivable, almost as though some natural law had been broken; if the evidence weren't up on the screen, he wouldn't have believed it. But there it was, right in front of him. It had happened on a Sunday, when the equipment was down, maintenance work going on, units disconnected, cables missing.

And yet someone had managed to get the equipment turned on – using jury-rigged cabling – and then taken photographs of the displays. He shook his head, part in despair, part in admiration. It was one of the cleaning women. Burnish brought in vetted ex-FBI employees, whom he got from an employment agency in Washington that specialized in supplying custodial help for secret agencies of government. One of them had been a fake.

They'd at least gotten the camera back; there were thirty-six exposures in it of computer displays. The matron had spotted it hidden under the 'cleaning woman's' dress, as she was leaving for the night; the matron managed to get the camera but not the woman, who ran out through the group of other workers to a waiting car.

They still hadn't been able to track the woman down; her operation had been almost flawless. Whoever she was, she knew too much about the Library. The patch job she had done on the plug panel was ingenious. How could she know to do that? Harry preferred to believe that the information had somehow been gotten from the manufacturer of some of the equipment, but the awful possibility remained that there was a spy in the Library. It had to be considered. It reinforced his feeling that getting Charley Eberhart's successor on the job was the number one priority. Eberhart's job was the insurance policy, far more

42

important than Beebe's; *he* could only act after the fact. Harry began to gnaw away at the problem of how he was going to break the news to Coolidge, when Coolidge's face suddenly appeared on the screen, superimposed on a weather report giving the current atmospheric conditions over the Soviet Union's one hundred largest cities.

'You know, Harry, your telephone operator really knows how to track a guy down,' Coolidge said.

The Reward

On his way back to the Library in Yeager's limousine, Coolidge had enjoyed the fake smell, sipped Yeager's brandy, called the weather on Yeager's telephone. It didn't matter that it was turning into a thirty-hour day: victories canceled out fatigue, cleared the head, toned the muscles, eased bowel movements. Getting the best of someone could stand a dying man on his feet, ready for action.

And you had to expect thirty-hour days when you worked for Harry Dunn. Conventional time meant nothing to him. The world was always at stake and so Harry was always working. *Dunn Paratus* could have been the family motto; *Semper Harry* was the way his employees put it. Worst of all, there was no place Harry couldn't find you. Whom Harry wanted Harry got.

When Coolidge reached Harry's private screening room, Dunn was overseeing the world. Watching here, there, keeping track, always on red alert. The lights in the room were low and the tiered seats rose into blackness, so it took Coolidge a few seconds before he could make out Harry's bulk, defocused by the darkness, seated at the control board.

'I deeply admire competence,' Harry said right off. 'Above everything else in life I admire competence. God damn it, I can like anything if it's done well.' There was a sudden shift of tone that only Harry could keep from sounding ludicrous, because it fit right in with his problem-solving nature, the necessity for accuracy, the importance of qualifiers. 'Except for baton twirlers,' he said, with an explosive little laugh. 'Even competent baton twirlers bore me.' Fast switch back to the apocalyptic mood: 'This country needs about four percent competence to run and we

44

barely make it, barely; it's always hanging in the balance. So when I find someone who's competent *and* has the courage of his convictions, I know I've got an asset.'

'You're not talking about me, are you, Harry?' Coolidge said lightly, sitting down in the second row, twisting in the seat to aim his words in Harry's general direction.

'Damn fine piece of work,' Harry went on, ignoring him, almost mumbling, as though talking to himself. 'Sticking to your guns like that. That's in the noblest tradition, not abandoning the guns.'

Oddly enough, at the same moment the screen was showing Eritrean fieldpieces firing somewhere in the Mogadishu. The thought occurred to Coolidge that conceivably the house on Adams Mill Road was big enough for Harry to drop on them at the next Intelligence Board: USDA-approved bureaucratic meat and potatoes, good for budget, good for the administration, good stuff to lay on the watchdog committee and maybe even shut Senator Garvey up for a while.

'You figure that place really has major implications, Harry?'

'What place?'

There was an edge of impatience in Coolidge's voice. 'The place you just called me at.'

'Tst, of course. Pardon me, I was already on to the next thing. Look, that was valuable in its own way. It shows what we can do. It makes them all sit up and take notice, and that's all to the good. So as an exercise, I think it paid off handsomely.'

'An exercise?'

'Yeah, an exercise.'

'What do you mean, an exercise?'

'Don't you know what that place is?'

'How would I know what it is? Do you know what's in there? Of course you do – you know everything.'

On the screen, Egyptian tanks were training in the Sinai.

'It's a Nuclear Regulatory Commission operation,' Dunn said.

Coolidge was deflating rapidly. 'An NRC installation?' he said without enthusiasm. 'How did you figure that out?'

'I made a few phone calls while you were on your way

here. I'll tell you something else. There's nineteen more of them around the country.'

Coolidge stared stupidly at the screen, watching scenic views of the Khyber Pass. Dunn explained it to the back of Coolidge's head.

'Whole thing is preposterous, really. *Decades* ago, the AEC set up an apartment or home in each of the twenty largest cities. The idea was to monitor the effects of a nuclear blast in case of an exchange between us and the Russians. It was a way of at least getting research data out of a disaster. When AEC became NCR, those funny houses slipped through the bureaucratic crack, which happens to be an infinitely malleable aperture. Nobody ever mentioned them to us. I think they're going to be more careful in the future.'

Son of a bitch, Coolidge thought. That magnificent problem turned out to have a stupid answer. 'The garbage was out there to fool the neighbors into thinking it was a normal household,' he said joylessly.

He could see the whole ridiculous scene. Somewhere in the NRC there were people bringing garbage to work. That's how you got totally irrational garbage, twenty-three adults and half a child in a three bedroom house. 'I guess that's why it was so pure,' he said to Harry.

'What was so pure?'

'The garbage.'

'Can we get on to why I called you here?'

The bureaucrats bringing their garbage to work were bringing in only the good garbage. The bad garbage was being thrown out in the garbage. Or maybe they had gotten self-conscious about garbage now and were throwing it in the Potomac.

'I want you to take on an additional assignment,' Harry said. 'A very important assignment.'

'Okay.'

'I'll tell you right up front it's a funny kind of assignment and you're not going to like it. I don't know – maybe you will, maybe you won't. Most people would say they didn't like it. And maybe they would and maybe they wouldn't. Maybe they'd just feel obliged to say they didn't like it. Do you know what I mean?'

'No.'

'I guess I'm taking forever to get to the point.'

Coolidge yawned. 'Why don't you just tell me what the job is, Harry. It's going on three o'clock.'

'I want you to monitor personnel.'

'Monitor personnel,' Coolidge said, starting to come awake, his eyes squinting as he mentally searched for land mines; the terrain looked harmless so far, even boring.

'It's the true garbage, Walter.'

Coolidge was rapidly coming back to full alertness, still looking off at the periphery, trying to decode the bureaucratese, but not having enough to work with yet. 'What would my duties be?' he said, attempting with the conditional 'would' to insert the thought into the conversation that it was all voluntary, whatever it turned out to be, and that it would be well inside the limits of decent behavior to refuse the assignment.

Dunn's voice got harder. 'It means exactly what it sounds like,' he said, then ending any possibility of it being conditional, added, 'Stop trying to get out of it. You're good and you're stuck with it. It's the good ones who have to carry the others. You will monitor them. Same way we monitor anything and anyone else. Films, tapes, trash, mail, phone calls, everything.'

'Surely not everything, Harry.'

'Let's get it out in the open right away. You're going to have to watch them doing things.'

'You mean like to other people?'

'That's right. Exactly. That and anything else. Anything and everything.'

'Harry, I'm not a voyeur,' Coolidge said.

'The thing to be is detached and objective, and I'm convinced you're the one who can do it. It's data and that's all it is. Data.'

'What am I looking for in the data?'

'Failure of nerve. Quitting. Leaking. Defecting. Before it happens, of course. Nervous breakdowns. Suicides. We put them through a lot, Walter. We make them face the facts. That's rotten. Human beings aren't really made to face the facts all day every day day after day. Human beings need escape and we can't escape. Everywhere we turn, it's the truth staring us in the face.'

47

Coolidge made a face. 'Spying on your colleagues. An imperative of the cold war.'

'Sure it's an imperative. Ninety-eight percent of life is an imperative. How much discretionary life do you think you really have? Don't kid yourself; it's close to nothing.'

'You're worrying too much about them, Harry. They're damn good people. All of them.'

'Yeah, I worry about them too much. I worry about drinking, about drugs, about slips of the tongue. I worry about weakness. I worry about change. The cold war's gone on too long.'

There was a rare tone of weariness in Dunn's voice, as though he himself was facing a problem he couldn't solve.

'Too long, way too long. Much longer than anyone figured. It's exhausted people. How long can you sustain a sense of emergency? A reliable official anonymously mails a damning memo to a congressman. Or rats to the *Times* or *Post*. Or Xeroxes the Bombing Encyclopedia, for God's sake. You can't count on your own people anymore. I think you could see it starting around Korea. That war was not fought with enthusiasm. Nobody marched on the Pentagon, but it was a flat war. Now, hell, people all over government are leaking stuff. Selling it. Even *giving* it to the Russians. I don't have to remind you about the break-in, do I? We still don't know who did it or why. We don't know if that woman had inside information or not; maybe she'd picked things up on previous Sundays. But we have to at least consider the possibility of a foreign agent in the Library.'

Coolidge found himself slipping away, forgetting scruples under the battering of Harry's salesmanship, beginning to see, against his own better judgment, Harry's point of view.

'Now I want you to look at something,' Harry was saying in his didactic tone of voice, the professor of apocalypse, the indefatigable problem solver lecturing on jeopardy and the unthinkable and constancy. 'I want you to watch carefully,' Dunn was saying. 'I'm going to show you what killed Charley Eberhart.'

The True Garbage

Yeager really appreciated a good leg; he'd even codified his admiration into Yeager's First Law: If the length of a woman's calf equaled the length of a woman's thigh, her knee thereby being the bisector, Yeager could put up with a lot of crap.

He looked over at Sybil, who was sitting on the couch talking on the phone, legs crossed, dress high, long catenary thighs curving away like the cables of a bridge toward, variously, the Pink Palace in the Black Forest (before) or the Entropy Express (after). Sybil had two telephones, one at each end of the couch. the white one was personal, the black for commerce. She was talking on the black one while Yeager, sipping straight vodka, pores sucking in perfume, stood across the room casing the place.

The apartment was cool and dark. Sybil used orange lights exclusively. It was so dim the red warning light on the empty humidifier stood out like a beacon. There was an inviting dish of peaches and cherries and apricots sitting on the long, narrow coffee table in front of the couch, but they were all candles. The bacon and eggs on the round table in the dining area was a candle too. Even the tall, slender cylinders that tapered to a point on either side of the stereo were candles.

Sybil finally hung up the phone and broke her classic cross-legged pose to get Yeager a fresh drink. Now she became the confluence and concatenation of Newton's and Yeager's laws, the physics and metaphysics of a heavenly body in motion, a heavenly body with its knees in the right place, the flimsy fabric of her dress alternately hugging and flowing, hugging and flowing, her buttocks swinging and bouncing and shaking, the crease in her dress going back and forth. It reminded him of the escapement in a watch, tick-tock, tick-tock, but attached to a time bomb, tick-tock, quarter-pound standard stick of dynamite, tick-tock, tick-tock, wired to an M-4 fuse, Mk I, tick-tock. . . . She handed him a straight vodka, freezing with a twist, and he made a kiss sound.

While Yeager was sipping his drink, Sybil pulled her dress up and elaborately straightened first one stocking, then the other. Her perfume was like an especially piquant vermouth for the vodka, and he drank it all in, congratulating himself on being such a good comparison shopper. He rated them on:

1. Leg structure
2. Inverse sullenness
3. Faking ability
4. Drink quality
5. Afterglow diplomacy

in that order. So far, Sybil looked like Four Stars, a Best Buy, Recommended for the Weary Traveler. She really seemed eager to please. She was smoothing back that skin-tight dress, charmingly getting another eighth of an inch in length out of it. But she kept right on smoothing, around the buttocks and thighs, her hands finally slipping up to her breasts, cupping them and squeezing the nipples. She winked at him.

'Would you like me to strip?'

Yeager sipped at his drink, playing for time. He couldn't decide if he was feeling visual or tactile. His nose was starting to twitch and he was on the point of giving up laid-back for laid. He had trouble getting his drink down on the coffee table without spilling it.

'Or you can do it if you want. I love being undressed by a horny man,' Sybil whispered in his ear, caving in against him, bumps and curves pressing everywhere. He got a buttock in each hand and pressed her even more, squirming against her, licking her lips, breaking it off only to follow his hands south, slowly curving down the rear of her thighs to the hem of her dress. Her dress was so tight it

50

was hard to slide his hands up under it. He started working the dress up her body, a delicious struggle that ended when he had to unzip her in back to get it past her breasts, then suddenly whipped it up and off her, like a magician producing a woman, materialized out of nowhere.

She was wearing a black bra and black half-slip. 'At times like this I stop being a leg man,' Yeager said to her. 'Now I'm an everywhere man. All flesh is created equal.' He was drawing his mouth across her midriff in one marathon kiss. Then he descended even lower pushing her slip up, talking to her thighs, kissing the flesh between her stockings and panties. She was wearing a garter belt because he didn't like panty hose, as no red-blooded man did; they were imposed by mindless manufacturers and gullible women who put mere utility ahead of male satisfaction. He was kissing both thighs just below the panties when he said, 'Know what I think?' voice quavering, cool gone, still trying to hold on to it out of conditioned reflex built deeply into his nervous system, but gone, gone.

'Follow me,' Sybil said.

They went toward the bedroom, Yeager shedding clothes like a pinwheel while intently studying the slip hugging Sybil's rear, loving the static cling. By the time they got to the bedroom, Yeager was down to a pair of plaid shorts. Sybil, soft computer, programmed to a move, sat on the edge of the bed and then dropped back to her elbows to watch Yeager, with infinite relish, push her slip up and begin pulling her panties down, giving an assist by lifting up at the right moment, beige silk with black lace looking devastatingly ravishing at her knees.

'Oh, God.'

'Now don't overreact.'

'This is crazy. I can't do it.'

'Sure you can. Now take it easy. Live with it. You haven't lived with it.'

'I've seen enough. I respectfully decline the assignment, Harry.'

Dunn hit a button and froze the frame. 'O-kay,' he said slowly. It wasn't an okay at all, merely an acknowledgment type of okay, meaning that, intellectually speaking, he had understood the words.

51

'I mean it, Harry.'

Yeager's face was all bulging eyes and flared nostrils and his tongue was hanging out; worse yet, the fish-eye lens of the microcam, which saw wide-angle, threw in some distortion and it made Yeager look vaguely like a scared horse. Sybil had a look of bemusement. Her head was lifted off the bed and she seemed fascinated by Yeager's face, as though pondering what all the excitement was about. Up on Harry's screen, Sybil had an odd look of innocence. She had this body which men got crazy over, but deep down she really didn't know why; men were a constant but they were a mystery, and she was watching carefully each and every time as though hoping that one day she'd figure it all out.

Coolidge's right hand was holding up his chin as he stared at the screen. 'This is un-American,' he said. 'A man should be allowed to fuck in privacy. It's in the Constitution. I know it for a fact. Benjamin Franklin put it in.'

'This is what All Eyes means. Somebody had to do this. You have to do it.'

'You've got this stuff on everybody in the Library? You've got it on me?'

Coolidge was thinking about what he'd been doing to whom lately. And, worse, what he'd been saying about whom, especially the Head whom sitting in the back of the room. Coolidge could hear Dunn moving for about three seconds before he saw anything start to happen. Then Harry's bulk loomed large in the dimness as he struggled out from behind the console and seemed to float gracefully down the few steps to where the screen was.

'You think I give a shit about this stuff?' he said, pointing to Sybil, although he did an unconscious double take because Sybil was the stuff middle-aged dreams were made of. 'How people get their kicks is irrelevant to me. Okay? It doesn't affect my opinion of their usefulness one way or another. Hell, this is kindergarten, for Christ sake. You're going to see a lot worse than this. My only concern is national security; that's all that counts up there on the screen. By the way, our friend Yeager blew it. Did you catch it?'

Coolidge rubbed his eyes, which had already been open

too long for one day. 'He left his ID in his pants on the living room floor,' he said disgustedly.

Dunn smiled, satisfied with his man.

'I'll want reports on little things like that. I intend to spot-check.'

Coolidge was looking at satin and lace up on the screen, panties around her knees, sex exposed, trying to be honest with himself about her and himself and Vera and everybody. Everybody. Dissertation titles flew through his brain. Did he have raw material?

'This is what killed Charley Eberhart,' he mused.

'Do it for a year, that's all I'm asking. By that time I'll have searched out a doctor or a psychiatrist or some kind of professional we can train as a full-time monitor.'

'How do you know *I* won't kill myself?'

'I'm gambling.'

'Terrific.'

'You won't. You're used to garbage. Sort through it, make observations, get rid of it. It's the same old stuff, facing the facts. Just don't make it bigger than it is.'

She still had her shoes on. Coolidge knew that high heels were erotic, but he never understood why. On the other hand, how could you understand sex intellectually? Were shoes any crazier than breasts or asses? On the other hand, nature hadn't invented shoes. Who had discovered the high heel?

'I can't decide if this is a compliment or an insult,' Coolidge said. 'Why me, Harry?'

Dunn stopped pacing, a dim image of lace panties on his forehead. He looked at Coolidge with a blank expression on his face and started pacing again, dredging up the logic that he'd already forgotten.

'In the first place, you're relatively unimportant,' Dunn said, solving problems now, oblivious to delicate feelings, pure manipulator of equations. 'You're like the butler in an old mystery story. Your background isn't "hard" science. You were something of an experiment to begin with. Nobody takes trash covers seriously. This thing with the NRC will make you look good, but it'll be like the dog on its hind legs; it's amazing that you can do it at all, know what I mean?'

'Yeah.'

'You're not threatening. That's a great asset; that's money in the bank. Nobody would ever dream that *you* were monitoring personnel. That's assuming they even know that Library personnel are monitored. They may not.'

'I didn't,' Coolidge said ruefully.

'Then there's your record. You probably don't realize how good your record is. Want to know what your most outstanding characteristic is? You read the *New York Times*, but you don't write for it.'

Coolidge was trying to look modest. It was no problem.

'And you've had opportunities. By God, have you had opportunities. You've been on the periphery of a few major fuckups.'

'Yep.'

'You saw it coming, you warned your superiors, they did nothing. Neither did you. You didn't go around kicking over ashcans, like Ellsberg or Fitzgerald. You stayed on the team. You never claimed to have revealed knowledge from God. Do you know what that's worth today, Walter?'

It was an ice-cold analysis, which made Coolidge blush. The way Harry was talking, he wasn't sure if he was blushing with pleasure or shame, but he was doing his best to look pleased. After all, Harry was praising him. It was a rare moment. Coolidge hadn't gotten this much praise in his entire life. The important thing to remember was that Dunn was being sincere, it wasn't some kind of administrator's act. Coolidge was a highly valued employee of the U.S. government and that's all there was to it. It was no small accomplishment. It wasn't just any clod they would trust with the job of Federal Voyeur. It was a struggle for him, but it was crucial and he managed to get it out with the right intonations and appropriate facial expressions.

'Nice of you to say that, Harry.'

'Sure.' Harry hit a switch at one of the seats and made Sybil go away. 'Listen,' he said as he headed for the door. 'You start to get any funny thoughts, you talk to me, okay?'

'Hell,' Coolidge said.

54

II   The Doctor

This Place Is Leaking

Trash bored Tice. It aroused no analytical emotions in him; it was the garbage, the whole garbage, and nothing but the garbage. he was counting the days until he got off the trash run. His wife had given him a magnum of cologne for his birthday. She wouldn't even talk to him at night until he'd spent twenty minutes in the shower. Tice wasn't sure, but he had a definite feeling that trash was a punishment tour for some sin he'd committed, or hadn't.

The truck was moving quietly through quiet early-morning suburban Maryland streets. Which in itself was a classic Holmesian dog-in-the-night clue for the paranoid and the quick-witted: it was a garbage truck that didn't go out of its way to wake people up. Butterworth turned the truck into Ambrose Street and Tice spotted the next pickup. The garbage cans had already taken on personality for him. This one was a green plastic fluted job with a black lid. It was really loaded with goodies this morning and the lid wouldn't stay on straight. It was tilted at a rather rakish angle that reminded Tice of a beret. It gave the can a devil-may-care look, almost as though it were aware of its four-star rating, VIP trash, more pregnant with meanings than the usual run of congressional, bureaucratic, or foreign consular garbage. In the ingrown convolutions of Washington, that had to be a covert status symbol of some kind or other.

Tice dropped out of the right-hand seat easily, the truck still moving. He was only few feet from the green and black can when he realized that a second garbage truck was easing quietly up to the curb, nose to nose with Butterworth's. Tice had come to know garbage trucks in approximately the way F-14 pilots knew MIG-23s. It wasn't

Library. It wasn't even county. It was an International, and the county didn't use them. Besides, who'd ever heard of a county garbage truck showing up an hour ahead of schedule?

Butterworth had reached the same conclusion. He was inching up on the other truck, gunning his engine loudly. It sounded threatening as hell. The second garbage truck began to roll backward, until its driver started gunning *his* engine, fighting back. They were like two woolly mammoths, butting heads, forcing each other backward and forward in a ritual battle over territory.

In the meantime, Tice found himself staring at a bad face across the black plastic lid. They both had their arms around the can. Tice tried to yank it free, but the other guy went with the flow and Tice ended up backpedalling off-balance.

'Go back to your racing form,' the other man said. 'I'll take care of this.'

Was four-star garbage so important that agencies were starting to fight over it in the streets? Tice knew he was supposed to deliver the goods, but he wasn't supposed to draw attention or engage in bloodshed that people would notice.

'Who are you with?' he whispered, attempting to negotiate.

'You want to be a vegetable? It's okay with me.'

'Don't talk like that,' Tice said.

'Let go.'

'What's your authorization? Who are you with? Let's talk about this.'

'I'll give you three seconds.'

The sound of the garbage trucks was getting noticeable, two goliaths roaring at each other in first gear, not giving an inch. Tice was trying to arrive at the correct bureaucratic decision, when a lady in a housecoat went by, led by a dog about to make his daily contribution to the plague. Suddenly the two opposing garbage collectors went into an act, as though they'd rehearsed it for weeks, cooperatively carrying the can toward the rear of Tice's truck, while the lady glared at big government: two grown men and two vehicles for one paltry garbage can. When she was half a block away, the man said, with an air of finality, 'Okay, this is it. This is your big chance to grow old.'

The man's intensity astonished Tice. And he was no kid. He had to be sixty if he was a day. What was going on? Tice was determined not to yield. The Library was number one priority; the Library yielded to no one. And besides, the man was reaching for something in his jacket. It was time to stop thinking, and Tice handed himself over to his spinal cord in total confidence, trusting his reflexes to handle matters.

Tice let go of the garbage can, grabbed the man's arm with one hand and produced a .38 from a pocket in his pants leg with the other. He pushed the pistol up against the garbage can, planning to shoot right through it, the garbage serving as a silencer. He was already tightening his squeeze on the trigger when the other man's face started turning blue and he was gasping for air.

The man had been reaching for his heart.

Tice quickly slipped his pistol under the lid onto the garbage. The man's eyes were going up to his head and, still gasping, he made a tiny gurgling sound and went limp, his body sagging over the black lid of the garbage can.

The second driver saw it all. He backed up and roared away, outnumbered. Tice, still fighting for appearances, struggled to hold the man in a vertical position, without spilling the garbage all over the sidewalk, until Butterworth finally got over to him. Then the two of them made a superb team. It was as if they had been doing it all their lives. They took a fast look up and down the street – the lady seemed fascinated by her defecating dog – cased the windows for witnesses, and then tossed garbage and man into the back of the truck with one very professional, bored garbageman's pitch.

When Coolidge saw the item in Senator Oliver Garvey's trash, his first impulse was to ball it up real small and chew on it. Swallow and Forget, a new security classification, since forgetting it seemed infinitely preferable to facing it.

It was a scrap of paper, a note Garvey had been given by one of his aides, reminding him of an appointment. Below the aide's writing Garvey had doodled. He'd doodled the nation's biggest single secret, O.F.F., an acronym that only the top of the elite were privy to. The Joint Chiefs, the secretaries of state and defense, the President, and Ives. And the Library. Even the thousands of men involved in the various aspects of O.F.F didn't know they were part of it. O.F.F. resembled the Manhattan Project in that respect, and was far more important. It was the Library that had brought it all together, had made it possible, had created what was easily the rarest acronym in government, and now it had turned up in Garvey's garbage. He'd even thrown it away!

The really strange part about it was that Garvey didn't seem to know what the letters meant. He was amusing himself with it. 'Office of Fiscal Foolhardiness,' he'd jotted down. 'Office of Foreign Failures,' 'Office of Federal Fuckups.' Garvey knew, but he didn't know. All he knew were the letters. How come Garvey knew only the letters? How could he know that much and no more? What kind of screwball leak was that?

Thinking hard, Coolidge looked over at Jake.

'In the first place, you never saw this,' Coolidge said, putting the doodle in his jacket pocket. 'Never was, never happened. Give yourself a microlobotomy. You could pass a lie detector test. Right?' He looked into Jake's eyes, watching for the quality of the response.

'My mind has always been weak,' Jake said. 'I can't retain anything.'

'Fine.'

Coolidge started pacing around Jake's office, which wasn't the sanest place in the world; it looked like a thirties movie lobby. There were posters and photographs all over the place. Clark Gable, James Cagney, Errol Flynn in *They Died with Their Boots On*. Which was about the best possible face you could put on a piece of military insanity. Two hundred cavalry attacking ten thousand braves. But then, men had done stranger things when running or, as in this case, galloping for President.

Now that he thought about it, Jake's office wasn't that irrelevant. Hollywood was a subset of politics, or vice versa. Louis B. Mayer, behind-the-scenes boss of MGM party, restlessly in search of the corniest possible denominator. Agents were the campaign managers. The stars were the candidates, bankable when hot, after which they became bit players on the evening news. Coolidge looked for a decent place to sit down. Everything was a salvaged movie seat. He dropped into one of them. sensing a strong smell of buttered popcorn coming up from his unconscious.

'Can you think about other things now?' Jake asked.

'Maybe.'

'That guy who had the heart attack. He was a retired CIA agent. Sixty-four years old. No known affiliations. CIA says CIA had nothing to do with it.'

'Heh,' Coolidge said. There were a lot of former agents, with a lot of devious skills still at their command, loose on the streets.

'Other than that thing I can't remember, there was nothing special in the trash.'

Coolidge could usually spot Garvey's trash from twenty feet off. It was in the center tray on Jake's worktable by the window. The stuff struck Coolidge as classic political garbage, it gave off a distinct odor of ambivalence. It was on both sides of the street, or aisle. It was the stuff Garvey cast off to achieve his middle-of-the-road position.

Jake handed the Trash Report to Coolidge.

TRASH REPORT: #85-10-3
CASE NUMBER: 104759
ABANDONED PROPERTY DONOR: Senator Oliver Garvey (residence)
  1. Assorted left wing fund requests, most unopened.
  2. Assorted right wing fund requests, most unopened.
  3. Document: plans for fund-raiser. Estimated cost. Hall. Four-course dinner. Waiters. Estimated ticket prices. Estimated profit.
  4. *N.Y. Times* and *Washington Post*, today's issues. Articles clipped: nuclear arms negotiations, Social Security story, profile of Presidential Assistant Eugene Ives, NATO military requirements, insurgency in El Salvador.
  5. Mail:
     Invitation to address War Registers League.
     Invitation to address Right to Life.
     Invitation to address Peace Through Strength.

Invitations to speak at UCLA, Columbia, University
of Miami, Michigan State, University of Michigan,
Indiana State.
6. Heavily annotated copy of *On Thermonuclear War*,
by Kahn. Pages torn out: 19, 86, 337-49, 402, 619-22.
7. Twenty-dollar bill used as bookmark.
8. Marked-up copy of Senate Bill S-2019.
9. Copies of letters from constituents, assorted requests.
10. Notes on scrap of paper.
11. Copy of letter from the Egg Association, requesting
affirmative vote on S-2019.
12. Copy of letter from Sec State requesting support for
foreign aid bill now in joint committee.
13. Used lipstick; shade: Dawn Pink.
14. Pair of run panty hose, black.

Garvey's trash was a physical realization of the politician's survival equation, the equation with all factors fac-
tored in, all variables accounted for. It revealed what lay
behind total stasis. The stasis, zero force and zero thrust at
the middle of the road, was in reality the vector resultant
of countless pressures and forces, all canceling each other
out to produce a quivering immobility. It also included the
elusive W factor that all successful politicians needed – W
for winds, the hot streamlining winds of political evolution which destroyed any politician whose weather factor
wasn't sufficiently flexible, who couldn't tell the difference between, say, southeast by east and east-southeast.

'Cross out item ten and have the page retyped. No, ink it
out. Black ink.' Coolidge was holding his head in his
hands, staring at the rug, which looked like something
from a vintage Loews movie palace. 'No. Cut it out of the
list with a razor and then have it retyped and give me the
piece you cut out.'

Garvey had access to the Library; somebody was talking, leaking, giving things away. Coolidge's first thought
was that it was inconceivable. Obviously impossible. The
only people who knew were 100 percent reliable. He'd
barely thought this when he realized it was wrong. Of
course it was conceivable; why else would some poor slob
have to do Eberhart's job of monitoring personnel? He
went over the few possibilities. First, the politicians: the

President, Ives, the secretary of state, the secretary of defense. That was all; even the Vice-President was in the dark. Common sense ruled out these four – it would be political suicide for them if O.F.F. were leaked to the public. Second, the military types: the four Joint Chiefs. But the Joint Chiefs were gung ho; O.F.F. would be their greatest achievement. They and their predecessors had been preparing it for decades. Maverick, turncoat generals simply didn't make it to the Joint Chiefs. It couldn't be a Joint Chief, it had to be a Librarian.

But all Librarians knew everything; that was the first rule of the Library. It was a conundrum. Anything the Library did to find out who the spy was would be known to the spy. It would make an interesting little problem in paradox for the great problem solver on the ninth floor. Call it Harry's Paradox. Of course, Dunn might have a stroke when he heard the news. Dunn's blood chemistry had to be a mess, considering the number of pounds that blood had to do housekeeping for.

Coolidge hated to be the bearer of the news, even if it did make trash look more or less indispensable. The happy bureaucrat in his soul fought with the realist. It could tear the Library apart. How did you go about solving the problems of hunting the Spy Who Knows Everything?

He figured he'd have a paramedic standing by when he broke the news to Harry.

Dunn's Conundrum

Coolidge nodded at a pair of Beebe's guards and pushed open the door. It was humming right along. The Reference Room. The place of inputs, all inputs, where connections were made that could be made nowhere else, where mere data became information on its way to truth – or, at least, policy.

The beacon shone bright in the darkened room and he homed in on it: the red light of the coffee urn Burnish kept going like an eternal flame. He watched the coffee pour hot and black into the cup, vaguely aware of the buzzing behind him as they talked, observed, commented, differed. Specialists quietly conferring about the patient, which was the planet.

He forgot the saucer, like a good bachelor, and went to his place at the table; it was round, Harry adamantly insisted, for practical and aesthetic rather than symbolic reasons. Harry was there, of course. Harry was always in the Library. Why would you want to be anywhere else when you had the Library to go to?

Coolidge sat down at his assigned place next to Charley Eberhart's empty chair, in a black mood that was a murky concoction of anxiety and anger. Anger at the guilty party, whoever he – or she – was, and anxiety about what would happen to the Library once Coolidge dropped his bomb on them. Whereas the others were on a high, which tended to be the normal emotional state in the Library.

They got high on data, working at the leading edge of reality, out where national interests intersected, where national power clashed against national power, where the real frontiers, as opposed to mere lines on a map, existed. They enjoyed the rush of facts, enjoyed being first, like being the first to fly a jet plane or walk on the moon or talk on the telephone. But the Library's firsts were far bigger than these. In the Library, they were the first to have one and one make two.

Vera was there. And Ma Bell. Mike Barber. Leo Gardella. Alex Hopkins. John Burnish, of course. Harry Dunn, of course. The rest of the Librarians were off in their own departments, pursuing their own specialties. As long as Dunn had four Librarians plus himself he was happy, there was 'ignition,' things would happen.

The computer was doing NATO, throwing statistics and data onto the projection screens that ran around the walls. Coolidge looked over at Vera and got a funny look back. They hadn't made love in weeks, since Coolidge had found out that personnel were monitored. You couldn't even do it in the dark; the damn things were sensitive to infrared. The hotter you got, the clearer the picture. Coolidge hadn't had the time to work out the details of a 'safe bed' yet. He was trying to look professional and all business, but as he looked at her the capillaries in his crotch were starting to expand, or contract, or whatever it was they did.

Vera turned away. She was in the middle of a debate going on about a magnetometer reading from a satellite pass over Eastern Europe. The magnetometer detected the presence of metal, and it was up two percent over Naumburg in East Germany. Coolidge watched Vera talking, trying to picture how she might talk to Oliver Garvey, what she might say, why she might say it. But his imagination failed him.

How could you conjure up a scene like that when it went against everything you previously knew about the individual? He could imagine Vera doing the Hong Kong basket job, but he couldn't picture her giving information to Oliver Garvey.

Or Johnny Burnish, sitting next to Dunn. Burnish was the only old-fashioned aspect of the Library: whenever Harry wanted something done, Burnish made notes with a pencil on a yellow legal pad. This was the best job Burnish had ever had, a high-level, well-paid gofer's job that required not too much in the way of thinking, only energy. He was almost pathologically loyal to Harry Dunn, who'd brought him along from Dunn's Ticonderoga Institute, where Burnish hadn't been making it. If anything, Burnish was even more improbable than Vera.

Coolidge sipped some of the hot coffee and, while waiting for his big moment, desultorily went through a pile of printouts Burnish had left at his position. One of them was an ID photo of the dead CIA agent, along with his dossier, including the names of those he'd worked with and for in his eighteen years at CIA. An investigation was no doubt well under way, although the Library left such matters to others. There were tens of thousands of people working on every single item of intelligence that came into the system. The Librarians were after bigger game: juxtapositions, signs, portents, messages in the tea leaves, or in the sky.

'A two percent change in the magnetometer readings is change,' Vera was saying.

'No, it isn't.' Harry was sympathetic but unmoved. 'Two percent is a lurch. Two percent is noise.'

'Two percent is a new shipment of cigarette lighters to the PX,' Mike Barber put in. 'It's small. Vera. Very small.'

'It's not the size, Mike, it's how you use it,' Vera replied sweetly.

'Oh, well,' Barber said, 'that's different. In that case, let's by all means pursue it until Vera is satisfied, if that's possible.'

Leo Gardella stifled a dirty laugh, shaking his head. He winked at Vera. Gardella. His only problem, aside from keeping his beautiful young wife happy, was a low tolerance for the irrationality of others. Gardella and Garvey? Gardella would have nothing but contempt for Garvey. He would mortally insult him within five minutes of meeting; Gardella had reserves of anger to draw on when needed.

It couldn't be Gardella. Or Barber, for that matter, sitting there in his perfect clothes. Dark brown corduroy pants. Rep suspenders. Deep blue shirt with brown stripes, plus a vaguely orange tweed tie. His eyeglasses glistened. Barber would never be caught wearing eyeglasses whose plastic frames had gone dull. Barber had to be perfect, because he had no ego. None. Everything he owned had to be perfect, everything he did. It was necessary for Barber to be invulnerable. Coolidge couldn't believe Barber would take the chance of exposing himself, not so much to danger as to criticism, which would destroy him far more quickly than a bullet from Beebe's automatic.

And Harry. Harry was looking at Vera with that problem-solving look of his. His blood pressure was probably a thousand over six hundred. 'What are we arguing about? Let's take a look at Naumburg,' he said, Obvious. Go right to the heart of the matter. Would Harry destroy his own baby?

Vera did input at her keyboard, and all five screens of the main display directly across from Coolidge were suddenly wiped clean and replaced by a satellite shot of classic German countryside. Hills, valleys, picturesque little toy towns not much more than a kiloton apart, as the Pentagon was fond of putting it. Vera selected one small area of the picture and blew it up to fill the five screens.

'79TH GUARDS TANK DIVISION,' the computer printed out over the picture.

They could see soldiers walking along wooden paths toward a mess hall. A blurred ambulance was speeding along a road toward the hospital. There were quite a few tanks in the tank park. Heavies. About seventy-five of them. They could read the numbers on the tanks. One tank was undergoing maintenance, with an open instruction manual on the turret. They couldn't quite read it.

'It's a week old,' Vera said, looking at the displays behind Coolidge, which duplicated those on the other side of the room, so no one had to twist to look. She kept her eyes on the screens. 'We lost the latest picture. The C-130 missed the weekly film drop, so we've got to reshoot and try again.'

'Then all we've got is the two percent,' Hopkins said.

Hopkins's manner was to be obnoxious, although you weren't supposed to take offense. He was three inches short of a basketball player and thin almost to the point of invisibility. His gray sideburns squirmed around to the edge of his jaw and continued on down, framing his face and going critical at his chin, bursting into a Vandyke.

'That's right,' Vera agreed. 'We've got no proof there are more tanks now than there were last week.'

'My dear, you're taking our time up with ephemera,' Hopkins, looking like the perfect shirt ad, said dryly.

'It's change,' she persisted. 'Something is stirring.'

'It's two percent, Vera,' Harry said, shrugging his shoulders.

'I wouldn't want to hang by two percent.'

Hopkins's brain had sponged up enormous quantities of data. He was in charge of electromagnetic transmissions. That included any and all messages that were propagated through the air. Radio and TV broadcasts. Diplomatic transmissions. Military. Citizens band babble. Telemetry. The chatter of taxi companies in Leningrad. Control tower conversations. Hopkins sometimes babbled like a madman, describing what it was that came into the computers day after day. Now he put his knowledge to work, interrogating the computer.

'CODE NAME CIA NAUMBURG?'

'SAWDUST II.'

'LATEST REPORT SAWDUST II?'

'EXPECTED ARRIVAL 645TH GUARDS TANK REGIMENT ON SCHEDULE. TOTAL WILL BE 45 TANKS, 600 ASSORTED VEHICLES, 4000 MEN.'

'There's your two percent,' Hopkins said. 'You got a reading as the relief was beginning to take place. Temporarily, they've got more vehicles in Naumburg.'

'Nice piece of work, though, Vera,' Harry, the good administrator, said. 'Russians move in a few vehicles and you catch it. Not bad. Next.'

Vera was giving Harry her best bitchy smile as he was talking, but she was thinking hard. Coolidge could tell. He always knew when Vera was thinking. Sometimes she did it at funny times, but he could always tell. So he wasn't surprised when she went into a fast dialogue with the computer, and the computer began answering in German: they were hearing a telephone conversation over the speakers placed around the room. Vera inputted for a computer translation; it lacked elegance, but there could be no mistaking the meaning.

It was a conversation between a woman and a man in Breslau. She was ordering more girls for one of the chain's bordellos. The one in Naumburg.

Vera smiled at the round table.

'More boys means more girls, otherwise the boys get

rancid. Gentlemen, they're reinforcing the whorehouses.'

'The two percent must be the metal clips on the garter belts,' Hopkins said.

'You owe her a lunch,' Gardella said to Hopkins.

'An extra tank regiment in Naumburg,' Harry was musing. 'Interesting.' It was easy to see the wheels turning in his head: he was going to beat CIA to it.

'Now that you've had your fun, there's something I'd like to discuss,' Coolidge said.

'By the way, Vera, let's be sure and see the new satellite footage as soon as it arrives,' Harry said.

'This next one isn't so nice,' Coolidge said.

'If that C-130 pilot can manage to catch it,' Vera said.

The computer had already left Naumburg, as well as Coolidge, behind and was heading south and east toward NATO's right flank. Diogenes Station, the American listening post in Sinop on the Black Sea, was being threatened by demonstrating Turkish radicals. At the same time, the Soviet's main missile testing site near Tyuratam was showing signs of increased activity, indicating that a missile test might be coming up. Did that mean Turkish radicals were being run from Moscow?

Barber asked the computer where General Yeremenko, who was running the SS-45 missile program, happened to be at the moment.

'GENERAL YEREMENKO LEFT MOSCOW LAST NIGHT ABOARD AN ILYUSHIN 21. DESTINATION: TYURATAM.'

Gardella immediately checked to see if the monitoring stations on Cyprus, on Midway, and in the Aleutians had been alerted for a forthcoming test. They hadn't. Furthermore, the computer had no data on the Turkish radicals. This needed exploring, and Burnish was making notes for the President.

Watching, Coolidge shook his head in admiration. They were smart. Cross-trained. Fantastic instincts. They could sniff out possibilities on the barest hints of data. Harry had hired well. Wasn't this the right way to do it? Turn them loose on the problem of the leaker, put those minds to work on it, let them make their combinations and their connections. But he hesitated.

Coolidge wasn't a spy, or even an intelligence man for

that matter, not born, anyway – thrust upon, perhaps – but he knew how insidious his little item was. Would they continue to sit there spinning off ideas with the freedom they had now, or would the process dry up, wrecked by the convolutions of suspicion, which were endless in any case. Suspicion and intelligence went together. Was it worth warning the leaker?

Weirdly, Senator Garvey suddenly appeared on all screens. Garvey had Computer Importance.

Coolidge's eyes flicked around the room. It told him nothing; the darkness in the room prevented any kind of psychoanalysis.

Garvey was sitting on a park bench in Lafayette Park, across the street from the White House, where protesters often gathered. It was odd. The date and clock superimposed on the display indicated that this was real time: Garvey was out there *now*, sitting with a former director of CIA, Herbert Purefoy.

'You heard, I suppose?' Purefoy was saying.

'I heard,' Garvey said.

'I had nothing to do with it, Oliver.'

'Who?'

'The general.'

'The general.' Garvey said it as though it were a disease.

'His last assignment was with DIA and I think it went to his head. He somehow got the idea there was a trash cover on you, Oliver. He wanted to protect you.'

'Who steals my trash steals garbage,' Garvey said. 'Tell him to mind his own business.'

'I've already leaned on him; it won't happen again.'

'That's what you said after that stupid break-in attempt at the Library. You've got to keep the general under control. Discretion is everything.'

'I'll do that, Oliver, but discretion is not everything,' Purefoy replied. 'We want to get moving. All the Emersons do. They want to act. Now, Oliver.'

('Who the hell are the Emersons?' Harry said. 'The Emersons hereby have Computer Importance. Make a note, John.')

Garvey's chin was leaning on the handle of his umbrella as he gazed off at the White House, which he no doubt

70

wanted rent-free someday. Garvey was a man who actually had a fondness for inaction, for whom the abstract contemplation of possibilities was the real game, the fun, who held back and held back from the actual step into reality until he'd seen certainty.

'Be patient. I need a little more time,' Garvey said.

'There is no more time.'

'Who says so?'

'The Bishop, for one.'

'Now I've heard everything. The Bishop.'

'And the Rabbi.'

('The Bishop and the Rabbi, huh? Sounds like an Agatha Christie novel,' Harry said. 'What the hell's going on? Computer Importance. Rabbi and Bishop. They must be code words.')

'The Bishop and the Rabbi,' Garvey said. 'The experts in political timing.'

'Will you listen, Oliver?'

'I'm listening.'

'Would you mind telling me what you're waiting for? I've got to have something to tell the others.'

'We're waiting for the Doctor. Tell them that.'

'How long?'

'Not long.'

'Who is the Doctor?'

'The Doctor is the one who's going to supply the cure.'

'How's he going to do that?' Purefoy said, a faint, skeptical smile appearing.

'The Doctor's on the inside. On the inside of the inside, in past the last layer of the onion. I know what I'm talking about. We'll wait for the Doctor.'

'Oliver,' Purefoy said, 'you're not chickening out on us, are you?'

'I am not.' Garvey looked offended, which didn't come easy to him. 'We're going to drop a bomb on that whitish house across the street, but it has to be done surgically. We'll wait for the Doctor.'

('Doctor. Computer Importance,' Harry said.)

Purefoy sighed and stood up. 'Oliver, don't you think I'm entitled to know who the Doctor is?'

'I'll think about it,' Garvey said.

Purefoy strolled off while Garvey remained seated, chin on umbrella, face impenetrable, portrait of a man who covered his tracks so carefully that he had to stop now and then in order to get in touch with himself. When Garvey stood up, the all-knowing computer cut away to NATO's northern flank, the Swedish naval base on Muskö island, where the Swedes were assembling a task force to locate a suspected Soviet submarine lurking in the waters nearby.

Harry was licking his lips with pure appetitive lust. Senator Oliver Garvey was on the point of doing something indiscreet, committing himself to a course of action, taking a chance! It was an opportunity to get him. 'Now we know where all the trouble's coming from. I want to know everything about the Emersons – who they are, what they're doing, what their goals are. By tomorrow, if not sooner.' He looked around at them. 'Any thoughts?'

It was the moment.

Harry was waiting for his geniuses to produce insights. The time had come to tell Harry that the Doctor worked in the Library. Coolidge liked to do things by the book – it was the best way, the safest way. And yet Harry's Paradox blurred the issue. Dunn's Conundrum: in the Library, where everyone knows everything, betrayal must be kept a secret by whoever learns of it until the betrayer is exposed.

Thus making it less of a Library, isolating a bit of data – along with whatever flowed from it – from the others. Which would get complicated, one item leading to two, the two leading to four, eight, on and on, branching out in all directions like forked lightning. If there was to be any chance of success, it would have to be done quickly, otherwise the rapidly branching facts would sooner or later intersect with some other fast-moving branch, and exposure would result. And what would exposure lead to? Would Harry believe him? Would Harry believe in Dunn's Conundrum? Or would it look as though Coolidge had been playing some kind of game? It made no difference. Were you responsible? If you were, there was no choice. You had to do your work.

You had to go find the Doctor.

Trash Report: #85-10-5

CASE NUMBER: 104759

ABANDONED PROPERTY DONOR: Senator Oliver Garvey (residence)

1. Pack Alexandrine brand scented cigarettes.
2. Lipstick, Dawn Pink.
3. Twelve bottles Beck's beer.
4. Bottle private label Scotch, 1.75 liter.
5. Bottle nose drops.
6. Two plastic ice cube trays, inoperative.
7. *Washington Post*, folded to TV page.
8. Penciled memo re dates to call H. Dunn before sub-committee.
9. Clipped issues of *Time, Fortune, Foreign Policy, Armed Forces Journal, Wall Street Journal, N.Y. Times, Washington Post, Playboy.*
10. Copy of speech apparently intended for private party at Houston home of Harvey Stubbs, chairman of Texarkana Oil.

Trash Scenario

On Tuesday evening, Senator Garvey had two members of his oversight subcommittee to his home for drinks. They were Senator Buchanan (item #3, twelve bottles of Beck's beer) and Senator Quincy (item #1, package of Alexandrine brand scented cigarettes). Subcommittee business was discussed (item #8, rough memo with several proposed dates for 'Dunn testimony'). No conclusions were reached about the nature of the Library's activities (item #8 was balled up and discarded).

73

After the senators left, Garvey's favorite girl, Melanie Smith (item #2, Dawn Pink lipstick) arrived. She left at approximately 12.30 A.M. (item #7, TV schedule in *Washington Post*, starting time for *The Candidate* circled in ink, known to be Garvey's favorite movie).

Notes

Item #10, an oddly impolitic speech that has not been delivered so far, and isn't likely to be, is a curiosity. It is totally out of character for Senator Garvey, or any other American politician for that matter. A fragment, recovered from torn-up, partly burned pages, is reproduced here.

. . .and that's what a Republican gives you when you ask him for half a buck for a cup of coffee (*Pause for laughter*.) But, seriously, I did want to touch on one important matter tonight before I let you get back to the barbecue.

We often use the term 'free world.' It seems on the surface to be straightforward enough. 'Free world' distinguishes those countries which are free from those which are not free, or Communist. And yet, surprisingly, it is a widely misunderstood expression.

The confusion arises because most Americans tend to think of the personal freedoms when the word 'free' is used. Freedom of the press, freedom of speech, freedom of assembly, and so forth. It is this definition of 'free' that causes the problem, because many of the countries of the 'free world' are not 'free.' South Africa. Guatemala. Paraguay. Many others.

How can a country be 'not free' and yet be part of the 'free world'? That is the contradiction I wish to resolve tonight. Indeed, the answer is basic to our understanding of the arms race.

Very simple, 'free world' does *not* refer to the basic freedoms. It refers to non-Communist economic arrangements within various countries which permit the freedom to invest. That, after all, is what distinguishes a Communist country from a non-Communist country. Freedom to invest, to develop, to expand. Freedom to make a buck. Freedom to, literally, *stay out of the red*, and that, my friends, is what the arms race is all about. . . .

Who Is the Doctor? What Is He?

Beebe was a breast man.

The impulse was unusually strong in him. In fact, the breast impulse didn't come any stronger than it did in Beebe; it suffused his entire personality. He was always sucking on something. Scotch. Coffee. Cigarettes. Cigars. It was as though Beebe had never lost the one instinct human beings are born with, had never outgrown it, had to go on obeying it again and again and not be turned away no matter what happened, because something deep down in the lower brain kept repeating the same message over and over: Suck or die.

When he met Madeline, he was instantaneously turned on. She had two qualities that aroused him. Her breasts were slightly too large for her body, so they had a captivating air of excess, plethora, abundance; inside her bra was survival itself. She was also over fifty, with the fading quality of the ex-good-looker which did something to Beebe. It appealed to his competitive instincts: he would be the best, the absolute tops of what had to be a long line of lovers.

There was the added advantage that Madeline combined business with pleasure. She worked with undecodable messages at NSA, mainly from Communist countries. Even the National Security Agency's experts were unable to decipher them. But they were still considered data; sometimes information could be deduced merely from the volume and direction of the traffic flow. All such messages were routed to the Library for storage in the computer; the day might come when NSA cracked the codes. Since Madeline was liaison with the Library, she was automatically interesting to the Protector of the Data, thereby giving Beebe two reasons for taking her to dinner.

While Madeline was making the drinks, Beebe wandered around the one-bedroom apartment, looking at the art on the walls, the books in the bookcases. Nothing unusual. Typical government intellectual. The latest book of interviews with Mexican peons. A *Foreign Affairs* subscription. A shelf full of unread-looking books on statistics, which was probably part of her background in cryptanalysis. No portraits of Che Guevara.

She came out of the kitchen with the drinks, on a tray, no less, and set them down on the coffee table. Bending over was a good test of a woman's shape, and hers was still damn good. She dressed well too. She knew how to make the most of everything. He watched her walk across the room to the stereo. Beebe remembered one line from one poem. It had stuck in his brain in high school. It was something about the liquefaction of her clothes when she moved. He never forgot that word, liquefaction; it became his favorite word. It said something about women and the way they moved and the way their clothes moved when they moved, with booze thrown in. He was sure she was looking for a little. She had to know he wasn't going to be satisfied with a Mozart quintet. By the time she sat down next to him on the couch, Beebe had forgotten about the Scotch; he was too close to the real thing.

'You like Mozart, huh?' he said, a hand onto her left shoulder, then sort of walking across the back of her neck to the right shoulder.

'Yes,' Madeline said, pretending she hadn't noticed the beginning of the invasion. 'Do you?'

'Take it or leave it.'

Beebe's finger was toying with her far ear while he started kissing the near one. He started getting a good reaction almost immediately: All she was doing was staring at her ice cubes. He reached over to her far thigh, sliding his hand lightly back and forth, preparing for the final assault on the twin peaks, and felt a gratifying response as her hand slipped onto *his* thigh, squeezing slightly. Beebe was so excited at being so close to those big luscious breasts that he had a 100 percent erection, which Madeline made unexpected contact with because it was farther down his pants leg than she'd expected.

'There's something I ought to tell you,' she said.

Beebe was about to say what's a little blood between friends, it seals the pact, when Madeline added, 'I hope you're not a breast man.'

Beebe was in the middle of nibbling and caressing, sliding here and there. He felt a momentary surge of anger, but he went on licking the convolutions in her ear, thinking it over.

'Tst.'

Madeline was trying to soften the blow by sliding her hand up along Beebe's erect penis, but the blow had already been softened; it had withdrawn northward.

'I'm going to get silicon implants, but I have to wait for my vacation. You can't get sick leave for it.'

'Uh huh,' Beebe said. It wasn't the first time he'd run into this.

'Like to have a rain check?' Madeline said.

'You got any false eyelashes?' Beebe replied. There was a slight quaver in his voice.

'Any what?'

'False eyelashes. You know. False eyelashes.'

Madeline giggled. 'Sure. What are you going to do with them? Put them on?'

'Yeah,' Beebe said, a crazy toothy smile on his face.

While Madeline was poking around in her vanity drawer, Beebe attended to security matters. When she wasn't looking, he slipped his small social gun out of the ankle holster and hid holster and gun in one of his size thirteen shoes. Then, after fighting off Madeline's attempts to hang it in the closet, he hung up his jacket, with his ID in it, on one of the bedposts at the head of the bed.

'Here you are,' Madeline said seductively, handing him the false eyelashes.

'Where's the cement?' Beebe replied. 'And lipstick. Oh, and a mascara brush and eyeliner.'

'Really?' she said.

'Yeah, yeah. Come on.'

'That's funny,' she said. 'I wouldn't have figured you for the type.' She went back to her vanity.

Tristan und Isolde – the Prelude and Liebestod – was now playing on the bedroom speakers. The lights were about as low as the dimmer was capable of. To Madeline's intense relief, Beebe had asked her to lie on her stomach. It had become her favorite position since her operation. She was only hoping that Beebe wouldn't ask her to roll over so she could admire his makeup. Then she felt the eyeliner moving around on her lower back.

Beebe seemed to be drawing on her. First with the eyeliner, then with the lipstick, then with the cement brush. She couldn't imagine what he was doing, what kind of oddball male fantasy he was acting out, and she wouldn't know until after Beebe had gone, when she could take a look in the full-length mirror on the door of her bedroom closet and find a face staring back at her: blank, staring eyes made of eyeliner, rimmed with heavily mascaraed eyelashes, plus a big ruby mouth, badly smeared, and two smeared red nipples drawn on her buttocks.

But while it was happening, Madeline wasn't able to figure it out. All she knew was that Beebe became suddenly passionate, caressing her buttocks as though they were breasts, kissing them, sucking on them, whispering to her back, passionately kissing it, moaning. Then she felt her hips being drawn upward and discovered that whatever the hell was going on was working just fine, oh real fine.

Coolidge hadn't started out with sex. He'd started out on the more lofty plane of ideas, beliefs, conscience – the realm where people were able to justify any acts, no matter how antisocial or inhuman. But conscience was a funny area. There were plenty of intellectuals in government who had no problems with conscience. When political truth conflicted with absolute truth, it was easy enough to decide that political truth, in its way, was as much truth as absolute truth. You could shade matters in the interests of everyday practicality and functioning within the system, as well as of making the kids' tuition payments.

But there were some whose consciences would bend only so far, and that's when the copying machines went to work. Occasionally one of them would even go public. But

Coolidge shied away from it. It was too messy, too complicated. Conscience wasn't photogenic; it didn't show up easily on the microcams. He gravitated toward easier solutions, solutions that could be documented. Cash money, for example.

He'd spent long hours at the terminal in his basement office, checking up on everyone's finances. Bank accounts, stock and bond holdings, insurance, real estate, venture capital deals. He looked for losses and debts and sudden large withdrawals and deposits. He went back over financial histories, searching for patterns. Nothing. No gambling losses, no margin calls, no catastrophes on Wall Street, no looming insider trading scandals. It was spelled out in the data: Whoever he was, the Doctor was solvent and honest. Coolidge was impressed. What other group of people could have withstood such an investigation?

So he'd gone to sexual blackmail, the other banal reason for betrayal. The sexual revolution hadn't reached government yet; people would still be opposed to leather freaks serving as high officers of government. Coolidge went on the prowl to see if the Doctor was selling out his country to keep from being a juicy feature story in a supermarket tabloid.

As he did it, he kept telling himself he was becoming a better person, tolerant of human variations. He wouldn't even call them deviations. Deviations from what? What was the norm? All the acts you could imagine, and many you couldn't, were going on constantly. He kept telling himself that he wasn't spying on them; he was looking out for their own good, like a therapist. He was ensuring that they were innocent. Innocent, anyway, of betraying the Library; any other sin was acceptable.

And the PPMP (Personnel Personal Monitoring Program) was definitely tuned in to sin. It had been given the ability to reject and ignore banality and everydayness. Whose turn it was to visit Grandma in the nursing home. How much to tip the baby-sitter. The computer was looking for perversion and kinkiness with the relentless intensity of a Puritan preacher hunting wickedness and degradation. As soon as it smelled sex it made a mental note, and after the scene was over it would back up the sequence long enough to provide an introduction to the action and then catalogue it under the appropriate participant's name. The computer understood the concepts of blackmail and exposure, of respectability and fear. It knew that those entities called people had to be themselves, at least part of the time, or else they'd go sour and awful, and it kept careful watch for those unclosed moments.

Unclosed, that was the word. A verb form. To uncloset, to reveal oneself. Coolidge wanted to catch the Doctor in the act of unclosing, catch him in the act of being himself, which was where he would be most likely to slip. So he watched all the varieties of sin, relentlessly, fighting to reduce the period of time during which he was holding back a fact from the Library.

He prowled through bedrooms. He made random rounds of bordellos and sex parlors. He saw on his terminal the colossal gap between the intellect and the crotch. Gardella liked to run around the floor on all fours, like a puppy dog, being told what to do, being disciplined. Gardella also beat his wife, a beautiful woman who was trying to become a model. Coolidge knew something Gardella didn't: she was going to leave him in a few weeks, right after she got her first modeling assignment with a small Washington advertising agency.

And Hopkins. The shirt ad seemed to be indifferent to the sex of the person he was having sex with. Coolidge watched Hopkins doing it with a young girl on his living room couch. Then a quick jarring cut, different clothes lying on the floor, but same couch, same Hopkins, and now it was a writhing man under him. An orifice was an orifice. After all, if you liked someone, what did the plumbing matter?

Coolidge cruised. Shanley was a heterosexual transvestite who liked to be seduced by butch women. Farnsworth liked delicious young girls. Real young. He was beginning to break the sound barrier of eighteen, heading for trouble. Was he already blackmailable, and therefore a Doctoral candidate? Coolidge decided to go into the historical footage on Farnsworth, which was anything more than three months old. And Shanley too, while he was at it;

Shanley didn't look half bad in an evening gown. Johnny Burnish was one of the boys who go to whorehouses for laughs, booze, and incidentally to get laid. All this was starting to desex Coolidge. As for Vera's footage, he couldn't bear to call it up.

Sex was beginning to look paleolithic to Coolidge: two creatures of the dawn writhing around the edge of the swamp in a life and death struggle.

Ambassador Zhu smiled at Yeager and said something in Chinese, bowing her head shyly. She had a reputation for being a roughhouse negotiator, so it seemed that progress had already been made; she looked as if she was willing to make a few concessions. Even so, her coy words sounded like a Chinese waiter calling out an order. It was Ambassador Zhu's interpreter, referred to affectionately as Ling-Ling, who brought the proper tone to it in English.

'Ambassador Zhu says it was very kind of you to come to the reception.'

They were honoring the newly arrived Australian ambassador. Yeager was playing a junior UNESCO representative. Harry had told him the mission was about as important as the one Nathan Hale blew, but Yeager never took that kind of stuff seriously. You had to concentrate on the nuts and bolts. Ambassador Zhu, in this case. And Yeager seemed to be picking up encouraging vibes. Who needed language? Wasn't civilization a steady advance into the spaces between the lines? He looked deep into Ambassador Zhu's brown eyes and then his eyeball radar swept over her body very fast, no lingering, a mere blink, obeisance to the body beautiful, an acknowledgment that lust was a possibility if only life and circumstances were different and affairs of state hadn't come between them. Ah, well.

'Tell Ambassador Zhu that I'm extremely delighted to be here, since I find the Chinese embassy to be a place of unusual exquisiteness.'

Yeager was surprised; the place didn't smell of MSG at all. Although all the furniture turned up at the ends. So, however, did Ambassador Zhu. She had the high-cheekbone look everywhere.

81

There was a chatter of Chinese, in which Yeager could discern the word 'martini.' He found that he was already breaking the habit of looking at the person who was talking, Ling-Ling, so as to maintain contact with the target. It was the ultimate test, really. Content zero, style everything. Done with eyes, lip muscles, eyebrows, tilt of head. Yeager remarked that he would prefer wine, inasmuch as the ambiance was intoxicating enough. The demands of diplomacy, after all, required sobriety.

Ambassador Zhu nodded and smiled and departed, trailing Ling-Ling behind her, for her other guests, but she left Yeager a glance that seemed to say: This is the Year of the Fox.

Yeager wandered. He discussed the leg muscles of soccer players with an Englishman, listened to a Japanese tell a dirty joke in German to an Italian who had trouble keeping up, faking a laugh a good three seconds after the joke was over; took an occasional indescribable hors d'oeuvre; and generally stayed relaxed, not expecting a junior member of UNESCO to be especially interesting to anyone. He was right; nobody paid him any attention.

When the place finally started emptying out, Yeager got worried. He was convinced the old radar had picked up an echo, but nothing was happening. In a few minutes he would be verging on the impolite if he didn't show signs of leaving. Could the AN/APS-21 Airborne Sexual Radar Set be in need of a tuneup? He drifted down the central staircase to the coatroom and took forever getting into his topcoat.

He decided to shake every Chinese hand he could find, bowing and scraping. He was actually moving toward the front door when he saw Ling-Ling heading in his direction. Ling-Ling wasn't bad-looking herself, in that translator's self-effacing way of hers.

'If Mr. Yeager wouldn't be thrown off his schedule too much, would he care to have tea with Ambassador Zhu?'

They went up to the third floor in a tiny elevator, made even tinier by the heavily framed portraits of the current Beijing pecking order. Ambassador Zhu was sitting prettily on a couch in her apartment. The tea things were set out, for three, on the table in front of her. Of course they *would*, Yeager thought, have to talk first.

While Ling-Ling was pouring, Ambassador Zhu made sounds like a sewing machine and Ling-Ling said: 'Your government is highly ungracious not to have sent you here on other occasions, since you are such a pleasing emissary.'

Yeager leaned forward on the couch, establishing a molecule of knee contact, saying that the ambassador was far too kind. It would have to be considered a rare privilege – quick longing glance at her thighs now – to be invited at all.

Ambassador Zhu's reply was instantaneous. 'It is now time to drop the language of diplomacy,' then she added, uncircumlocutorily, 'Do you have any more engagements this evening?'

'As a matter of fact, I'm free for the weekend.'

Ambassador Zhu thought that was very funny. She had lovely, even teeth, Chinese miniatures, and her tongue was a delightful stroke of pure red. Yeager increased the knee pressure by another two molecules and said, 'Does Ambassador Zhu have anything in mind?'

Buzz, buzz, buzz.

Ling-Ling reported. 'I just thought we might get better acquainted and thereby have a smoother working relationship.'

'Splendid idea,' Yeager said, looking for the auguries deep in Ambassador Zhu's eyes, and the auguries looked terrific. 'I have a feeling we'd work very smoothly together.' Ling-Ling had hardly repeated it in Chinese when the phone rang and she went into another room to answer it.

Yeager didn't waste any time. He kissed Ambassador Zhu's hand. He smiled. She didn't. He decided to risk an international incident. He kissed her on the cheek. No response. He kissed her on the lips. Nothing. He slid an arm around her shoulders and kissed deeper, slowly separating her lips with his. Something. Her lips started talking to his. She put a hand on his hand, which was on her knee. She put her other hand around his neck. He heard Ling-Ling fooling around with the tea things. Ambassador Zhu's hand moved off his neck into a tighter grasp on him, pulling Yeager forward.

Then, rat-tat-tat.

It was impossible to guess at the emotional content. Yeager had to wait for the vote to come in.

'Would you like me to undress?' Ling-Ling said.

Yeager looked at her.

'Says Ambassador Zhu,' she added hurriedly.

Yeager smiled and his eyes bulged, knowing that Harry wbuld be proud of him: mission accomplished. When they got to the bedroom, the indispensable Ling-Ling busied herself turning down the bedclothes and lowering the lights, Yeager hoping against hope that she wouldn't put some soft Chinese music on the stereo. In less than a minute he and Ambassador Zhu were climbing into the bed and embracing in the same motion; they *were* working smoothly together. Yeager's hand was wandering over her body wantonly when Ling-Ling whispered in his ear, 'Squeeze my nipples.' She said it soft and quavery. She was good at her job, having definitely got the hang of duplicating the emotional tone of the original.

Yeager found that he was now tuning out Ambassador Zhu. He wasn't even hearing the rush of Chinese in his left ear; he was responding entirely to Ling-Ling's soft urgings in his right.

'You are a sweet lover,' Ling-Ling whispered. 'I knew you would be like this.'

'Take me,' Ling-Ling whispered passionately, lying down beside them. Yeager didn't look at Ling-Ling. He had a feeling that she was naked and that looking at her would be disloyal to Ambassador Zhu. He wasn't sure now which of the two he felt closer to. As he eased into Ambassador Zhu, he couldn't even be sure which of them had groaned, but there was no doubt whose arms and legs were wrapped around him.

'Ah,' Ling-Ling translated. 'Oh,' Ling-Ling said. 'Higher,' Ling-Ling urged. Ambassador Zhu began to writhe deliciously. Ling-Ling seemed to be doing an attenuated version of it, moving in fits and starts, like someone with sudden uncontrollable itches.

'Screw now,' Ling-Ling said. 'Now in. Ahh. Now out.'

But Ling-Ling was like a stock ticker falling behind on a bullish afternoon. Yeager no longer needed feedback. He and Ambassador Zhu had reached back to preliteracy.

And so, as it turned out, had Ling-Ling, who was even forgetting her training, calling out, 'She say faster,'but not really speaking for Ambassador Zhu anymore, the three of them coming together in one titanic mattress-wrenching convulsion, and Coolidge switched off the monitor and went out for a double Canadian on the rocks.

The Japanese Howard Hughes

Reinhold Kunstner was trailing his employer, Glenn Ingalls, through the San Francisco International Airport, making notes. It was the usual controlled chaos that Ingalls seemed to thrive on. Calls to make, memos for the staff, interviews to set up. Social engagements to make, postpone, cancel. Ingalls was a substantial winner in Silicon Valley, but it was a terrifyingly fast-moving business and Ingalls seemed to be always running, trying to stay ahead. There was no way to predict when someone might come up with something new that would obsolete everything you were doing. It was Ingalls's nightmare, which was why it was Reinhold Kunstner's point of attack.

Although Glenn Ingalls was giving all the orders, and Reinhold Kunstner was scribbling furiously in his notebook and saying a lot of yes sirs, it was in fact Reinhold who was pulling the strings; without knowing it, Ingalls was doing exactly what his assistant wanted him to do.

When the time came to board, Ingalls shook his assistant's hand and told him he'd be back the next day. Reinhold waited only until the plane began to taxi out toward the runway, then he sped back through half a mile of corridors to another airline and caught his own flight to New York.

For Reinhold Kunstner, the criterion for the perfect undercover operation was 'untouchability.' Untouchability required the severing of connections, the distancing of cause from effect, unrelatedness. Of course, you could rarely achieve 100 percent untouchability. It was something you could only aspire to, but this time he was getting close. It was going to be like a chess game between an international grandmaster and a wood pusher, in which the master's present move had no apparent relevance to the queen capture coming in six moves. The problem was to separate Glenn Ingalls from his briefcase, a task which on casual inspection seemed impossible.

But not for an international grand master. To get from one point to another, you simply broke it down into the necessary substeps, computer-like. You set up an algorithm, which was one of Glenn Ingalls's buzzwords. However many steps it took to get from A to B, you specified them, you took them, one at a time.

Ingalls never parted with his briefcase, except to put it in his safe. The thing was old and wrinkled and cracked, but Ingalls hugged it like a teddy bear, up until the moment of clicking his safe shut on it. The safe was too much for Reinhold; it wasn't his field. And anyway, a safecracking operation was too complex, too touchable. Reinhold preferred indirection. Avoid the frontal assault. Finesse it. He'd brooded about it for days, until he saw in the *San Francisco Chronicle* that Yamashiro, the Japanese microchip czar, was coming to the United States. Everything clicked in a moment. It had wonderful qualities of untouchability; it was exactly what he was looking for, the means to get into Glenn Ingalls's briefcase.

Two nights later, at a cocktail party in Palo Alto, Reinhold commenced operations. The first step of the algorithm consisted of starting a rumor, mentioning it to a total stranger sitting at the bar, already half in the bag. The rumor was that Yamashiro was ready to go into production of a megabit chip. If true, it would mean the biggest leap in computer memory yet made. It would mean a new generation of computers years ahead of time; it would be a catastrophe for the Americans in general and Glenn Ingalls in particular. It took all of twelve hours for the rumor to work its way back to Ingalls, who promptly ordered Reinhold to locate Yamashiro and get an appointment with him. If there was such a thing as a million-bit chip, Ingalls would have to license it or die.

When his plane landed at JFK in New York, Reinhold hurried to check arrivals and departures. There had been slippage. He was thirty-five minutes behind Ingalls.

Variable winds – *that* was something you couldn't get into the algorithm. But the limo was waiting and he had a high-speed ride into Manhattan, going straight to an athletic club on Central Park South. When he stepped out of the car, he was wearing a mustache and eyeglasses.

Reinhold had already set up the locker room attendant, which was a point of touchability, granted, a falling off from 100 percent, but it was vastly superior to taking on a safe. He went straight to the locker room.

'You're ten minutes late,' the attendant said, taking out his keys. He'd kept an entire aisle of lockers empty so there'd be no one around. Before opening the locker, he held out his hand and Reinhold handed over the second five hundred. Then, at last, the end of the algorithm, the inevitable, foreordained result of the program: the attendant swung open the locker door and Reinhold had the beat-up old briefcase in his hands.

Untouchability and indirectness: Yamashiro was the Japanese Howard Hughes. He liked to conduct business meetings, not in men's rooms, as Hughes had, but in saunas. Ingalls would be in there now, sweating about megabits. Reinhold had a collection of keys; the fifth one opened the briefcase; there were to be no scratch marks from a pick. He found what he was looking for and sat down on a wooden bench, leaning back against the lockers to read. The attendant was twitching, having a quiet epileptic fit, but Reinhold read slowly, savoring every word. It was fascinating. He was surprised. So that's who the Doctor was. He would never have guessed. But then, who would have guessed about Reinhold Kunstner?

Reinhold returned the pages to their precise location, closed the briefcase, returned it to the attendant, and left without saying goodbye. The limo got him back to Kennedy with minutes to spare for the return flight to San Francisco.

He'd earned his pay for a lifetime.

The Clue

Coolidge had unconsciously developed the evasive actor's look; he was doing everything to avoid looking into the camera eye. He didn't want to face them; he knew too much about them. He'd become a de facto mind reader, which was the net effect of monitoring personnel and being a professional fly on the wall. He knew, to the extent *they* knew, which in some cases wasn't a whole lot, what they were really like. And he knew what they thought about him, Coolidge.

Beebe called Coolidge a fuzzy-wuzzy. Coolidge had watched Beebe say it on the monitor any number of times. A fuzzy-wuzzy was a snot-nosed, *soft*-nosed, soft-*headed* intellectual who had a college degree for a cock. Beebe was personally guarding the door of the Reference Room when Coolidge arrived. He did the duty himself now and then, just to keep his hand in and to remind everyone that he, Beebe, was the Protector of the Data and don't you forget it.

As the Garbageman went past him, Beebe wrinkled his nose; Coolidge thought about making a suck sound but restrained himself. Beebe wouldn't have gotten it anyway; Beebe didn't know he sucked, which was the problem with humanity.

Coolidge beamed in on the coffee urn, poured sloppily, then slipped as unobtrusively as possible through the dimness to his seat. He was careful not to look at Hopkins, who thought of Coolidge as an antisocial snob educated beyond his intelligence; he'd said it to Kraus one night in a bar. Nor did Coolidge look at Beatty, the reformed orgiast now a born-again Christian, who thought Coolidge was arrogant, touchy, defensive, and a mortal sinner. He avoided exchanging glances with Johnny Burnish, whose wife thought Coolidge was good-looking but cold; all brain, no feelings. John Burnish himself thought that Coolidge was good-looking but cold; all brain, no feelings. Mike Barber, who sought perfection in every way, thought Coolidge was sloppy, careless, head-in-the-clouds, spaced out, a loser. Emil Kraus didn't trust him. Shanley liked him but considered him a hopeless square. Coolidge had become the man who knew too much.

Except for one thing. He hadn't found the Doctor in the bedroom. In spite of all the wild sex scenes, the Librarians were somehow managing to be discreet. There were no signs of entrapment, no outraged husbands (or wives, in some cases). It wasn't sex. It wasn't sex and it wasn't money. What was next?

The coffee was beginning to revive Coolidge, who had spent too many consecutive hours in Sodom and Gomorrah and had monitor fatigue. He began to realize that there was an unusually large number of people sitting around the table. He looked around finally and was amazed to see it was a full table; all Librarians were present, which meant eleven, with the tall back of Charley's empty chair sticking out like a tombstone.

There was a Doctor in the house.

It slowly dawned on the exhausted Coolidge that all Librarians were present because it was an occasion; the latest Naumburg satellite footage was about to come up on the screens, the C-130 pilot in the Pacific having managed to snag it as it parachuted down from space.

While waiting for Naumburg, Harry was wandering around with a printout in his hand, peering at monitors, throwing out questions, suggestions, problems, ideas. He had all ten of them to play with; he was having a ball. Anything was possible with this staff. And all kinds of weird stuff was coming up. The Western Shoshone Sacred Lands Association was going to make a big flap about possible sites for the MX missile. This produced jokes about drawing up the missile trailers in a circle.

Harry said it was no laughing matter. Simultaneously, the National Indian Youth Council was making a flap about unshielded uranium tailings on tribal lands. The Navajos and the Pueblos were stirring up trouble, trying to block uranium exploration. The Apaches were on the warpath again: the Chiricahua, the White Mountain, the Mescalero. All raising hell at the same time. About what? Geronimo's grave. Sure. Plus those crazy Indian land claims. Was it all a coincidence?

Everything had to be faced, the questions had to be asked. Was there an Indian conspiracy? Was there foreign influence? You had to at least *consider* it. If there was even a remote possibility of un-American activities, the federal agency in charge of Indian Affairs – oddly enough it was called the BIA – wasn't up to the job. Maybe CIA should open a case number? Harry smiled. He had the composure to say things that sounded ridiculous and not feel ridiculous.

The craziness rolled on.

McDermott Beebe III had officially requested the use of olfatronics equipment as a defense system for the Library. According to Beebe's memo, the body's own 'natural effluvia and exudates' would serve as a positive identification for all personnel. It was temporarily deflected by requests for the effects of shaving cream, aftershave, Vera's perfume, and onion burgers on the equipment.

News of the federal opium stockpile had leaked out. There were 71,000 pounds in stock and the government was looking for more, canvassing medical supply houses all over the country and Western Europe. It was to be used for painkilling in the event of a nuclear war, and it told the public too much about the nature of the post-Bomb environment.

The chancellor of West Germany had suddenly quit smoking and lost twenty-three pounds. Did that mean a change was in the offing? Farnsworth proposed that CIA steal a sample of his urine.

Then there was Kyshtym. No one yet knew what had happened at Kyshtym. Some thirty Russian villages had suddenly been deleted from all maps of the area, and a river had been rerouted to avoid it. What kind of accident had it been? Nuclear? Nerve gas? Anthrax? It was important to know what the Russians had been working on.

Kyshtym was given Computer Importance.

Listening to the byplay around the table, Coolidge realized that he didn't even have prejudices, much less clues. Maybe, except for Vera, whose footage he hadn't looked at yet, his problem was that he knew too much about them. How could you suspect one of the major cases of satyriasis in the Western world – Farnsworth – of being the Doctor? Or Shanley, whom he'd last seen on the monitor wearing a black cocktail dress, a long, beautiful brunette wig, and high heels?

Nobody seemed to be holding back. They all looked open and at ease, probing themselves for associations, solutions, problems. On the other hand, the classic double agent had precisely that ability, to exist on two planes at once, totally at home in either.

Looking around at them, he felt that if there were anyone who could handle that kind of weird existence it would be Kraus. The master simulator. The constructive paranoid. He had once simulated a missile attack on the United States, complete with Minuteman 1 malfunctions that produced a nervous breakdown in a promising young brigadier general; Kraus had found his weak spot. He had also faked a bombing attack on the USS *Eisenhower* with captured MIGs. The carrier commander as well as the air wing on board had so botched the situation, they were unable to get a single F-14 launched; the captain of the ship had to be given six months medical leave.

Kraus also had the job of watching the CIA. He kept track of every operation on and off the planet. So he knew with great precision what America's real international agenda was, as opposed to what you read in the newspapers. He knew more about the CIA than the director of Central Intelligence.

Kraus was ambitious. He was trying to make up for his height. He had become a millionaire with his own consultancy company in Maryland, advising corporations with risk analyses on overseas investments. When he came into the Library he had carefully put all his money into municipal bonds; if and when he ever left the Library, he'd be in a position to capitalize on his overseas knowledge.

It was also possible that Kraus was ambitious for more than money. He was by nature a giant-killer. It was possible that he wanted to be director of the Library. It had occurred to Coolidge that there was something of the simulations quality to the Doctor and the Emersons. It was possible that Kraus was rigging the whole thing to discredit Harry Dunn through some involuted sick plot and then arrange to put himself forward as the logical successor to Harry.

Coolidge looked over at Harry, who was oblivious to the situation. He was too busy enjoying the intense satisfactions of vindication. ONI and DIA had produced intelligence estimates on Yugoslavia which flatly contradicted CIA's estimates of separatist tendencies among Albanian Yugoslavs. The computer demonstrated, by actual word comparisons, that ONI and DIA had bought a CIA disinformation campaign. It would make a lovely little note for the President. Coolidge was actually feeling sorry for Harry. At the moment of the Library's triumph, the seeds of its destruction had been sown. Which was when, literally off the wall, there came a ray of light.

The daily Garvey trash report.

It brought instant giggles and lewd remarks. Jake had processed it himself and it was all up on the big screen, all neatly laid out on white paper, garbage gone, only trash remaining, the usual Garvey castoffs, but with one exception. It was a greeting card with the line: 'Where is my goozy lover?' Jake had anticipated the inevitable interest; he'd made a copy of the inside, which was a drawing of a sexy lady in a negligee and was signed 'Shanghai Lil.'

It was more than a blush, actually. Her cheeks were incandescent. He looked at her, sitting across the table from him, praying she wouldn't say anything. He shook his head from side to side by about an eighth of an inch. Vera had sent him the card three days before and Coolidge had tossed it out the next night.

Somebody had a trash cover on the Garbageman.

Vera was as close to being one of the boys as any woman ever is, but she was suddenly looking girlish and modest and Coolidge had hopes that she wouldn't blab it out all over the place. His next break came two seconds later: it was the German countryside, which now had number one Computer Importance, and there were five screens of it, through the miracle of the latest satellite photography.

'All right, Vera,' Harry said impatiently.

She was still looking at Coolidge. He winked. She didn't wink back. But she broke off the stare and turned to her keyboard, looking rattled. Nevertheless, she did input at sixty miles an hour, cut out the unwanted terrain, and brought up the previous shot of the tank park, juxtaposed now against the latest version.

There was total silence in the room as they sat there counting tanks.

There were forty-two new tanks, all with different regimental markings.

'The magnetometer reading is up eight percent,' Vera commented to the quiet room.

Coolidge glanced instinctively at the O.F.F. display. It was now reading 49.63 percent. It had been gaining substantially lately.

'Let's don't start World War Three over this, huh?' Hopkins said dryly. 'It *is* only forty-two tanks. It could well be a sluggish replacement procedure.'

The biggest possible advantage an army could achieve was to mass at a point where the opposing army hadn't. Was this the beginning of massing? Of piling up tank superiority at one point so there'd be irresistible power for the fabled drive on the English Channel?

'Negative on World War Three,' Harry replied. 'But maybe it calls for Seventh Army to go to DefCon Four.' DefCon was defense condition; DefCon 5 was peace, DefCon 1 was war.

They haggled over how to phrase a memo for the President, but Coolidge had stopped listening. He was staring at Vera, psyching her into silence. He was running his hand over his face. He needed a shave. His exhaustion was beginning to fade into pure energy. He was back in his own element now; he knew what had to be done.

The Doctor had made his first slip.

Vasilyev

Admiral Andrei T. Vasilyev looked at his face in the mirror. It was 6 A.M. and the pouches under his eyes looked deeper and darker than usual; he had been up all night reading reports. His wrinkles seemed to be deeper too. It was necessary to undo forty-five years of experience, pulling his skin back tautly, in order to shave. He liked to think that he could identify each wrinkle. This one was the siege of Leningrad. That one was the sinking of the *Yaroslavets* in a thousand meters, with all aboard. Then the next three were Stalin's, when Stalin had gone through a period of deep distrust of Vasilyev, and the entire Soviet Navy was in jeopardy. The last one the Americans had given him, the incipient bit of flab slowly developing into a fold over the last three years. One way or the other, he had the feeling it was going to be his last wrinkle.

At times of crisis, he couldn't help going back to Stalin's day. The crises came one after another then; at this hour, the meetings would still be in session, having gone on all night: and there would still be plenty of eating and drinking ahead. Drinking. Stalin had a connoisseur's appreciation of oblivion. Everybody else's as well as his own.

But they were bureaucrats now. Things were more defined. Less capricious, less frightening, less exhilarating. There was nothing of the quality Stalin had, the feeling he gave you that you were walking into the wolf's lair.

Vasilyev made a face at himself in the mirror. The wolf's lair. That was Hitler talk. Maybe they were all alike. Hitler, Stalin, who else? No, they weren't all alike.

Hitler and Stalin, they were alone. Possibly Ivan the Terrible, Robespierre, a few other lovelies from the past.

He checked for hairs up his nose, plus those vagrants growing out of his ears, and did what he could. You would think he was going to meet a woman. He went back into the bedroom to put on his uniform. The vodka bottle was on the night table. He hesitated and then poured a good one. After all, he'd been up all night; it wasn't the same as having it for breakfast, which would have been a bad sign. He tossed off the vodka and licked his lips, braced for the meeting.

He hated bringing bad news, even to bureaucrats.

He'd sat in the big room during many crises. Some had threatened the very existence of the nation. Few of them had had to do with the navy, which had never been important enough to Stalin. Still and all, he'd sat in on the operational plan for Stalingrad. The defense of Moscow. The attack on the German Army Group Center. The various Berlin crises. Hungary. Czechoslovakia. Poland. East Germany. Afghanistan. What a litany of disasters! Litany. That wasn't a good Marxist word; it smelled of incense.

Vasilyev had his briefcase on the table in front of him, but no one asked to see the reports. This was Vasilyev's field. He went on for ninety minutes, and the mood in the room began to feel like Moscow in 1941, when they were throwing workers into the front line.

'Very well,' the President said when Vasilyev was done. He was efficient, precise. The cool executive who never perspired in public. 'The problem is quite clear. Now what are your thoughts, Admiral?'

Stalin had often sat at the same place, asking the same difficult questions of his military people. Vasilyev had always gone well prepared for Stalin's questions, career hanging on every answer, possibly life itself. Now he had no answer.

There was none. There were no options. Geography worked against the Soviet Union. Geography had them trapped. You couldn't move continents, islands. If Greenland were only two hundred miles farther from

Norway, it might be a different story. He must be getting senile, slipping into fantasies while meeting with the Defense Committee.

'Surely you have a contingency plan,' the chief of the Soviet general staff said, sarcasm shading the word 'contingency,' an implication that things weren't as bad a Vasilyev had said and that in reality it was a budget maneuver, which was yet one more attempt at not facing the facts.

'Do we have friends?' Vasilyev asked. 'Then this is the time for calling in debts. I think,' he added, satirizing Stalin deliberately so as to shock them into reality, 'that even the Pope's divisions might come in handy now.'

The defense minister was scornful. 'We cannot concede anything that would reflect on the system.'

Or on the defense minister, Vasilyev thought. He had been warning them it could happen, would happen. He had seen it coming for years. The fools didn't understand geography. So the Soviet Union's last hope, the strategic submarines, the retaliatory force, was in jeopardy. Once the Americans were certain of their ability to destroy them, there was nothing they wouldn't attempt against the Soviet Union. Nothing. The socialist experiment would be over for good. He decided to impress upon them how desperate the situation was.

'As I see it,' Vasilyev said to the members of the Presidium, 'apart from any pressures you could bring to bear, there is only one meaningful course of action.'

The defense minister, defensive, said, 'Remember that the only thing the Americans understand is strength. We must deal from strength.'

The foreign minister cut in. 'What do you recommend, Vasilyev?'

'We must play the trump card,' the admiral replied. 'We must talk to the Doctor.'

They all sat there looking into space, thinking, until the President finally broke the silence.

'Do so,' he said.

The Observatory

The Library, a slender, triangular brick building nine stories high, was located on 18th Street, N.W. There was a small parking lot at one end, with space for fifteen cars, for the twelve Librarians, Yeager, Beebe, and one left over for couriers and deliveries, including trash.

The rest of the several hundred workers in the building who supplied ancillary services for the Librarians had to park elsewhere; the Library wasn't supposed to look important.

Coolidge had the basement and sub-basement for his trash operation. Vera had the sub-sub-basement, which was deep enough to lie below the utility lines running under Connecticut Avenue. It enabled the Library to expand out under the adjacent streets, to provide Vera with the tremendous space she needed for monitoring the Soviet Union.

He found her in orbit over Naumburg. He'd come down the stairs quietly and stood leaning against the railing at the Siberian end of the room, watching her work. She was out on her little platform, peering down through a telescope, designed by the National Reconnaissance Office, at a tank park in East Germany, he assumed.

Coolidge walked back along the platform that ran high up around the perimeter of the big room, which was about as long and as wide as a football field. The satellite photographs were projected upward from below. The projectors were computer controlled so that she could call up any photograph of the millions in the inventory for comparison purposes; some of them, taken from German aircraft, went back to World War II.

He strolled along, worrying about it, but there was

really nothing to decide. There was no way out. He was going to have to trust her. It wouldn't do any good to make up some cock-and-bull story about the greeting card. Lying was futile; she'd catch it.

He hated having to trust her. It just got him in deeper. And her as well. They'd be going further and further away from doing it by the book, taking more and more chances. Coolidge had no idea what the consequences might be. The data tree was branching out fast. Vera had slipped out of the Reference Room, claiming she wanted to study the satellite footage more thoroughly. Coolidge had stayed behind only long enough to contribute his bit to a mess in Somalia. She was concentrating so well he'd gotten as far as Murmansk before she spotted him.

Vera's movable platform cruised in his direction. She inspected the photos from twenty feet up through small binocular telescopes. The platform moved on tracks that ran across the short dimension of the room; the tracks themselves moved lengthwise, so she had total access to the entire Soviet landmass out to Siberia, and to the satellite countries all the way to their western borders.

Coolidge climbed over the railing and got into the second seat. They sailed out over the void, in orbit. When they were due south of Moscow – in the middle of the room – Vera brought the platform to a stop.

'Okay, we're out of gas, honey. Come across,' she said.

'Keep your voice down.'

'We're in the middle of nowhere,' she whispered. 'What the hell is going on?'

'I don't know what the hell is going on.'

'What does a U.S. senator want with your garbage?'

'It's my trash he wants.'

'All right, your trash. Why?'

'I don't know why.'

'Why haven't we told Harry about this?'

'I know why I haven't told Harry. I don't know why you haven't told him.'

Vera sighed. 'They'd be calling me Goozy Girl for life,' she said.

'*I'm* the one they'd be calling Goozy,' Coolidge said. 'What the hell does goozy mean, anyway?'

'I'll tell you sometime.'

'All in all, fear of being thought goozy doesn't seem like a good basis for making national security decisions,' Coolidge said.

'You threw that card away awfully fast. You're not very sentimental, are you, Walter?'

'I got the message,' he said, a blank and logical look on his face.

'And where the hell *have* you been lately? If you hadn't done a disappearing act, I wouldn't have sent the damn card.'

That was the question Coolidge was afraid of; it required a lie. He couldn't tell Vera about monitoring personnel. He couldn't tell her that he figured that he wouldn't be able to cope with making love on camera. She would, but he wouldn't. He was starting to line up potential trysting places. Hotel rooms in the right hotels on the right floors.

'Let's not have a lovers' quarrel this far behind enemy lines,' Coolidge said.

'All right, we'll stick to strictly business. We're *Librarians* and we're *concealing something*. That means trouble.'

'You haven't heard the half of it. You know that guy the Doctor? The one Senator Garvey was talking about? The man that's going to solve all their problems? The one who's going to surgically bomb the White House?'

'Go on,' she said skeptically.

'He's a Librarian.'

Vera paled. It was shocking to watch. He cheekbones were high and usually red, even when she wasn't blushing, which she didn't do very often. Now her face had gone gray. Then she belched.

'Now don't throw up all over Russia.'

'How do you know that?' she said quietly.

Coolidge handed her the scrap of paper from Garvey's trash, the one with O.F.F. scribbled on it.

While she was studying it, he looked down at Russia. The colossus. The enigma wrapped in a riddle. Almost incomprehensibly huge. He aimed the telescope at Moscow. At the western approach to the city, he could make out the monument they had erected marking the farthest advance of the German Army in 1941. They'd gotten as far as the first suburban bus stop, but they were skeletons by then. He looked off in the distance at Stalingrad; that was where 300,000 German soldiers got down off their high horse and ate it. His eyes swept back across the room toward East Germany. The distance was so great the German infantry had worn their intestines smooth walking it. Maybe that's the kind of thing that had gotten to the Doctor: seeing the inevitable craziness that was part of running a government, the *Drang nach Osten,* in this case – the push to the East.

'The crazy bastards,' Coolidge murmured.

'Who's crazy?' Vera asked.

'The Germans.'

'You mean the Russians aren't crazy?'

'They're crazy too. So are we. Everybody's crazy.'

Vera was still staring at the scrap of paper.

'I don't suppose it could be the Joint Chiefs.' she said.

'Be wrecking their own game plan.'

'What about State? You think that oaf could have slipped on his tongue?'

'If he did, he'd be so guilt-ridden he'd come crawling to the President to confess. Needless to say, you can forget about Old Iron Balls at Defense.'

'Damn,' she said.

'So I figure it's got to be one of us.'

'I think you better show this to Harry.'

'It wouldn't be *logical* to show it to Harry. Harry could be the Doctor. It's possible.'

'That's absurd.'

'So is this room.'

Vera was wonderfully integrated. It was impossible for her to separate international politics from her body, her sexuality, her verve. 'How do you know I'm not the Doctor?' she said, radiating all kinds of stuff at him.

'I don't know. You could easily be the Doctor. Frankly, I wouldn't be surprised. If it weren't for that card turning up in Garvey's trash, I would never have told you about the leak.'

'That's fine with me,' she said. 'And I don't know that you're not the Doctor.'

'Yes, you do. You know it can't be me. I wouldn't be telling you about it if it were me, now would I? That wouldn't make any sense at all.'

'You could be subtle. You can be subtle, you know.'

He focused tightly on her eyes before springing it on her.

'Are you the Bishop?' he said.

Nothing funny appeared in those carbonated eyes of hers, just independence of spirit.

'I'm a Bishop.'

'I'll take your word for it for the time being.'

'Thanks.'

'All I know is that this doodle can't be entered in the computer. And it can't be reported to anybody who is a suspect. *You* are the only suspect who knows about it because I couldn't avoid you. *After* I find out who the Doctor is, *then* I'll tell Harry. Assuming Harry doesn't turn out to be the Doctor.'

'Who do you tell in that case?'

'Ives, I guess. I don't know.'

'Ouch.'

Vera was letting the platform drift southwestward, out over the great plains of the Ukraine. It was superb tank country. It was no wonder the Russians had 39,000 tanks. They passed over Kursk, where the greatest tank battle in history had been fought. Then Kiev, on the great sweep of the Dnieper River, where the Russians had surrendered 650,000 prisoners. Everything about the country was outsize. But Vera was getting practical.

'Do you really think that you, the Garbageman, can solve this?' Vera caught herself. She had a faintly stricken look. 'Now I didn't mean that the way it sounded.'

'Yes, you did. I'm only the Garbageman, what do I know? Well I'll tell you what I know. I'm the one who discovered it. The Garbageman. Found a *leak*. In the *Library*. In the *garbage*.'

'What are you going to do about it, Walter?'

'I'm going to cover the guy who's covering my trash. Follow him. Find out what's what and who's who, find out how it gets to Garvey, assorted data of that kind.'

'But you're not an operational type,' she said. 'You're dangerous. Yeager said so.'

'I can follow somebody. What does that take?'

'Training.'

'I'm a fast study.'

'Walter, I love you, but if you fuck up, I'm going to Harry.'

'Fair enough. Deal. And I want to thank you for your confidence.'

Vera was steering for the West German end of the room.

'Drop me off at Bulgaria, would you?'

'Walter.'

'Yes, Vera.'

'Could I interest you in some Chinese?'

Coolidge leaped up to the railing and climbed over.

'Sorry, I've got a date with a garbageman.' He started back toward the stairs.

'Think everything through, Walter,' she called after him.

'Yes, mother,' he said.

The Anthropologist Experiences Déjà Vu

He was intelligent, but he wasn't Intelligence. He was a strayed anthropologist. Perhaps 'fallen' would have been closer. It might explain how a man of reasonable intelligence but questionable Intelligence was sitting in his four-year-old Plymouth station wagon a block and a half from home, waiting for a stranger to collect his garbage.

He was barely listening to Chopin mazurkas on the radio, wondering if following someone was anything like the way it looked on television. Most of the time they did it badly. They were too obvious, they stayed too close, so the cameraman could get both cars in the shot. Coolidge had brought along the pearl opera glasses he'd inherited from his grandfather; it was a trick for following at a distance that he'd seen on *The Rockford Files*.

Oddly, Chopin had segued into Garvey. It was the hourly news. Coolidge shook his head in amused despair. When Jake Shoemaker imitated Garvey he did Charles Laughton. The 'news' was an excerpt from a patriotic speech Garvey had made the previous day. It was the kind of trash that Garvey didn't throw out in the garbage: middle-of-the-road-right-down-the-white-line-at-twenty-five-miles-per-hour, crowding everybody else off onto the right and left shoulders.

He snapped it off. There was a garbage truck coming down the street. He watched it with a curious professional eye. They had the right truck, the standard District model, but they didn't even try to fake the rest of the street. They drove right up to the three-story building Coolidge lived in and the man who got out was in a spotless uniform and totally lacked the professional indifference of a real garbageman. He was too interested in his work; he picked the

104

garbage cans up as if he'd just won them in a raffle.

That was encouraging. They'd sent amateurs to pick up the Garbageman's garbage. But as Coolidge started his engine, he reminded himself not to get overconfident. Everyone had his area of specialization. What might these guys be good at?

The truck took off too rapidly and sped unprofessionally around the corner. Coolidge got his grandfather's opera glasses out of the glove compartment as he was pulling away from the curb; he intended to watch the truck at the far end of the focal length.

He'd expected them to head south, back toward Washington and the big flights of steps, but instead they got on the Beltway, which circles Washington and goes through Maryland and Virginia. Coolidge was starting to feel lonely. It hadn't even occurred to him to bring a gun; the best he'd be able to muster in an emergency was a jack handle, which was floating around loose in the back of the station wagon. It was all for the best. His total experience with handguns was with a .45 in Army basic: they'd let him fire eight rounds.

The truck was approaching an exit, slowing down, giving a turn signal. Coolidge was about to take his foot off the gas when there was a loud explosion. He snatched a fast look to see if there was blood on him. His car was slewing over the highway at sixty miles per hour, thumping loudly, trying to spin. They'd gotten a tire. Coolidge twisted the wheel back and forth like a windshield wiper, trying to regain control; his car didn't have MacPherson struts, meaning the driver himself had to straighten the mess out.

Coolidge was trying to remember if you were supposed to brake or not. Just a little? It could make matters worse, but on the other hand, he had kinetic energy to get rid of. If he didn't brake, the whole experience was going to last longer, with more opportunities to get hurt. The landscape was whipping past at the periphery of his vision and Coolidge tapped the brake. The car promptly went into a fast spin, doing 360 degrees while slewing to the right. As the right-hand wheels got onto the shoulder, the car started over, as though forward motion had somehow become translated into rotation. The car was slowing but tipping toward the right side.

It was like a carnival ride, rising suddenly, stomach left behind, but the ascent of the Plymouth reached a peak and then it started down again. The peculiar thing was that Coolidge could still hear the animal scream of brakes and as his car slammed back to the ground, finally at rest, another car, braking hard, pulled off the road directly in front of him, blocking any movement.

Coolidge acted not out of the conditioned reflexes of an agent – he had none – but with what was even faster: logic. Since all he had was a jack handle, there was obviously only one thing to do: attack.

He reached back for it and was out of the car, racing for the other driver's door. He got there just as the door was swinging open, and he raised the jack handle over his head.

'It was a *flat*, Walter. Stop acting like a secret agent,' Vera said.

Coolidge lowered the jack handle. He was relieved. He was also embarrassed. But he was more relieved.

'You're unorthodox and that's good,' she said, getting out of her car. 'But you're also dumb, and that's bad. I could have drilled you full of lead by now.'

'What, you didn't think I could take care of myself?' Coolidge said.

Vera walked back to Coolidge's car. 'Look at that,' she said, pointing to a tire. 'It's a baldy, Walter. Are you nuts? You've got sixty thousand miles on these things. And you probably haven't had a lube job in fifteen thousand miles. Yeager is right about you; you're dangerous.'

'You're wonderful,' Coolidge said finally. 'Gee, I hope you don't turn out to be the Doctor.'

'Let's go; we can still catch up.'

Coolidge started to hustle around to the passenger side of Vera's car.

'Your car keys,' she said.

'Oh, right.' And there were his grandfather's opera glasses too.

Vera got up to speed with remarkably little fishtailing. Her car was brand-new and she enjoyed showing what it could do. She slowed up slightly, taking the exit to Route 50, and headed east. After she'd cut a swath through traffic at the top of the cloverleaf, she settled down to flying straight and level. Coolidge took out the opera glasses and began scanning the horizon.

'Now tell me why you followed me,' he said, the glasses up to his face.

'I told you. You're dangerous. You need help. Two heads are better than one. In your case, one head is better than one. Walter, you're not a man of action.' Pause. 'I was hoping to keep you from getting killed.'

'You're very sweet.'

'I'm sweetness flecked with realism.'

'I feel ungrateful saying this, but you could also be trying to throw me off. Maybe you're just being superclever.'

'How would you like to walk home, honey?' she replied.

'Slow down. I can see them.'

Coolidge had picked up the truck, chugging along at fifty-five. They settled down into a slow rhythm, trailing a quarter mile behind, occasionally putting on a burst of speed when they hadn't seen the white truck for a while.

Coolidge sat back, stretched his legs, idly gazing at the scenery, outside and inside. The line of Vera's thighs. The plush new upholstery. He smelled the car. He smelled Vera. Vera and the car were a good combination. They were both plush and aerodynamic, with a lot of scooch. He was slowly getting possessed by the traveler's disease, living interruptus, in between, drifting along.

The truck was headed toward Chesapeake Bay, which was clearly not your usual garbage run, so something was happening. He couldn't imagine why Senator Oliver Garvey of the great state of Nebraska would have a trash cover on him. And how that might lead to the identity of the spy in the Library, the so-called Doctor, whoever he was. A blackmailed Farnsworth? Kraus? Gardella gone off the deep end? Hopkins blithely selling out the country for some perk or other? Each possibility seemed possible, then each seemed impossible. But only Beebe and Yeager could be ruled out; they had no access to data and wouldn't know about O.F.F.

The scenery was changing. They were getting close to

water. People were hauling their boats home for the winter. The roadside decor was one seafood restaurant after another. They went over the four-mile Annapolis Bridge spanning Chesapeake Bay, past Kent Island, then on to the Delmarva peninsula.

'Maybe they're going to dump it in the ocean,' Vera said. 'We can get them on an environmental charge.'

The truck finally turned off the highway into a small town, Oxford, and went slowly along the narrow streets, looking provocative, a cruising garbage truck. Vera slowed and held back as far as possible. It wasn't more than a village, situated on a river, and probably had more ducks than people. The ungainly truck, twisting through side streets, made a turn and disappeared. When Vera followed, they came out onto a ferry landing.

The garbage truck was slowly pulling onto the small ferry.

'Now what?' Vera said.

Coolidge looked at the possibilities. No bridges were in sight. There were boats tied up all over the place and conceivably they could pay someone to take them across, but then they'd have no car.

'If we've been any good at all, they won't know we're following them,' he said. 'And if they do know, it won't make any difference. Go ahead.'

Vera pulled in behind the garbage truck, trying to pretend it wasn't there. She turned on the radio. They talked to each other. Once she caught the driver looking at her through his outside rearview mirror, but that could have been a normal male ogle. After the ferry filled up, it took only ten minutes to cross the river. Now Vera stayed even farther behind, because they had had a good look at her car.

It was more of the same – farms, pines, weeping willows, rolls of hay stacked near the highway. Beyond the next town, St. Michaels, the truck turned off the highway into a pinewood and was suddenly out of sight. Coolidge focused in and out with the opera glasses, trying to find it through the trees.

There was an asphalt road where the truck had turned in. Signs were everywhere: Keep Out. No Trespassing.

Entry Positively Forbidden. Vera wound slowly through the woods, past nothing but scrub grass and pine cones and brown pine needles strewn over gray sand. The asphalt gradually disappeared and the road turned into hard-packed sand, but there weren't any truck tracks. They went around a bend and the pine forest fell away.

There was nothing in front of them but sand.

Woods behind, woods on the right, woods a long way off in front. To the left, northward, there was nothing but grayish sand, and no truck.

They continued for another minute, slowly, baffled. Vera stopped at a tall wooden marker stuck in the sand, with a small red pennant flying from the top of it.

Coolidge got out and wandered off.

'There are no miracles,' he said. But it was a problem. One garbage truck had vanished. What were the possibilities? He strolled northward, trying to absorb the problem into his unconscious. He looked off at the trees rising above the dunes far away to the north. All he could think of was that they'd missed a turnoff. But there was something eerie about the scene. The place looked vaguely familiar, even though he knew he'd never been there before. It was so quiet he could hear the air.

'Let's go find a nice French restaurant. Walter, are you listening to me?'

Coolidge was trying to reach back into his unconscious; he knew there was a connection in his past to this place. What was it? Then the mystery deepened: he heard a *sound* that was familiar. He knew he'd heard that sound before, but he couldn't remember where. It had to be a coincidence of some kind, something sounding like something else, the same way a person looked like someone else. Then he heard the sound a second time, only seconds after the first one.

Coolidge was all ears, and eyes, his psyche on tiptoe, looking north.

When he heard it a third time, he knew. It was the pattern of three that got through to him. His basic training finally accomplished something useful. He whirled around and ran toward Vera, tackling her and then crawling over her, covering her body. The sand helped; the rocket sank in a few inches before detonating, but the sound was terrific. He figured it was 80-millimeter high-arcing mortar rounds, fire three for effect, that were coming in. The second one was closer; it was raining sand. The third one caught Vera's new car and blew it into a million pieces.

A Proposition

Vera's car had given a good account of itself; it went up
spectacularly. Disassembly had been so rapid, the gas tank
didn't get a chance to explode until it was seventy-five feet
in the air. Then it went off even louder than the mortar
rounds, as though the car were firing back.

Bits and pieces of it were still burning fiercely, the smell
of burning rubber and oil and upholstery staining the air.
Then, sounding at first like the ghost of the recently
departed, the quiet distant hum of a motor. Coolidge, still
lying on top of Vera, looked up over her head and saw a
jeep bouncing over the dunes, coming in their direction.

'You okay?' Coolidge said.

'I told you we should have gone to a French restaurant,'
a voice said from beneath him.

They slowly got to their feet, dusting off. Coolidge kept
an eye on the jeep. There were two hulks sitting in it. They
looked like trouble. He suddenly realized he hadn't taken
into account the lawlessness inherent in clandestine
fieldwork. He experienced a moment of panic, seeing that
he had blundered into anarchy, where there wasn't a cop
on the beat to protect your interests. He looked at Vera.
As usual, she was closer to the moment than he was; she
looked terrified.

The jeep pulled up. The passenger was talking into a
radio. 'We got them. Alive.' He hung up the microphone
and smiled. 'I can't make up my mind if you folks are
lucky or unlucky. Get in.'

An aggressive notion flitted through Coolidge's brain.
They didn't seem to be especially alert. There were no
weapons showing. He looked at Vera with a raised eyebrow, propositioning her.

111

She gritted her teeth back at him. 'Get *in*,' she said.

They got in back and the driver spun the jeep around and headed over the dunes. While Vera was gazing back longingly at the debris that had been her new car, Coolidge was thinking that if he only knew a little karate, it would be over in seconds and they'd have themselves a jeep. But that was absurd. Yeager was right; he was dangerous. He sneaked a look at Vera. Did her collision insurance include colliding with a mortar shell?

Before wofg they could see the top of a garbage truck sticking up over a dune and he found himself shaking his head in amazement at the sight of the Senator from Nowhere, out in the middle of Nowhere, old Computer Importance himself.

Oliver Garvey was standing in front of a tent with a Scotch in his hand, Davey Reed alongside him, and another man, whom Coolidge didn't recognize. A black limousine was parked off to the side, next to the garbage truck. About two hundred feet off to the right there were half a dozen mortars set up on bipods, all aimed in the general direction of Vera's car. Three empty rocket cases lay in the sand. As the jeep came to a stop in front of the tent, Garvey, looking appalled, said, 'Jesus God, have we gotten off on the wrong foot.'

'You mean you weren't intentionally lobbing mortar shells at us?' Coolidge replied. 'That was an accident? Oops?'

'I'm not liable,' the third man said, pointing a finger at Coolidge. 'It's not my fault. This is a federally inspected and approved firing range. It's posted in accordance with regulations. You people ignored all my signs. You parked right next to the target.' The man was badly flustered. He was rapidly going through all his pockets in search of something. 'Here,' he said, producing a card. 'Talk to my insurance company. Oliver, I'm sorry I got mixed up in this thing.'

'Relax, Arthur,' Garvey said. 'This is Arthur St. Claire. He's a good friend of mine who happens to be a merchant of death. He loaned us this place for a private meeting.'

'Thanks a lot,' St. Claire said.

'You missed the turnoff, Walter, that's it in a nutshell.

We thought it was obvious. Big deep ruts, easy trail to follow. I mean, if you got this far, we figured it would be easy. You ended up at the wrong end of the range. Can we please pretend this never happened? Is that possible?'

Coolidge closed his eyes. Being mortified was worse than being mortared. They had dangled Vera's goozy greeting card for bait in Garvey's garbage and he had followed it all the way.

Reed cleared his throat. 'Aren't you forgetting something, Senator? Uh, was that your car I saw in the sky?' he said to Vera.

'I intend to find the odometer before I leave here,' Vera said. 'That will be important in the suit. It had only two hundred miles on it.'

'Suit? No. No suit. No necessity for that,' Garvey said quickly. 'The courts are overloaded. Arthur just bought her car, didn't you, Arthur? It gets wonderful mileage. Isn't that right Arthur? Cheaper in the long run, Arthur.'

St. Claire shrugged.

'There we are,' Garvey said. 'Settled. All over. Now why don't we step inside to Arthur's place here and have ourselves a relaxing little drink and forget all about this?'

Coolidge didn't like the idea of Arthur St. Claire paying for Vera's car. It seemed reasonable and morally ambiguous at the same time. As he sat down at the camping table in the tent, Reed handed him a white wine on the rocks. How did they know he drank white wine on the rocks?

'Touché,' he said, looking at Reed.

'Now all we *wanted* to do was have a little chat,' Garvey said. 'That's all. Talk. Explore a few things. Important things. I admit to a degree of deviousness in how we went about it. It seemed like a good way at the time.'

'What he's getting at,' Davey Reed put in, 'is that you weren't followed, nobody knows you're here. The car ferry at Oxford was the pièce de résistance. Only locals got on behind you. It's the only reason we picked Arthur's place to meet at. What I'm saying is you're clean as a whistle.'

'I don't need you to tell me I'm clean as a whistle,' Coolidge fired back.

'I stand corrected,' Reed said humbly. 'Madam?'

'Two fingers straight up,' Vera replied.

Coolidge was finding the wine intensely restorative. He'd have to watch that he didn't get too restored. It was peculiar sitting in a tent with the enemy. It was evidently supposed to be a little moment out of time, off the record, never happened. Two generals meeting under a white flag of truce on neutral territory. But the tent made him think of the Civil War, and before long it sounded like it, as Arthur St. Claire test-fired a few mortars.

'If you want to chat,' Coolidge said, 'chat with Harry Dunn. He's the director of the Library. I can arrange it for you.'

Garvey sloshed the ice cubes around in his glass. 'Harry Dunn has watched me on *Face the Nation* too many times. He's gotten too good at evasion and escape. I consider him my prize pupil.'

Vera was holding up her glass for someone to fill and Reed went around replenishing drinks.

'It was a cheap trick, getting us here,' Vera said.

'Absolutely,' Garvey replied. 'Well, you do what you're used to.'

'You don't deal with other agencies of government this way, do you?'

Garvey gave her a genuine smile, not the election kind. 'Usually not,' he said. 'But then, you're not just another agency of government; you *are* the government. Or you will be before long. If all you are is an intelligence-collating agency, what's Harry doing there? Harry is a high-pressure guy.'

'Let's put it this way,' Davey Reed said, still fussing with bottles and ice cubes. 'Thomas Jefferson didn't know about computers. Computers have changed the nature of government. Computers are a watershed in the forward march of civilization. Now there's a first: mixing a metaphor while mixing a drink.'

It was Garvey's turn at bat. 'Look, the Library is an enormous power center not covered by the Constitution. There aren't any fundamental checks and balances, the way there are in the Congress and the judiciary and the executive. A lot of knowledge is a dangerous thing, Walter.'

'Not *bad*,' Reed said. 'A lot of knowledge is a dangerous thing. You finally wrote a good line.'

It was salesmanship. A real vaudeville act they had going. Coolidge put his hand over the top of his glass so Reed couldn't refill it.

The mortars were going again.

'It's hard for me to believe that you believe Vera or I would give you classified information about the Library. I mean, it's hard to take this scene seriously. You must know that. What are you up to?'

Garvey had been watching Coolidge closely, looking into his eyes as he spoke, head nodding, agreeing completely with Coolidge as fast as Coolidge could get the words out.

'I understand what you're saying,' Garvey said. He thought about it for a moment. 'I guess that just shows how important this meeting is to me. I know it must look ridiculous. I'm willing to risk looking ridiculous.'

'What's so important?'

Garvey thought a moment. 'Because I want to be President.' He smiled. 'Okay? Have we gotten that out of the way? I also have a personal, selfish, vested interest in saving the planet, because that includes me.'

Coolidge looked at Vera. 'This is "the treatment",' he told her. 'I've heard about it. In private, as opposed to his fake-solemn, sanctimonious public persona, Senator Garvey here comes across as totally honest, disarming, winning. How could a man that honest be anything but trustworthy?'

'I like the tone of this conversation,' the senator replied. 'I think we're getting down to marrow.'

'We're not getting down to anything.'

'Look, Walter, it's barely possible that with all your knowledge you don't understand what the hell's going on. There's a lot of opposition to the Library. I'm not just talking about American Civil Liberties Union bleeding heart liberal New York Jewish intellectuals. There are plenty of worried conservatives too. They figure that if a collation agency like the Library were used improperly, it could give the President too much power, both domestically and in foreign affairs. For the moment, we're especially interested in foreign affairs. They want to know what's going on. They're entitled.'

It was mind-boggling. Garvey was speaking with precision, terseness. He wasn't wandering around in subclasses and mutually canceling prepositional phrases, slipping away in conditionals, covering his tracks, working both sides of the street. He was actually communicating.

'You're interested toward what end?' Coolidge said.

'Well, I suppose you might refer to all these people loosely as the American peace movement. They're afraid the President has too much nuclear power at his fingertips and is too willing to use it. If it's ever used, there won't be a vote taken first; we'd like to have a *little* say in that.'

Coolidge sat back on his folding camp chair. 'The American peace movement?' he said. He looked at Vera, who was wearing a smile that could have cut hard salami. 'You?' Coolidge scratched his head. Garvey came from a conservative state. It was politically dangerous to be thought of as a dove. It was non-middle-of-the-road, totally out of character for him. It was pathetic. It was insulting. Did Garvey think he would buy that?

'That sounds impossible, right?' Garvey said.

'It smells impossible, is the way I'd put it. You're tampering with an official of a highly secret government agency' – 'Trying to,' Garvey put in dryly – 'instead of going through channels. You've got a trash cover on me' – 'You trashed me first' – 'and you have the sheer gall to say that you're doing it in the name of peace? Is it possible the good conservative senator has got himself mixed up with some radicals?'

'No. No, Walter. You've got it all wrong. In fact, you've got it backward. You guys are the radicals.'

'We are a legal agency of government, duly authorized by Congress.'

'Not so duly.'

'It's on the books.'

'Something's on the books.'

'What *you're* doing *isn't* on the books. What *are* you doing?'

'Just trying to get the government back in the hands of the people,' Garvey said.

'Oh, that's a good one,' Coolidge replied. 'That's hallowed. It's all-purpose.'

116

Coolidge had never believed in the *Seven Days in May* scenario. When power was played with in America, it was always done with the outward semblance and trappings of legitimacy and democracy. Otherwise the peasants would *spot* it. But now the Senator from Nowhere seemed to be vaguely hinting at something like that. Garvey's eyelids were back to their normal hooded position, and he tossed it off casually, as though asking about the latest hot lunch program: 'What about O.F.F., for example?'

'What's O.F.F.?' Coolidge said, looking into Garvey's blue eyes. He had the distinct feeling that Vera was trying to breathe and couldn't.

Garvey looked back at him from somewhere under his eyebrows and over his Scotch, then smiled good-naturedly. 'Okay, I don't know what the hell it is.'

'Whatever it is, it's 23.75 percent,' Reed said. 'O.F.F. is 23.75 percent. I can't tell you why, but that's scary to me. Is it supposed to go up or down, Walter? What happens when it gets there? Are we all going to be happy when it gets there? Am I going to be happy?'

'My name is Walter Coolidge, Social Security number 107-22-1025,' he said, wondering why the Doctor wasn't keeping them up to date. O.F.F. was now almost 50 percent.

Garvey laughed again. 'I knew we couldn't fool you, Walter. Hell, we don't want to fool you.'

'Yes, you do. You've already fooled me once today. You must think I'm a double fool to have forgotten that you made a fool of me only a few minutes ago.'

'I can't help it,' Garvey said. 'It's an occupational hazard. I don't suppose you could just up and tell us what O.F.F. is?'

'You wouldn't want me to violate my oath, would you? I could get in trouble for that.'

'Walter.' Davey Reed was feigning patience. 'You're *supposed* to answer questions like that. You could get in trouble for *not* answering questions like that.'

'Then call me before the committee.'

'I hereby declare this a hearing room for the Senate Select Subcommittee on Oversight for the Intelligence Collection Agency, meeting is called to order, witness will be sworn,' Garvey said in the monotone of a bailiff, holding his face up with one hand, fiddling with his drink with the other.

Reed pulled out a blue, drink-stained Gideons Bible. He held it out in the dim light of the tent. 'Do you swear to leak the truth, the whole truth, and nothing but the truth?'

Garvey grimaced. 'Davey, God damn it, I wish you hadn't used that word. Okay, we're asking you leak. There, we said it. But to a properly constituted government body. And in the interests of the republic.'

Coolidge looked at the Bible, at Vera, at Reed, at Garvey.

Reed put the Bible back in his attaché case. 'I knew this was a waste of time. God only works in public.'

'Will you at least think about it? Consider it? Let it simmer on the back burner for a while?'

Coolidge wanted to knock him off balance. He gave in to an urge. It was irresistible.

'Maybe you ought to go see your rabbi,' he said. 'Talk to him about your problem.'

Garvey's big frog eyelids opened for the first time in years. Reed put his drink down without making any sound. They looked at each other in amazement and despair.

'I think you've had too much to drink, Walter,' Vera said.

'I don't think I've had enough to drink,' Reed said quietly.

Coolidge was watching their faces. They were stunned. End of vaudeville act. Garvey was looking bleak; no more smile, no more big honesty routine. He fell back on what he knew best.

'No comment,' Oliver Garvey said.

They were awkwardly moping around in the sand outside the tent, when it finally occurred to them that without Vera's car, they had a transportation problem.

The men who drove the garbage truck would have to stay behind to load the jeep with the weapons, the equipment, the tent. That left the limo. 'I doubt if Walter and Vera would want to ride with us,' Arthur St. Claire said delicately, 'although I suppose we could drop them off at a bus stop.'

Reed, long and thin, shoulders hunched, hands buried deep in his pockets against the chilling breeze coming in from the bay, smiled bleakly and said, 'I have a thought.'

Coolidge had seen it coming. He was prepared for it. It was the final indignity of a preposterous day. He held his hand out. 'Give me the key,' he said.

The Garbage-Lovers

It was his fate. It was written. It would have been pointless trying to avoid it. The mature individual recognized such circumstances when they arose.

'If anyone deserves this, it's us,' Vera said.

Coolidge had driven a truck for a while in the Army; shifting and double clutching were a permanent part of his nervous system. He was able to get the feel of it while driving from Arthur St. Claire's test site out to the highway. Thereafter it was easy, although the wheel took a lot of handling. They went rattling along at fifty, St. Claire's limousine soon leaving them far behind, tiny red dots disappearing for a final time over a distant hill.

'Alone at last,' Coolidge said.

'Isn't it romantic? If we make any garbage, all we have to do is toss it over our shoulder.'

'Now, now, you *know* you like to do new things.'

'Open the window,' Vera said, rolling hers down. 'I'd rather be cold than smelly.' Then she started laughing, quietly at first, covering her mouth, then letting it blast, as she rocked around on the slab seat of the garbage truck.

Coolidge merely drove.

'Walter,' she said finally, 'I would rather you slept with other women than go on operations again. Ever.'

'We haven't found out who the Doctor is.'

'See no evil, Walter.'

'Be the easy way, certainly.'

'Have you been screwing around, Walter?'

'No, I haven't been screwing around.'

'You've got to know this thing's too big for you. I mean, something basic is going on. Powers are coming up against each other. It's a basic clash. Don't get in between, Walter.'

120

It was getting to be twilight, on a chill autumn day. Seven Days in October, Coolidge was thinking. Will you plot against me in October like you do in May?

'But there does seem to be a plot against the U.S. government,' he murmured. 'There *seems* to be. All kinds of characters involved. Including a U.S. senator. And they know something about O.F.F. They're worried about O.F.F.'

'Who isn't worried about O.F.F.?'

'How can we ignore it?'

'I think I'm tight,' Vera said.

'They've even got access to weapons. A lot of weapons. Arthur St. Claire has warehouses full of them. He's even got light tanks, for God's sake.'

'No tanks, I'll just eat,' Vera said.

After a while the highway served up a diner. Coolidge pulled off the road and drove into a crowded parking lot. The truck took up two parking spaces and jutted out into the lane. Coolidge and Vera climbed down ignoring a few stares, and strode into the diner, trailing sand.

'We're going to Harry,' Vera said when they were sitting at a table. Coolidge took the side where he could keep his eye on the truck.

'The hell we are.'

'What else is there to do?'

'I don't know yet. But we're not going to Harry.'

'I'll think about it.'

When the waitress brought the hamburgers, Coolidge looked down at them without enthusiasm.

'It's not exactly Chinese,' he said.

'But it'll do in a pinch,' Vera said wickedly, chomping down on hers.

'You can't go to Harry because it could be Harry. It's a logical possibility. You don't want me to think of you as an illogical woman, do you?'

'You're overdoing this logic stuff, Walter. How could it be Harry? The Library is Harry's baby. He loves it. Passionately. There are situations in life, Walter, that cannot be approached logically.'

'Yeah,' Coolidge said, eating absently, listening absently. He couldn't tell her what he'd been doing. He'd decided on ideology. It was next after sex and money as you worked north from the crotch. He'd gone on a witch hunt, looking for a Communist in the Library, starting with Harry.

It had been more countless hours at the terminal in his office. He was neglecting trash entirely now, giving it all over to Jake Shoemaker. He'd checked back to the original vetting done on Harry, the first time he'd ever gotten a government security clearance. Then he'd branched out, checking all the people who'd given Harry a clean bill of health. Then he'd repeated the procedure for every one of the Librarians.

Minor flirtation with Marxism at college was the most he could find on anybody. Peculiarly enough, Harry himself had been a Marxist during his freshman year. But it was merely intellectual with him; there had been no fervor. For Harry, Marxism was interesting because it was such a clever attempt at solving a problem. Then he'd dropped it for the much cleaner, clearer fun field of nuclear physics.

The Doctor wasn't a Communist or even a sympathizer. Damn, it was getting back to the worst, the hardest to find: conscience. The man of conscience who had decided that everyone else was wrong, and had acted accordingly.

'Stop brooding and eat,' Vera said. 'You're dangerous when you brood. You're going to hatch something ridiculous.'

Coolidge was going over the crazy scene in the tent, trying to remember every word spoken to see if there was a clue about the Doctor. Something accidental that might have slipped out sideways. There was one obvious flaw in Garvey's armor. Davey Reed drank too much. Maybe Coolidge could do something with that. He wasn't much of a drinker himself, but he'd seen on microcam what it could do to people. When they were self-pitying, they'd say anything. It was a thought anyway, a possibility for future action, a chance.

Back on the highway, he said, 'I haven't seen your legs in weeks. It just occurred to me.'

'I know how preoccupied you've been.'

'You're wearing pants these days, aren't you?'

'I am not. Except for today, because I was going on a

mission. You just haven't been paying attention, Walter. Walter, are you fooling around?'

'No, I haven't been fooling around.'

'Honest?'

'Honest.'

Coolidge couldn't take his eyes off the road because traffic was picking up, but he heard a zipper go zip. When he dared look, she was sitting there, very office down to the waist, but then just panties and long creamy legs, her slacks down around her ankles.

'Now what were we talking about?' Vera said brightly.

It was the privacy, Coolidge realized. No microcams to worry about. No bugs. Or, as they were called when located in bedrooms, fugs. It was releasing him, rather suddenly. He looked over at those tightly crossed legs and almost went onto the shoulder.

'Walter, I've never done it in a garbage truck, have you?'

A few impatient miles ahead, they suddenly came upon a rest area. Coolidge careened into it, burning rubber all the way, and then brought the truck nose in at the farthest corner, away from the few parked cars. He got out of the truck and walked around, casually surveying the scene. They'd raised a few heads, but then everyone had gone back to their thermos bottles. He was totally erect before he got back into the truck, on Vera's side.

Her panties were hanging from the rearview mirror and she was pulling at his belt buckle as soon as he sat down.

'Did you put out the Do Not Disturb sign?' Vera was saying as she pulled his pants down.

She sat on top of him and eased on. 'Oh-oh,' Coolidge said right away. This was going to be major; the garbage truck was going to move. He'd been saving it up too long. So had she, from the looks of things. Coolidge sat there, upward while Vera oscillated, nice smile on her face that kept breaking up, at first intermittently, then more often, until there was no more smile at all. None. She looked as though she were trying to remember something deep down. Something crucial. And Coolidge was jogging her memory. Then her face had a look of discovery and it all came back to her in a flash.

Trash Report: #85-10-7

CASE NUMBER: 104759

ABANDONED PROPERTY DONOR: Senator Oliver Garvey (residence)

1. 1962 Dumont 19 inch TV set, inoperative.
2. Clipped issues of newsletter: Institute for Policy Studies.
3. Copy of original legislation creating Library.
4. Membership plaque, Benevolent and Protective Order of Elks.
5. Cuff links with built-in wristwatch, new.
6. Photocopy of H. Dunn's *Who's Who* entry.
7. Minutes of House Intelligence Committee.
8. Bottle private label Scotch, 1.75 liter.
9. Three packs mentholated cigarettes.
10. Copy of speech intended for delivery to Senate.

Trash Scenario

On Thursday night, Roger Castleman, legal counsel to Garvey's oversight subcommittee, paid a visit. There was a long late-night session (item #9, three packs of mentholated cigarettes), with intense discussion of constitutionality of the Library (item #3, copy of original legislation creating the Library, heavily annotated. Numerous question marks in orange grease pencil. Comments in many places: 'Legislative intent?' 'Don't remember this wording.' 'We've left the barn door open,' etc.).

The legal counsel's opinion was that the Library is legal (item #7, testimony of attorney general re Library before the House Intelligence Committee). The senator was greatly annoyed (item #6, photocopy of H. Dunn's *Who's Who* entry, acidulous comments in margins).

Notes

The peculiar speeches continue to appear. Along with Garvey's refusal to deliver them. Garvey has a shredder in his home, which required a large number of man-hours for reconstruction of item #10. Could this somehow be rendered inoperative?

Based on the other sources of information, it is apparent that the writer of these speeches is Davey Reed. He can't be writing them when drunk; they're too coherent. But why would he write them when sober? There isn't a politician in the country who would level like this with the public. Item #10. reconstructed in its entirety, is reproduced here.

Members of this body, I come before you today gravely concerned about an issue of critical national importance. I am referring to the increasing level of criticism being directed at the weapons systems the Pentagon is purchasing. In particular, comments about the ineffectiveness of these weapons systems, or their redundant character, seem gratuitous and damaging to our defense posture.

Such unthinking comments also betray a fundamental misunderstanding of what the arms race is supposed to achieve.

I think we might well refer to the arms race as Operation Potlatch. Yes, potlatch, a word invented by ancient American Indians living on the Pacific coast.

One might go so far as to say that the arms race was invented by these early Indians.

Now potlatch, as you doubtless know, meant that competing chiefs would demonstrate their mightiness by their willingness to destroy their tribe's worldly goods. The two competing chiefs would sit by the campfire and take turns tossing the good things of life into it – blankets, bows and arrows, food, skins. The 'atomic bomb' of such contests was to burn down one's entire village. They were bent and determined to find out who could afford to lose more. The chief who was endlessly willing to destroy goods thereby acquired the reputation for power and majesty and was the greater chief.

This analogy shows us the self-defeating nature of criticisms of our weapon systems. The actual military usefulness of a particular weapons system is secondary. Indeed, I might even go so far as to say (*pound podium here*) irrelevant!

Does it force the Russians to throw something into the fire? Are they forced to build a similar weapon? Are they coerced into building a counterweapon? Must they alter their command and control systems? If they do, thus tossing more worldly goods into the campfire, then the weapon has *already* succeeded in its mission. It is only when the Soviets *don't* spend money to counter it that the weapon is a flop. I fervently hope and pray the Soviet leadership never understands this.

Therefore, gentlemen, I propose that the members keep the good of the country in mind and temper their criticism of our weapons systems hereafter. Someday, the tribe across the ocean, hungry, cold, deprived, will rise up against their chief and then Operation Potlatch can be declared a success. We will then be seen as the mightiest of all nations and can begin to keep our own worldly goods out of the campfire.

Thank you, Mr. President. I yield to the gentleman from South Carolina.

The Scenario Comes to Life

Cables were starting to fly back and forth between NATO capitals. There'd been crises before in NATO: over Poland, Hungary, Czechoslovakia, East Germany. But there had never been the remotest approach to a tank buildup at Naumburg. That was what they'd been talking about and gaming for decades; there were hundreds of scenarios in the files.

Could it be a Soviet threat? Or, worse, a Soviet intention? Or was each side misreading the other? The French were already discussing whether or not they would commit their army to NATO, or stay out of it and guard their own borders, backed up by their strategic *Force de Frappe*, one hundred warheads for one hundred Soviet cities, which would mean the end of the Soviet Union. They were also talking to the Germans about participating in a forward defense in Germany, without committing themselves one way or another.

There was no unanimity of opinion in NATO. The West Germans and Great Britain were, for the moment, supporting the buildup. Belgium and the Netherlands were, for the moment, opposing the buildup. The French were undecided. Greece and Turkey were abstaining.

Harry Dunn himself had an entire weekend in which to think and stew in his garden, dozens of hours in which to worry, use foresight, insight, hindsight, be apocalyptic and fretful. To Dunn, the weekend was one long two o'clock in the morning: sweaty palms, snapping at the wife, nipping at the brandy, anxieties piled up, control lost, nothing to do. He spent the entire time a hair away from calling them all in for an emergency session. But he kept forcing himself to wait, husbanding his resources. If things were moving the way he thought, they were going to have long hours for a long time. It was best to give them their weekend, let them have their rest; they were going to need it.

On Monday at 7 A.M., NATO was given All-Importance, the highest category, all other matters to be excluded, and the pursuit of indications, signs, portents, omens, juxtapositions, combinations, permutations, began.

In response to the Russian buildup in East Germany, NATO high command had brought the U.S. independent 14th Armored Brigade to full alert and had begun to move it into position south of the gap at Fulda, to serve as a flank threat to any Russian breakthrough. The Russians had responded by adding the 27th Armored Shock Army, about the size of an American armored division, to its strike force near Bad Hersfeld. It was all over the satellite photos, and Vera spent ten minutes moving the electronic pointer across the displays, picking out the tanks.

They listened to a conversation (translated) about tanks and women between two naked, vodka-drinking Russian generals in a bordello on Pletskaya Street in Moscow. The women part concerned their poundage preferences; the tank part was about the new type, the model referred to in the West as Juggernaut, which was built to survive in atomic, biological, or chemical environments, and had the new 160-millimeter gun. The first models were to be deployed in East Germany, as part of the 125th Guards Armored Division.

O.F.F. had broken into the fifties for the first time. Coolidge was amazed at how fast it was moving. It reached 54.75 percent before sixty-mile-per-hour winds in the eastern Mediterranean subtracted a mandatory 7 percent, dropping it back to 47.75 percent.

Coolidge was having concentration trouble. Which had the higher priority, World War III or the Doctor? He had been watching his fellow Librarians as much as the data screens. Kraus, Farnsworth, Harry, Vera, Barber, Hopkins. The least likely suspect was Burnish, who seemed too simple to be involved in a plot, so he watched Burnish a lot. No, the least likely suspect was Beatty, who was leading a 100 percent clean life. He was having sex with only one person. His wife, of all people. His only peculiarity, if it could be called that, was that now and then she'd lie face down on the bed and Beatty would slap her buttocks. She seemed to like it more than he did. Marriages had been based on thinner strands than that.

Beatty was assigned to resources. He kept an eye on all the strategic resources the U.S. had to import. Oil particularly, but also molybdenum, tantalum, bauxite ore, manganese. He looked for potential threats, political or military, that might jeopardize America's supply lines. Because of oil, he was also an expert on the Middle East and could talk for hours on the complexities of tribal politics and the influence of religious prejudice on world affairs. Beatty considered NATO a second rate theater of war; the real action was at the Strait of Hormuz, through which most Middle East oil had to pass to get to the West and Japan.

Beatty was as gung ho as Harry Dunn. There was a fanatical quality to his anticommunism. It was mixed up with religion, his born-again Christianity. It was mixed up with money; the French branch of his family had lost a fortune in rubber plantations in Vietnam, thus eliminating the life of a rich man's son for Beatty. Beatty was so gung ho that of late he had become impatient with Harry. Harry was too cautious. So was the President. They both wanted to know too much before acting. 'If we're not willing to take risks, we shouldn't be here,' Beatty kept saying. At home he scornfully imitated the mannerisms of Harry, Vera, Hopkins, and Coolidge. He was like a predator hot on the chase, nose full of scent, but frustrated from closing in on the kill. Was Beatty's fanaticism and loyalty so intense that he could no longer be trusted? Coolidge rubbed his eyes. He had too much data. He had managed to take the least likely candidate and make him a serious suspect.

Then he forgot about Beatty. There was aerial footage of a dogfight up on the screens, Russian MIGs mixing it up with American F-15s, and the F-15s weren't doing so hot. For a moment it seemed as though the war was on, until he realized that the MIGs were from the Air Force's 1500th

Fighter Training Group, which consisted of crack American fliers piloting MIGs that had been flown out of Russia and satellite countries by defectors; the MIGs had done too well against the USAF 137th Fighter Wing. The expensive American planes were supposed to be able to deal with superior numbers of the cheaper Russian planes. But the larger American planes created fat radar echoes that were easy to lock onto, whereas the smaller Russian planes were more elusive. The MIGs of the 1500th could only be defeated in dogfights with at least equal numbers on both sides. The personnel of the 137th were now returning to their base in Mannheim, tactically chastened but wiser.

A brief, unsatisfactory exchange on the hot line between the two Presidents was flashed on the screen exactly as it went out over the hot line teletype.

PRES U.S.: 'Your tanks must be removed from the general area of the Fulda Gap. Anything less than total compliance would be regarded as a grave threat and could not be tolerated.'

PRES U.S.S.R.: 'You are picking a fight. If you continue, you will certainly get one. You have taken a minor redeployment of Warsaw Pact forces and have pretended it's a crisis. We will never abandon the defense of our Warsaw Pact allies.'

It went on hour after hour, a major crisis building before their eyes. Tanks were on the move everywhere in Europe and debates began to move into tactical questions rather than strategic ones. Was Fulda Gap a feint? A buildup at the obvious place to conceal a more subtle thrust being prepared somewhere else? There was always the Von Mannstein brilliancy to remember: moving the German panzer divisions through impossible tank country, the Ardennes, thereby taking the French by surprise in 1940, showing up behind French lines with ten tank divisions.

World War III or the Doctor, Coolidge kept thinking, vainly trying to decide which should get Coolidge Importance.

The Priests

The Library wasn't operational, it was advisory. They were concerned with the big picture rather than with the nuts and bolts of operations. So it didn't have to stand guard over situations in quite the same way as, say, the CIA Indications Center, which was manned twenty-four hours a day 365 days a year. So although Harry didn't care for it, after about twelve hours of playing with data, Librarians began drifting in and out.

Coolidge picked up the phone and called across the table.

'Could I interest you in a little Chinese tonight?' he said quietly.

'Chung jung gung.'

'One order with sweet sauce coming up.'

After they got out of the building, they changed their minds about Chinese and decided to have French, which was every bit as good for Chinese as Chinese was. The French chef at the 211 Club was a genius. The Club had the advantage that it was nearby, plus the fact that it was one of the rare places in Greater Washington that was off limits to microcams. As they followed the maître d' to their table, Coolidge was spotting celebrities all over the place. Only the top people in Washington were members, and the President himself had put the Club on the small list of 'free-talk zones.' Coolidge and Vera belonged only because Harry had got them all memberships; Librarians were important.

There had to be a place like the 211 Club, Coolidge thought, winding his way past the movers and shakers. It was essential to the workings of a democratic form of ruling, even though the idea seemed fishy to any proponent of good government: it was the meeting ground between official power, that designated by the Constitution, and unofficial power, that produced by the random forces of society. The 211 Club was where congressmen and lobbyists met on neutral territory, where people seeking to influence power met people with power.

Former Secretary of State Henry Kissinger, who existed almost alone in a special realm of once and future power, always got the best table in the dining room. It was the one that gave Kissinger the best possible view of the other diners, as well as serving as a showcase, since it also gave the other diners the best possible view of Kissinger.

Vera was ignoring significance. Vera was hungry. When her Little Neck clams arrived, she didn't eat them so much as absorb them into her system, each little beauty turning into an impulse.

'My place or my place?' she said.

Coolidge was precisely titrating half a drop of hot sauce on each and every clam, a job he finished before replying.

'I'm always very concentrated when I'm squirting hot sauce,' he said, looking her right in the eye.

'Oh-oh.'

'You're the seventh clam, lady.'

Fluttering of eyelids and fake vibrato: 'Really?'

'We're not going to your place or my place. We're going to nobody's place. I've made a hotel reservation. It'll save time.'

'And it's much more illicit.'

He was also sure the room was free of microcams. Coolidge looked at her and smiled. He still hadn't checked her footage. Not that he expected to see anything terrible. He didn't have any expectations one way or another. She was over twenty-one. She was an active woman. She was alive. She spent a good part of her life out at her nerve endings. She was the opposite of Coolidge, who spent most of his time imagining how other people felt, which was safer.

Sooner or later Coolidge was going to have to watch the two of them going at it in her bed. He wanted to see himself even less than he wanted to see her. He was also convinced that he'd never be able to perform sexually in any place where he knew there were microcams. The penis was an absurd organ; you could never tell what mode it was going to be in. It was capricious, perverse, blind, insensitive, lazy, energetic, fussy, undiscriminating. It was a random, uncontrollable maniac. What could you say about a creature whose brains were in its balls?

Coolidge was trying to keep his mind on Vera and on clams, which went so well together and were a good antidote to the tank armies on the move that he was trying to forget about for a while. He was also trying to forget about his abortive one-day career as an operational agent, but it kept popping up.

'Are you thinking about me or the world?' Vera said.

'The world.'

'You can't screw the world, Walter.'

'Don't be so sure.'

'Okay, let's get it out of the way.'

'Get what out of the way?'

'I was going to wait until, uh, afterward,' she said coyly, 'but maybe it's better now. I want to tell Harry.'

'No, you've got it backward. You don't want to tell Harry.'

'The whole thing is preposterous; we've got to tell Harry.'

'Preposterous is Harry's word.'

'I don't care whose it is. Do you realize we spent an hour in a tent with Oliver Garvey, getting propositioned?'

'I'll grant you it's preposterous.'

Vera was buttering a small piece of French bread with clam sauce.

'We just can't let that ride,' she said. 'We'll have to tell Harry. Now don't try to stop me, Walter.'

'Will you listen to me for a minute?'

'Take two, darling.'

'Let's assume for the moment that you're not the Doctor, okay? Or the Bishop.'

Vera took out a pack of cigarettes, lit one slowly, blew smoke at Coolidge, narrowed her eyes.

'Okay, let's assume that.'

'Okay. If you're not the Doctor, whoever *is* the Doctor won't know that two of us are watching for the least little slip. He won't know unless you blab it to the Library. And with all the Library's resources at our disposal, we're bound to find out who it is. It's inevitable.'

'Suppose I *am* the Doctor. What do you do then?'

'If you're really the Doctor, you're going to live clean from here on out. Because you know, sweetheart, that I'll get you. So if you're the Doctor, you're neutralized, and I'm willing to forget your past sins.'

'Walter, the truth is I'm not the Doctor. I'm what the Doctor ordered.'

'Yeah,' Coolidge said. But as they clinked wineglasses, he picked up a large moving blob in the corner of his eye. Harry Dunn had just entered the main room of the restaurant.

'Vera,' Coolidge said threateningly, his wineglass still touching hers.

'Damn,' she said. 'I don't know what to do.'

'When you don't know what to do, don't do anything.'

Fortunately, Harry was taking his time getting across the room. He was like a movie star, shaking hands, patting people on the back, touching bases. The Senate minority leader, John Mulrooney. The chairman of appropriations for the House, Jasper Brown. The assistant secretary of defense for procurement. It went on and on. The executive secretary of the Sugar Council. The chairman of the board of Boeing. A man whose name was Lockheed but who was international vice-president of the Tinsmith, Welders and Solderers Union. At least it enabled Coolidge to finish his clams in peace before Harry got there.

'Mind if I join you?' Harry said.

Coolidge didn't even get the chance to answer, but it wasn't a question. There was even less point in asking, How did you know we were here? Nodding at the maître d', who was suddenly all snapping fingers and smiles, Harry proceeded to join them in his fashion: they were quickly moved to a bigger and better table, as well as a bigger and better wine – a '74 Montrachet that, according to the maître d', was drinking well.

Coolidge was trying to stare Vera down. Harry was looking unusually tense as he dug into the bread and butter. As soon as the waiters had moved off, he leaned across the table.

'The Second Armored Division in Mannheim has just been put on full combat alert,' he said. 'This country is now at DefCon Three.'

'Something happen in the last half hour?' Coolidge asked.

'The Russians are reinforcing again. They're playing some kind of game. We're going to win it, of course. Vera, after dinner you're coming back with me. In the meantime, let's get fortified; it's going to be a long night.'

Then the maître d' was there with recommendations and Harry was ordering for the three of them, Vera and Coolidge slumping in their chairs, Harry missing the gesture completely.

'The new film is in?' Vera asked weakly, when the maître d' had gone.

'In processing,' Harry said, chomping.

'That's a break,' Vera said.

'We're going to get those tanks out of Naumburg, folks,' Harry said. 'They're going to turn tail. Guess what's now 66.38 percent and rolling? It's going to be our biggest moment.'

'You don't mean we'd use O.F. – uh, that is, uh, *it*?' Coolidge said.

'I certainly do mean *it*. Of course, we'd use it in the way it was planned to be used. Which is to employ its threat value. When the threat is made plain to them, it'll be like the Cuban missile crisis. They'll back out. If it were up to me, we'd have a display of *it* in the Kremlin and let them keep track same as we do. We could call it the Kremlin Mood Controller. Anytime they start to think aggressive, all they'd have to do is look at *it* to become instantly tranquilized. It's the answer to everything.'

Waiters were advancing rapidly from all sides; they were like dismounted cabdrivers, making time, cutting corners. The order was filet of sole meunière for three and the maître d' was surreptitious about the béarnaise sauce. He placed a small pitcher of it on the table, while looking around to see if anyone noticed. Harry put béarnaise sauce on everything.

'See the service I get?' Harry said, spreading the béarnaise sauce on top of the lemon butter. 'And I'm not

135

that big a tipper. I'll tell you something. Nobody's allowed to pick up my check here. If I didn't have that rule, they'd be fighting over it.'

'How come, Harry?' Vera asked. 'All we are is an unimportant intelligence collation agency.'

'Two and two makes four,' Harry replied. 'Everybody can count in this town.'

Harry started into his priest speech. They were high priests of information. Purity was the order of the day. It was necessary to fend off the power hungry, the money hungry, the prestige hungry. Anyone with power had to remember that it wasn't you that interested them, it was the power, only the power, never forget it, beware of friendliness.

Harry was really full of himself. Naumburg had turned him on. His normal enthusiasm was distilling out to an even higher proof. He went on about jealousies among the intelligence services. How the DIA had information on Afghanistan that it didn't bother telling anyone when it might have helped. The way the armed forces fought each other for budget and prestige and areas of responsibility. They would leak fake scenarios to the public at budget time in an attempt to reduce each other's importance. Then they'd hold a peace meeting in the Pentagon cafeteria and agree on a common scenario, with everybody's interests figured in.

'It's the kind of thing that went on endlessly before we came on the scene. I tell you, the Library is the answer to all of it. The cold war. The arms race. Problems around the world. You know what we are? You two, me, the others, the data? We're the Department of Peace and Quiet. That's what we should be called. Peace and quiet, that's all we're after. That's our organizational mission. It's worth struggling for. And now you see why I picked the meanest son of a bitch in the country to protect the Library, defend the data. *The* meanest. So I'm not worried about the physical security of the Library. That's always the easiest part. It's people that's the problem. The Emersons, they're a problem. This Doctor character, whoever the hell *he* is. A problem.'

Coolidge reached across the table and lit Vera's shaking cigarette.

'Okay, we *are* getting the names now,' Harry went on. 'That's all to the good. Herb Purefoy, ex-CIA. Glenn

Ingalls, computer chip manufacturer. Admiral Dutch Anderson, an oddball retired officer. General Rudolph Witek, another oddball. We don't know who the Bishop is yet, or the Rabbi, But that's all right; I've sent Gardella on a rampage. A few more microcams, a few more bugs, we'll find out. Then there's the leader. You figure it. Emerson Foster, for Christ sake, a conservative, an investment banker. I don't get it. Do you get it? Any thoughts, connections, guesses?'

'They come on as though they're some sort of peace movement,' Coolidge said. 'Is that remotely possible?'

Harry threw his hand out in disgust. 'Everybody uses peace. Hawks, doves, even SAC, for Christ sake: Peace Is Our Profession.'

Coolidge cleared his throat, avoided Vera's eyes, glanced over at Harry's disappearing cheesecake. 'Uh, who do you think the Doctor could be?'

'Could be anybody, Walter. Could be anywhere. Garvey's the Porkbelly. He's been doling out pork for over twenty years. He's got a trunkful of IOUs. He's campaigned for everybody on his side of the aisle, plus a few on the other side. He has pals in every agency of government. He's got friends in this room. God knows how many people owe their jobs to him.'

'Then I guess finding the Doctor,' Coolidge said, 'justifies almost anything. This is one of those cases where we break the rules, right?'

'Anything goes,' Harry said. 'In fact, I hereby start a new policy. Rewards. First Librarian to identify the Doctor gets a five-thousand-dollar reward. Make it seventy-five hundred. We'll get him. I've got the eleven best bounty hunters in the world working for me. I mean ten. Anything goes, Walter.'

Coolidge and Vera were still inspecting each other's eyeballs when they heard the sound of loud voices coming to them from across the big room. It was a disturbance at the Kissinger table. The former secretary of state was gesticulating, his Germanic voice penetrating to all corners of the room. But the Kissinger magic wasn't working. While Kissinger was in the middle of a telephone call, the maître d' had personally pulled out the telephone plug. Kissinger looked stunned, unbelieving. He was actually speechless, groping for phrases as though, at a time of grave emergency, he'd lost his acquired tongue.

The maître d' walked away from him, carrying the phone. He brought it to Harry.

'The President is calling, monsieur,' the maître d' said, plugging in the jack and picking up the receiver for Harry. Harry winked at them while cupping his hand around the mouthpiece so no one could lip-read. Harry was right. He had power.

When Harry got off the phone, he advised Coolidge to get a good night's sleep. Then Coolidge found himself alone with his coffee cup, as Harry and Vera went back across the big room, Vera turning to wave weakly.

Coolidge was in an odd state. Disconnected. In over his head. Having second thoughts. Who was he to be at the center of things? He was an anthropologist who liked to piece out the way ordinary people worked at the tasks of living. He could as easily have been an archaeologist, piecing out the way ordinary dead people had worked at the tasks of living.

Coolidge always began to have morose thoughts when things got too irrational. A first-class crisis was shaping up in Germany. The worst that had come along in many years. It looked as though there was a movement inside the U.S. establishment that was directed against the Library. And then there was O.F.F., which hovered over everything. A baby playing with a hand grenade: that was the status of mankind. Nice baby, leave the little hand grenade where it is. Pretty, isn't it?

It was going to be the Library's finest hour. It was a chance to one-up the Senate and the House and the CIA and all the others, as well as, incidentally, the Soviets. Assuming the Doctor didn't screw up everything first. Coolidge felt as though there ought to be something constructive he could do, but he didn't have the faintest idea what. His thoughts were interrupted by the approach of the maître d'.

Harry had stuck him with the check.

138

The Visit

By the time Oliver Garvey got to the hotel room, things were well along. For a writer, Davey Reed was a reasonably good organizer. The holes were already drilled in the walls and the camera guys were getting set up. A man arrived right behind Garvey with a case about twice the size of an attaché case. He took out a vacuum cleaner and went to work on the plaster dust.

'There's a message for you from the President,' Gretl, the senator's secretary, told him. 'They won't repeat it over the phone.'

'Fine,' Garvey said, taking off his coat. 'He can wait.'

Gretl had a pile of messages. She'd been using the hotel room as a command post for two hours. 'There's a roll call vote on the postal bill coming up at four-thirty. The dairy lobby wants to see you again – '

'Skip it,' Garvey said, taking off his jacket and tie. 'What do you think, Davey?' he said. 'Is he going to show?'

Reed had been working hard on a speech in spare moments. He was sitting on the couch, drink in front of him on the coffee table, notes everywhere on small pieces of paper.

'I'd say it's a damn good maybe. I think he's serious because he went to a lot of trouble to spell out the room. McArdle Hotel. Any even-numbered room below the tenth floor, any odd-numbered room above the tenth. What the hell that means, I don't know. They can't have half the hotel bugged, can they? I mean, that's overload. They couldn't handle it all.'

'I'm not going to think about that now,' Garvey replied, unbuttoning his shirt. 'We've got to figure out how we're going to talk to him if he does come. He's smart. We can't fool him. We're going to have to level. What do you think?'

Garvey was fussing around, unusually nervous. Reed had never seen Garvey unhinged before. He was poking around at the bar. 'Do we have white wine? We don't have any white wine. I told you to get white wine.'

'It's behind the Scotch,' Reed said, rubbing his eyes.

'Oh, good. Is that a good white wine?'

'No, it isn't. It's the kind he's used to. A good white wine would look like a bribe.'

Garvey was hanging his shirt up. 'Hey, Davey, you're improving. I'm really bringing you along. You're getting goddamn subtle. You're turning into a politician, Davey.'

Reed smiled and sipped. 'One more crack like that and I go home to mother.'

'She wouldn't have you.'

Garvey was taking his shoes off when his 'director' came in. He plugged a video monitor into the wall and started ordering unseen people around through a microphone. 'Camera three, give me a shot of the couch.'

'How do we know he's going to sit on the couch?' Garvey said. 'I mean, you think he never heard of cameras in walls before?'

'Camera two, let me see that zoom,' the director said.

'Relax,' Reed said. 'He's got it covered.'

'The zoom, the *zoom*. Camera two!'

Garvey was hurrying out of his pants. 'Gretl, call the office. Have Dominick call Ives and find out what's on the President's mind. Hey, suppose he decides to sit on that table over there. You never know where people are going to decide to sit down. Davey, don't just sit there, make me a Scotch. Lots of rocks.'

'You can't let him sit on the table,' the director said to Garvey, who was stalking around the room in T-shirt, shorts, and socks. He was old-fashioned in one respect: garters were holding up his socks. 'That's the one wall we can't cover. Unless you want a cameraman standing out in the hall.'

'Then put the table in the tub,' Garvey said, as though it were the most obvious thing in the world. 'That way he won't be able to sit on it.'

Reed handed him his drink. 'And suppose he goes in to pee,' Reed said. 'You want the great senator from Nebraska to look like a screwball? A table in the bathtub? Oh, yeah. He likes to work even when he takes a shower.'

'No, you're right,' Garvey said, looking dangerously close to a basketball balanced on top of a medicine ball. 'All right, then we'll have to maneuver him away from sitting on the table. Davey, that's your job.'

'Sure, sure,' Reed said, gathering up the notes for the speech.

'But remember. We've got to take it easy on him, to start with. He'll probably feel as though he's betraying his colleagues. He's an idealist. We have to appeal to his idealism. He takes his job seriously.'

'That type is a cinch,' Reed replied.

Garvey was putting on his dressing gown and slippers. The idea was that he'd look less formidable in a bathrobe. More human. Nicer. Regular. They were playing every percentage point.

'It's for the good of the republic,' Reed suggested.

'Please,' Garvey said, pained. 'Don't use that one.'

'Loyalty to the Bill of Rights? Not to whatever hack poly happens to be sitting in the White House at the moment?'

'That's better. Use poly, don't use hack. Hack is too much. How do you know how he feels about the President? But it's good to remind him that the President isn't George Washington; he's merely another gentleman in the politics industry.'

Garvey was brushing back what little hair he had and trying to make his eyebrows look less diabolical than usual.

'Okay, camera one, that's the spot; lock it.'

'The tobacco people want to talk to you,' Gretl said.

'Tell them he's in with the No Smoking Alliance people.'

'Tell them I appreciate the call and I'll get back to them tomorrow. Afternoon. Ish.'

The director was pulling out the monitor when the phone rang again; this time it was one of Garvey's troops downstairs.

Gretl looked at Garvey with wide eyes. 'He's in the lobby,' she said.

'Ah,' Garvey said. 'Thank God. We've got him. Okay, everybody out. Gretl, when you get downstairs, tell the desk to hold my calls. Hey, fellah, do me a favor. I don't want this to look like that crummy Abscam footage. Keep it in focus, okay?'

'Sure, and keep your foot off the microphone. It's on the rug underneath the coffee table.'

They were now all picking up possessions and scurrying. Gretl was really loaded down. The phone rang again and Reed got it. Reed hung up. 'He's in the elevator.'

'Get *out* of here,' Garvey said to Gretl.

Reed pushed her through the door and then ran around straightening the place up. Garvey ran into the bathroom and emptied his drink in the sink. Then he ran back and plopped down in the big chair and grabbed the latest Senate bill to read. He put on his rimless glasses, which gave him an avuncular, intellectual look. There was a knock on the door. Reed took one last long look around at the room and then swung it open. Charley Eberhart walked in.

Coolidge froze the frame and studied Charley's face. The face looked alert, wary, unafraid; it was the face of a man who knew he was taking a chance, but had worked to make it as safe as it could possibly be and was now willing to throw the dice.

The computer had relegated Charley's footage to a storage category; Charley had Computer Unimportance and was fading fast. Coolidge had only checked because Garvey's knowledge of O.F.F. had been twenty-six percentage points behind current events.

Coolidge let the scene run through again, and Charley stepped into the room, looking at every object, including Garvey and Reed, as though they were land mines. There was an air of confidence about Charley that came as a total surprise to Coolidge. Another mystery of the psyche; he had known Charley as a quiet intellectual, a master of strategic theory and war-game scenarios, but not as one who took chances in his own life. Charley crossed one-way streets looking both ways. But he sat down now on the chair that was covered by camera two in the bedroom.

'I can't stay long,' he said.

'Suit yourself,' Garvey's off-camera voice replied. 'I want you to be comfortable.'

'Ever heard of O.F.F.?'

'It's more alphabet soup. What is it?'

'If you'd heard of it, you'd know it.'

'Then I guess I haven't.'

'You ought to find out about it,' Charley said.

'Fine with me. Let's start now. What is it?'

Charley smiled a faint turned-on smile, the kind self-

143

conscious people put on for the camera. 'It's 23.75 percent,' he said.

'Is that bad?'

'Look, I don't know about these things. It's beyond me.
If that's what the people want, then that's what they want
and I don't suppose anybody can do anything about it.
But maybe they don't want it. That's your department.'

'You're not giving me much to go on, Charley. I might
well be opposed to it if I knew what it was. Maybe I could
do something about it, who knows? Let's start with your
telling me what it is. What is O.F.F., Charley?'

'Nose around. You'll find out. It's bigger than life. It's
everywhere. You know how to use this town. If you look,
you'll find it.'

That was it. That was all Charley would tell them. He'd
never even touched his wine and left in five minutes, going
out the same way he'd come in: confidently negotiating a
minefield, unaware that he'd been skunked, the scene
ending with Garvey calling out to the walls, 'Shut those
goddamn things off.'

Watching it, Coolidge felt his cheeks get hot, not out of
anger that Charley had been duped, but out of embarrassment. The whole scene had been a classic example of how
the amateur could get set up. Eberhart had picked a good
room; it was clean of microcams. But Garvey had friends
in the CIA who were willing to set up the filming and do
the processing. Of course, Garvey had got skunked too.
None of them seemed to realize that the Library automatically got copies of everything. The Library was firmly
plugged into bureaucracy and you had to use dynamite to
unplug it. In fact, Garvey had been doubly skunked. He
hadn't found out what O.F.F. was.

Coolidge stared mesmerized at the blinking cursor on
the blank monitor screen. Charley Eberhart. Son of a
bitch. He had never given Charley a thought. It looked
like the ideal way to end the problem. Call Charley the
Doctor, let it go at that. The problem was that Charley was
already dead when Garvey was talking about the Doctor
to Purefoy. The situation seemed impossible. Charley
Eberhart had leaked to the senator. Now *another* Librarian, the Doctor, was leaking? Statistically, it seemed

crazy. *Two* out of the twelve carefully selected Librarians, all of whom were considered among the most reliable people in the establishment, had turned?

Everyone was a mystery. All the surveillance with all the microcams and bugs couldn't find that out: that inner smoke that was the human personality. Charley Eberhart had walked into a hotel room to blab the biggest secret in the inventory. Why? What could have changed him from the man you could always count on, the least likely candidate among the twelve least likely candidates for betrayal. It said something fundamental about the ultimate flaw in security procedures. You couldn't pin the human psyche down like a butterfly. It had too much capacity for change.

To make things more opaque, Charley *hadn't* given away the biggest secret in the inventory. Only the initials. He had skunked Mr. Greaseball from Nowhere, but what the hell for? Coolidge was exhausted. He had developed a nifty case of insomnia. Between Naumburg and his monitor, he had been getting by on less and less sleep, but he had reached the stage where being tired seemed irrelevant. There was a possibility to pursue. Did Charley leave some kind of documentation behind that Oliver Garvey was looking for? If he did, it was still possible that Garvey was thinking of Charley when referring to the Doctor. In that case, Charley's wife might know something.

There were five telephone slips in his desk with Estelle Eberhart's name on them. He had been ignoring them for days. It was time to face her. She picked up the phone on the eleventh ring.

'Hey, you're a pretty hard guy to get in touch with.'

'My apologies. I've been busy.'

'You people are always busy. It used to take six messages to get through to Charley.'

'What can I do for you?'

'You wouldn't believe the half of it.'

Coolidge had met Estelle Eberhart at two or three parties at Johnny Burnish's house. She was totally unlike Charley. An open, easy manner. A flirt. Nothing too much on her mind.

'You name it,' Coolidge said.

'Actually, I have something for you. It's a message. From Charley.'

Coolidge worked at keeping his voice calm, although he couldn't be sure what tone was going to come out when he spoke. 'What is it?'

'Are you kidding? A message from one of you guys to another of you guys over an open telephone? You'll have to come out here.'

'Why, I think I could spare some time,' Coolidge said, his voice cracking only on the word 'spare.'

When he had first gotten Eberhart's job, Harry had ordered him to look at personal footage going back a month before Charley's death, just to be on the safe side. So Coolidge knew all the angles.

He had peered along those sight lines a half dozen times at least. He knew, for example, that there had to be a microcam in the Degas print on the southeast wall of the living room. It was a case of life imitating art: he was seeing the place through the camera, instead of from where he was seated in a white leather easy chair next to a steel and glass coffee table, with Estelle Eberhart five feet away on the couch. The Degas microcam was undoubtedly photographing her crotch at this very moment, because she had a pronounced tendency to sit loose, legs spread, dress pulled up carelessly, or some delicate combination of both.

'Can I get you a drink?'

'Too early,' Coolidge said.

It was unfair; he knew so much about her. She didn't have the slightest idea that he knew so much about her. Coolidge knew enough to be rather critical of the way she made love. Love was supposed to be slow, a race in reverse. The tortoise was love; the hare was a whore. Estelle Eberhart was a hare in bed. On the other hand, Charley had been no slowpoke either. Between the two of them, lovemaking looked like a pit stop.

'Come on, have a drink,' she said. 'I'm looking for an excuse to have a drink. Hey, I've got a special recipe, you'll love it. It's called a penis colada. Okay? Done?' Estelle swept out of the living room, giggling.

146

Coolidge accepted the fact that it was going to be a while. She was holding on to attention. She was lonely and the kids were teenagers, meaning they were more fit for dragons and dungeons than for humans. She finally came back with the big drinks after fumbling around in the kitchen forever, and she said, 'I mean, can you tell me what the hell Charley did for a living?'

Coolidge was looking suspiciously at his penis colada. 'I can't tell you,' he said.

'Can you tell me what you do for a living?'

'I can't tell you.'

'Ask me what I do?'

'What do you do?'

'I can't tell you.'

One thing she wasn't doing was taking care of the house. Charley's wife was a totally incompetent housewife; she had been overwhelmed by the objects in her life. It was the kind of place where you could find inexplicable stains on the ceilings. It was disorganized, filthy. He knew for a fact that she kept out-of-season clothes in the refrigerator. The kitchen stove probably took walks in the living room while she was out shopping. But, like taking a blood sample, Coolidge had long since pronounced her garbage normal.

'The last time I saw you,' Estelle said, being shy and friendly at the same time, 'was at Johnny Burnish's. You had a very attractive lady with you. Did you marry her?'

'No.'

'Are you going to?'

'I can't tell you.'

They smiled at each other; they were getting past the embarrassment of death in the family. Charley was on his way to becoming a secret.

'What are all you people looking for? Was Charley in trouble?'

'No. Not at all. But he did kill himself. Do you happen to know why?'

'No, I don't know why. I never understood my husband. I never even understood why he married me. I mean, we had nothing in common.'

Coolidge looked at her. Whatever her hang-ups, she

spoke the truth, to the extent that she could see it, anyway. Estelle lived in a world where all that should have been obvious and clear and went without saying didn't, wasn't. It simply didn't happen that way. So she saw the world as perverse, inexplicably upside down, even accepting it as a weird kind of norm, although she would make sarcastic remarks about it now and then.

'Was Charley worried about anything?' He could almost hear his own words reechoing, as he would hear them a few days from now in the Library, sounding cruel and detached.

'Sure.'

'What?'

'Everything.'

'Uh huh.'

'I went through all of this with Harry Dunn.'

'I know.'

'Did anything in particular stand out?'

'Not that I noticed.'

There didn't seem to be anything else Coolidge could ask without breaching security himself.

'What's the message Charley left me?'

'I don't know.'

'What's that mean?'

'It's in code.'

Coolidge was surprised. NSA did codes. Secret agents did codes. Charley knew that Coolidge didn't know about codes. What could he have been thinking of? Was a perverse side of Charley's character beginning to emerge?

'Where is it?' he said to her.

'Upstairs. In the bedroom safe. Come on, Walter, you're not afraid to walk into a bedroom with me, are you?' She took his hand and led him up the stairs, Coolidge's mind racing ahead. When they got to the bedroom, he acted as though he didn't know where everything was. The only unknown was the safe; he had never heard them mention it. Estelle went to a Utrillo print over an old-fashioned cedar chest. She took it down and stood it on the windowsill. It was pathetic. Charley had actually believed in safes. It looked as though you could stare at it and it would fall out of the wall. Estelle screwed up the combination and had to do it twice; she probably always got wrong numbers when she dialed the telephone. She finally got it open and handed Coolidge an envelope with his name on it. One end had been torn open.

'Naturally I looked,' Estelle said.

It was code, all right. There was a single line of typing in the center of the sheet:

56921113# — $8905691114**!

It looked like a cartoonist's idea of cursing; a secret agent's version of the envelope 'To Be Opened in the Event of My Death.'

'This is it?' he asked her.

'Great. You don't know what it means either,' Estelle said, showing obvious satisfaction that all these big shots with their big secret jobs didn't know what they were doing. 'He left you a message in code and you don't have the code.' She giggled.

It looked to Coolidge like a computer entry. It was the only association he had. He'd try it as soon as he got back to the Library. It was possible that Charley had salted something away in the computer under a protective code. If so, he'd find it soon enough. When he looked up from the code, Estelle was standing in bra and panties, smiling.

Someone was going to have to tell her about panties; she was wearing the violet ones with the red flowers. There was so much bad taste in panties. Women didn't seem to understand what really excited the male. Coolidge looked for the scar on her left thigh. He'd noticed it a number of times. He found it provoking; women had all kinds of things they didn't know about.

There was a slide bolt on the bedroom door, just in case the kids, through some miracle, actually came home. Estelle went over and locked it, then leaned back against the door.

'Life must go on,' she said.

Her stomach was way too big. She really needed exercise; about twenty thousand sit-ups would do it. And there was the problem of performing for the unseen audience. He figured one microcam had to be in the crack of the folding closet door. Another one was on the radiator cover by the window. Then there was Gardella's favorite installation angle: the ceiling light fixture. Coolidge had his doubts. They had grown even bigger since he'd begun watching other people's footage. Love was a lot of things, but it wasn't photogenic; it didn't look at all like what it was. Maybe this was as good a time as any to start getting used to it.

He took his clothes off, then got rid of her ridiculous bra and panties. She was good at kissing. Real good. She meant it. But the maniac between his legs was playing hard to get. It didn't do things like this. It went to church on Sunday and read books. It was interested in the higher things of life. All of a sudden it wanted to listen to 'Jesu, Joy of Man's Desiring' on the harpsichord.

'What the hell,' she said after a while of serious trying. It was a losing year for her and everything was probably going to go the same way. She put on a sloppy bathrobe and went over to close the safe.

Coolidge rolled out of bed. Putting on your clothes after a failure in bed was the greatest antidote to war he knew of; it was the cure for omnipotent ways of thinking. This particular failure was even on tape; taped evidence to be stored away in the U.S. Government Archives for all eternity.

And all he'd gotten out of it was Eberhart's curse, whatever that was.

The J Factor

It struck Coolidge as entirely possible. You get an already opened envelope from a safe you could crack with a good sneeze and it turns out to be the key to everything. He took a chance on his balding tires and pushed to get back to the Library. In his office down in the second basement, he punched in Eberhart's curse, waiting for illumination to come up on the monitor.

There was nothing. It produced no output, caused no error message. He tried reversing some of the characters, thinking Charley might have made a careless error in transcribing the code. But when he did that, the computer caught it.

'INCORRECT CODE,' came the response.

Which meant that Eberhart's curse *was* a computer code. Exactly as written. The computer would permit no changes in it. But it was apparently yet another of Charley's little peculiarities. He had bequeathed a computer code to Coolidge which the computer accepted but did nothing with. It seemed to be Charley's modus operandi; it was the same thing he had done to Senator Garvey. Told him something he couldn't use, something that titillated and oppressed the mind, but was otherwise useless.

There was data missing. Why would a man try to leak a major government secret, you might say *the* government secret, and then not leak it, telling them to go find it out for themselves? What did it mean? Coolidge hated to drop it without knowing more. He had the feeling that if he continued to poke around, he might stumble onto the meaning of Eberhart's curse. *That* had to mean something. It was his inheritance from Charley, willed and bequeathed to him. He couldn't believe that a man on the point of suicide would be in the mood for a practical joke that the recipient wouldn't even know enough about to *get*.

Idly, he punched Davey Reed's name into the computer, probably because Reed was the weakest link in the chain. He watched as a lot of bar scenes went flipping by in real time: he wasn't seeing history; he was looking at the present moment. He slowed down the scan rate to a crawl, to see if he could spot the thin, seedy-looking character. But it was impossible; it was the magic hour and there were crowd scenes everywhere.

He tried Eberhart's curse again, simply because he had nothing to do. There was nothing. He was sitting at the end of the big pipeline, plugged into the entire town, the country, the world. The data was flooding in from everywhere, all available, a state-of-the-planet report updated every second. And the one thing he was interested in brought up a blank screen.

He sat there looking at it, his mind wandering. Whatever he was, the Doctor was no ordinary character. The son of a bitch was a wizard. He seemed to leave no trace whatsoever. It seemed to Coolidge that if he was ever to uncover the Doctor, he would first have to understand him, practically psychoanalyse him; only then would he know what to look for: there could be so many possible reasons for betrayal.

There would be different explanations for different people. It might be nothing more than ego. A megalomaniac (like Hopkins) playing God, someone who had found an issue big enough to equal his neurotic sense of importance. Or its opposite, someone with no ego at all (like Mike Barber), who might feel that he was justifying himself, his existence, his oxygen consumption, who went ahead doing the 'right' thing in spite of the evil going on around him.

But along with that, ego or no ego, a certain kind of strength: that would be the common denominator. A willingness to go against numbers, the tide, the grain, the current wisdom. Somebody accustomed to being in the minority, a loner.

152

One thing was obvious. The Doctor had to have been true-blue when he first got to the Library, and had been changed by something. But what? These weren't the kind of people to drop value systems in the blink of an eye. It would have had to be something major.

Unfortunately, there was a lot to pick from. When you were on the inside, you saw the bad stuff. The stuff that was hidden away from the public, or disguised. Hiroshima, for example, which had nothing to do with World War II; it was the first shot of the cold war, fired across Stalin's bow. Unless you wanted to give that honor to Dresden, a medieval toy city in the path of the Russian Army which was destroyed by Churchill to demonstrate what a fleet of bombers was capable of.

Western leaders played for keeps, Coolidge thought. Were they wrong? He wouldn't know. They were ordinary men, after all, working under pressure. All he knew was that you couldn't stand on the sidelines, criticizing. Somebody had to make decisions, somebody human, fallible. Presidents did the best they could with what they had to work with, but the results, sometimes, would be awful. Was it that which had gotten to the Doctor? Was he someone who couldn't bear the realities of power once he was exposed to them?

Coolidge's fingers were moving over the keyboard, searching for something to enter, and without even realizing what he had done, he looked up at the terminal and saw that he had entered a number he'd been avoiding ever since his little chat with Harry Dunn. It was Vera's personal code. He hesitated. He thought of Henry Stimson's famous criticism of cryptography: Gentlemen don't read other people's mail. The world had moved a long way. Now he was being disloyal to Harry Dunn and to the United States of America for as long as he avoided spying on his sweetheart.

Did he trust her or didn't he? If he trusted her, he wouldn't have to look. On the other hand, if he trusted her, there should be nothing to worry about. If he really trusted her, he wouldn't have held off so long. There was also the fact that it was what he was getting paid to do.

He hit the RUN key.

The screen looked like a Vegas slot machine for a few seconds, footage flying past, a mélange, Coolidge hoping he wouldn't hit the jackpot, the computer skipping everything that lacked Computer Importance. He found himself breathing shallowly. There was that one category with Very High Importance. The computer could spot sex either verbally or graphically. It knew all seventy-seven basic positions, and it contained a longer list of synonyms for sex than even the Vatican Library.

Lemons came up.

Coolidge got a migraine on the spot, a hand squeezing his brain, his insides starting to shift around. Vera was in her living room, fully dressed, but kneeling in front of her couch. Harry was in front of her, his grotesque, partly naked bulk seated and strung out, having a problem solved for himself.

Coolidge watched them, unable to look away even though every stroke was pounding in his head. He could hear the sounds her lips were making. He was forcing himself to face facts. That's what his job was. That's what they all did in the Library. They looked at the world as what it was, not what it was supposed or alleged to be. They were anti-delusion as much as they were anti-Communist. Face it. Fact: Vera was sucking Harry off. Was that the best way of putting it? How about: Vera was sucking off Harry: a much more elegant communication. It didn't delay the crucial fact – Vera could have been sucking Harry's siphon hose to fill his gas tank. It was much better to get 'off' in there as early as possible instead of holding back until the end of the sentence.

Coolidge was beginning to see colored lights in his head; it was going to be a bad one. He put his hands over his eyes and tried to cool his forehead with his fingers. He didn't dare move with a headache like this; he'd spill his guts in a second. He was suddenly thinking of Charley Eberhart. Did Charley have a devastating moment like this in front of a monitor? What had finally gotten to Charley, what little fact had pushed him over – about his wife, about himself, about the world? There was a value ignorance. Survival value. Garvey had said it: A lot of knowledge is a dangerous thing.

154

Vera and Harry went back a long way, he knew that. She had been one of the stars at Harry's Ticonderoga Institute, one of the earliest think tanks. Vera had told Coolidge all about it. She had been dazzled by Harry's brain. The planet was Harry's chessboard. He saw everything, calculated everything, pondered all possibilities. The Library was a physical realization of Harry's brain: the knowing of everything so as to be able to make stunning connections that no one else could.

Harry's famous book, *On Winning*, had pushed him to the top of his profession. He had become a superstar in the world of think tanks, of Pentagon defense consultants. The telephone calls he fielded in the course of a single day were astounding. Harry had become a power solely because of his brains. Although some people considered it an American version of *Mein Kampf*, *On Winning* – meaning in the East-West confrontation – had been so encyclopedic and persuasive that it had won Vera. Vera began sleeping with the biggest brain in the establishment. But it had ended years ago. At least so she had said. Harry had become too interested in power and influence and prestige. Truth for Harry was gradually metamorphosing into 'policy.' And the more it did, the fatter Harry got. Vera was disillusioned and went back to being merely Harry's employee; even though the sharp edges of his intellect were being rounded off by politics, he still played the most exciting game in town.

Sitting motionless to avoid nausea, Coolidge was wondering how Harry could have been so dumb as to forget Vera's apartment would be a minefield of microcams. The lights in his head were flashing in different colors like UFOs coming in for landing. The footage was dated the previous night: maybe it wasn't an oversight. Maybe Harry had done it deliberately, as a way of telling Coolidge something.

It would be just like Harry, turning sex and betrayal into a propaedeutic experience. Now do you see what kind of objectivity is required here, Walter? Emotionality comes in a bad second. Strip away the irrelevant reactions, stick to what is essential, do not be distracted, call things as you see them, and above all *see* them, see the

155

unseeable. In a sense, Coolidge was eating it as much as Vera was.

In between the throbs and pulses in his brain, Coolidge realized that in one act Harry had tied it all together. Vera was sucking O.F.F. O.F.F. meant Opportunity For Fucking. Whoever had O.F.F. could fuck the world; that's what O.F.F. was. Do you see, Walter? That's another aspect of it. Now we know who's in charge. Now you understand my power, our power, *the* power.

Coolidge switched off the monitor before Harry could have his big moment. Coolidge's brain was having a reverse orgasm. He was afraid to move a muscle. He sat before the blank screen, hands over his eyes, trying not to groan. A doctor once told him that he got headaches when he didn't want to face something. Now he was getting one in the act of facing something. Maybe he didn't want to face what it was he'd like to do to Harry and Vera. Was it the mere fact that she would do it with anybody when she had the great lover Coolidge on the string? Was it a love headache or an ego headache? He sat there without moving for two hours, until the colored fireworks gradually went away and the squeezing hand began to relent.

He stood up. Everything stayed where it belonged.

He left the Library, head still hung over, and drove to a bar for the second-level cure. It was on the way home, a place called Tiny Tom's, a hangout for medium-level bureaucrats postponing the trip home after work, on the lookout for a stray secretary or simply to obliterate the frustrations of a day in government. He was going to have a few and figure out very precisely how to tell Vera and Harry to go O.F.F. themselves. He sat down on a stool at the far end of the bar, trying to forget his head. Then he heard the last thing he wanted to hear. A friendly voice.

'I can't believe this is a coincidence,' someone said. He didn't even look around. He didn't want to know anybody. He wanted to sit there quietly and hate. But he recognized the timbre. A hand put down a Scotch and soda next to him. The hand was connected to Davey Reed, who plopped down on the adjacent stool, which was, unfortunately, empty.

'Tell me the truth,' Reed said. 'Between us folks. Won't

breathe a word. Have you guys got a direction finder up my ass?'

Reed was smiling. He was his usual friendly, intense self, the violin-string extrovert: taut but with a warm tone. 'I bet you guys could have a direction finder up my ass and I wouldn't even know it,' he added.

'No, Davey. I just came in here for a drink. On impulse.' As he was saying it, Coolidge remembered seeing the name, Tiny Tom's, flip past on the monitor earlier while he was looking for Reed.

'Well, okay,' Reed said. 'I guess it's still theoretically possible for coincidence to exist in Washington. I'll even buy you one to show you there's no hard feelings.'

'That's okay. Don't worry about it. Everything's fine. Don't let me keep you from your friends.'

'You look like hell.'

'Nothing seven or ten drinks won't fix up.'

'I'll tell you what. I'm not going to pry. Now is that a reasonable offer?'

'Touché,' Coolidge said, sipping his wine, wishing Reed would go away.

He was down in the dumps, which was appropriate for the Garbageman. He was forever poking around in all kinds of stuff. That was his profession. What was the surprise? If you looked for garbage you found garbage. It was all right to look at other people's garbage and play intellectual games with it. See them doing everything, catch them all with their hair down, unbuttoned, all closet doors open, psyches hanging out. There were no private parts anymore; it was all in the public domain. So how could he complain when it got close to home?

Harry was a pig and he'd really like to see him wallow in the mud. But was he working for Harry or for the national interest? The first ten amendments. Democratic institutions. An image of apple pie skittered across his brain, but there was residual nausea and he almost threw up.

He slowly turned his aching head and looked over at Davey Reed. Reed was half in the bag and in a talkative mood. It was an opportunity. Only a few hours ago, he had eagerly been looking for him. And anyway, he was curious for his own sake. He wanted to know.

157

The place was noisy as hell and the bartender had only one arm, so he was kept pretty busy.

'How did you like working with Charley?' Coolidge asked, staring straight ahead.

Reed put on a really well-done straight face, which Coolidge caught in the bar mirror.

'Charley who?'

'Yeah, him. That guy. Charley who.'

Reed attempted a you-must-be-on-something look, then hid in his glass of Scotch.

'I mean, he didn't tell you very much. He goes to you guys with some trade secrets. Tantalizes you. Gets your blood up. Then doesn't put out. Half a leak, really.'

'Half a leak, half a leak, half a leak onward,' Reed replied, now trying lightness.

'A little here, a little there – I know, it adds up.'

Reed rubbed his eyes and then shook his head as though to clear out the fuzziness. He looked at Coolidge for a long time and then seemed to accept the inevitable.

'There are some things you are very bad at,' Reed said, 'but there are some things you are very good at.'

'Why didn't he tell you everything?' Coolidge said.

'Good question.'

'You don't know, huh?'

'I had a theory about it.'

'I'm all ears.'

'Pure speculation. I mean, I don't know what I'm talking about. What do I know? I'm low man on the totem pole.'

'Speculate.'

Reed first glanced up at the television screen, which he'd been keeping a close eye on. It almost looked as though he were afraid of being overheard. It was the evening news and the President was sitting on a couch in the Oval Office, meeting with a group of House and Senate leaders.

'Okay, here's how I see it,' Reed began. 'I figure that thing – I won't even say its name out loud, okay?– that thing must be a really funny thing. I try not to let my imagination go crazy when I think about it. But I figure it's got to be first-rate, off-the-wall craziness. I mean,

158

when a government gets its act together with everyone on the team, they're capable of genius. Take the Hundred Years' War. Who but a government would think of fighting a war for a hundred years? See what I mean? It's going to be something like that. Anyway, I figure that Charley figured that Garvey *would* figure, once he'd found out what that thing was, that it would be too something to touch.'

'Too something, huh?'

'Too big. Too crazy. Too frightening. Too something.'

'You mean, then he'd *forget* about it?'

'Walter, this is politics.'

'Okay.'

'So maybe Charley wanted to be sure it got out. In a respectable way, not *necessarily* public. I mean, Charley was a complicated guy. So I figure that he figured he would tantalize us with it. Drive us crazy. And then maybe the senator would ask around, say, at a subcommittee hearing. Have a few people hear about it that way, if only the other members of the subcommittee. Have it propagate out through the government at a high level, get everyone asking the same question: *What is that thing?*'

'Wouldn't it have been a lot easier to take it where they all do? The *New York Times?*'

'You know better than I, Walter. Maybe Charley thought it was too something for the *New York Times*. What do you think? Would the *New York Times* print it?'

While waiting for an answer, Reed picked up a paper napkin and held it out to the bartender, who was speeding by. He had a bottle of Bloody Mary Mix tucked under his stump and a liter of Stolichnaya in his hand. He poured about an eighth of a shot of vodka onto the napkin, without even slowing down. Reed began to clean his glasses.

Coolidge, getting aggressive, figuring Reed was now a drink older, said, 'Suppose Charley *had* told Garvey what the thing is? Suppose I tell him? What do you think he'd do with it?'

Reed looked very cool and judicious, almost Solomonic, but he dropped his eyeglasses in the Scotch. He was trying to retrieve them with a tiny bit of aplomb, when he was interrupted by his boss.

'The security of this nation must always take precedence over partisan politics,' Garvey was saying. He was standing outside the West Wing of the White House, half a dozen microphones stuck in his face. The other congressional leaders were posed stony-faced in the background. With his usual fine instincts, Garvey had managed to step through the doorway three seconds ahead of the others.

'Politics, as the old saying goes, stops at the water's edge.'

Reed began to mouth the senator's words, having written them that morning.

'. . . and it is to be fervently hoped that the men in the Kremlin understand the nature of American unity. While we may differ on many issues, we always draw together behind the head of state at times of external threat. We will not allow ourselves to be intimidated at Fulda Gap.'

Reed kept at it, imitating Garvey's delivery, even though they'd cut away to the weather report. 'You see, ladies and gentlemen, the politics of this great republic of ours can be described with only one word. My fellow citizens, that word is vodka. American politics is straight, pure vodka. Although it goes under different labels, it's all one-hundred-percent political grain neutral spirits. Tasteless, of course. Odorless, perhaps. Colorless, certainly. And yet, in spite of all, having the power to intoxicate. Bear in mind, however, that only the labels are different.'

'You trying to lose me around the bend?'

'Walter, if politicians were like Scotch instead of vodka, this would be a better world.'

Coolidge was holding his head delicately, as if it were a condor egg. He closed his eyes.

'I can see I'm going to have to be honest with you,' Reed said.

'It would help the rapport, Davey.'

'Yeah. Well, we want to help the rapport. That's always a prime objective for a politician. Okay. I don't know *what* the hell he'd do with it.'

Coolidge found himself almost liking Reed. Of course, some people were experts at coming on honest. It was a technique with them. It basically required the salesmanship emotion, and Reed was an ex-advertising copy-writer. He was adept at telling you what you wanted to hear. He had gone straight from selling dog food to selling a politician, conceding that the senator was more interesting and it was a definite step up in life, but that the techniques were the same. Whatever his motivation, his theory about Charley Eberhart wasn't bad. It was better than anything Coolidge had come up with.

Coolidge pushed his glass toward the speeding bartender. 'I'm buying this round, just to keep things on the up-and-up.'

Reed waved a hand. 'I'm putting in for it. We're talking committee business.'

Coolidge wasn't getting anything usable. He turned to Reed, the headache following a second later, crashing into the side of his skull.

'What are you guys really up to? What's the bottom line?'

'Peace on earth.' Straight face. 'Good will toward voters.'

'Why don't they go public? What's all the sneaking around for? Playing at secret agent, pretending you've got a trash cover on me. That whole ridiculous scenario.'

'It's John Doe's fault, Walter.' Big ingratiating drunken smile. 'It's the problem of a democracy. Everybody is afraid to tell John Doehole the truth. To be a peacemaker in this country, you risk looking like a tool of the KGB. You can be a hawk and you're okay, but if you're a dove you got to watch your ass. John Doehole doesn't like fairies.'

'That's all there is to it, huh?'

'The whole problem, Waller. Bringing the news to Doehole. He's in for a real shock if he ever finds out what's going on. Johnhole Doehole is in for a real shock.'

'You're lecturing.'

'Sorry. When I drink, I lecture. When I'm sober, I write crazy speeches that Garvey throws out and you read. Do you know that you're my biggest fan, Waller?'

Coolidge made a final stab at it, knowing the odds were low.

'Can you tell me one thing, Davey? What are their loyalties? What holds them together?'

'The logic of this situation calls for another round.'

Reed sat there ostentatiously thinking, lips pursed, waiting for the drink and inspiration, presumably trying to find a way to express the inexpressible. The drinks came and he was still struggling, nose wrinkled up, head going from side to side.

'Look at it this way, Waller,' he said at last. 'There's a sort of higher mathematics of loyalty.'

Coolidge listened.

'It's like the square root of minus one. Mathematicians call it the J factor. It doesn't really exist. There is no such thing. There is no number such that, when multiplied by itself, produces minus one. It's imaginary, inexpressible, an idea in space. It is given existence in order to be manipulated. See what I mean? That's what loyalty is. That's what you're asking me about. The square root of minus one.'

'Ask an ineffable question and you get an ineffable answer.'

Reed giggled. 'Nice word, effable. I like it as an adjective for girls. *In*effable girls, on the other hand, are a waste of time.'

Reed was deteriorating rapidly. Coolidge had decided to go to another bar and catch up on his drinking all by himself, when he felt *another* one sit down next to him and order a drink with a familiar voice. Coolidge's brain at first refused to process the data. He was having a problem with reality. It was ridiculous. Or was coincidence still possible in Washington?

'Black Johnnie,' was what he'd heard McDermott Beebe III say. 'Straight.'

The Opportunity of a Lifetime

Beebe liked to surprise people. Sadistic surprises only, of course. Pop up out of nowhere, suddenly breathing on you. Omnipresence was his game. You can't escape me: Live clean or die. Had Beebe been following him? Coolidge didn't even want to *look* at Reed. Beebe could easily put a suspicious construction on Coolidge's meeting Oliver Garvey's closest aide in a bar. But Beebe didn't even seem to know who Davey Reed was. Beebe was only Protector of the Data; he never got to look at it.

'Okay, let's go,' Beebe said.

'Let's go where?'

'You'll find out.'

Coolidge looked at him. Beebe's large, oval face was constructed of insolence and intimidation and contempt. His Scotch was already gone. Beebe had some kind of spring action in his drinking wrist; it was barely possible the glass never left the bar and that he caught the stuff on the fly.

They were total opposites. Coolidge was liberal; Beebe was conservative. Coolidge was a masochist; Beebe was a sadist. Coolidge liked Chopin; Beebe liked country. Coolidge read; Beebe watched. Coolidge was an ass man; Beebe was a breast man. Coolidge was white collar; Beebe was blue collar. Coolidge was garbage; Beebe was Old Spice.

Coolidge glanced at the bar entrance and saw the usual two attaché cases standing there: Beebe's troops. Beebe never went anywhere without two of them along. They always carried attaché cases, in which, Beebe said, they 'had all the answers.'

He decided not to make a scene. It would have been a

disaster. Beebe was safe; Coolidge was dangerous. He checked Reed in the mirror behind the bar. Reed was hiding behind his glass, ashen. It was hard to tell if he had figured out who Beebe was. As Coolidge stood up, he heard Reed murmur to the bartender, 'Execute Plan B,' which Coolidge knew, from microcam footage, meant that Reed was totally bombed and the busboy would have to pour him into a cab.

There was a limo outside. One of the attaché cases was the driver, the other was riding shotgun. Coolidge climbed into the back, feeling hemmed in, the huge Beebe bulk forcing in behind him, calling out to the driver to move it, wheels in motion, no way to undo it. He sat back, trying to imagine what Beebe was thinking. Or planning. Or feeling. Beebe was smiling a lot, which was a bad sign. What would please that psyche?

'How did you know where to find me?' Coolidge asked, trying to start a relationship.

'You mean even though you didn't leave word where you'd be, like you're supposed to?' Beebe said.

'Yeah.'

Beebe just stared off into the night in disgust.

'Where are we going?' Coolidge asked.

Beebe looked at him expressionlessly for a moment. 'We're going to work – what the hell do you think?'

Coolidge looked at him sideways, putting Beebe on a slide, trying to focus in on the essential bit of DNA or whatever it was that distinguished Beebe from himself. He wasn't afraid of Beebe's strength so much as Beebe's irrationality. Beebe was a fanatic. Beebe had all the answers. Beebe could commit irrevocable acts without second thoughts. It was impossible to retain your dignity around Beebe; there was no way of dealing with him unless you were willing to go the limit, and Coolidge wasn't.

They sat in silence, except when Beebe got impatient; he didn't like people getting too close to his car. Now and then he'd pick up the intercom and talk to the attaché case at the wheel. 'Will you lose that son of a bitch?'

It took twenty minutes to get to Georgetown, the attaché case double-parking with the motor running in front of a three-story brown-stone. Money was being spent on it; even at night it stood out from the rest of the block. Beebe let the way across the cobblestones down to the basement door and had a fast exchange with a voice coming out of the speaker.

The door buzzed open on a narrow corridor with an elevator at the far end. There were little circular metallic flanges at intervals along the walls. They could have been eyeholes or gunports or merely Georgetown decor. Beebe pressed the elevator button and they stood there awkwardly for a few minutes. At least Coolidge was awkward. Beebe seemed to have come alive with anticipation. The mean mien had faded; he almost looked mellow.

When the elevator finally came and the door opened, Beebe had a big smile on his face.

'I just love ringing for this elevator,' he said to the girl.

She was topless. High heels, black net stockings, the cutest garters ever made, black bikini panties, and dangling earrings. Beebe couldn't take his eyes off her. Beebe and the girl were like a cobra and a flute. Coolidge took the initiative. He stepped into the elevator and said, 'Where are we going, Mac?'

'To heaven. Take him, darling.' He was still staring as she tantalizingly closed the door on him.

It was a small elevator. It was a slow elevator. Her presence expanded to fill the available space. Coolidge was afraid to inhale. On the other hand, it might not sound too good if he started breathing through his mouth. The situation appealed to the anthropologist in him. What were the rules of behaviour in naked elevator relationships? 'Where am I?' he asked.

She was facing front, with one hand on the control, but she managed to turn around full. 'Why, this is the best hospitality suite in Washington, D.C.,' she said charmingly.

Coolidge felt it would have been gross and impolite and perverted to totally ignore her breasts, so he gave them a quick flick of the eyes as he said, 'I'm going to take your word for that.'

A hospitality suite. That's the kind of thing they had at conventions. Of course, Washington was a year-round convention plus permanent floating circus. What the hell had that bastard Beebe gotten him into? It couldn't be a practical joke. Never. It was impossible to conceive of McDermott Beebe III consciously making a joke of any kind whatsoever. It had to involve that bastard Dunn.

'Here's your floor, sir,' she said, 'courtesy of your hard-working Wisconsin dairy farmer.'

Coolidge promptly forgot her. There were a lot more where she came from, at least half a dozen more. They were doing hostess duties at a cocktail party. It was an unusually long room for Georgetown, and it was unfamiliar, which meant there weren't any microcams; it was a free-orgy zone. Coolidge stood there a moment, swiveling around slowly, stopping at an occasional breast, recognizing quite a few congressmen, looking for why he was there.

He found them at the far end: Harry Dunn and Eugene Ives, managing to look busy.

He strolled through the crowd toward them, trying to decide what he wanted more: his job at the Library or satisfaction. Harry and Ives were sitting on a couch, coffee table in front of it, two telephones on it, papers spread everywhere, a portable typewriter, Ives on one phone, Harry's secretary, Phoebe, on the other. As Coolidge approached, Harry looked at him and they tracked eyes for three seconds.

'Thanks for coming,' Harry said. 'Have a drink, Walter. We've got something big.'

Coolidge flopped down in a big chair. The three of them looked bleary-eyed, working on reserves. They had probably got fed up sitting in the same room for sixteen hours and had transferred operations to the hospitality suite just to stay awake and sane. He could see right off how Harry was going to handle the problem with Vera. Harry was going to avoid the whole thing. How could Coolidge be small enough to let a piece of ass get between him and the fate of nations? That wouldn't be professional. Events were taking over. Emergencies. Coolidge was mixing apples and tomatoes.

'Fuck you, Harry,' Coolidge said quietly.

'Fine. Does that make you feel better? Get past it, Walter. Get it *done* with. I can't explain it. I don't know

166

how it happened. We've been putting in bad days.'

Harry was squirming. His own truth machine was making trouble for him. He was getting caught in subjectivity. It was interfering with more important matters.

'This Germany business has us all unhinged. I don't know what the hell I could have been thinking of. If I could undo it, I would.'

Ives, talking on the phone, had picked up vibes and was half listening in, without understanding what was going on.

Coolidge didn't know how to handle it. What did you do about someone who first stabbed you in the back and then apologized abjectly? Of course, it was just manipulation; Harry didn't really feel apologetic. He was doing whatever had to be done, whatever the situation required.

Ives had got off the phone and was looking nervously at the two of them. 'Hey, Walter, how are you? Have a drink; it brings one of the girls. Wallace is on his way, Harry.'

Ives was trying to lighten the atmosphere, to ease the conversation. He was looking drained. His tie was actually pulled down and his collar button was open. He even seemed to have forgotten his TV makeup. Only the Russians could do that to Ives. He waggled an eyebrow at one of the girls, who came bouncing.

'Are you going to tell me I'm going to get used to this?' Ives said to them.

'That's what Dostoyevsky would say,' Harry replied.

'That Communist. Bring this man a white wine on the rocks,' Ives said to the girl, 'but just bring the wine; he's already got the rocks.'

Coolidge smiled wanly. He didn't have the rocks; he was turned off sex. The girl's eyes searched around for an ice bucket before she flowed away.

'The amazing thing is that they're all made out of french fries,' Ives went on, obsessed. 'French fries and tacos and pizza. *That's* the real power of nature.'

Harry and Ives were a fine team. Ives didn't even know what was going on and he was playing the perfect role. Charm, wit, hospitality.

'We've got the assignment of a lifetime for you,' Harry said suddenly.

'I thought I already had the assignment of a lifetime,' Coolidge said.

'No. It's all been preparation for this one.'

Harry looked serious. On the other hand, Harry always looked serious.

'The tank buildup in Germany is getting critical. Crit-i-cal. They're reinforcing, we're reinforcing. The President just ordered tactical air up to forward fields.'

Now Coolidge understood why Ives's collar button was open. The NATO battle plan looked suspicious to the Russians to begin with. It called for all tank and infantry divisions to be kept close to the frontier with East Germany. Nothing was held back to be used as a reserve in case of a Russian breakthrough. NATO's reason for not having a reserve was that Germany insisted on it. Germany didn't want to become the battleground for World War III; the war would have to be fought on the frontier. This looked like a classically unsound strategy. No reserve? To the Russians it meant that if NATO didn't have a reserve, NATO wasn't worried about a possible breakthrough. Therefore, ipso facto, NATO was following an offensive strategy and would attack first.

It *was* possible to consider tactical fighters as the reserve. Any Soviet breakthrough would presumably be stopped or slowed down by waves of tactical fighter bombers armed with tank-destroying missiles. Once again, moving up the tactical fighter bomber squadrons could look to the Russians like the equivalent of massing on the frontier for offensive purposes. It was a fundamental ambiguity of war: When was a weapon offensive, when defensive? It was why war could break out from sheer nervousness, strain, the misreading of intentions. It was the World War I syndrome, when five empires destroyed each other by accident.

'This thing could be moving toward O.F.F.,' Harry said. 'Hopefully only for threat value, but who the hell knows?'

Miss French Fries leaned over with the drinks and serious thinking came to an end until she was gone.

Coolidge's headache knocked on his skull just to remind him it was alive and kicking. They were sitting in a crazy hospitality suite talking about the planet being at risk. A hundred million dead minimum. One society wiped out, conceivably two. Plus postattack syndrome, people dying all over the place. There was also the bare possibility that all this was Harry's way of getting Coolidge's mind off Vera.

'The assignment we've got for you is totally unorthodox. It even breaks *my* rules, and that's going some. You're going into the field, Walter.'

'Trying to get me killed off, Harry?'

Dunn responded to the comment but ignored the implications. 'You're going to be protected. As thoroughly as any man has ever been protected. You've got to do this job, Walter. We *can't* give it to anyone else; you're the only one who can bring it off. I'll go back to the beginning.'

Ives had both phones going now and was dictating to Phoebe at the same time; she was taking it down directly on the typewriter. Harry, sitting on the edge of the couch, resumed the briefing.

'There's some back-channel communicating going on. We're talking, unofficially. There seems to be a lot of disagreement in the Kremlin about how to handle this thing. They've got their doves, their hawks, their crazies. It's murky as hell. So we don't even know the significance of the talks.'

'That's not my kind of scene, Harry.'

'Listen to me. The meetings are taking place in a shack a few hundred yards inside the East German border.' Harry's face took on the intense look of the problem solver, the intellectual angle-merchant on the prowl. He looked positively radiant as he said it. 'We've got a microcam in there. The pictures started coming in a couple of hours ago. It's not much more than a one-room shack, little ell off to the right. Phoebe, where's that photograph?'

It looked like the typical military command post, set up on the run in a deserted outbuilding. Drop lights hanging from the ceiling, a portable telephone switchboard off to the right with attached enlisted man, cables running outside through a window, presumably to an engine generator set. There was a crude wooden table in the center of the main room and a large map of the Germanies on the wall behind it.

'Notice the wastebasket,' Coolidge could hear Harry saying from across the coffee table. 'Against the rear wall, slightly to the left of the table. If you got lucky you might get the chair next to it. We can't count on that, of course. The Russians will decide the seating arrangements.'

'We're cooking,' Ives said, hanging up one of the phones. 'We've got the plane.'

'Now don't worry about a thing,' Harry said to Coolidge. 'Seventh Army is supplying the escort. I wouldn't let you go if I didn't think it was absolutely safe. This is going to be a diplomatic negotiation; you'll be protected by custom and international law, not to mention the Fourteenth Armored Brigade.'

'Harry, what do you expect me to do?'

'I want you to walk past that wastebasket, look in, and keep on walking. Come back and tell us what you saw.'

'What do you think I'll see?'

'I have no idea.'

Coolidge sat back in the chair and took a triple sip of wine.

Harry edged even closer, practically sitting on air. 'They've got to be throwing secure documents in there. An enlisted man takes it outside for a burn on schedule. One little fact could be fundamental to our understanding of the situation. If you can get more than one, fine. We're going to schedule a meeting with them for right before the burn time. It'll be loaded. Just get a look in there, Walter.'

'Harry. Uh. Is it possible you're overestimating me?'

Ives hung up another phone. 'You don't seem to realize what a reputation you have, Walter. Even the President talks about you now and then. Remember Axelby?' Ives said to Harry. They both chuckled. 'Jesus, that was good,' Ives said. It was as if he and Harry were talking about their favorite halfback from college days. Ives concentrated, dredging it back up. 'What was it you did? You spotted him throwing away something. As a result, we dropped his nomination to the SEC like a hot potato. Sure

170

enough, three months later the guy was nabbed for trading on insider information and had to fork over three hundred and fifty grand. That was magic, Walter.'

'That was trash magic,' Harry said admiringly.

They were really selling. Building him up. He'd been sitting in the same airport waiting room with Axelby, and he'd noticed him balling up a blue American Express receipt and tossing it in a trash can. Coolidge wondered why a man in Axelby's position would toss away a possible tax deduction, so he retrieved it as he was walking out to the plane. It was for lunch at the Four Seasons. A little investigation turned up the fact that he had bought lunch for the chairman of Union Steel when he was supposedly having a job interview. The prospective employee never pays for lunch in that situation; he was actually getting insider information, a stock tip.

'And what about the Case of the Empty Thorazine Bottle, eh, Watson?' Ives said to Harry. They both broke up like a couple of madmen. 'I mean, you saved the Pentagon that time,' Ives said, 'not to mention the next election.'

They were laying it on thicker and thicker. It wasn't that brilliant. Coolidge seemed to have good instincts about trash. He'd been visiting old friends at HEW. An under secretary there, Joseph P. Kinderman, was about to be named under secretary of defense. Coolidge had been strolling toward the water cooler. Kinderman was already there. As he turned to go, he tossed a medicine bottle into the trash. It was a prescription for Thorazine. Kinderman, it turned out, was a nervous breakdown case who wasn't over it yet and was a bad candidate for a killing job.

'You're trapped, Walter,' Harry said. 'Face it. You're the Garbageman. If I know you, you'll have half a dozen different scenarios worked out by the time you're sitting' – he gestured at the photograph – 'at that table. Anything, Walter. Anything at all. A phrase. A name. A word. There's no telling what the payoff might be.'

Coolidge had saved the obvious for last, hoping to embarrass them with it. It was so obvious, it was a sign of deterioration. Maybe Harry was on the point of a stroke or, better yet, galloping senility.

'Harry, if there's anything in there, it's going to be in

Russian Cyrillic, Harry. It'll be gibberish to me.'

Harry closed his eyes in disgust. 'Come on, Walter.'

'Just in time,' Ives said, pointing.

Two of the hostesses were escorting Norman Wallace across the big room. Wallace had solved the problem of dignity by putting on a big act of subtly stealing glances at the girls. He was thin, slightly gray, slightly bald, and wearing a slightly gray suit. He had State Department written all over him.

'Everything okay?' Ives said.

'Sure is.'

Wallace took out a packet from his inside jacket pocket and plunked it down on the coffee table. They were flash cards for teaching the Cyrillic alphabet.

'У нас много работы,' Wallace said to Coolidge. 'That translates as: "You and I have a lot of work to do." '

Trash Report: #85-10-9

CASE NUMBER: 104759

ABANDONED PROPERTY DONOR: Senator Oliver Garvey (residence)

1. Bottle Southern Comfort.
2. 1.75 liter bottles private label Scotch, quan. 4.
3. Unopened crate of soybeans.
4. Numerous clipped newspapers and magazines. Clippings obtained from identical copies and added to file.
5. Videocassette movie, *The Candidate.*
6. Senate bill S3018, annotated.
7. Broken vase.
8. OMB document #30852.
9. Copy of speech intended for delivery to the American Library Association.

Trash Scenario

The Vice-President visited with Senator Garvey on Sunday evening (item #1, bottle of Southern Comfort; item #3, the usual crate of soybeans – in this case unopened – which the Vice-President gives everyone). They discussed the proposed soybean landmark program (item #6, marked-up copy of S3018). Garvey indicated his willingness to support it. In exchange, he got a look at next year's budget request by the Library (item #8, Office of Management and Budget document 30852).

They also discussed the Vice-President's isolation from the President and his lack of information about various policy matters (item #7, broken vase, plus the V-P's well-known temper).

Garvey's home document shredder is now inoperable. Item #9, however, seems to have gotten a soaking in Russian dressing while in the trash. Chemists at the University of Maryland have been asked to analyse the action of Russian dressing on typewriter ink. Only a fragment of item #9, reproduced here, was recovered.

. . . and while your convention is dealing with the question of information retrieval, I would prefer to confine my remarks to the nature of information. We inevitably think of information, data, facts, as inherently good. An asset. Something positive in our lives. Who would deny this? Information gathering, perhaps more than food gathering, has permitted the advance of civilization. And yet it is my belief that not all information is beneficial. Not all information represents a positive step forward. Some information is clearly negative.

By negative information, I don't mean that which is, say, critical, adverse, nay-saying. I use the word 'negative' in its arithmetical sense. I will define my terms.

Negative information is that which, immediately upon acquiring, causes the recipient to know less than he did before.

Negative information is that which subtracts from one's store of knowledge and wisdom, hard-earned from the experiences of life. Each atom of negative information annihilates one atom of common sense, emitting an alpha ray of stupidity in the process. The more negative information one is exposed to, the less one knows. At some critical point in this process, one ceases to think. One is thereafter 'playing back.'

Perhaps I should give you some practical examples of what I mean by negative information. I will start with a phrase used frequently during the Vietnam War. It is a rather exquisite example of what I am talking about: 'surgical bombing.'

174

The beauty of this phrase is that it cancels out one's background and experience with the word 'bombing', which is commonly thought of as a violent and unfriendly act. By connecting a healing word like 'surgical' with a destructive word like 'bombing,' one gets what sounds like a healthy bombing, a beneficial bombing, a Blue Cross sort of bombing, which will cleanly excise the cancerous cells and leave the body better off than it was before it got bombed.

Another rare find goes all the way back to Robert McNamara's term as secretary of defense in the sixties, when he used to refer to the 'bombing program' in Vietnam. The bombing program was on schedule. The bombing program was succeeding. The bombing program was a really outstanding program. Indeed, like a poverty program, a model cities program, a hot lunch program, a bombing program sounds like merely another piece of liberal do-goodism.

Here is a fine example of negative information: 'bargaining chips.' Weapons systems are never called weapons systems. Weapons systems are always called bargaining chips. In this way, the Pentagon has managed to get massively expensive and militarily destabilizing programs through Congress and past our citizenry by claiming that, as bargaining chips in an arms reductions talks, they would result in great reductions of armaments at a vast saving in dollars.

And of course there is the biggest bit of negative information of all – the atomic bomb of negative information, as it were – the notion that nuclear war is fightable, winnable, survivable.

What defenses do we have against negative information? How can we fend off these high-speed particles of ignorance emitted by our leaders? How can we shield ourselves from the alpha rays of stupidity showering down on us? Here's my idea . . . .

Delenda Est Carthago

Coolidge felt tempted to smile and wave at the crowd. People were peering in, trying to see who the celebrity was in the back seat. It happened often enough in Washington, of course: a foreign head of state, an important ambassador, occasionally even the President. But he had to ignore his public; Norman Wallace was keeping him busy as their motorcycle escort wound slowly through double-parked Georgetown streets. Wallace was swaying slightly from side to side in his jump seat, intent on the flash cards, not wasting a moment, determined to teach Coolidge – as he put it with one of his State Department jokes – 'acrylic.'

Б.

'B,' Coolidge said.

С.

'S.'

Coolidge hated to admit it, but the more he thought about it, the more he realized Harry was right: it *was* the opportunity of a lifetime. In a crazy kind of way. A screwball assignment concocted by people in power who had resources to deploy and couldn't resist deploying them. At the same time, it was pretty serious stuff for the Garbageman. It was going a long way beyond the droppings of the ghetto or the refuse of a congressman. Coolidge had made garbage respectable, had turned it into an instrument of national policy. He'd gotten it to the point where garbage might even head off World War III and thereby save the planet. Hell, he *was* a celebrity.

Ц.

'Ts.'

Ч.

'Ch.'

It was going to be a long twenty-four hours. That's when they were supposed to arrive back at Dulles, according to the neat schedule Phoebe had already typed up and distributed to all parties concerned, including a telex to the American Seventh Army in Germany. Out of that twenty-four hours, he was going to have, at most, three or four seconds to glance into a wastebasket, which wasn't even long enough for anything to register on the brain. It was going to be in his eyeballs only, a shimmer of light sweeping along the retinal cones and rods; he'd need another good five to ten seconds to recognize and memorize what he'd seen after he'd seen it. It would push his technique to the extreme; the whole thing was marginal. But, he told himself, the margin was where things happened. He'd have to prepare himself not to be distracted by oddments of exotic Russian garbage that would kill a second or so pointlessly. Ignore the garbage; concentrate on the trash – that's where success lay.

'We're making progress,' Norman Wallace said. 'Now here's a new one.'

Щ.

'Look familiar?' Wallace said.

'It looks like sh. Except for that little thing on the bottom.'

'Good. That little thing on the bottom turns it into shch. Which is getting a lot of mileage out of one little thing on the bottom, don't you think?'

'Certainly.'

Wallace went on flashing cards, while other things went flashing through Coolidge's brain. Eberhart's curse. Eberhart. The Doctor. Garvey. Vera.

Going to Germany was a good antidote for it all. Germany was a chance to concentrate on technique and forget about people, all of them. He wasn't good at people, anyway. It was a fact of life: He was more at home with garbage. The objective details, the effluvia, that which they were trying to be rid of. What they held on to was, by definition, nongarbage. But only by their definition. There was really only a hairline temporal difference between what was garbage and what wasn't; nongarbage was garbage not thrown out. Ergo, everything was garbage. Including Harry Dunn.

The sirens seemed to be getting louder.

Coolidge tore his eyes away from Ж and saw a fresh phalanx of motorcycles out in the passing lane of the Beltway. It looked like they were getting reinforcements, until another limo appeared. It was a second motorcycle escort, and they seemed to have the right of way, as though there were a kind of hierarchy of motorcycle escorts. Wallace even forgot about his flash cards. As they watched, both entourages left the Beltway at the next exit and lined up on a narrow side road, sounding like a bikers' convention.

Coolidge got out of his limo just as Harry Dunn lumbered out of his.

'I got worried about you,' Harry said.

Coolidge didn't believe for a moment that they were calling it off. A phone call to the airport could have done that. No. It was the way they did things in government, improvising, patching together at the last minute. He was wondering what the new wrinkle was going to be, and then he saw Beebe climbing out of the other limo.

'He's going with you,' Harry said. 'I've made him responsible for you. You're going to be in Communist territory; you're entitled to the best.'

Coolidge watched that bad face walking along the roadside, carrying his own attaché case for once.

'Just an extra precaution,' Harry was saying. 'I don't want to take even the remotest chance of losing the best garbageman in the free world.' He smiled. But there was a curve on the smile. It wasn't a wide-open, all out smile. There was a thought interfering with that smile.

Coolidge flicked his eyes at Beebe again and understood the situation. Beebe was an imperative. Harry Dunn was touching all bases. Beebe wasn't there to protect Walter Coolidge; his job was to protect the United States of America. Was there even a statistical whisper of a bare possibility that a Librarian might be taken by the Russians? Then close off that possibility. Have a Beebe on the scene to, alternatively, save Coolidge's life or take it.

'Except for what happens inside the negotiation shack, take your your orders from Mac. I'm putting him in charge of this little expedition. So you've got Mac and you've got Wallace, and they're both good men.'

178

Coolidge watched Harry watching Coolidge. It wouldn't do to let Harry, and therefore Beebe, know that he had figured out Beebe's real assignment. It might give him a small advantage somewhere along the line. He put on an act of gratitude.

'Thanks, Harry. I appreciate it.'

Beebe came up to them and started climbing in the open door of the car. 'We're three minutes off the schedule,' he said over his shoulder.

'Mr. Efficiency,' Harry said. 'See you tomorrow, Walter. Bring us back something, huh?'

Coolidge got in and settled back. He looked over at Beebe, who'd gone so far as to give Wallace a nod. 'I hope you're going take good care of me,' Coolidge said.

'You betcha,' Beebe replied.

Wallace, still on the jump seat, was keeping his eye on the ball. He held up Φ.

'F,' Coolidge said.

Beebe established his authority in a hurry. He wouldn't let them drink. They had the entire 747 to themselves, and there were some rather good wines aboard, with two black waiters to serve. But they were going into combat, the front line. They'd have to be at their best.

It was odd hearing it come from Beebe's lips: Beebe who was not an intellectual, whose lips were built for drinking and tough talk, quoting a Roman orator. '*Delenda est Carthago*,' Beebe said, enunciating toothily. 'Carthage must be destroyed.' He said it with considerable relish, then went off by himself to clean his guns – two automatics that he carried on him, plus a disassembled sniper's rifle in his attaché case, which had a snooperscope attachment so he could kill even in pitch darkness.

Wallace and Coolidge resumed the study of acrylic.

Coolidge was definitely improving. There were only thirty-three symbols to remember, and they hadn't stopped working since they left Georgetown. He was even finding time to worry about Beebe in between flash cards, distracted by the sounds Beebe was making with his guns. Built into Beebe's assignment was the unmistakable bureaucratic reality that it would be safer for him to overreact than to underreact. Beebe would be in hot water if Coolidge ever ended up as a guest of the KGB, but he would only get a slap on the wrist if he had to kill Coolidge to prevent his capture.

He wondered what Beebe would be like once they were over the East German border.

At Mannheim in West Germany, the 747 rolled past dozens of Lufthansa and Air France and Swissair jetliners and up to a waiting helicopter, blades idling; they were airborne again in seconds, picking up two minutes on the schedule in their race to beat the trash burn. Ives had arranged to have heavy flight jackets in the helicopter for them; they'd come in handy in the chill fall air.

'Never go into Russia in summer uniform,' Beebe said as he put his on.

The helicopter took them to a rarely used emergency landing field only five miles from the East German border. The rickety wooden control tower, unmanned, looked World War I. Alongside it were a few small wooden buildings and a landing strip that didn't look long enough to take a Piper Club without arresting hooks; otherwise there was nothing but pine trees as far as the eye could see.

As the helicopter descended through the dusk, they saw a line of military vehicles driving off a highway onto the field; it was Coolidge's escort. The chopper sat on the ground long enough for them to get out and then went fluttering back to Mannheim.

The three men stood on the runway watching the convoy approach. Brigadier General Arlington C. Prager was in the lead jeep. As it pulled up to them, Prager looked at his watch.

'We're ninety seconds off the plan,' he said to them. 'We'll have to move right along.'

Prager was CO of the 14th Armored Brigade. He was also one of the two unofficial negotiators for the U.S. He was West Point, and high on the list for major general. He had been to staff colleges and had a master's in foreign relations from Columbia University. In the event of combat, his command would probably be the first unit committed. Prager was medium height and wasn't doing his exercises; his belly was looking down over the edge of his belt. He watched Beebe start climbing into the back of his jeep.

'You Coolidge?'

'No. Beebe.'

'Then you wait here with Wallace. The Russians are expecting Coolidge, my driver, and me. That's it.'

Coolidge brightened. Things were beginning to look up. General Prager was holding his hand out. 'I guess you're Coolidge. You must be a pretty important man. Seventh Army Headquarters has guaranteed your safety. That means your insurance company is ahead on the deal.'

'I believe you, General,' Coolidge replied happily.

'All right,' Prager said, 'we'd better move.'

Beebe was still standing there with his attaché case, unaccustomed these days to taking orders from a mere brigadier general, looking frustrated as Coolidge climbed into the back of the jeep. Even Norman Wallace was getting clued in on Beebe's moods, he saw it coming. 'Okay,' Beebe said to the driver. 'Out.'

'Uh, perhaps I should handle this,' Wallace put in hastily. 'General Prager, it seems as though Mr. Coolidge isn't permitted across the border unless he's accompanied by Mr. Beebe.'

'Nobody said anything to me about it,' Prager said.

'I realize that. It was a last-minute agreement between the State and DoD, Now if your driver could catch a ride with one of the other vehicles . . .'

Prager had heard enough. The mention of DoD told him what his orders were. 'Okay, Sergeant.'

Wallace responded to a dirty look from Coolidge with a subtle raising of his hands, his shoulders, his eyebrows. He was only following orders.

The column of jeeps, weapons carriers, and armored personnel vehicles quickly sped back to the highway. General Prager, sitting next to Beebe, turned to Coolidge and pointed. 'That's only a small part of your bodyguard, Coolidge. They're the best troops in Europe.'

Coolidge nodded. He liked Prager's solicitous attitude. But as far as he was concerned, the best troop in Europe was sitting behind the wheel of the jeep. Coolidge was perspiring. He took the heavy flight jacket off and laid it on the seat next to him, then started going over his ABC's a final time. T hour was approaching. He also had his scenarios to work out. He stayed totally absorbed in trash fantasies until he heard Prager's voice in the darkness.

'Another part of your bodyguard, Coolidge. Vehicular homicide, I call them.'

He could make out the giant shapes of M-60 tanks in the moonlight, all lined up along the border with East Germany, guns all pointed eastward. Beebe left the road, drove between two of the goliaths, and headed out across an open field.

Harry had underestimated a little. The negotiation shack was more like half a mile inside the German Democratic Republic. There was a break in the treeline at the far side which gave access to a small road. A Soviet T-72 blocked the way. The massive tank had its turret swung around to the rear, pointing at the jeep. A young lieutenant was in the turret, scrutinizing them. He had the look of a peasant who was tasting power and liked it and could very easily be provoked into exercising it. There were also four soldiers on foot, each of them taking up a position at a corner of the jeep.

The lieutenant flashed a light on his watch and said in perfect English, 'You're exactly on time, gentlemen.'

Beebe turned back to Coolidge and sneered. 'Cheap Russian watches,' he said out of the corner of his mouth. They were forty-five seconds late.

The narrow road led off through pinewoods and the entourage proceeded at walking speed. Coolidge had stopped doing acrylic; now he was working on how to be. He was so cold he couldn't stand it anymore, so he put his flight jacket back on.

He was supposed to be State Department and he was trying to feel like Norman Wallace, cool and efficient and resourceful and in good emotional control. He was going to play a role, the way spies did. He wasn't a spy, but it didn't worry him. At bottom, almost everyone was a secret agent, harboring thoughts, playing games, living to hidden agendas. Coolidge was as ready as he was ever

182

going to be. He was shivering, but he was going on the assumption that it was from the cold.

The jeep was now rolling past the barrel of yet another T-72 tank. As they turned past it, the turret swiveled, following them; someone was getting in a little gunlaying exercise. They began to notice Russian troops; they were posted all over the place. They were like recruiting posters, dripping morale, looking to the future.

'That T-72 is rigged for chemical and gas warfare,' General Prager murmured. 'But we've got the right antitank gun. I have to admit I'd enjoy the test.'

'You don't happen to have one *on* you, do you?' Coolidge replied.

Beebe had stopped in front of the shack. The door opened and they could see General Dmitri B. Ronzhin standing there silhouetted in the light. He had been a company commander in World War II and he'd seen plenty of fighting. Which was then matched by decades of infighting inside the Soviet military and civilian bureaucracies. Ronzhin looked it: he was combat ready.

Coolidge glanced back as he went up the steps. Beebe was beginning to look lonely out there all by himself, but Beebe versus a platoon of Russian mechanized infantry was probably about even-steven.

It was time for the Garbageman to go to work.

The Masterpiece

Coolidge was pretending to listen; they were doing their work, he was doing his. Ronzhin and Prager were playing war games with each other. Sergei P. Kalyanov, a civilian, was sitting listening, making an occasional note in a pocket notebook, staring up at the ceiling most of the time. Coolidge had lost out on seating: the Russians were sitting backs to the wall, which put Kalyanov next to the wastebasket. Prager and Coolidge had their backs to the microcam installed on the inside of the front wall. An electronic interrogator hidden in the jeep was constantly scanning the chip memory and retransmitting the data to a larger transmitter across the border. Coolidge would be doing his act live, in real time, via satellite. Harry and Ives and the others would be watching.

'You people are killer pedagogues,' Ronzhin was saying. 'You're itching to teach us a lesson. I need hardly remind you, however, that should one NATO tank cross the border, you will be presenting us with the right of hot pursuit. I could be on the Rhine in a week.'

'Certainly,' Arlington C. Prager replied. 'That's where we have already built our prisoner-of-war cages.'

They weren't ranting and raving. The tone was gentlemanly, quietly speculative. It was more like two retired generals from opposing armies sitting, say, in an outdoor Paris café, tossing out delectable possibilities at each other.

As for Coolidge, he was trying to establish a relationship with the wastebasket. The question was how. He had brought cigars with him, for the cellophane wraps. He had got them from Wallace, because the 747 only had genuine Havanas in a humidor. He had a pack of cigarettes with

184

one cigarette in it that he had got from the helicopter pilot. He had cough drops, each one individually wrapped. He had Beebe's reading glasses, surprisingly delicate, rimless, intellectual-looking, which he could drop near the waste-basket and bend over to pick up.

But they all had a touch of fakery. They were labored. He was praying for nature to take its course. It should be natural, unpremeditated, guileless, convincing. Coolidge had his watch on the inside of his wrist so he could glance at it surreptitiously. It was only twelve minutes to burn time, and he was going to have to commit himself.

He looked over at Kalyanov, who was sitting quietly, staring down at the table now, making an occasional note, not saying anything. The wastebasket, to Kalyanov's right, Coolidge's left, was standing against the rear wall. It was about a four-foot throw from where Coolidge was sitting. He took out one of Norman Wallace's cigars and toyed with it for a few minutes, pretending to be intensely interested in the conversation while doing so, still undecided about what scenario to use.

The café generals were still at it.

'From a defensive point of view, NATO strategy makes no sense whatever,' Ronzhin was saying. He leaned across the table, smiling, a patronizing tone in his voice. 'You leave your tactical nuclear weapons up close to the border, where they're vulnerable to capture? Come, come, Arlington, we're both military men.'

'Conceded,' Prager replied. 'That's a factor you people don't understand because you don't have the problem. We can't tell our Germany what to do the way you can tell your Germany. Our Germany wants its territory defended at the border. Surely you can understand that, Dmitri.'

'I understand that only offensive weapons are kept close to the border. They are to be used before any possibility of capture. Use them or lose them, as you people so neatly put it. They are for the purpose of blasting a path.'

Ronzhin slapped the tabletop on the word 'path.' He spoke idiomatic American. So did Kalyanov and the young lieutenant outside. On the plane, Wallace had spun out at great length the possible significances of the fact that from the very first meeting the Russians all spoke

English. The potential for interpretation seemed infinite. It was an insult, showing how crude and uncultured the monolingual Americans were. It was a sign of eagerness to talk, making it easy on the Americans. It was all things in between. It was the kind of web spinning diplomats did ceaselessly.

Coolidge didn't want to use the cigar. He still had five minutes left. He was studying Kalyanov, trying to figure out what kind of man he was. He was going to have to do it right under the man's nose. He vaguely recalled having seen Kalyanov somewhere, possibly on the microcam in the bordello on Pletskaya Street in Moscow. For a man to be in any kind of high position in the Soviet Union, he had to have bitten a few bullets in his time. Bitten them, chewed them, swallowed them, savored them, smiling the while. Although his face didn't look it; it was remarkably unlined. His cheeks were almost baby cheeks. Four minutes to burn time. He had to move. The cigar wrapper plus dropping Beebe's glasses would give him a few extra seconds over the wastebasket, but it involved a lot of fumfering around. It was busy, busy.

'The only positive aspect in all this,' General Ronzhin was saying, 'is that winter is approaching. It is difficult for me to believe that, once again, the West would be so monumentally infantile as to invade the Soviet Union in winter. But perhaps your President is game, Arlington? "The Volga, here we come," eh, Arlington?'

There was the sound of a sneeze.

'Gesundheit,' Ronzhin said jovially.

Coolidge smiled at the general and took out his pocket pack of tissues. He wiped his nose, balled up the tissue, leaned slightly to his left, and hurled it straight into the wastebasket.

Ronzhin meanwhile had stood and gone to the map. 'Let's even assume that your high command knows what it is doing. You would attempt to cut through here and here.' He glanced at Arlington Prager and smiled, as though to say: See? We know what your plans are. It's quite obvious, old man. 'Then you will attempt a linkup here, thus cutting off the Twenty-seventh Shock Army. A little Kiev, eh, Arlington? Tens of thousands of Russian prisoners streaming to the rear. Chaos. Open country ahead. What we might call a reunification attack, stopping at the Oder-Neisse line for a generation to digest your meal.'

Coolidge's square yard of sinus cells were producing like Stakhanovite workers, having been spurred on by the cold ride in the jeep with his jacket off. He fired the second tissue into the wastebasket and then sneezed discreetly into the next one. The operation was shaping up. It was a potential masterpiece. Subtle, convincing, no straining for effects. He sniffed loudly, to keep a drop from spilling onto his lap.

'It is not the intention of NATO to attack East Germany,' Prager said, counterattacking. 'But if we did, it would not be at Fulda.' Then he went on to analyse exactly how the Soviets would attack West Germany.

It was one minute to burn time. The relationship was established; it was time to move. Coolidge fired the opening salvo, as it were: he blew his nose as loudly and convincingly as possible. It was so messy, he had to wrap the tissue in another tissue and then wipe his hands. He casually tossed the tissues at the wastebasket and missed. He stood up, feigning interest in the exchange taking place between the generals, and moved around the corner of the table.

At that moment, Sergei Kalyanov spoke up for the first time. 'Bah,' he said. He tore the page out of his notebook in disgust, balled it up, and threw it into the wastebasket. 'This meeting is ridiculous. You gentlemen are talking nonsense. All this talk and excitement over a few tanks? Let me tell you something, gentlemen. You may not like this, but you might as well face the fact that tanks are going the way of the horse. Rapidly. The missile has finished them. They are obsolete. Frankly, right at this moment, I believe the horse to be the superior weapon of war.'

The outburst was timed beautifully for Coolidge's purposes. He bent down to pick up the tissues and toss them into the wastebasket. As he did so, his hand took over and acted independently of his brain, working out of his spinal cord. There was nothing to read in the wastebasket. The

187

papers were standing up almost vertically because there were so many of them. Instead, his fingers coiled around the balled-up note page that Kalyanov had thrown away; he had Kalyanov's own notes of the meeting.

He was still pulling out his chair, back at the table, when the enlisted man went by him to pick up the trash. It occurred to Coolidge that he had a piece of contraband in the palm of his hand and that he would have to not only read it but digest it, literally. The distraction Kalyanov had unwittingly created had been perfect; the two generals were now attacking Kalyanov's military expertise. Coolidge added to the general noise level by moving his chair into place, sniffing, clearing his throat, all to cover the crinkling of the paper as he spread it out in the palms of his hands. Then he tilted the chair onto its two rear legs, ostensibly listening to the generals, eyes up on the map, then eyes slowly descending, passing the face of Kalyanov, who, his outburst over, was staring at the ceiling as the generals harangued him, finally down past the edge of the table to his clasped hands holding the spread-out sheet of notepaper. When he read it, he almost went over backward. It was in English.

'I must speak with you. Cooperate in what follows. I know you are the Doctor.'

The Doctor's Assignment

Coolidge raised his eyes from the crumpled piece of paper and looked across the expanse of table at Sergei Kalyanov's inquiring face. He had a tough chin and a tough nose, as well as intelligent blue eyes that confronted you with unusual directness. Kalyanov seemed to be searching for some sign of unbalance in Coolidge, as though wanting to know how he was taking it all. Coolidge was working hard not to show his reactions; he'd been taken to the cleaners.

He had been made to look like a fool, a child playing stupid games in a pathetic attempt to deceive the grownups. He had been revealed as the Garbageman. He was probably known to be a Librarian, one who was in possession of All Knowledge. A prize catch and not even a field man, an easy torture case: one fingernail and Coolidge would blab.

Kalyanov had even managed to proposition Coolidge in real time on microcam, and Harry Dunn, sitting on his fat ass back in Washington, wouldn't know it. Or Prager or Ronzhin. It was big league all the way. The only flaw in Kalyanov's performance was a beaut: through God knew what involuted turn of events, he had mistaken Coolidge for the Doctor. Coolidge was now in a position to find out what the Soviet Union wished to tell the Doctor. The implications were fascinating.

'I have a proposal to make,' Kalyanov announced, apparently having decided that Coolidge had survived the shock. 'It is time to relax for a few moments. We will have tea. Perhaps we will even leave the generals to themselves, eh, Mr. Coolidge? Would you care to escape all these words for a breath of night air?'

Coolidge nodded while pretending to take a cough drop; it was actually the balled-up note he had slipped into his mouth. He chewed it thoroughly before swallowing, while trying to figure out some of the implications it contained, and the two things almost seemed to go together, as though, through his mastication of it, he might learn its essence.

They knew the code word 'Doctor.' That meant some kind of connection with the Emersons, or an infiltration of them. Charley Eberhart? Senator Oliver Garvey of the great state of Nebraska? It was all craziness. And the craziest thing of all was that while Kalyanov seemed to know a lot, he didn't know he was talking to the wrong man.

Even assuming Coolidge *was* the Doctor, what did they think the Doctor could do about an incipient tank battle in Germany? Coolidge didn't fool himself for a moment. He was in over his head. He *needed* a Doctor. He put his flight jacket on, followed Kalyanov out into the biting air, and ran right into the inevitable Beebe.

'What's happening?' Beebe asked.

'Nothing's happening. Nothing at all. Mr Kalyanov and I are going for a stroll.'

'Okay with me.'

Beebe followed as they went across the clearing in front of the shack. He was carrying his attaché case. Kalyanov looked at him as though he were a microorganism.

'Tell me, Mr. Coolidge,' Kalyanov said. 'What is the rank of this gentleman?'

'The general's driver is a sergeant,' Coolidge replied, looking straight ahead.

Kalyanov snapped his fingers and the lieutenant materialized with two men.

'Where is your Soviet hospitality?' Kalyanov said. 'See that this man has hot tea. And biscuits. And cigarettes. Play the host, Lieutenant!'

'Yes, sir.'

Beebe's face was expressionless. Which in itself conveyed volumes; he didn't know what was going on, but he was making notes.

'Stay in sight,' he said, lips hardly moving.

The two men walked slowly through the brisk German air, a few stars out, barely, mainly low-flying clouds, turbulence on the horizon, a storm on the way. They stopped at the treeline thirty yards off, well out of Beebe's hearing. He was now leaning against the jeep with a cup of tea in his hand and a tray of biscuits on the hood, the attaché case on the ground between his legs.

'First let me congratulate you. The Garbageman's reputation has not been exaggerated. Your performance was superb, your timing extraordinary. I tell you, I was totally absorbed in it.'

'Garbageman? First you call me the Doctor; now you call me the Garbageman. Which is it?'

'In the Library, you are Vladimir, the Garbageman. To the Emersons you are the Doctor. Oh, don't worry; your secret is quite safe. You saw the melodramatic way I chose to communicate with you, so the oafs in uniform wouldn't know. Your oafs as well as our oafs.'

Coolidge's problem was that he didn't know who to be. He didn't know what Kalyanov expected of the Doctor. He didn't know what the Doctor was supposed to know. Or how the Doctor was supposed to feel about things. He had no base to work from. The only thing he could think of was to blow his nose.

Kalyanov nodded. 'It's a genuine cold,' he said. 'I wondered about that. Magnificent. We knew the temptation would be irresistible. You are the foremost observer of garbage in the Western world. The Eastern too, for that matter. Once your people saw our trash receptacle, we assumed that, inevitably, *you* would put in an appearance.'

'I confess. I am Vladimir, the Garbageman.'

'You are also the Doctor. The Emersons' Doctor. Which isn't quite an apt code name for you. Mathematician would be better.'

Coolidge sniffled. They seemed to know everything.

'The subtle hair-splitting mathematician of human responses, ways of being. The algebraist. What you do to one side of the equation, like any mathematician, you do to the other. This is a remarkable and troublesome characteristic when applied to human affairs. But, in the end, I suppose Doctor is better. You're the Doctor coming in the night to save the patient.'

'Sergei, I think you are exaggerating my significance.'

'Perhaps. Let me say right off, Vladimir, that I want you to feel completely at ease. We know you are a Librarian. We know you know quite a bit, perhaps even the secret of life. Who knows what you've got in that place? Nevertheless, you are immune here. We know that you are an American and that your loyalties are American. We accept that. I am saying this so that we may speak frankly. Admiral Vasilyev insisted on those terms when he sent for you.'

The plot thickened. Admiral Vasilyev had 'sent for' Coolidge. Vasilyev, the venerable father of the Soviet Navy, a military man whom Kalyanov apparently did not consider to be an oaf. Why would an admiral involve himself in a tank battle, four hundred kilometers from the nearest body of water?

Coolidge couldn't wait to hear the rest. 'By all means, speak frankly,' Coolidge said.

'In the first place, you and I both know that this confrontation is an obvious fake and pretense. It is the familiar American vaudeville act, feigning fear of a Soviet attack.'

Coolidge smiled. 'You mean my government isn't concerned about those tanks you've got over here?'

Kalyanov made an obscene kissing sound.

'The whole thing is absurd. You people are well aware that the Soviet Union cannot count on the Warsaw Pact countries for offense. Do you really believe we would put our reliance on Polish divisions? Or Czech? German? Hungarian? On offense? Listen, my friend, we ourselves are the people who taught the world the worthlessness of satellite armies in the offensive role. We captured the elite German Sixth Army at Stalingrad precisely because they entrusted their flanks to the Rumanians and Hungarians.'

Coolidge glanced back toward the shack. There was no sign of Prager and Ronzhin, only Beebe leaning nastily against the jeep. It was a Russian strangeness, this desire of civilians and military not to talk in front of each other.

'Then there is the China front,' Kalyanov continued. 'A

million of our men stretched along forty-five hundred miles of that monstrous frontier. As your Pentagon well knows, the Soviet general staff would never willingly engage in a two-front war. It is the most intelligent thought they have ever had. Therefore, it is quite clear that, apart from the crazies, NATO is not concerned about an attack by the Soviet Union. The very idea is preposterous, my friend.'

Dunn's word. Preposterous. It brought back old times. Come to think of it, talking to Kalyanov wasn't all that different from talking to Harry. They both had an open-and-shut way of laying out a situation, all variables accounted for, all conditionals touched on, only one conclusion possible for a reasonable man.

It was cold standing still; Coolidge's hands were dug deep in the flight jacket's pockets. He had done too good a job. Was it possible to die of a cold?

'We'll walk,' Kalyanov said, noticing. 'I can tell you that neither is the Soviet Union staying up nights because of your vaunted Fourteenth Armored Brigade. Those tanks of yours across the border have nothing whatsoever to do with the Soviet Union; this entire affair is a dialogue between your leaders and your public. A monologue, I should say. You are looking for an excuse to start it, are you not?'

They were passing within fifteen feet of a staring Beebe, his swiveling head following them, wondering.

'An excuse? For what?' Coolidge asked.

'For pushing the button. Getting it over in an afternoon, as some of your people put it. And some of mine. The dominion of oafs extends across both international boundaries and ideologies. It is a dangerous country.'

'Possibly you are being preposterous now, Sergei?'

'Possibly.' Kalyanov raised a pointed finger. 'It is just barely possible that your President understands that fallout will not be confined to the Soviet Union. But if it isn't a first strike you are planning, it is something almost as serious.'

'What could possibly be almost as serious as a first strike?'

'Humiliation.'

Coolidge inspected Kalyanov's eyes and the lines around his mouth.

'Kennedy humiliated us in Cuba in 1962. What had we done? We did in Cuba what the U.S. had already done in Turkey. But Kennedy said to us, "Take those missiles out of Cuba, or else," and we took those missiles out of Cuba. *This* is power. Certain circles in the U.S. have been aching to get back to that position of power again, you know. It is the old nineteenth-century gunboat diplomacy. Sailing a gunboat into a port anywhere in the world, to intimidate the natives. Today your imperialist gunboats are missiles. But you know all of this, of course.'

They were far enough away from Beebe now for Kalyanov to allow his voice to rise.

'This humiliation is a dangerous game. There is no telling how it will end. You have your generals, we have ours. And the crazies. And the ideologues. It could get out of hand. You are trying to corner us, and it is a dangerous business. It is not the Four Horsemen of the Apocalypse, my friend; it is the Four Hawksmen: Missilery, Megatonnage, Radiation, and Overpressure.'

'Why did you send for me, Sergei?'

'Because now is the time to do something about it. It is time for action, Vladimir. Tell your Emersons. *Use* them. Do not stay in reserve anymore. You're the leader of the American peace movement, Vladimir. Commit your forces. To wait any longer is to waste them.'

Coolidge paused as though seriously weighing it. He was being judicious and responsible, as befitted the leader of the American peace movement.

'I'll think about it,' he said, busily thinking about the Doctor, the invisible man, that damned elusive Pimpernel, who now seemed to have done something uncharacteristic: he'd blundered spectacularly, outsmarted himself; was so preoccupied with concealing his identity that he'd apparently left some subtle trail implicating Coolidge as the Doctor, and had managed to fool even the Russians, thereby missing an important meeting in which he was to have been given his marching orders.

'Whatever you do,' Kalyanov continued, 'do not let the generals know. It will make matters worse. They will call it

194

a bluff. A desperation bluff. They will say, "Aha, now we have really got them; now is the time to squeeze them good!" Also keep it from the defense intellectuals. They will laugh. They think threats are neat and calculable. So many missiles here versus so many missiles there, ergo victory without firing a shot. But you, Vladimir, you are the real mathematician! You know that some things cannot be calculated. No, not the think tankers.'

It was a neat bit of Jesuitry. Kalyanov had eliminated all military expertise from becoming involved in what was a purely military problem.

Coolidge went fishing. 'What do you recommend I do?'

'That is for the Doctor to figure out.'

They were moving back toward the shack now and a badly needed cup of hot tea. To Coolidge, it was a total mess. He wouldn't even begin to try to sort it out until they were on the long flight back to Dulles.

They were almost in earshot of Beebe. Coolidge paused.

'Sergei, why are you so convinced my government wishes to humiliate your government?'

'I thought I told you that, forgive me. Admiral Vasilyev says so. He says there is no question about it. Vasilyev is never wrong about such matters.'

There he was again: Vasilyev, the land admiral, the commodore of tanks. The man who had 'sent for' the 'Doctor.' Then a light began to dawn. It must have been the effects of the cold on his brain, not to have seen it sooner.

O.F.F. was over 80 percent and climbing. The activity was worldwide, after all.

Vasilyev had noticed.

A Beebe Too Many

They were rolling slowly along in darkness, the headlight beams diffusing through an increasingly murky night, the moon dropping out more and more, the air beginning to acquire a killing chill. The T-72 was leading the procession back toward the border, the same four soldiers marching along in convoy.

Coolidge, freezing in the back seat, was bracing himself for another big change of scene as he built the foundation of a colossal case of jet lag; jeep to helicopter to Mannheim to Dulles to Harry. What was he going to say? How could you summarize what Kalyanov had said; what was the essence? It was going to be an off-the-wall report. The formal meeting had ended the way meetings between Russians and Americans had ended for decades, without agreement on much, other than that there would have to be another meeting. Ronzhin had seen them off, cordial, hand-shaking, summoning the escort, personally assigning each soldier to one corner of the jeep.

'He's afraid we might go sightseeing,' Prager had murmured. 'He's too late. They've got 122-millimeter self-propelled howitzers over in those trees and BM-21 rocket launchers behind the shack. Could tell by the tracks. The T-72s don't worry me. Coffins that do forty miles per hour.'

They were past the treeline and in the open field when the T-72 stopped. The lieutenant climbed down and approached the jeep. He switched on a flashlight. Then he reached into the jeep past Beebe's insolent glare and switched off the ignition. He turned the flashlight on Coolidge.

'You will hand it over, please,' he said, his open hand

outstretched, up close to Coolidge's face. It was like the third degree, staring up into a bright light glaring out of the darkness, barely able to see your interrogator's face. The officer had a lawless quality that reminded Coolidge of a Soviet Beebe. He had been given an assignment; he was going to carry it out no matter what was required.

Prager looked back at Coolidge. Coolidge shook his head.

'What are you talking about, Lieutenant?' Prager said.

'It is necessary that this man return the document he stole.'

'I have no document.'

'You removed a document from the burn can. Private Gavrilovich saw you when he went in to remove it. If you return it to me now, the incident will be considered closed. I must have the document, is that clear?'

'I have no document.'

The Russian shrugged as though it made no difference to him either way.

'Then you will all have to be searched.'

Beebe delicately rubbed the corners of his eyes with thumb and forefinger. 'Perverse bastards,' he said.

'You're out of line, Lieutenant,' Prager said. 'You are close to creating an incident that will not be too good for your career.'

'He means Siberia,' Beebe put in. 'They'll have you making ice cubes out of glaciers.'

The lieutenant smiled. He had his orders from General Ronzhin; all discussion was pointless, a waste of everyone's valuable time. To Coolidge, the incident seemed to grow out of the vast differences that existed between at least some of the Soviet military and some of the civilians. The lieutenant was being provocative. Was he trying to pick a fight? To justify a shooting? Was Ronzhin so concerned about what might have passed between Coolidge and Kalyanov?

'Why did you wait until we were out here?' Beebe said. He was looking straight ahead into the night, not deigning to exchange glances with the officer, who now turned his full attention on Beebe, as though knowing that's where the action lay, one Beebe recognizing another.

'It is Soviet tact,' he said. 'This way it doesn't have to be an international incident. Everyone can blame me, you see. Or you can decide to forget it altogether. You are, of course, supposed to have diplomatic safe-conduct. But you have stolen a document belonging to the Union of Soviet Socialist Republics. That is espionage. The two tend to cancel each other.'

'They do not cancel each other,' Prager said.

'General Ronzhin says they do.'

'Mac,' Coolidge said under his breath. 'I'm clean. Do it and be done. I think he's looking for a fight. Don't give it to him.'

The lieutenant switched the flashlight to his left hand and used the right to draw his pistol.

'You first,' he said to Beebe. 'Step out of the vehicle and strip.'

Beebe laughed. It came from deep down in his chest, and it scared the hell out of Coolidge. Two of the soldiers moved behind the officer with their Kalashnikov rifles unslung. Beebe was still looking straight ahead. There could be no more palaver; it was decision time.

'Don't make a federal case, Mac,' Coolidge said. 'Do what the nice man says.'

'Shut up, Coolidge. I'm in charge of this expedition.'

'I wouldn't quite put it that way, Beebe,' General Prager said. 'We're outgunned. Question is, is he bluffing?'

'Yeah,' Beebe said. 'Is this jeep well tuned?'

'Like a Swiss movement.'

'If you don't get out right now, we will physically remove you from the vehicle,' the lieutenant said.

'You and what army?'

'The Red Army.'

'Oh, that's different. The Red Army. I didn't know that. Why didn't you say that in the first place? I thought maybe you guys were the Bulgarian Army. I mean, you dress like Bulgarians.'

There was a disinterested, uninflected quality to the way Beebe was talking. His mind wasn't on it. He was rehearsing something. He'd been working on it all along, choreographing every movement and moment, flexing his muscles, running through it mentally, working down through some kind of countdown. Coolidge could see

198

Beebe's shoulders moving slightly as he rehearsed. Then he saw where the man's monumental self-confidence came from: the actual performance was done with flawless grace and éclat.

'Okay, you win,' Beebe said. But as he started out of the jeep, he kicked the headlight switch off with his right knee, knocked the flashlight away from the lieutenant with his left hand, sending it spinning end over end into the blackness twenty feet away, at the same time poleaxing the lieutenant with his right fist, the officer taking two of his soldiers with him as he crashed to the ground. Suddenly there was total blackness and no opposition.

'Damn,' Prager said admiringly.

The engine caught on the first quarter turn of the starter motor and they were racing across the open field toward the border, four hundred yards away. It was good black German soil, which grew potholes by the thousands; Coolidge was hanging on with both hands. Bullets were flying. They were shooting by ear, since there was nothing to see. For the first time in his life, Coolidge heard funny little rushes of air going past his head.

General Prager found out, the hard way, a bit of intelligence that he had always assumed but had never actually confirmed: the Soviet T-72 had a snooperscope. It had to; it was the only way they could have done it on the first shot. There was the sound of 160 millimeters exploding, which was a miss, but a near one, and both left wheels went airborne. As the jeep started to go over, Coolidge lost his grip and went flying into the night, while the jeep converted its forward motion into crunched metal.

Coolidge was on the ground, getting a facial in East German mud. His ears were ringing loudly and the insides of his shoes felt damp, but that could have been imagination. His parts all seemed to move, but both shoulders hurt; he had probably landed on them. He could hear Russian voices not far off. They were searching the area, but there weren't any lights and the shooting had stopped. It felt like no-man's-land and Coolidge was getting lonesome in the blackness. He was suddenly back in anarchy, where there was no cop on the beat and force was on the loose. He felt the classic powerful urge to urinate; there was nothing more violent and terrifying in life than state power unleashed. Then he heard a voice nearby, as calm as a control tower.

'Flash Two, this is Flash One,' General Prager was saying.

Coolidge rose to his feet cautiously, testing for breaks, listening for bullets. He homed in on Prager's voice and found him alongside the jeep, which was lying on its side. Beebe was still in the front seat, but in the crash had somehow managed to get turned around. He was stretched across the seat, with his head down near the ground and his feet sticking out over the top.

'You're alive,' Prager said to Coolidge. 'Good start. Are you in one piece?'

'More or less.'

'Flash Two, this is Flash One. Where are you?'

A flare went off somewhat to the north and they could see a Russian platoon searching for them. Three rounds of 160 millimeters went off 150 yards to the left. Now that the jeep was stationary, the snooperscopes weren't much help.

'Flash Two, this is Flash One. Come in.'

Prager was getting impatient. He and Coolidge could simply walk away from the whole thing, but that would mean abandoning Beebe. Beebe was a good excuse. Beebe was too good a man to lose. Saving Beebe allowed Prager to show the Russians that there was a price involved in shooting at a diplomatic party, not to mention a U.S. general. Coolidge could see Prager's teeth in the darkness. He was smiling.

'Fourteenth Armored still guarantees your safety, Coolidge.'

'Flash One, this is Flash Two,' the radio said.

'We're under fire. Advance azimuth one hundred degrees, range approximately two hundred yards. Do not fire until fired upon.'

It was like Le Mans, engines starting everywhere, steel treads going into motion. Now there was no chance of Coolidge walking back to the border; he'd get run over by a tank in the darkness.

'Looks like they got us,' Beebe said, half talking to himself.

'It's okay, Mac. We're out of trouble.'

There was a dirty smile in Beebe's voice. 'Hey, Walter, cut it out, will you?'

'Do you hear those tanks?'

'That ain't the Bulgarian Army; that's the Red Army.'

'It's our army. Relax. We're fine.'

Coolidge heard the hammer on Beebe's .45 being cocked back. To be fair about it, it was possible he was getting ready to take on the Red Army.

'What do you think we should do, Walter?'

Beebe hadn't called Coolidge Walter in all the time they had known each other. The Russians began to fire at the advancing tanks, and the 14th Armored returned it.

'Speak louder, Walter. I can't hear you.'

Beebe's form was just a blur to Coolidge, but he could imagine how he must be holding the gun, half conscious, aiming it upside down out into the darkness, trying to get Coolidge to talk so he could find him. Coolidge wondered. It was all deduction. He didn't know for a *fact* that Beebe was instructed to kill him if it looked like the Russians were about to capture him. It was ambiguous. But the .45 wasn't ambiguous. The tanks were getting closer and the firing was increasing in intensity.

Coolidge decided that conceivably he might be able to deal with being caught in the middle of a tank battle, and conceivably he might be able to deal with McDermott Beebe III, but he couldn't do both at the same time.

'Keep coming, Flash Two.'

Coolidge had been standing stock-still so as not to give his exact position away to Beebe. But Coolidge knew precisely where Prager was. He grabbed the radio out of Prager's hand and slammed it down where he figured Beebe's head was. It was none too soon; a second later, a Russian flare went off and made daylight.

For the first time, General Arlington C. Prager looked shocked. Coolidge was poised with the radio held high, ready to strike again at an unconscious Beebe lying upside down in the jeep, aiming an upside down .45 out into nowhere.

Coolidge shrugged. 'He was getting delirious. Say, how do I get the next flight out of here?'

An Account of a Battle Between the Soviet 27th Shock Army and Walter Coolidge

The hissing red and white flare was slowly dropping to the ground. Tank shells were dropping too. Russian shells, American shells. Coolidge decided it was time to drop something himself. A name.

'Any cooperation in getting me to the airfield would be appreciated by the White House,' he said to General Prager.

Prager didn't know where to look first. The Russian tanks, his own tanks, Beebe, Coolidge.

'Was he trying to shoot you?' he asked.

'He *was* pointing it at me.'

'Christ, you *are* important. Nobody would kill *me*.' He looked deflated.

A jeep came careening to a stop beside them; it was Prager's aide, a young captain. He looked appalled. 'Excuse me, sir, but those Russian tanks are advancing.'

'We *are* in East Germany,' Prager replied. 'I've got to talk to corps headquarters. Where's the COMM van?'

'Right behind me.'

'Give this man your jeep. Know the way back, Coolidge?'

Coolidge hustled behind the wheel. 'If you could manage it,' he said, shifting gears, 'it might be worthwhile if you could save him.' He nodded in Beebe's direction. 'But I wouldn't take any big risks.'

'Would the White House appreciate that too?' Prager called after him.

Coolidge backed out of East Germany, taking the last two hundred yards in reverse so he could watch for muzzle flashes from Russian tanks. The sounds of battle were terrifying. It was hard to believe that anyone could survive

202

such explosions. Or that human relations had deteriorated to the point where people would actually throw things that devastating back and forth at each other. Nasty little concentrated packets of state power. As he backed onto the road in West Germany, a shell exploded thirty yards away.

It had to be a Russian stray. Coolidge shifted into first and floored the accelerator, wanting to put distance between him and the battle. But another shell followed, and another. Someone was ranging in on him. He looked back and saw a Russian tank clanking onto the roadway.

Where the hell was Arlington C. Prager and the 14th Armored Brigade? There was a man standing in the turret. Coolidge had the eerie feeling it was the same guy Beebe had poleaxed a few minutes before, maniacally determined to carry out orders and now invoking the right of hot pursuit, which dissolved the sanctity of borders.

Whoever he was, the Russian meant business. Coolidge headed for the airfield at top speed, but the road began twisting and turning through the German hills. He wasn't a good enough driver to take the curves at high speed, and the tank wasn't all that slow. By the jeep's speedometer, they were doing a hair over forty. On the other hand, Coolidge had a couple of hundred yards on them, and the curves were keeping him out of direct sight of the tank gunner most of the time, so they couldn't get a good shot at him.

The tanker responded by taking a shortcut, estimating Coolidge's position and shooting at him through the trees. Shells began screaming out of the forest from totally unexpected directions. At one hairpin turn, the shell came at Coolidge from in *front*. His counter was to accelerate, up and down, to throw the gunner's judgment off. But it was costing him speed; the tank was inching up.

It was mania. The tank commander was a true believer. Tunnel vision through the barrel of a gun. It was insane for them to come this far; they would end up like a beached whale somewhere, unless the 27th Shock Army was following close behind. It suddenly occurred to Coolidge that he was leading the tank straight to the airfield.

Coolidge was exhausted, hurting, his head clogged, and

he was having trouble holding the road when he sneezed. It was an unfair competition. He had no resources, nothing to fight with. He rejected the easy way, running until the tank was out of gas. That was pure escapism; sooner or later one of those shells was going to connect. How much longer could he go on being lucky? No, he had to face it. He was going to have to engage them in combat and defeat them. Use karate. That was how you defeated a superior opponent; use their own strength against them. Simple. Blow them up with their own cannon. Karate was krap. What else? What other master strategies for survival were there? He thought of *Wasser* because he had a terrible thirst. *Wasser* could be the way.

Where was the *Wasser*? There had to be *Wasser* somewhere. He didn't remember any from the last time he'd been along this road. But they'd passed a little town. He decided to gamble; when he got to it, he left the highway, frantically looking for *Wasser* and finding it in the town square. Flowing *Wasser*. With a concrete bridge over the *Wasser*. The sign on the bridge over the *Wasser* said '10 Tonne'. Beautiful. The karate chop. Coolidge took the bridge at fifty. By the time he had gone down a side street on the far side of the square, he was hearing a fascinating new sound: the sound a forty-ton tank makes during a panic stop on asphalt, skidding to a halt, sparks flying, fishtailing, a monster at bay.

A searchlight came on. It searched around. They found the sign. Long pause. Coolidge backed out into the square. Don't let a little thing like that stop you, he thought. Come on, Lieutenant, you'll be derelict in your duties if you stop now. He honked his horn at them.

He would never know if that was the deciding factor, but the tank started up, inching over the bridge at half a mile per hour. Forty tons on a ten-ton bridge. Coolidge watched them like a pedestrian waiting for someone to jump out of a window.

The bridge was starting to snap, crackle, and pop. The tank kept coming. They were probably figuring on a safety factor of four. It was possible, but it was iffy. It reminded him of the old joke about the Pullman sleeping car, the woman in the upper berth saying to the ironing board salesman in the upper across the aisle when he said he had something long enough to crawl over on: In the first place I doubt it; but in the second place, how would you get back?

It was melodrama. They were doing about an eighth of an mph now, trying to minimize stresses. They wouldn't dare fire their gun. They were trying to put ten pounds into a five-pound bag. The concrete was being mortified. It wasn't going to put up with it much longer; it wasn't being paid to do things like this. There was a crunch and then another crunch and then a tremendous snapping sound. The tank began to sink, rear end first.

Coolidge cruised back up to the bridge. Their guns were all pointed skyward now and couldn't be depressed enough to get him. He felt a surge of righteousness. It was a fitting end for fanatics; Lieutenant Ahab and his whale were going down together. He turned for the airfield, driving off to the sound of failing concrete, and of steel tread slowly scraping backward along the tilting roadway. He honked his horn three times by way of saying taps.

When Coolidge arrived at the airfield, an executive jet was sitting there. It looked gorgeous; it could take him to Mannheim in no time. He drove up to it, but there was no one around. He raced the jeep over to the two dilapidated buildings and ran inside the nearest one. A weather tele-type, a phone, and a few pieces of broken furniture. It looked as if there hadn't been anyone there in years.

In the next building, he found Norman Wallace and the pilot. They were sitting at a card table drinking German beer and playing five hundred rummy. Wallace was his usual cool self. 'You look like hell,' he said. 'How did it go?'

There was a third bottle of beer. Coolidge grabbed it and sat down at the card table. 'I started World War Three.' He took a long swig of the best beer he'd ever tasted, a primal beer; it brought him back to the very first nose-tickling sip he had ever taken.

Wallace discarded. 'Conventional or nuclear?' he asked.

'Conventional. Extremely conventional. Which is to

say, totally fucked up. Fourteenth Armored Brigade invaded East Germany to rescue me. They got into a shooting match with the Twenty-seventh Shock Army. I don't think Fourteenth Armored is doing all that well. I left one of the Russian heavies around the bend three minutes from here.'

Wallace's rummy hand dribbled through his fingers. 'There's a Russian tank three minutes from here?'

Coolidge practically gargled the remaining beer. 'I *think* I totaled it, but I'm not sure.'

The pilot tried to suppress a laugh, but it came out through his nose. Wallace was looking stern. 'I think I know you well enough to know that you wouldn't kid about a thing like that,' he said, looking Coolidge in the eye.

'You are quite correct, Norman.'

'Then we better get the hell out of here.' He reached for his topcoat. 'By the way, where's *Delenda est Carthago?*'

'I left him in old *Carthago*.'

'Really? Whew. Listen. Quickly. Did you get anything?'

Coolidge looked at the pilot.

'Don't worry about him.'

Coolidge had been trying to think of how to sum up the entire incident at the shack. He couldn't possibly do it justice in less than an hour of discussion, but he was in a hurry to get airborne.

'Vasilyev is worried,' he said.

'Vasilyev? Vasilyev? That's far out, Walter. I mean, that doesn't make any sense. Is worried?'

'That's right. Vasilyev. Is worried.'

'No.'

'Yes.'

'You must have gotten it wrong.'

'Vasilyev.'

'Vasilenko, perhaps. Vasilevsky. Veklishev! What about Veklishev?'

Coolidge leaned across the table and bore down on Wallace, who was distractedly trying to get his topcoat buttoned. 'Vasilyev.'

'Okay. Vasilyev. Next. How did you get here?'

'Prager gave me a jeep.'

'Okay. You take the plane; I'll take the jeep. That way,

we'll have backup for delivering the message.'

'Why don't you use the phone next door?'

'Doesn't work, and I wouldn't use it if it did.' Wallace was heading for the door. 'If you prefer,' he said, 'you take the jeep and I'll take the plane.'

Coolidge had had enough of armored combat. 'I'll take the plane,' he said.

'Take good care of this man,' Wallace told the pilot. 'He may not look it' – Wallace cocked a sly eyebrow at Coolidge – 'but he's very important.'

'We'll be in Mannheim in half an hour,' the pilot said. 'Although I don't know what he needs me for if he can total a T-72 all by himself.'

They hurried outside and Wallace got behind the wheel of the jeep. 'First one back wins a drink,' he said, driving off.

Coolidge strolled out toward the plane, hoping he wouldn't go down in history as the cause of World War III. With any luck at all, he could blame it on Beebe.

Escape

Ernie Goldberg, the pilot, was up in the cockpit mumbling to himself, going through his checklist, solo, flicking switches with two hands, a one-man band. He didn't have a copilot. Coolidge preferred pilots who did things by the book; on the other hand, if Goldberg were the type to do things by the book, he wouldn't be here. His copilot had caught a bug in Munich and he had taken off alone to do the job of ferrying Coolidge. Because of a NATO-wide alert, there was a sudden shortage of aircraft.

Coolidge was in one of the passenger seats, bruised, exhausted, drooping, hung over from too much reality, totally confused, at the end of his rope. And then he heard the bad news. It was unmistakable over the small sounds Goldberg was making. Coolidge had become an expert at it: the clank of steel treads.

Goldberg had heard it too. 'Strap in,' he called back, as both engines fired up.

Coolidge was on the starboard side of the plane and saw the monster coming onto the field, a stegosaurus looking for a meal. It was about halfway down the field, a few hundred yards away from the strip. How had those maniacs gotten off the bridge? Another nice contest loomed, armor plate against a wisp of an airplane.

The plane was already moving rapidly down the strip, but it was within easy range of the 160-millimeter gun. Coolidge saw the muzzle blast. The addition of velocities of plane and shell gave the impression that the shell was arcing horizontally to the right, headed straight at Coolidge's seat belt. It looked like a perfect hit and he felt a terrific bump, thinking, *That goddamn Harry Dunn: Coolidge was supposed to be back in twenty-four hours.*

But instead of total disaster, there was only another bump. Goldberg had attempted a premature takeoff, practically standing the plane on its tail so that the shell would go underneath the fuselage. Then the plane dropped heavily back to the strip, still on its takeoff run.

There was time for a second shot. The turret was following them. On the other hand, Goldberg must have known something about how long it takes a tanker to reload his gun. How would a pilot know something like that? Strategic, tactical – two different worlds; they couldn't even talk to each other. The tank got off a second shot, which went singing down the runway. But the airplane wasn't on the runway. Goldberg had taken it off the strip and for the last fifty feet it was rolling on full power through overgrown weeds. Then the plane seemed to bounce into the air and was over the treeline and out of sight.

Coolidge opened the seat belt, and took a long exhale. He sat staring into space for about a minute, thinking of absolutely nothing, then staggered up to the cockpit. Goldberg was flipping switches all over the place.

'You just did a couple of things with an airplane that I never heard of before.'

'Neither have I. Hey, I'm looking for a copilot. Want a job?'

Coolidge slipped into the right-hand seat. He was still letting out more air than he was taking in. It had required genius to get him away from his nemesis. He wondered if Norman Wallace had managed to elude the 27th Shock Army. With his command of the languge, maybe he could pass for a commissar.

Goldberg was still flipping switches and tapping meters and flying the airplane. 'Look,' he said. 'When the nose goes down, you ease back on it like this. When the nose goes up, you ease forward. See this? It's the artificial horizon. The idea is to keep it horizontal. If this end tips up, you go like this, and if that end tips up, you go like that. Always easy, always smooth. Okay?'

'Why are you telling me this?'

'The autopilot isn't working. I think we took splinters from the shell. I've got to make a damage assessment.

Keep her at a thousand feet until I come back. See this thing here? It's an altimeter. That's a thousand right there. You now qualify as a command pilot in the U.S. Air Force.'

Coolidge stiffened in the seat and laid his hands on the wheel, tentatively. Then he grasped it. He looked over at Goldberg, who was holding his own hands half an inch off the wheel. Coolidge tried going up a little. Then he tried going down a little. Going down a little was scarier. 'You're a real gambler, Goldberg,' he said.

'You work with what you got. You almost totaled a T-72. Now that tells me you got something.' Goldberg climbed out of the left-hand seat and vanished.

Coolidge decided to ignore the world outside and play a video game; it was too dark to see anything, anyway. He shuttled his eyes back and forth between artificial horizon and altimeter. The plane responded easily. He even began to relax a little. It was sort of dreamy flying along through the murk, the plane held up entirely by Ernest Goldberg's faith. Maybe there was a way out of everything. Maybe he hadn't started World War III. They could always blame it on hotheaded local commanders. The Russians could shoot Ronzhin, and Arlington Prager could be stuck in a broom closet in the Pentagon. Call it pilot error, like the airlines always did. *If* both sides wanted a peaceful solution, there could be a peaceful solution. But it was dangerous. Classically. It had been preceded by a period of tension. Everything was strained to the limit: tempers, organizations, bladders. Human rationality was tenuous at the best of times.

Goldberg wasn't crazy; he was back in sixty seconds.

'There's damage, but I'm not sure how bad. The radio is out, autopilot is out, the gas tanks are, maybe.' He had the wheel back and was climbing. 'I'd prefer to stay low and avoid East German radar, but it could look like we're avoiding West German radar. We'll get out in the clear so the F-15s don't shoot us down by mistake.'

They bounced up through the turbulence and found the moon at eight thousand feet. Goldberg was flying and solving the navigation problem at the same time. Coolidge sat there looking out at sky and thought thoughts. Zombie thoughts, all the nightmares quickly surfacing. A montage of disasters. Vera and Harry, Beebe trying to kill him, a tank chasing him through the night, trying to kill him. Admiral Vasilyev directing the battle of Fulda Gap from a submarine. And over it all, the enigma: the Doctor.

He didn't know how long he had been wandering when he was brought back by Goldberg.

'That's funny.'

'What's funny?'

'Out there.' Goldberg pointed to the windshield.

Coolidge looked. 'There's nothing out there.'

'That's what's funny. We should have been intercepted by now. There should be a fighter on each wing. I can't talk to Mannheim, so I'm a UFO as far as they're concerned.'

'I thought you filed a flight plan.'

'Doesn't matter. I could be a Backfire bomber, for all they know. I think it's time to get down.'

Coolidge was peering out past the windshield wipers, waiting for a panorama to unfold in front of him, like a medium-size city with lights in parallel rows going toward a vanishing point. Or maybe nice baby-blue landing-strip lights. But it was too much to hope for. When they broke into the clear, Goldberg groaned. He leaned forward for a better look and then stood the Gulfstream on its port wing and made a 135-degree left turn.

There was nothing but mountains. Goldberg was back to tapping dials. 'They're not the Alps,' he said. 'I know the Alps. They're not the Black Mountains either; they're too young.'

'Then whose the hell mountains are they?'

Goldberg let out a long sigh. 'They've got to be the Carpathians.'

Coolidge nodded. The Carpathians. Czechoslovakia. It was the end of a perfect day. He was behind the iron curtain in an airplane that maybe was running out of gas, that would be lucky if it *got* to run out of gas before a MIG happened along and shot them down. They had to be on someone's radar by now.

'Compass must have got screwed up and I didn't realize it,' Goldberg said after a while.

'Think we've got enough fuel to get back?'

'I can't tell. I don't know if the gauge or the fuel tank was hit.'

There was nothing to say and they flew in silence for a while.

'If we see a fighter, I'll drop the wheels,' Goldberg said finally. 'Agreed?'

'I guess so.'

More silence.

'I can't figure out how I did it.'

'The plane was damaged. It isn't your fault. If it weren't for you, we'd have crashed on takeoff.'

'I shouldn't have trusted anything. Nothing. I should have known better.' Goldberg suddenly stiffened, as though he had sensed something through his pores. 'Get in the back.'

'What?'

'Get in the back.'

'You need a copilot.'

'I need a goddamn miracle. Get in the back. I'm responsible for you. Take the rearmost seat. Buckle in as tight as you can. Bend over double. Move it.'

Coolidge slid out of the seat. 'Put it down as neatly as you got it up, huh?'

He went all the way to the rear and got in the seat nearest the door. It was a hell of a place for a staff man. As he buckled in, he realized that Goldberg had indeed sensed something. It had gotten quiet in the cabin. The engines had flamed out.

III   O.F.F.

The Defection of Walter Coolidge

Ives had faked enough reports himself to know better. You could say nothing in a highly polished manner, using all the right jargon and buzzwords, the report serving to cover your flanks rather than inform the person for whom the report was intended.

So he wanted to see their faces. He wanted to be able to cross-examine, watch their eyes, be conspiratorial and confidential and man-to-man, it's us against the creeps – which was why they were performing live, via satellite, from Mannheim.

In Beebe's case, there wasn't much face to watch. He was lying on the hospital bed with his head bandaged, sedated out cold. General Prager and Norman Wallace were seated to the left of the bed, looking into the camera. Prager, stone-faced, didn't know yet if he was a hero or a bum. The tanks were now all pulled back and everyone was in his own Germany, at least for the time being. It wasn't World War III after all; it was only an incident. Prager had done his job, protecting Walter Coolidge, whereupon the man for whom he had gone into combat had apparently defected to the Communists. Prager seemed so confused about the meaning of the situation that there was no possibility he would lie now, since he had no way of knowing which way to go.

'What was your reaction to Coolidge and Kalyanov going for a walk?' Ives said to the big screen. He was sitting in the front row of Harry Dunn's screening room, up close so he wouldn't miss any subtle twinges in their faces. 'Were you suspicious about that, or what?'

'It was nothing unusual,' Arlington C. Prager said. 'I understand that sort of thing is common at negotiations with the Russians.'

'I don't care what you understand,' Ives replied testily. 'How did you feel about it? What was your reaction at the moment?'

'It struck me as off-color,' Prager said.

'Why?'

'The two of them had sat there hardly saying a word. Not to each other, to Ronzhin, or to me. All of a sudden they're going for a walk like old buddies.'

'But you didn't do anything about it?'

'Ronzhin got talking about antitank missiles. Maybe he roped me in. I got pretty involved in that aspect. I forgot about Coolidge. After all, my instructions were to protect him. I had no reason to be suspicious of the man.'

Ives was desperate for something, anything. 'How did Coolidge look after the walk?'

'Worried as hell. And confused. Like he didn't know how to act anymore.'

'Did he give you any idea what it was about?'

'No, sir. I certainly had no thought that the man was on the point of defecting.'

'What would you have done if you had?'

Prager looked hard-assed. 'I think he would have died a hero's death in battle.'

Ives took out his cigarette holder and sucked on it. He was getting nowhere. He had to have something to tell the President, who was seething in the White House. Ives glanced around at Harry Dunn, who was in his usual place in the last row, but Harry was out of it.

Dunn couldn't take his eyes off the unconscious Beebe. It was like seeing the Colossus of Rhodes on its ass. And toppled by the Garbageman! He had been fooled completely by Walter Coolidge. Underestimated him, misdiagnosed him. He had thought Coolidge was an open book, a bright man who lacked the courage to be devious and was therefore a straight arrow. He would never have entertained for a moment the thought that Coolidge might be a potential defector.

It just showed you. The quicksilver human psyche. You never knew what the hell it would do. The uncertainty principle all over again. The fact that you were interacting with it changed it. Had he gone too far with Vera? Damn.

216

He hadn't thought anything could touch Coolidge that much. In his soul Coolidge was an anthropologist; people were data, Washington was in its pre-Pompeiian phase, and Coolidge had the wonderful opportunity of examining the artifacts *before* the lava hit. Did anything really touch Walter Coolidge? He hadn't thought so. He was wrong.

'Look, I'll get you off the hook,' Harry said. 'I'll resign. Blame it on me.'

'Will you stop resigning, for Christ sake,' Ives replied. He was busy with the display, studying Wallace. Wallace, State Department poker player, was sitting there calm and unreadable.

'What do you think, Norman?' Ives said to him. 'I mean, on a gut level. Let's forget what's on paper.'

Wallace glanced at the prostrate Beebe and there seemed to be the merest idea of the beginnings of a smile on his face.

'On the one hand, I have to agree that it looks suspicious. Before Mr. Beebe here took his pills, he told me about the conversation Walter had with Kalyanov. Apparently it was an engrossing little chat. It seemed to Mr. Beebe to be more than passing the time of day. Furthermore, he felt that he had been deliberately excluded from the conversation. Then there was Walter's claim to have totaled – that's his word – a Soviet T-72 tank. That's improbable, but I never got a chance to ask him how he'd done it. In any case, no one could find the wreckage of a T-72. Maybe the T-72 was something he had cooked up to get me out of there in a hurry, although he might have come up with a more plausible lie than *that*. Okay, then there's the pilot, Goldberg. He's got a reputation for being something of a flake, I understand. You could make a case. Mannheim radar, of course, tracked them going straight for Czechoslovakia until they went out of range. That certainly looks bad. On the other hand, he didn't seem the type.'

Ives was holding his head in his hands. Mannheim tracking them to Czechoslovakia looked bad. The phone was going to ring any second and he had nothing but on the one hand and on the other hand. The really odd thing was that Coolidge's message seemed right. It was the ideal news from America's point of view, from an O.F.F. point of view. Vasilyev was worried. Terrific; Vasilyev was getting the message. Russian knees would be shaking. Russian will would be eroding, crumbling away. There would have been jubilation in the White House if Coolidge hadn't disappeared. Did that mean the message was compromised and Vasilyev *wasn't* worried?

The door opened. It was Vera, in from the cold of Connecticut Avenue, three-in-the-morning cold, which was the time you were most likely to die. Hands deep in her coat pockets, she walked briskly up the stairs to the rear of Harry's screening room, where the console was, and sat down without taking her coat off. Directly in front of her, Harry was catatonic, working on a nervous breakdown, there being no analysis to make, no problem solving to do. A Librarian had defected to Russia; that was the beginning and the end. It was worse than the Mitchell and Martin case, when analysts for the National Security Agency had turned up on Moscow television. Coolidge knew much more than they had.

Beebe, Prager, and Wallace were taking up only three screens on the front wall; there were two more to play with. Vera started playing, doing input with the speed of a pool typist, pulling in data from everywhere.

'GULFSTREAM II
'FUEL: 200 POUNDS
'AZIMUTH 135°
'RANGE 175 MILES'

Then satellite photos began to fly past on her two screens. Ives found himself watching in fascination; it was like being in a Mach 3 airplane flying over East Germany into Czechoslovakia. Vera began to slow down. There was a natural tension building, although Ives couldn't figure out what was going to happen. The pictures were clicking on, slower and slower, staying up on the screens longer, getting more scrutiny from Vera's educated eye. He sensed that behind him even Harry was stirring from his torpor. There was a purpose to what Vera was doing and it was a relief to get away from the uncertainties and watch like a spectator. Finally she stopped on one picture. She blew it up double. Then double again. Then double and double and double again.

The phone rang and Ives picked it up absently while still looking at the screen. 'Holy shit,' he said, and then had to apologize to the President before exultantly describing what was up on the screen.

Alert again, Harry Dunn lumbered to his feet and floated down to get a close look at the screen, at a faint grainy smear somewhere in the Carpathian Mountains: it was a crashed airplane with the word 'Vera' painted on the starboard wing.

'Latitude fifty-one degrees forty-three minutes north, longitude thirteen degrees seventeen minutes east,' Vera said to them. 'I'll have photomaps made of the area.' She was coming back down the stairs, her hands buried in her pockets again. 'He's got a cold,' she added. 'The rescue team ought to take along some chicken soup,' and she was out the door.

The Carpathian Blues

Warm feet was Goldberg's profession; it was his firm belief that as long as your feet were warm you were alive. He was sitting on a rock letting the tiny fire play over his boots, extracting every last Btu possible. Coolidge, squatting, was trying to keep everything warm so that his cold wouldn't turn lethal. The sun, strained through miles of haze, was yielding as much warmth as the moon. The temperature was on the mortal side of zero.

Goldberg shook his head. 'You really screwed up with that T-72,' he said. 'You don't have the killer instinct, Walter. You were trying to let nature take its course and do the job for you, when you should have gone in and finished him off. They were helpless. There is no more desirable military target.'

Coolidge glanced over at the ridge a mile or so to the south and watched the line of brown ants moving along it.

'Easy enough for a big-shot military type to say,' he replied. 'My jeep was a piece of Swiss cheese. I had no weapon. If I'd had a grenade, I might have crawled out on that bridge and dropped it down the turret. I'm not sure. Maybe. Give me the benefit of the doubt. But I didn't have a grenade.'

'If you had the killer instinct, you would have thought of something.'

'Okay, killer, what would you have done?'

Goldberg checked to see if his feet were on fire and squinted his eyes for a moment. Then he yawned. 'I'd have made a Molotov cocktail with the jeep's gasoline.'

'What would you have put the gasoline in?'

'Hell, there must have been something lying around. The fluid jar for the windshield wipers.'

'Damn.'

'Face it, Walter, you're just not tough enough. You don't do what has to be done.'

'Look who's talking.'

Goldberg, who had once been a B-52 pilot, said, 'Well, I used to be tough.'

'What's it like?'

'I forget.'

Coolidge was keeping his eye on the ants. They were getting to be big ants. Before too long they were going to turn into the Czech Army. A helicopter had flown over the wreck for a close look, but Goldberg had pointed his .45 at it and they had scrammed. After that, the helicopters came down on the other side of the ridge; Goldberg's .45 had put the fear of God into them.

He looked over at Goldberg. Short, stocky, powerful. He was lighting up the last of Coolidge's prop cigars with a burning twig. Coolidge was awed by the fact that Goldberg had ferried twenty megatons in his bomb bay for eight years, until they were dropping them by accident so often that SAC finally had to store the bombs away for a rainy day.

Goldberg had good instincts. At thirty-eight, he was probably at the peak of his abilities. Crash landing a plane in the middle of a mountain range took instinct. It was like speed chess, too fast for thought; your nervous system knew how to do it or it didn't. The plane had plowed up huge clouds of snow laced with rocks, the rocks bouncing back and forth between the ground and the fuselage like machine gun fire. With his head down, Coolidge kept staring at his seat belt, fascinated by it, hoping it could stand the gaff. Then the turmoil had stopped and quiet returned; they were on the ground, alive. Coolidge was still staring at his seat belt when Goldberg came heeling and toeing back down the aisle, looking pale. 'Thank you for flying with us,' he said, passing. 'Have a nice day.'

Then, when they'd dropped out of the airplane and scrambled through the snow for fifty yards, Goldberg suddenly stopped and looked back. He did his phony rabbi's voice. 'One advantage of running out of fuel,' he pronounced sagely, 'is that in the ensuing wreck, there's nothing to burn.'

Now, puffing on his cigar, Goldberg smiled.

'That's pathetic,' he said, pointing to the plane about a hundred yards from where they were huddled, sheltered against the wind. There were rocks on the starboard wing spelling out 'Vera.' 'That's like putting a message in a cornflakes box and dropping it in the Arctic Ocean.'

'That just shows how far behind the times you are, Ernie. I mean, you're really out of date. It's like sending a telegram.'

Goldberg looked out at the approaching ants, which were getting distinctly bigger. 'You mean to say you think we're going to get rescued before they get here?'

Coolidge's head rocked from side to side as he considered it. 'I'll put it this way. Something's going to happen before they get here,' not believing that a Librarian would be allowed to fall, still breathing, into the hands of Communists.

'My ass is theirs no matter what happens,' Goldberg said, sounding morose for the first time. 'The Russians get me for an overflight. Or the USAF gets me for doing it accidentally instead of on purpose. They'll be calling me Wrong Way Goldberg.'

'You know, I think I've got you figured out, Goldberg. You're a sore loser.'

'What did I lose?'

'You lost out to missiles. You're a bomber pilot in the missile age. You've been obsolete for your entire professional life. I'll bet that's what your problem is.'

Goldberg blew out a cubic yard to smoke and steam and stared at the end of his cigar, which was going fast. 'You're wrong, Walter. It's the missile that's obsolete.'

Coolidge had to smile; the absurdities were piling up. Where would it all end? 'I didn't know that,' he said.

'The missiles are a farce. Anybody with any sense knows that.' Goldberg was speaking the obvious. His voice was casual; it was old hat as far as he was concerned. 'There's never been a successful test of a frontline, Minuteman silo, and they've tried. Or an MX. All those things do is provide billets for more generals. I thought everyone knew that. The Russian SS-18 is even worse. Liquid fuel, for God's sake. We stopped making those in the nineteen fifties. No, that's not my problem.'

Coolidge sniffed. He was out of tissues. 'Are you saying Minuteman and MX are no good?'

'No, I'm saying no one knows whether they're any good or not. They've never been successfully tested in an operational silo, only test silos. It's elementary engineering, Walter. You never know you can do something until you actually do it. The B-52 is the only reliable weapon in the inventory.'

'That sounds nuts.'

'It is nuts. The Pentagon is cracked.'

'They can't all be cracked.'

'All of them. Cracked. I'll tell you, I don't even know what everybody is worried about. The Russian SS-18s leak, their nuclear subs are noisy as hell and don't have anyplace to hide, and their bomber force isn't worth a damn: one hundred fifty bombers, and fifty are prop planes.'

'But if tne Pentagon is cracked, the Congress has to be cracked too. They appropriate the money.'

'That's right. The Congress is cracked.'

'And the White House.'

'Cracked.'

Coolidge sniffled.

'I'd much rather talk about coffee tables,' Goldberg said. 'I'm figuring on getting me a place on the ocean somewhere and making coffee tables.'

'Ernie, maybe you ought to start beating your arms together.'

Goldberg looked serious. 'I'm going to make the coffee tables out of driftwood. There's some pretty good driftwood floating around. People get their hands on it, they put it in the fireplace. They don't know it's valuable stuff. I'm pretty good with wood.'

'You intend to make a living out of driftwood?'

'I figure fifteen hundred bucks per table. People will pay it. I'll sell them through fancy designer places. A table and a half a month and I could swing it. I'd need about a six-months stake to get started. To collect wood and my head.'

'Hey, I've got a name for your operation. The Flotsam Furniture Company.'

'It isn't Italian enough,' Goldberg replied.

The Czech Army had now crossed a significant, if imaginary, point. They were in easy rifle range, in a position to shoot down helicopters, which meant that the rescue option was losing its plausibility. The easy way out, destroying Walter Coolidge, was growing more likely with every passing second. The thought occurred to Coolidge that at this point he might be safer if he ran down the slope and joined the Czech Army.

'The status quo isn't going to stay status,' he said to Goldberg. They were both standing now, watching the troops approaching. He was shaken but not surprised when he saw something falling through the dim haze. Something winged, something maneuverable. 'It's a cruise missile,' Coolidge said. 'They're taking us out with a cruise missile.' It was the logic of the situation, inevitable, an imperative of state power.

Goldberg shook his head. 'The angle of approach is all wrong for a cruise missile.'

Coolidge was baffled. Was there some kind of flying maneuverable bomb he had never heard of? Had the Pentagon managed to slip one by everybody, not directly funded, paid for out of various contingency funds?

'It's a man.'

'What is?' Coolidge said, still baffled.

'Your missile. It's a man. A sky diver. There's no piece of ordnance that could fall like that. Question is, is he one of theirs or one of ours?'

The Czechs opened fire on the sky diver.

'Ours,' Coolidge said.

The sky diver was pushing his luck. He was holding back, holding back, in a hurry to get down. He was made out of balls. He didn't pull the rip cord until three hundred feet off the ground, and the chute didn't open fully until seconds before he hit. As he touched down hard, his crash helmet flew off and they could see that his head was bandaged. They'd sent the best: it was Beebe.

'I told you it was a telegram,' Coolidge said.

It was spellbinding to watch Beebe at work; among his many accomplishments, he was a master parachutist. Even the Czechs looked amazed; they were close enough for Coolidge to see their faces. They actually hesitated a few seconds, watching him, before taking aim. It was as though even his least movement had been rehearsed until it was rote. Beebe had the harness off and was doing a limping run toward the Gulfstream. He had jumped with explosives on him; he was assembling charges and detonators as he ran zigzag to avoid the bullets that kicked little puffs of snow around him. Goldberg and Coolidge, spectators, immobilized, watched him disappear into the broken fuselage for ten seconds; then he was out, running toward them.

'This way,' Beebe shouted, going past them doing his tilted, off balance run like an eccentric cam. He knew exactly where he was going; Vera must have briefed him on every footstep. Goldberg and Coolidge looked at each other with a mixture of amazement and panic, then took off after the disappearing Beebe, shots beginning to ping against the rock of the ledge they had been hiding behind.

Beebe was going up ridges, down ridges, along ridges, plowing through snow as he careened down into shallow vales, twisting, turning. Coolidge lost all sense of direction until he heard the Gulfstream blow up. The trend was mainly downhill or Coolidge wouldn't have been able to keep up; he was running a bad third. This made no sense since he was the one the rescue was about, but he ignored the contradiction and lumbered on, gasping.

Beebe had picked the site with the eye of an infantryman. It was behind a low ridge, windblown, only a few inches of snow, a clear field of fire, roughly seventy-five yards, which the Czechs would have to attack across. He took out orange marking tapes from the lower left pocket of his jumpsuit and made a big X in the snow. Then he produced a radio out of the lower right pocket.

'Come in,' he said into it, and then threw the radio away into the snow.

They had been hovering somewhere out of sight, out of

earshot. Now the two choppers clattered in over a ridge to the west and were on the ground in seconds. Coolidge was sitting on his heels taking big breaths, while Goldberg stood next to him, panting.

'You get more important all the time,' Goldberg said between pants. 'A helicopter tanker. I didn't know there was such a thing. They must have invented it for you.'

The pilot of the smaller chopper was already out and running a hose to the bigger troop carrier. At the same time, Beebe was deploying an eight-man army along the ridge, facing east, waiting for the Czechs. They had machine guns and mortars. Ammunition cases were lying in the snow everywhere. The two mortars were being quickly leveled on their base plates, bolts were sliding home, clips clicking into place.

'Demonstrate first,' Beebe called out to them. 'Is that understood?'

The Czechs were now visible a hundred yards off, hesitating before the big white empty expanse in front of them. Coolidge crawled to the ridge. A few helmets were visible agaisnt the snow, and one man, probably the officer, was peering through field glasses.

'Commence firing,' Beebe said.

It was a convincing demonstration. They raked the field mercilessly with machine gun and mortar fire. Any sane troop commander would have to have visions of World War I as he contemplated charging through all that steel, and there wouldn't be enough time to take the easy way and flank Beebe's position.

Coolidge was beginning to feel optimistic; if the idea was to avoid Czech casualties, thereby reducing the scope of the incident, then there mustn't be a war on in East Germany. It seemed logical, anyway. The barrage continued for five minutes until the tanker pilot signaled that he was finished.

Goldberg shook his head in admiration. 'Piece of cake,' he said. 'We'll disappear over the ridge, come up a couple of miles away, pick up a flight of F-15s, and sail home.' He climbed into the chopper.

Coolidge hesitated while Beebe planted charges on the now empty tanker; there wasn't enough fuel to get both choppers to West Germany. As he came hustling back, Coolidge said, 'Is there a war on?'

Beebe grimaced. 'Climb in and eat your damn chicken soup,' he said.

The President's Kneecap

'You look positively terminal,' Yeager was saying, sipping coffee, eyes oscillating back and forth from Coolidge to the other tables, checking for points of interest, threats, whatever. 'Are your affairs in order?'

Coolidge took a big swallow of scalding coffee and was reassured when it hurt going down: it meant he was alive. He had reached the point where his fatigue had bottomed out; additional fatigue caused no further change, hardly seemed to matter. His nose was stuffed and his ears still ached from all the flying. He had gone from the Carpathians to Mannheim (where he'd left Goldberg with his commanding officer and Beebe back in the hospital), and then on to Dulles in Virginia, where Yeager had picked him up for the quick flight to Roanoke. Both of his knees were bandaged because of gashes he'd received when his jeep went flying in East Germany, and again when his plane stopped flying in Czechoslovakia. The dry fall weather had brought the eczema back on his legs and arms, but he was too tired to scratch.

'It's the eyes they watch for,' Yeager was saying quietly. He meant the Secret Service men sitting at the next table. They were all in a private lounge at one end of the airfield, awaiting for the President's plane. 'The killing impulse appears in the eyeballs before it reaches for the weapon. Those guys are like psychiatrists who only handle one kind of patient.'

There was an Air Force major too, seated alone at a third table, keeping very much to himself, eating a sandwich and drinking coffee right-handed because his left wrist was chained to an attaché case.

Things were upside down. For a while, Coolidge had

been worried that he had started World War III. It was pleasant to find out he hadn't. But as soon as he landed at Dulles, Yeager told him the President was rehearsing a procedure that would only be used in the event of World War III. He was airborne in NEACP, the National Emergency Airborne Command Post – or Kneecap, as it was called. Kneecap was going to be in Roanoke for just about two minutes, long enough to take Coolidge aboard.

They didn't fool around when they were holding a Kneecap exercise. There were sixteen legally designated heirs to the presidency, and all sixteen would now be safely ensconced in shelters called Presidential Emergency Facilities, or PEFs, located along the Federal Relocation Arc, which extended north and south of the District of Columbia.

Yeager was periodically breaking up at the thought of old Chatterton, President Pro Tempore of the Senate and third in line. Chatterton, intermittently senile, intermittently sober, would be tucked away in a PEF somewhere, maybe the third basement of a brewery, wondering what in hell had happened; this didn't *look* like the Senate dining room.

The provoking quality of a Kneecap exercise was that they never made any attempt to keep it secret. Which would have been difficult in any case, since there was no way the sixteen successors could suddenly disappear from Washington without an anchorman noticing. But that was part of the exercise. It was at once a chance to see how the plan worked and a warning to the Soviet government: The U.S. government means business.

Coolidge was always astonished about people who didn't worry about such things. Like Yeager. Yeager was unconcerned. Yeager had faith. A nuclear alert was just an element in the mix. He was much more concerned with face. 'You know, I'm one-upped by all this,' he said. 'The President is interrupting his end-of-the-world exercise to land in this burg solely for the purpose of picking you up. While I take a tin lizzy back to Washington. I mean, let's face it – I'm more important than you are.'

A thousand-cycle tone sounded and all five men sitting in the lounge reached for their pagers. It was for one of the

Secret Service men. He got up and left the lounge, returned in a minute, and waved to them.

'Enjoy the party,' Yeager said, bored, abandoned, now free to have his first drink of the day.

'It's going to be a barrel of laughs,' Coolidge said, following the agents and the Air Force major out through the swinging doors of the lounge.

Coolidge stood quietly on the taxi strip in the dusk as Kneecap came in for a landing. He was trying to think of what to say. You couldn't hem and haw when reporting to the President of the United States. You were supposed to be brisk, terse, cogent. The only one of the three he felt like was terse.

How was he going to tell them they'd all been suckered by the Russians? That the Soviet garbage can in East Germany was bait designed to get Harry Dunn to dispatch Walter Coolidge (familiarly known as Vladimir in certain circles of the Kremlin) to East Germany at the request of a Soviet admiral, Vasilyev, and that all of it intersected with the question of a spy in the Library, the Doctor, the alleged leader of the alleged American peace movement. That, in short, the data tree had got out of hand and the forked lightning was reaching out dangerously in all directions.

Then there was the problem of trying to capture the essence of Kalyanov's words, tone, manner. That's what a good ambassador did, and Coolidge had been thrust into precisely that role. It was serious duty; it might change the course of events to the degree that it influenced that piece of disputed territory, the President's brain.

Kneecap taxied up and a small contingent of Air Force rolled the steps up to it. The Secret Service was still gimlet-eyed. The Air Force major was unlocking his wrist. As the door opened, Harry appeared waving. He quickly signed a receipt for the attaché case, then shook hands with Coolidge. 'Welcome back, Walter,' he said, giving it all the warmth he had. 'Come on, strap in, we're taking off.'

It was a small compartment with only six rows of seats. There was one double seat, which Harry could buckle into comfortably; it was the one used by the chairman of the

House Armed Forces Committee, who weighed in at 270.

Harry was looking squeamish as he unlocked the attaché case. The plane was already taxiing back toward the runway. 'I can understand why you did what you did to Beebe, and that's all right, no problem, but you didn't have to; he had no orders from me to do anything rash where you were concerned. I wouldn't want you carrying that idea around in your head.'

While he was talking, he was rapidly going through the documents in the attaché case. Coolidge sneaked a look and realized why they had been chained to the major's wrist; they were targeting maps of the Soviet Union prepared by the Defense Mapping Agency. It was terrifying to see them. They were for the Pershing 2 missiles that had been positioned in NATO countries. The maps provided steering data for the Pershing 2 computer and they were among the most secret documents in government. Coolidge didn't like the idea of seeing those maps on Kneecap; he had just escaped from a war. Harry closed the case and wrote a tag, which he attached to the handle. Things were continuing to stay upside down: The tag read, 'For Yeager.' Yeager was operational, not a courier. Normally he would have been the last man in government to get data like that.

The maps revealed the targets the Pershing 2s were programmed for. They were of the highest strategic – and political – importance. It was the kind of stuff the Doctor and the Emersons could have some real fun with, if they *were* a peace movement. Show aggressive American targeting doctrine, war-fighting rather than retaliation, destruction of Soviet command and control. If they did it right they could make a big splash. Maybe the Emersons *were* a peace group. Led by Doctor Harry? Why Yeager, he kept wondering. Yeager? He found himself staring at Harry in puzzlement; he would have to check the computer about that little operation.

But Harry was already on the move. They were only about five hundred feet up, but he unbuckled, ignoring the seat belt sign, and led Coolidge back through the plane, talking, talking. About how well the Game was going, how there weren't nearly as many screwups as in the past, how they were getting their act together, how the Library was now dominant, the President was listening to Harry more than to CIA, DIA, ONI, all of them. The Library was number one.

It was dim everywhere, which added to the sense of urgency in the plane. Kneecap was a stripped-down 747 reequipped with computers, radars, plotting consoles, and tons of communications equipment. It was the place from which the President could direct a nuclear war, presumably in total safety. The compartments were illuminated mainly by pilot lights and radar and computer displays. Like the lights, the voices were subdued. And busy. The Game was keeping them on their toes. Harry walked through the place as if he owned it, moving past one compartment after another until they reached a door with the presidential seal on it. He actually knocked before opening it.

The President and Ives were bent over a chattering printer, frowning. It was the only piece of hardware in the room. Otherwise it was quite livable. Couches, easy chairs, a bar, port-to-starboard carpeting. The President looked up, smiled, took his glasses off. 'The man of the hour,' he said, holding out a hand. 'How are you, Walter? Gene, the war stops while you make a drink for this man.'

Coolidge was getting the full treatment. A two-handed handshake from the President. Ives patting him on the back. Harry beaming proudly, his prize pupil having distinguished himself.

The President tore a sheet out of the printer. 'Harry,' he said, 'this is totally unacceptable. You guaranteed me twenty million maximum. I can handle twenty, maybe twenty-five. No more than that.'

'What's it running?'

'We're going to end up with forty-five million.'

Harry shook his head. 'Something's wrong.' He quickly scanned the printout, frowned, went to the tray where the printouts were piling up, and went through them rapidly. Coolidge stood there awkwardly.

'Here it is,' Harry said. 'They're underestimating MX accuracy. I don't know why they keep doing this. Circular Error Probable for the MX is 150 yards, *not* 225 yards.

232

Change these figures from 225 back to 150 and you'll be inside twenty million because you won't be destroying 98.32 percent of their warheads, you'll be destroying 99.98 percent.

'Well, let's get that straightened out, Harry. Are my missiles accurate or aren't they? Forty-five million would ruin me politically. And maybe the party too. Got any jet lag, Walter?'

'A little, sir,' Coolidge answered, fighting to keep his eyes open.

'I'll tell you a secret. I'd rather this didn't get out: The President of the United States *always* has jet lag.'

Ives handed Coolidge a triple Canadian on the rocks and the President put an arm around his shoulder, leading him over to a couch after maneuvering past a coffee table. Coolidge checked without even thinking about it; it wasn't made of driftwood.

'Another thing, Harry,' the President said. 'There's something perverse going on here.'

Dunn landed gently on a delicate-looking straight-back chair on the other side of the coffee table. He sagged over the sides.

The President sailed another printout across the coffee table. 'I don't understand these defense intellectuals,' he said to Coolidge. 'Supposedly, one of our best men is fighting a nuclear war with me right now and he doesn't blow up my capital. He drops two each on Houston and Dallas, but nothing on the Capitol dome. Does that make sense to you?'

Coolidge shook his head. Let Harry handle that one. Harry was busily reading the printout. There was a slow nod of recognition as his eyes traveled over the entries. 'It looks like the Shannon touch,' he said. 'I hadn't realized Shannon was in the exercise.'

'We can find out easily enough,' Ives said. A phone and a martini were on the bar next to each other. He picked up both.

'You see, Mr. President, there are some disagreements about Soviet strategic targeting doctrine,' Harry said. 'Let's say we reach 99.96 percent accuracy and they have only a dozen warheads left. How do they use them? What targets do they pick? What strategic thought would they use in picking those targets?'

Coolidge sipped at his whiskey gingerly, not wanting to wreck what little mental alertness he had left; sooner or later they were going to get around to him. How was he going to handle it? Through the haze of alcohol and exhaustion he was trying to find something he needed desperately: a point of view.

'Conventional wisdom has it,' Harry was saying, 'that the Russians would use their last dozen or so warheads to hurt us as much as possible. Washington. New York. Boston Bos-Wash, as they call it. Detroit. Chi-Pitts. S.F. Houston. So on. That way they'd hurt us economically and demographically. Maximum hurt.'

Ives put down the phone. 'You were right, Harry. Shannon is playing commanding general of the Soviet Strategic Rocket Force.'

Harry looked pleased with himself. 'It's written all over the printout. Shannon's idea is that the Soviets would be more rational about it. They wouldn't go for a maximum hurt, which would basically be a revenge firing. Remember, at this stage we'll have destroyed their weapons, except for those few warheads, so it's all over and they know it. The U.S. has won. The U.S. will dictate peace terms. The U.S. will dominate the postwar world. What can they possibly do to help themselves with those last few warheads? Shannon says they'd attempt to improve the postwar political environment by hitting only conservative cities. So they'd leave the northeast corridor alone. Bos-Wash would be untouched. They'd hit San Diego and maybe part of Orange County: San-San would become San-L.A. Chi-Pitts might even get off. They'd basically hit the South, some Midwest, some mountain states. That means San Diego, Phoenix, Dallas, Houston, New Orleans, Kansas City, Saint Louis, Omaha, a few others. The idea being that a nuclear war would end up turning the U.S. from a conservative country into a liberal country. A liberal country would be easier on the Russians in the postwar world than a conservative country would be.'

The President looked resentful. 'That's the god-damndest thing I ever heard of.' He was almost stut-

234

tering. 'I mean, that's fiendish. Do you think they'd really attempt to change the political character of the nation?'

Harry shrugged. 'Anything's possible, I suppose. If it were my decision, I'd go for GNP. Weaken America's economic base as much as possible. Power grows out of GNP.'

'Well, that's what I think. I mean, *two* warheads on both Houston and Dallas and nothing on New York? That's outrageous.'

'Shannon is something of a gadfly,' Harry replied. 'He likes to be unconventional. It's self-advertising.'

'Damn,' the President said. 'Look, I don't want to read about this on the front page of the *New York Times*. It's subversive.'

'Yes, sir.'

'The problems you run into,' the President said, shaking his head in bafflement. He turned to Coolidge. 'But this Vasilyev fellow seems to be running into a few himself. He's worried, huh?'

'Yes, sir.'

'You know we were all watching on microcam. Brilliant performance, Walter. Gene here was rolling in the aisle; your timing was unbelievable. I see it was a real cold.'

'Yes, sir.'

'Okay, now tell us what happened. First, what did you pick out of that trash can? We've been playing games with that one for days.'

He felt like saying: an atomic bomb. It was salary-earning time. How had a lowly anthropologist reached the point where he was flying in the President's airplane, about to blow the lid off a Library scandal? The Library, the Sacred Grotto. All Eyes. Harry's cozy little Department of Peace and Quiet. Shot through with a leak that went straight to the Kremlin. And with Harry himself as a possible candidate. He looked at them. All eyes were upon him. They almost looked like kids about to open a gift. He couldn't decide if the bravest thing was to tell them . . . or not tell them. It would be responsible not to tell them. That would mean taking it all on his shoulders. Harry could be the Doctor. Ives could be. The possibility was there. There wasn't any choice as it ran through his mind.

There was only one responsible way to handle it.

'It was nothing,' he told them. 'It was a doodle from Kalyanov's notebook.'

'Let's see it.'

'I ate it.'

Ives spluttered. 'You mean to say World War Three almost started over a doodle?' Then he fell back in a chair and had a crazy laugh.

Coolidge strained and managed to get the ends of his lips up in a smile. Then he told them about his walk with Kalyanov, leaving out only two words: Garbageman and Doctor.

'Did you believe what he was telling you?' the President said.

'I believed it,' Coolidge said. 'I don't think it was easy for him to talk about humiliation the way he did.'

'Uh huh.'

'He implied very strongly that humiliation might push them over the edge. In other words, if we pushed them too far, there was a possibility that their hawks might force a nuclear war. It might not be stoppable.'

'Tchk,' the President said out of the corner of his mouth.

'What do you know,' Ives said.

'We've got them,' Harry said.

Coolidge was sitting on a couch, flying sideways, a whiskey in his hand, three big shots peering eagerly at him. He felt as though he were getting a tan, with so much high-level attention; but they didn't seem to be getting the message.

'I had the distinct impression,' he said, 'that there are serious disagreements in the Soviet high command about how to handle the situation in Germany. There seems to be a degree of chaos. I feel I should point out that it wasn't the armored generals who sought me out; it was an admiral.'

'Well, naturally,' Ives said. 'The sea is the decisive factor. Without that we'd be nowhere.'

'What's O.F.F. now?' the President said.

'86.42 percent,' Harry replied with considerable satisfaction.

The President was thoughtfully holding his Scotch up to the light. 'How long is it going to take, Harry?'

'Not much longer. Few weeks. Months, maybe. There *is* an element of chance involved. It's an opportunity, remember.'

'Of course.'

Ives was aroused over the glittering prospects. O.F.F was making everything possible, *everything*. He couldn't sit down, thinking about it. 'You'll have the greatest foreign policy triumph in history,' he said. 'They'll build a Greek temple for you across Constitution Avenue.' Harry and the President were starting to laugh. 'I'm serious. We ought to set up a site committee. Figure out where to put your memorial. You're bound to get one. It's going to be as impressive as the Lincoln. Look what's coming up: We'll be rolling the Commies back in the Caribbean, Cuba, Central America. Then on to Africa. The liberals complain about conservatives wanting to turn back the clock? They ain't seen nothing yet. Nineteen seventeen, here we come!'

The President leaned forward on the couch and looked around at the others. 'Nineteen seventeen is ambitious. I hope so. The question is, can we at least get to Eastern Europe before I have to leave office? Unify Germany. Liberate Poland, Hungary, Czechoslovakia, Rumania, Bulgaria. Why should my successor get all the glory?'

'Do you really want to liberate Bulgaria, Mr. President?' Ives said, getting another laugh.

'What do you think about all of this, Walter?' the President asked. 'Sound crazy?'

Coolidge's political instincts were terrible, but he knew better than to spoil the party. It was not the moment for nuts and bolts questions, doubts, speculations. 'Sounds marvelous, Mr. President. I recommend *this* side of Constitution Avenue. The Ellipse.' The park behind the White House was the most prestigious piece of empty space in Washington, D.C. It would take nothing less than a combination of Lincoln and Alexander the Great to have it used as the site for a memorial.

'Very good, Walter,' Harry said. 'There's your first site recommendation, gentlemen.'

'Not bad,' Ives said. 'Walter, you can be on the site committee.'

'All I hope, gentlemen, is that I've accurately conveyed to you the essence of what I heard in East Germany.'

'Relax, Walter,' Harry said. 'I'm sure you have. In essence, you're saying that there's panic in the Kremlin. They're stuck. They don't know what to do. I'm not trying to downgrade your own importance in all this, but it's a measure of the panic they're in that they gave you the message to pass on to us. Why would they pick you? You were someone who'd shown up at the negotiations. I figure they had you pegged as, say, a deputy under secretary. Something at about that level, right? They were grasping at straws.'

It was a natural opening. Now was the time to tell them that, well, uh, no, Kalyanov hadn't exactly taken him for a deputy under secretary of state; Kalyanov thought he was the Doctor; Kalyanov thought he was negotiating with the Emersons. He let it go by, clinging to the principle of responsibility.

'Yeah,' he said. 'Deputy under secretary. Something like that.'

'Hell,' the President put in, sipping his Scotch contentedly. 'They aren't even a superpower. They've got half our GNP; they're not in the same league with us.'

Harry, ecstatic, raised his glass. 'Here's to the beginning of it. To when the Russians pull their tanks back from the frontier because you, Mr. President, order them to.'

'Cheers,' the President said.

'Amen,' Ives said.

They dropped Coolidge in Mobile, then soared away, continuing the exercise, Harry staying aboard because being with the President was the only activity important enough to keep him away from the Library. Coolidge found himself sitting alone in the airport waiting room, drunk from his triple Canadian, sniffling, ears aching again, no longer able to think, slowly becoming aware that his German trip was ending as it had begun, with a migraine.

But at least he knew now how to find out who the Doctor was.

238

A Doctor's Appointment

Coolidge got to his apartment after 2 A.M. and went straight to the painkillers he had left over from his last brush with a dentist. He took three of them, trying to head off the monster that was growing in his brain, and fell asleep. He woke up eleven hours later and took two more, stopping only to listen to his telephone answering machine before going back to bed. It was a babble. Vera four times; Harry's secretary, Phoebe, eleven times; Burnish twice. He went back to sleep for another nine hours. When he woke up the second time, it was ten at night, but his head was okay; his cold was almost gone and he had energy back. He didn't get to the Library until it was almost midnight, hoping to have the place to himself.

Burnish was there. He was worse than Harry; the Library was home to him. Burnish's *home* was his home away from home. He was cleaning the place up, which he'd decided was easier and safer than shutting everything down, drawing the drapes, and bringing in one of those FBI cleaning women. He was polishing the round table when Coolidge walked in.

'Hiya, sweets!' Burnish said in his joke gay falsetto. 'Everybody's been looking for you. You look fresh as a daisy; you haven't been sleeping, have you?' Burnish was serious. 'Welcome back. Have some coffee; I'll make it fresh.'

Burnish dropped his polishing cloth and went at the coffee urn with the grace of a short-order cook. If you were willing to put in overtime at the Library, he would do anything for you. Coolidge went to his position at the table, blew his nose, rubbed his eyes, took out the painkillers and nose drops, and put them alongside his keyboard. The screens were jumping all over the place; the world never slept. He cleared the big display up on the opposite wall, wondering how many hours it would take – or days or months – to find the KGB's connection to the Emersons.

Either the Emersons were a KGB operation or they had been infiltrated by the KGB. If it were a KGB operation, Kalyanov wouldn't have been pleading with the Doctor for help; he would simply have issued orders. Therefore it was infiltration. Furthermore, Kalyanov had to know that merely by admitting to his knowledge of the Emersons and the Doctor, he was compromising the infiltrator. It was an indication of how seriously the Russians took the situation in Germany. It also meant that by now the infiltrator would have been pulled out.

Coolidge entered the names of all the known Emersons. He called for a relationship tree, so the computer would expand its coverage to all friends, associates, and relatives of all of them. Then he asked for a correlation against all airline departures from the United States in the preceding week. It took the computer thirty seconds.

Reinhold Kunstner, executive assistant to California businessman Glenn Ingalls, who was known to be an important member of the Emersons, had flown to Paris aboard Pan Am flight 342 twenty-four hours earlier and connected there for an Aeroflot flight to East Berlin.

Coolidge asked for all biographical data on Reinhold Kunstner and the screen filled with what amounted to Kunstner's résumé: previous jobs, residences, education, military service. Coolidge began checking out each item in reverse chronological order. The Library's computer was plugged into Social Security, the banking system, the Census Bureau, all major data banks. Burnish interrupted with coffee and Coolidge, playing it safe, popped a painkiller. He kept chasing Kunstner through the labyrinth. Three years back, Kunstner's résumé began to fall apart. Nonexistent companies, residences no longer in existence. The military records computer in Kansas had no entry for a Reinhold Kunstner with the given birth date and Social Security number.

Three-quarters of an hour. The computer was earning its pay.

Coolidge sipped coffee and ignored Burnish, who was still puttering around. He was quietly amazed that the KGB knew more about the Emersons than the Library did. Glenn Ingalls owned a computer company in Silicon Valley; it was barely possible that Kunstner had been assigned the job of stealing technology from Ingalls and had then stumbled on the Emersons.

He decided to start with Ingalls, and fed in all the magic words: Garvey, Senator, Library, Emerson, Doctor. Then he asked for all of Ingalls's phone calls, correspondence, and telexes in which those words occurred. It was a big request, and the word PROCESSING immediately appeared on the screen. It would keep the monster busy for a while. Coolidge went to the urn for a refill.

'Okay, sweets,' Burnish said to him. 'See you in the morning. Don't forget to turn the coffee off when you leave.' Then he actually went out the door, to visit his wife in his home away from home. Coolidge drifted back to his place, glad that Burnish was gone. It was just him and the computer now. The computer was still stalling with PROCESSING while it churned its way through trillions of bits. Then PROCESSING went away and was replaced by the most exciting message Coolidge had ever seen. It was a telegram Ingalls had received the day before:

DOCTOR'S APPOINTMENT. TUES 4 P.M. D.R.

That's what I call data, Coolidge thought. He was going to get a chance to *see* the Doctor. But where was the appointment? D.R. had to be Davey Reed; the telegram had originated in Washington. He tried the same approach with Reed's messages but nothing came of it, so he went to graphics and inserted Reed's photographs into memory: profile, front view, close-up of face. He put it on rapid scan and watched Reed flip by. Reed working in the Dirksen Senate Office Building, Reed outside the Senate floor talking to other aides, Reed in bars, Reed at parties, Reed making out with a woman in his apartment, Reed in restaurants, Reed in the same bars again. The microcam footage kept moving because no one was saying any of the magic words. Reed at the Department of Commerce, Reed at the Department of Interior, Reed at the Office of Management and Budget, Reed at the Museum of Pre-Columbian Artifacts.

Coolidge pressed the STOP button. He ran the footage back to the beginning of the Pre-Columbian era.

Reed was sitting on a stone bench looking lost, surrounded by images of Quetzalcoatl and ferocious Aztec masks. He was sober and looked something like Stan Laurel, totally defeated by his environment. But it wasn't Oliver Hardy Garvey who came along and sat down next to him. It was none other than Herbert Purefoy, ex-director of the CIA.

'At the mansion, four P.M., Tuesday,' Reed said, lips hardly moving. Then he got up and strolled out, trying to look casual and coming off like a rapist on the prowl.

The other man sat for five minutes, checked to see if he was being watched, then got up and left.

Coolidge sat back in his swivel chair and looked at the ceiling. The Doctor's appointment was going to be fascinating. Coolidge longed to talk to the Doctor. All right, say it was conscience. Then why didn't you quit, walk away from it, refuse to take responsibility for whatever it was you didn't want responsibility for? Was your moral conviction that strong? But what gave you such *certainty*? That was the question.

Coolidge imagined himself pacing up and down in front of the Doctor, who would be seated in a chair. 'I'm not entirely unsympathetic,' Coolidge would say to him. 'Still and all, you've committed *the* sin in government. Even when your job description stated that your *function* was to look for funny stuff and then blow the whistle, even *then* it was the cardinal sin in government. You would be dead, professionally speaking. In this particular case you could be more dead than that. Why did you take such responsibility on yourself?'

The prospect was ravishing. Things were coming together. He had the KGB connection and he had a Doctor's appointment. The Garbageman was doing pretty good work. But there was still that fascinating tidbit: the

242

curious case of Yeager and the Defense Mapping Agency.

In a way, Ambassador Zhu reminded Yeager of a washing machine. She made love in cycles, invariant cycles: slow, fast, circular, slow, fast, circular. He wondered if Chinese regimentation had gone quite that far. Not that it made any difference. He thought of William Faulkner's line: while some whiskeys might be better than other whiskeys, there is no such thing as a bad whiskey . The slow, the fast, the circular. They were all Black Label, V.S.O.P. Hennessy, Châteauneuf-du-Pape '67. Ambassador Zhu was getting so frenzied on the fast cycles that he was having trouble staying in the driver's seat. He had never made love to an Oriental woman before and he realized he'd had some kind of crazy idea that doing so would be an exercise in politeness, delicacy, ritualistic slow movements.

Yeager's only problem was that Ling-Ling always bolted the bedroom door from the inside. How was anyone going to sneak in and do the job? But he couldn't afford to worry about it, because if he did, he might go soft and ruin Sino-American relations. And then there was Ling-Ling. She was caressing his shoulder and looking at him with soulful eyes. He had made a conquest there without laying a glove on her. She was devastatingly cute, and having her watch was the classic erotic scene; he just wished Ambassador Zhu were a little less selfish. Ling-Ling was simply too cute to ignore, so he tenderly rolled Ambassador Zhu over and resumed the slow cycle from the rear.

Ling-Ling took the cue. She sat up and leaned over and gave Yeager a soulful, loving, delicious, lingering kiss.

There was an explosion of machine gun Chinese from below, and Ling-Ling jumped back, terrified. Ambassador Zhu was outraged. Yeager dropped back to very slow, just enough to stay in business. He was embarrassed. He had been caught in flagrante delicto while he was already in it. Ambassador Zhu was going berserk; it was flattering. He could imagine what she must be saying. I give you a position of great trust and as soon as I turn my back, you do this? The tirade went on long enough for Ling-Ling to start firing back. They were rattling back and forth at ninety words a minute. It must have been what the Boxer Rebellion sounded like. Ling-Ling got out of bed, defiant, still chattering, then pulled the drapes around the bed, spitting bullets all the while, and in seconds Yeager and Ambassador Zhu were in lovers' solitude, Ambassador Zhu slipping into the circular cycle as though nothing had happened.

Yeager's toes were beginning to vibrate and he smiled; those darling lovely girls had figured out a way to do it. Ambassador Zhu had connections to the KGB, going back years to when the Chinese Communists and the Soviets saw themselves as two against the world. She still maintained a few of them, unofficially, even though the two governments were at loggerheads; it was a case of professionals helping each other out from time to time. Now she was about to pay back an important favor a KGB agent had done for her a year earlier. Mission, thought Yeager, in the throes of love, accomplished.

Ling-Ling took a few deep breaths, calming her various emotions, and then, still naked, went straight for the attaché case. She already had a camera in her hand; Coolidge hadn't even noticed her pick it up. Well, she *was* cute. Oblivious to the groans coming from behind the drapes, she opened the case carefully, muffling the lock catches before they could make a sound, then took out the papers and began photographing them with an inscrutable little camera that didn't even click.

Coolidge froze the frame. He centred the cursor on the papers and blew up the scene twice, three times. In spite of everything that had happened to him, he was still capable of surprise. It was the maps he had seen in Harry's attaché case on Kneecap. Maps from the Defense Mapping Agency, the maps that were already installed in the Pershing 2 missiles in Europe.

Harry had told a Communist power, and through them the Russians, exactly what the targets were for each and every Pershing 2. Purity had paid off; not defying Dunn's Conundrum was the correct strategy after all: Harry, not knowing he was a suspect, had gotten careless. A luscious possibility was beginning to emerge from the confusion.

244

Trash Report: #85-11-6

CASE NUMBER:104759

ABANDONED PROPERTY DONOR: Senator Oliver Garvey
(residence)

1. Mail, unopened: Save the Dolphins.
2. Mail, unopened: Save the Whales.
3. Mail, unopened: Save the Children.
4. Mail, unopened: Save America.
5. Mail, unopened: Save the Seals.
6. Mail, unopened: Save the American Way of Life.
7. Mail, unopened: Save Free Enterprise.
8. Bottle private-label Scotch. 1.75 liter.
9. One loose-leaf book labeled: 'The Collected Speeches of Ronald Reagan.'
10. Two dozen clamshells.
11. One jar, half full, glycerin suppositories, outdated.
12. Reservations list for 211 Club.
13. The 1976 Democratic platform.
14. One ladies' garter.
15. One tablecloth.
16. Rough draft of letter to John Leggett, Manager of Senate Personnel.
17. Fragment of speech for delivery to National Lexicography Society.

Trash Scenario

On Monday night, the head chef at the 211 Club, M. René Guillemin, visited Senator Garvey and cooked his favorite French dish, clams casino (item #10, two dozen small garlicky clamshells). They discussed the dinner H. Dunn had with E. Ives and Admiral Roscoe McQuade at the 211 Club last Thursday (item #12, reservations list at the club for the night in question; item #15, the tablecloth used at their table). The senator learned nothing of Admiral McQuade's significance to the Library – which is to say, to O.F.F. (item #15, the tablecloth, contained only unimportant naval budget figures.

In return for at least trying, M. Guillemin's granddaughter is to be named a senatorial page (item #16, rough draft of letter to John Leggett. Manager of Senate Personnel).

As M. Guillemin was leaving for the evening, he passed Melanie Smith (item #14, garter, mates with one found in Ms. Smith's trash, Case #111836) on the walkway and introduced himself (item #4 in M. Guillemin's trash, Case #127225, his business card with Ms. Smith's phone number written on back).

Notes

What can one say about Item #17? Perhaps it is nothing more than a running gag between Reed and Garvey, say a contest of sorts, to see if he can write the most unhedged speech in American political history. On the other hand, perhaps Reed is really trying to persuade the senator to make these statements to the public. Investigation shows that Reed has nothing odder in his background than membership in the Gregorian Chant Society at college.

A fragment of item #17 is reproduced here. Part was lost due to application of Crazy Glue before folding page in half.

. . . it is perhaps not too great a leap to go from our discussion of atomic warheads to what we might call an atom of language. A word. We all know, of course, that words can be as powerful as bombs. This particular atom of language surely is. It's dangerous, explosive, and produces fallout.

I speak, ladies and gentlemen of the National Lexicography Society, of the word 'nigger.' I believe it is a word that needs to be taken out of the closet. I believe it should be put back into everyday use. Indeed, it is a word we can hardly afford to do without, considering the parlous state of the world today.

Now we all know how language evolves. A living, vibrant language is molded, shaped, developed by the hot wings of society's evolutionary forces.

I therefore assert that, with the passage of time, 'nigger' no longer refers to skin color. That, in point of fact, far from referring to the shade of one's epidermis, the word has become internalized, as it were, and now denotes not the nature of one's outsides but, instead, the nature of one's insides. It is a phenomenon observed often enough in language: a word turning into its opposite. My observation is that the word 'nigger' should now be used to describe one's state of mind, one's approach to life. More specifically, I assert, the word refers to the quality of one's defenses.

Nigger defenses are obvious. Transparently defiant. There is overkill in nigger defenses. A willingness to drop the bomb, as it were, for minor slights.

White defenses, on the other hand, are subtler. Not necessarily weaker. *Subtler*. Indeed, the subtler one's defenses, the whiter one is. On the *inside*, I remind you. Easy examples come to mind. John Wayne. Clearly a nigger. Look cross-eyed at him and you got a punch in the nose. No one ever knew that he collected dolls. George Patton. A highly aggressive officer who wore ivory-handled pistols and made his men go into battle wearing ties. Nigger, I say. John F. Kennedy? White. Lyndon B. Johnson? Nigger. Martin Luther King, Jr., and Henry James? White. Harry Truman? Bantam cock nigger. And so on. You see my point. Quite frankly, it is a lot easier to find examples of niggers than of whites.

But what does all this have to do with atomic strategy?

Everything, my friends, everything.

Observe how the United States behaves in the international arena. We talk constantly about how our will is being challenged. Our resolve is being tested. We are quick to bristle, quick to go on the defensive, terrified of losing face. We have armies and fleets all over the world.

We have listening posts everywhere, looking for slights. Our radar sets are 'on' twenty-four hours a day, searching, searching.

In all honesty, I don't see how we can avoid referring to this as a nigger foreign policy. We are easily challenged. Quick to rise to slights, real and imagined, quick to fight. What awful thing does it mean to the American psyche to yield, to concede a point, to give an inch?

I think you now see the usefulness of the word 'nigger.' It puts the arms race in a clearer perspective. We are a nation of niggers with thirty thousand atomic weapons at our disposal. Sobering thought, isn't it? Remember that whenever an American President uses force overseas, his poll ratings go up.

Anyway, it's a thought for your consideration, and I do hope the reporters among you will not take any part of this speech out of context. Thank you very much.

Surprise!

Simultaneity does not imply causality, according to statisticians. Simply because two events occur suspiciously close together does not necessarily mean there's a connection between them. It is the statistician's antidote to paranoia.

Coolidge kept reminding himself of it. He was nervous and excited going into the Library the next morning because it was D day, Doctor day; he was closing in on the Doctor. But when he got there, he found out that the Library was throwing a surprise party for him between the hours of 1 P.M. and 3 P.M., which was just right for making him late for his Doctor's appointment.

Surprise parties at the Library were one of Harry's little games. You got one when you did something unusually brilliant. But it was also a test: How long would it take a know-it-all Librarian to find out that he was the guest of honor at a surprise party? Coolidge broke the four minute mile, figuring it out in 3:56 after showing up, immediately registering it with Burnish's secretary and claiming the record.

The big clue was that Burnish was late for work. This was a reductio ad absurdum, since Burnish was never late for work; Burnish was only late for home. It took one computer query to find out that he'd made two phone calls to a caterer and one to a liquor store, with a lot of attention given to the white wine.

There was an added little flourish. It was normal to rotate the parties among Librarians' apartments. This time Burnish had arranged for everything to be delivered to Vera's place. Simultaneity did not imply, he kept thinking. Be objective. Sift out the superfluous, stay to the basics, be insensitive, don't read anything into innocent acts; they may be innocent.

It was hard, waiting. He read through the latest trash reports at his desk, then dumped all kinds of extra work on Jake Shoemaker so Coolidge would have the afternoon completely free. He wanted to be able to give the Doctor his undivided attention. At a quarter to one, he left the Library and made the familiar drive to Vera's apartment, wondering how he was going to give the appearance of warmth. Vera was hard to fool. When she opened the door, he could see the others gathered behind her. He got a big red kiss while they all applauded.

'Hiya, sweets,' Burnish said, handing him a white wine.

'First-rate job, Walter,' Harry said, holding up his glass of club soda. He looked sheepish standing in Vera's living room; it couldn't have been his choice. 'Vera and gentlemen,' Harry said, 'we normally don't say this to his face, but let's drink to the Garbageman.'

Coolidge turned on a smile and sipped wine and looked modest and counted heads. It was a full house. Beautiful. Maybe the party would work in his favor. One of them would have to leave early and Coolidge would be right behind him It would be easier than waiting outside Herbert Purefoy's law office in a no-parking zone.

'Tell us how you took out that T-72, Walter,' Barber said. 'Maybe you've stumbled on a new principle of armored warfare.'

'Then I want to know how Beebe defeated the Czech Army,' Emil Kraus said, spearing an onion out of his Gibson.

'Have some shrimp, Walter?' Burnish said, making his rounds in an apron.

Coolidge had his eyes on them. His shoes were off and his feet were up on an ottoman; his jacket was somewhere and his topcoat was in the bedroom. Music was playing. Time was easing by. Librarians were relaxing. Except one, the Doctor. Except two, Coolidge. He had been carrying on a running census of the room while telling Vera all about Germany and pretending to be convivial.

250

Looking at them, Coolidge couldn't be sure what he felt like: father confessor (he knew all their sins); number one snoop and voyeur; marriage counselor; sex therapist. He had seen so much of their private lives that it was almost impossible for him to be casual with any of them.

Harry was over his ill-at-ease, and was being his usual voluble self with Farnsworth, Hopkins, and Barber. Coolidge looked at their faces. Farnsworth was still running amok with seventeen-year-olds. Hopkins was slowly developing a serious drinking problem. He hadn't started drinking until he was thirty-five and then discovered what he had been missing. Barber, the man without an ego, reacted to the world as though his outer layer of epidermis was missing. It made him ruthless; he was currently destroying his third wife.

The four of them were intently gaming a question: What would be the first civil affairs action taken after a nuclear exchange? It was typical party talk for Harry Dunn. They got to the answer in five minutes. Close the stock exchanges.

Burnish was wandering around offering hors d'oeuvres and drinks. Coolidge didn't even have to ask for a refill; it kept reappearing magically when he wasn't looking. Burnish had not only handled the catering; he was the bartender and the waiter. He had arranged with Gardella to have Vera's apartment swept for unauthorized bugs, and had got Beebe's permission from the hospital in Mannheim to have a few men discreetly guarding the apartment building. They would also carry home drunks, if necessary. Everyone had been under a lot of pressure and some might have to blow steam. Burnish was also going to stay after the party and clean up the place and get the deposits back on the bottles.

Gardella was sitting in a corner, depressed. His wife was leaving him. If he knew anything about the way she'd been fooling around, he'd kill her; he was much better off depressed. He was talking to Beatty; now and then Coolidge could hear Jesus floating across the room. As far as Coolidge could tell, Beatty was living a clean life. He was untouchable.

Vera was shaking his shoulder. 'Walter, you're not listening to me.'

'I am so. What did you say?'

'I said, have you spoken with Harry yet?'

'Of cabbages and kings.'

'How about physicians?'

Coolidge looked at her. He knew a lot, but he didn't know everything. Was she the Doctor's nurse? Hell, for all he knew, she could be the Bishop. He was hoping she wouldn't say the word out loud: they were on camera, which was an authorized bug.

'No,' he said to her.

'What are you waiting for?'

'I just got back. I've got a lot of crap to catch up on,' he said, which given his job – Collected and Reviewed Abandoned Property – was the literal truth.

Hopkins was now missing. It was after 2 P.M. Hopkins was the most vulnerable of them all. A bisexual en route to gay. Among Librarians he would be voted most likely to screw a congressional page of either sex. Coolidge had already reported him to Harry, who had given him a merciless dressing down about being indiscreet; you had to be merciless with Hopkins or he wouldn't notice.

'You know you're taking chances, don't you?' Vera said. She was talking softly, lips barely moving, so the others wouldn't hear. It was possible the microcam wouldn't either; it was directly across from them, in the bookshelves next to the bar. 'You're creating a second category of data. Things that only you know. That's un-Library.'

'You're forgetting Dunn's Conundrum, aren't you?' he said in the same lipless way. 'You wouldn't want me to be illogical about this, would you? That would be even more un-Library.'

Coolidge looked around the room. One of them was an unexpected genius. Kraus, Hopkins (back now; he'd been in the kitchen), Farnsworth, Barber, the others: could any of them be that good? It was so hard to believe, it occurred to him that perhaps the Doctor was not 'witting,' that maybe the Doctor didn't know he was the Doctor, and was somehow being used by others.

It was an awful thought. It would turn a genius into a fool and wipe out an intriguing question of ethics and morality. The Doctor unwitting? Confiding secrets of state in moments of tenderness to, say, a mistress supplied by another agency, another government – the hallowed, proven crotch approach to statecraft? It was hard to accept, but he had to concede it was a logical possibility.

Vera was looking at him funny. 'Walter, do you know things I don't know?'

'Of course not. What would I know that you don't know and how would I know it?' he said, wondering if she was wondering about the Doctor, or about fooling around with Harry, or about Yeager and Harry giving away the Defense Mapping Agency to a Chinese connection of the Russians, or about Charley Eberhart going to see Oliver Garvey, or about the Emersons being infiltrated by the KGB. Let's see, was there anything else?

'I don't know,' Vera said. 'I just have a feeling. There's something spacey about you. I mean, more than usual.'

Where was Kraus? Probably in the john, which would be appropriate. Kraus was vulnerable; he had to be one of the leading johns in the capital. He was short and ugly and women didn't take to him, so he bought the most expensive hookers around, sometimes two at a time, always chic, long-legged beauties who towered over him. Everything imaginable was human, commonplace; ravaged egos trying to keep from drowning in self-hate; that seemed to be the state of the race. As he looked around. Kraus came back into the room.

Then he noticed that Harry's tie was up. His sleeves were rolled down. He was putting on his jacket. His topcoat was across a bar stool next to him. He was making his move. Coolidge realized he was a little tipsy from the wine Burnish had been slipping him.

Harry, on the other hand, was holding up a chaste glass of club soda. 'Before we break up,' he said, 'I think we owe ourselves a toast. It's going to be a new world, folks, Walter's little adventure in Germany demonstrated that. The consequences of O.F.F. are infinite. The Soviet Union is finished; it's only a matter of time now. I give them five years tops, *maybe* five days. And we're the ones who made it possible. Us. The Library. We pulled it all together.'

'Hear, hear,' Hopkins said.

Coolidge was putting on his shoes as undramatically as possible.

'Aren't we entitled to a bonus or something?' Farnsworth asked. 'I mean, after all.' They speculated about how much it would be worth.

'If they paid us a billion dollars apiece, it would be a twelve-billion-dollar bargain,' was Harry's opinion. He had his coat over his arm. 'Cheap at half the price.'

'Hell, it would be half the price,' Hopkins said. 'They'd get half of it back in taxes.'

It was the kind of banter and camaraderie that Harry liked. He was smiling as he made his way across the room. The idea behind the parties was to generate team feeling in what was a new agency of government.

Coolidge wasn't ready yet. His topcoat was in the bedroom and he couldn't even find his jacket. There was only one way to stop Harry. Pose him a question.

'Harry, before you go,' he said. He was playing it very easy, sitting up straight, pushing at his back with his fists, stretching. 'In the event that O.F.F. is ever used, Harry, what about the forty-five million?'

'It isn't forty-five million,' Harry said patiently. 'It's twenty million. They were using the wrong figures on MX accuracy.'

'Okay, what about the twenty million?'

Harry smiled wanly. He dropped his coat and sat down on the nearest bar stool. Coolidge was looking for his jacket. 'What *about* the twenty million?' Harry asked back.

'It's a lot of people. And we're not going to get half of them back in taxes.'

'Ho, ho, *ho*,' Hopkins said.

'That's a maximum figure,' Harry said, obviously surprised at encountering skepticism of any kind at this late date. But that was okay; that's what Librarians were for. To probe, question all assumptions, leave nothing to the crazy maneuverings of chance. 'That figure allows for screwups,' he continued. 'Major screwups. Actually, we've got backups on top of backups in this thing.'

'Uh huh,' Coolidge said, spotting his gray tweed squashed in the seat of a chair. 'What are the possibilities of it being less than twenty million, Harry?'

'I personally feel it'll be a lot less. But I'll tell you what I'll do. I want you to be convinced. I want everybody to be convinced. Remember Brezhnev? Let's bring him back from the dead. He's a tough adversary. He's the only one we haven't brought in yet. I'm sure he'll enjoy getting a day's consulting fee. When I get done with Brezhnev, you'll have no doubts about the efficiency of O.F.F.'

It was 2:30 P.M. Harry waved and was gone, right on schedule.

'Guess I'll run too,' Coolidge said to Vera, moving for the bedroom to get his coat. She followed him and closed the door behind her.

'Hang around awhile,' she said, pressing up against him. 'Chung jung gung.'

'Sure you can.' Gentle pressure of a knee against him. Fiendishly sexy look on mouth and in eyes. 'You're the party boy today; you're entitled.'

He slid his hands down her back, but stopped in the nick of time. It was too tempting. When Vera turned up the wattage, Coolidge tended to go limp except for one place.

'Can't,' he said, buttoning his coat.

'Walter, are you up to something?'

'What could I be up to?'

'Are you fooling around?'

'No. Are you?'

She blushed, batting her eyelashes. 'I'm *trying* to.'

'I've got a headache, honey; try me again sometime.' He blew her a kiss and went out the door.

'You didn't even thank me for saving your damn life,' she said after him.

Coolidge was racing for the elevator. He stopped one just in time with his foot, but there were stops, arrivals, departures. It took forever to get to the basement garage. He got to his car in time to see Harry already rolling out of the exit and on his way. He had lost him.

All right. Plan B. Herbert Purefoy, ex-director of Central Intelligence.

Coolidge was moving along the windows with his grandfather's opera glasses, looking for signs of life. The light was wrong; he couldn't see in. Purefoy was in there and maybe the Doctor; there were two cars parked out front. Coolidge was having trouble keeping his hands from trembling.

The house sat on its own hill. It must have been sixty years old, with big Tudor triangles looming over the upper story, dark brown shingles covering the sharply raked roof, mullioned windows, built-in servants' quarters. He had managed to follow Purefoy to it without screwing up.

Purefoy had driven out of a basement garage in downtown Washington in a brand-new yellow Mercedes. Coolidge was getting the breaks for a change; it was like following a huge lemon sherbet. Twice Purefoy had gone completely around a block, looking for a tail, but Coolidge was staying so far behind him that it didn't matter. After that, Purefoy had taken the Beltway straight to Maryland.

Another car started up the long driveway. From his position crouched behind a row of hedge, Coolidge aimed the glasses. It was Glenn Ingalls, the California business man. Ingalls parked his car next to Purefoy's, then went to the front door and opened it without a pause, as if it were home.

Coolidge lay down behind the hedge for two minutes to give his creaking knees a rest. In ten more minutes, another car came up the hill. It was Garvey. He got out carrying a briefcase and stayed in daylight as briefly as possible. Ten more minutes went by. No one else showed up. It was 3.35 P.M. Coolidge had been hoping to catch the

Doctor on the way in. Now there was no choice. He would have to do some breaking and entering; it was time for his annual checkup, anyway.

Staying behind the hedge, Coolidge worked his way around toward the rear of the house. There were all kinds of doors and entryways, but a flagstone patio with double French doors opening onto it looked promising.

He waited for signs of activity. There was only the fine rustling of dried leaves. He stifled a newly born thought about going back to his car. The temptation was great. He stood up and shook out his knees, then went quietly and quickly up to the patio. One of the French doors gave. He stepped into a library and crossed the room to a closed door, pausing to listen.

There was a single sound. It was weirdly menacing. Labored breathing. Uuuhhhh. Pause. Uuuhhhh. The trouble with it was that it was coming from the wrong direction. There was an emphysema case standing right behind him.

'I'm going to try my best not to blow your, uuuhhhh head off,' a man said. 'You're inside the premises now, so it's uuuhhhh, legal. Follow me?'

'I get your drift.'

'If we work together, maybe we can save your, uuuhhhh, life.'

Coolidge's hands went up in the air, slowly and elegantly. In between gasps for air, the man had a rotten tone of voice.

'Lean up against that, uuuhhhh, wall.'

Coolidge could feel an insensitive hand moving over him, searching for a gun. It wasn't exactly delicate around the crotch. He felt his opera glasses leave his back pocket. It was frustrating. The Doctor was so near and yet so far. Having come this far, Coolidge couldn't bear the thought of failure. It tended to balance out his fear, all of it adding up to a surprisingly casual kind of desperation. He sneaked a fast look behind him. The man was dressed like a gardener and was seventy if he was a day. He was holding a .357 magnum. The only thing in Coolidge's reach was a bookcase.

'Turn around in slow, uuuhhhh, motion.'

Coolidge rotated slowly, taking *The Decline and Fall of the Roman Empire* with him. It had to be at least 1,200 pages. The remaining books on the shelf made a noise, but the man's hearing must have been about on a level with his respiration. Coolidge hit him on the head with five hundred years of history and the man's eyeballs rose to meet it. There was only one problem: Which objects would make the most noise hitting the ground? He grabbed the opera glasses, the gun, and Rome, and let the gardener fall.

Coolidge opened the door and peered out. It was a large entry area: heavy dark brown beams and joists, dark steps going up to the top floor, doors to other rooms, all closed. He moved carefully from door to door, listening, holding the barrel of the .357 as if it were a staple gun. He got to the double doors at the bottom of the stairs and put his ear against the dark wood. It was tantalizing; he heard the magic word: 'Doctor.' He put the gun in his right hand and slowly turned the knob with his left and hustled into the room, looking at all the faces, one two three.

Garvey, Purefoy, Ingalls.

No Harry, no other Librarian either. The three of them were sitting on leather chairs at a small round table in what seemed to be the sitting room. Coolidge closed the door behind him.

Purefoy looked him over with a professional eye and said evenly, 'Nice going, Coolidge. Nobody knew about *this* meeting.'

'Are you holding a gun on us?' Ingalls said, offended, wounded already.

Coolidge looked at the thing in his hand. 'You know, I'm not sure.' He moved farther into the room. 'Three esteemed, successful members of the establishment. Movers and shakers. Doing what? Plotting against the government? All you guys need is a candle stuck in a wine bottle.'

'We're discussing matters of civic importance,' Garvey said dryly. 'I'm in a position to know there's been no recent legislation passed making that illegal.'

'Oh, that's what you're doing.'

'Walter, I hope you didn't hurt that old man,' Garvey said.

'Where did you get him? The CIA retirement home?'

'Something like that.'

Coolidge shook his head.

'Do you have a plan, Walter?' Garvey said.

'No. Nothing much anyway. We'll sit here until the Doctor comes.'

'I see.'

The three men looked at each other. 'While you're waiting, would you like something to read?' Garvey's briefcase was lying on the table. He picked it up and tossed it to Coolidge, who dropped his gun catching it. He threw Garvey a dirty look while retrieving the pistol, then sat on the window seat across the room from them, balancing the briefcase on his knee, managing to open the clasp with one hand. Inside, there was only a single sheet of paper, with no letterhead.

WALTER COOLIDGE – AN ESTIMATE

There's only one man in the Library likely to serve your purposes. He is Walter Coolidge, occasionally referred to by insiders as the Garbageman. Why do I think he's a possibility? He's a misfit.

Coolidge has unconscious feelings of being above it all, which inclines him to be more of an observer than a participant in life. It follows that he tends to be ineffectual in the everyday issues of living. In his relations with people, for example, Coolidge is invariably the anthropologist observing the exchange. This has an adverse effect on spontaneity, fun, creativity.

Since he feels above it all, Coolidge does not invest opponents with feelings of hatred, loathing, fear, etc. He has strong powers of empathy. Almost too strong, almost self-destructively strong. One practical example of Coolidge in action: It is impossible for him to root for a baseball team, since he empathizes equally with both batter and pitcher. The only exception to this is the double play, the beauty and dynamism of which moves him to root for the fielders over the runners. Coolidge doesn't even see baseball as a team sport. It is an elaborately ritualized way in which some male adults earn their living by testing their abilities against other male adults. He is more interested in how an outfielder relates to groupies in the stands; what a base runner has to say to the opposing second baseman; how a pitcher feels about getting his instructions from the catcher. He watches a baseball game in much the way he would observe the people in a Bronze Age village going about the daily tasks of life.

It is possible that this attitude could also stem from an unconscious fear of losing. Whatever its cause, it makes Coolidge a poor competitor since he empathizes too much with the opposition. He has little team spirit. What is there to root for?

Coolidge doesn't run with the crowd and is satisfied to make his own mistakes. He has a pronounced tendency to reinvent the wheel. He lacks the killer instinct. He has a higher feminine component than most men. He's a bad judge of character. He doesn't know it, but he's a narrow technocrat, totally absorbed in his own field.

What all this seems to add up to is that Coolidge does not project his own personal hang-ups onto his work. He is the opposite of the fanatic or the ideologue, whose very psyche is threatened by adverse facts. Rather, Coolidge is something of a mathematician, one who takes into account all known quantities and variables without shutting anything off from view. Each term of the equation is present and undisguised and must be accounted for.

In summary, Coolidge would never doctor the results in order to force new data into a preconceived scheme of things. Rather, he is a Doctor whose diagnosis flows from the facts of the case and nothing else.

Which is why putting him into the Library was a serious mistake on Harry Dunn's part. In the Library, the Doctor will see things beyond his presently narrow purview. He will become educated. He will be exposed to new data. He will not be able to ignore this new data; to do so would jeopardize his entire concept of himself as dedicated and aloof truth seeker. Coupled with his loner tendencies and absence of a strong sense of loyalty to any group, he has the classic personality of the leaker. He is your only opportunity in the Library. It is the Doctor himself, however, who will have to do the persuading. The hard sell will not work. Easy does it.

Coolidge memorized it on the spot; he would have trouble forgetting it. He had never seen another person's evaluation of him before. He carried the briefcase over to them, dropped it on the table, and pulled up a chair. No one, including Coolidge, noticed that he had left the .357 on the windowsill. There was the distant rumble of a throb in the back of his skull.

He looked at them. A millionaire. An ex-intelligence man. The Senator from Nowhere. They were studying him just as intently.

'Who wrote it?'

'Charley.'

'How many people have seen this?'

'Only the three of us. I can assure you of that. The main reason we've been so secretive is to protect your identity.'

Garvey was pouring coffee for him; Purefoy politely passed the cream and sugar. They were treating him like an accident case.

'Walter doesn't take sugar,' Garvey said.

Coolidge's hand shook as he picked up the cup. It was too big a change to handle in so short a time. It was pure craziness. There was no Doctor. It was a myth based on a guess, built on a wish. Harry was in the clear, damn it to hell. He, Coolidge, was supposed to have become the Doctor, because he, Charley, *thought* he would. He was feeling about the way he had felt in Germany when Kalyanov pulled that fast one with the wastebasket. It seemed to be open season on making Walter Coolidge look like an ass.

No Doctor. There was a sudden void in him. His preoccupation, his obsession, had nowhere to go. His illusion that he, the Garbageman, would sooner or later discover the clever, elusive, intellectual, unselfish, idealistic Doctor was gone. Phffft. All his paranoid thoughts about Hopkins and Farnsworth and Burnish and Beatty and Harry were proved wrong. Thud. Mr. Coolidge, meet Doctor Coolidge, modern man plodding through data in search of himself. Doctor Coolidge, I presume. Deflated, he looked around at them.

'Charley was a nice guy, but he was a lousy psychologist,' he said. He nodded at the briefcase. 'That isn't me. You've made a big mistake. This won't matter much to you, but you've caused me one hell of a lot of trouble. If you're nothing more than a peace group, then do it out in

261

the open. Stop trying to infiltrate a secret government agency, or Harry will get you. You guys are playing with fire.'

'So are your guys,' Purefoy said.

'You don't seem to understand that we're already *in* real trouble,' Ingalls said. 'It takes one hundred strategic nuclear warheads to destroy the Soviet Union in a retaliatory second strike. We've got ten thousand of them, and we're building toward seventeen thousand. What are all those other warheads for?'

'Tell your friend the senator to call a few generals before his committee. I'm sure they'll be willing to answer your question.'

'Bull,' Garvey put in. 'Those guys are worse than I am. They lose you around the bend.'

'Okay, what do *you* think they're for?' Coolidge asked Garvey.

'I'll tell you exactly what they're for. The A-bomb and the H-bomb are America's answer to the C-bomb. Do you know what the C-bomb is, Walter? It's the Commie-bomb. It works like this.' Garvey shifted into a pretty fair Spanish accent. "Hey, Pedro. Tired of that shit hole you're living in? Want to give the kids three squares a day? Want to see your wife in a sexy dress? Then come with us, vote with us, march with us, fight with us – we'll take it from the rich and give it to you." That's the C-bomb, Walter. Scares the pants off the establishment. Most people in the world are peasants, remember. There are billions of them; billions of people who have nothing. Hell, we've been putting down other people's revolutions since *before* there was a Soviet Union. What could we say to those peasants that would have the same appeal? Not without clobbering corporate profits, anyway. So America's response to the C-bomb is the multiple, independently targetable reentry vehicle aimed at the fountainhead of communism.'

Coolidge's head was nodding up and down. 'That's the kind of thing you throw in the garbage when Davey Reed writes it.'

'Well, naturally.'

'You don't talk that way for publication. Mr. Purefoy

here didn't talk like that when he was running the CIA. Eisenhower didn't complain about the military-industrial complex until the day he *left* office. Rickover decided that what he really wanted to do was sink all the nuclear submarines he'd spent a lifetime building for the U.S. Navy. *After* he retired. Why is that, do you think?'

Purefoy set his coffee cup down without a rattle. 'Because we liked our jobs,' he said, looking right at Coolidge.

'And if I told you what O.F.F. was, you'd all sit on it. Just like Ike and Rickover and the others. You wouldn't know what to do with it. You wouldn't want to lose your respectability.'

'I understand what you're saying,' Purefoy said. 'You're right, that's what we would have done. In the past. But things were never this serious before. The world is getting down to decision time. We can't allow things to go on as they have been. Someone has to call a stop to it before it's too late.'

'He's talking about you, Walter.' It was Garvey now. '*Somebody's* got to do something and you seem to be the only possibility; you're the man on the spot; you could make a difference. It's your luck, Walter.'

'That's what you told Charley Eberhart; then you filmed him talking to you.'

Coolidge had really cut through the lard. Garvey was stricken. He did the impossible for a politician: he blushed.

'We never used it against him, Walter. We never threatened him. Nothing. That was solely to protect ourselves. We were on the best of terms with Charley until the end.'

'Until the end. Terrific.'

Ingalls pushed his coffee cup away in disgust. 'You're slipping away, aren't you?' he said. 'You're not buying. You're passing the buck.' He pushed his chair back, disgusted, and wandered around the room, thinking. 'All right, I'll ask you one question. Do you believe O.F.F. is good for the United States or don't you?'

'That's too big a decision for me to make.'

'I'm not asking you for a decision, God damn it; I'm asking you what you think.'

The three of them were poised, waiting.

'Walter Coolidge, civilian, Social Security number 107-22-1025.'

'That isn't funny, Coolidge,' Ingalls said. 'It's cheap.' He was standing near the window. He picked up the magnum and pointed it at Coolidge. 'Suppose we forced it out of you. Would that ease your conscience?'

Coolidge was looking at the wrong end of the magnum for the second time.

'Glenn, take it easy,' Garvey said. 'Put that thing down.'

'I don't even know why I'm talking to you people,' Coolidge said. 'You're in over your head, Ingalls. You're not competent at this. Go back to Silicon Valley.'

'We've got some of the best people in the country with us,' Ingalls said. 'We're not neophytes.'

'You're not, huh? Do you know you've been infiltrated by the KGB?'

There was nothing but large eyes, pale faces, and slack mouths in the room. Garvey's left cheek flinched. 'You going to leave us hanging on that one?' he said.

Coolidge worked hard to get his eyes off the gun and up to Ingalls's face. 'Your administrative assistant, Reinhold Kunstner, is a Soviet spy.'

Ingalls threw quick looks at Garvey and Purefoy. He didn't believe it, but he had a trapped, stunned look. Coolidge had access to information.

'That's the craziest thing I ever heard of,' he said, for want of anything intelligent to say. 'Reinhold's my right-hand man.'

'Do you happen to know where your right-hand man is?'

Ingalls checked his watch. 'He's using my Los Angeles office to talk to customers. Right at this moment.'

'The hell he is. He's in East Berlin on a one-way ticket. You've seen the last of him. He was planted on you years ago, probably to steal computers. You told him about the Emersons. You also told him about that thing Charley wrote about me. You told him I was the Doctor. Or you let it slip, somehow.'

'I didn't know,' Garvey said. 'I swear it, Walter.'

'That wasn't smart, Glenn,' Purefoy said tightly.

Ingalls had put the gun on a desk in the corner and was dialing the phone as Coolidge started for the door. He wasn't feeling like a hero, but he was out of trouble; he was a free man again. Son of a bitch. There was no Doctor. Before he reached it, the door swung open.

'Uuuhhhh.'

This time the gardener had a .45.

Purefoy sighed. 'That's all right, Ned,' he said. 'You can put it away. This man isn't dangerous.'

'Whatever you say, Mister, uuuhhhh, Purefoy.'

'Where's Reinhold?' Ingalls was saying desperately into the phone.

'Jesus God,' Garvey was saying.

Coolidge went out the door thinking that Purefoy had hit the nail right on the head. He wasn't dangerous. Not anymore. That's what he wanted. He had done his duty. He had been a good soldier. What could possibly go wrong now? Nothing. There was nothing. Except, maybe, World War III.

Waiting for Leonid

They were waiting for the resurrection of Leonid Brezhnev; he had a twelve-thirty appointment. They'd have to shut down for an hour or so while he was there, so Harry was pushing everybody to touch all bases beforehand. Scan the planet, make connections, recommendations, keep the President up-to-the-second, look into the far decimal places where improbabilities lurked.

The computer was twitching. It was simultaneously sensing different areas of equal importance. The crisis in Germany had implications that snaked around the world.

The Soviet SU-24 Fencer fighter plane was being deployed in greater numbers in East Germany, Poland, and Czechoslovakia. It was one of their best fighters; the display was giving the location of all new squadron deployments.

Two-thirds of the American F-15s were grounded because of a defective tail assembly. But the F-15 had been averaging 35 percent availability for a long time anyway, so the situation was normal.

The Soviets were moving their movable missiles: the SS-21, the SS-22, the SS-23. The computer was programmed to automatically consult the latest satellite footage in an attempt to spot the new locations. Not all were known yet.

Soviet artillery deployments were also active. The 203-millimeter atomic artillery, the 152-millimeter self-propelled atomic artillery, the 204-millimeter atomic mortars were all on the move and the Library's computer was moving with them, sometimes only minutes behind, sometimes hours.

In the event of a shooting war in Europe, the Middle

East would become a secondary theater of operations. The Marine Amphibious Force, MAF, was getting ready to move. Shipping was rapidly being assembled for 50,000 men, 1.8 million cubic feet of consumables, 758,000 square feet of vehicles and howitzers, and 225 helicopters of various types.

But there were now Soviet SAM-5 missile batteries at the Shinshar base near Mesken, east of Aleppo in northern Syria. With a slant range of 250 kilometers, they could easily be used to shoot down U.S. AWACS aircraft flying out of eastern Turkey. The SAM-5s were in turn protected by SAM-6, SAM-8, and SAM-11 shorter-range missiles, so it would be difficult to take out the SAM-5s. A special operation would be called for. With one of its left hands, the computer was rapidly poring through official Israeli contingency plans, looking for ideas.

The German Society for Peace and Conflict Research was making noises.

Colonel General Yevgeny S. Yurasov, first deputy commander of the Soviet Air Defense Forces, was reported to be in Krasnye Kamni, a health resort near Kislovodsk in the Caucasus, which indicated that he was not feeling well. It added 0.5 percent to O.F.F., which was now at 90.17 percent.

Two squadrons of Pave Mover aircraft had moved to advanced bases in Germany. The Pave Mover radar could spot armored and other vehicles as much as eighty miles behind the Warsaw Pact lines, and was the eyes for the new Assault Breaker missile. Assault Breaker was equipped with eighty precision-guided armor-piercing bomblets. The bomblets could penetrate any Soviet armor, and were guided by sensors even after release from their missile casing. Between Pave Mover and Assault Breaker, the NATO high command believed it could clean out all second-echelon tanks for fifty miles back into East Germany. Thus there would be no forces to exploit any possible breakthroughs achieved by the first-echelon tanks.

The computer kept jumping to the Caribbean because it was on the right flank of any sea lift headed for Europe or the Middle East. The status of the Cuban Navy, which was mainly fast-attack craft of the Turya and Zhuk classes and a few Koni class frigates, was displayed every half hour.

There was a flap over the combat readiness of the U.S. aircraft carriers. Only three had a rating of C-1, or combat ready. Two were C-2, minor deficiencies, five were C-3, major deficiencies. Three were at the bottom, C-4, meaning not ready.

A World War II British fighter base in southern Egypt had been activated during the Iran hostage crisis; now it was being beefed up with two squadrons of tactical fighter aircraft, plus an AWACS group.

The National Warning System, designed to alert the public to nuclear attack, had been cut off from the city of New Orleans because of a flood in a basement. The model 4ESS long-distance switching computer had been knocked out. The Library computer was checking the background of everyone working at the switching center.

It was like being in the control room of spaceship Earth, where all variables were monitored. The pace was dizzying, the scope gigantic, and the thought occurred to Harry that he might have to start worrying about Librarian fatigue, when suddenly all the displays went blank except for a large HOLD in the center of each screen. It was Burnish's doing. Harry dropped a four-foot-long printout he had been scanning; the morning had gone by so fast that he'd forgotten about the main event.

It was time to give the third degree to Leonid Brezhnev, long-deceased General Secretary and President of the Union of Soviet Socialist Republics.

Suckers and Suicides

Leonid I. Brezhnev came into the conference room slowly, feebly, a dead surrogate. He had already been succeeded by Andropov's surrogate and by those of Andropov's successors.

A surrogate was a CIA analyst who had been assigned the task of specializing in the life of a foreign leader. There were surrogates who had spent their entire professional careers studying a Sukarno, a Castro, a Khrushchev, a Nasser, in some cases even before these men had achieved real power. The analysts immersed themselves in all aspects of the lives of their chosen subjects. The idea was to learn how important foreign leaders thought, how their mental processes proceeded, so that it might eventually be possible to predict their reactions to events before the fact.

Brezhnev's surrogate had been unusually skilled, and was considered invaluable by the CIA. On numerous occasions he had reacted exactly the way Brezhnev had. He had predicted the invasion of Afghanistan (although no one believed him at the time). He had regularly foreseen Brezhnev's positions on arms control and policy toward NATO and trade with the West. He seemed to have acquired a direct connection to the real Brezhnev's unconscious.

But Brezhnev was an unusual surrogate in other respects. He was Russian. He was the same age as Brezhnev would have been. He even looked like Brezhnev, and as the years went by, the resemblance grew. In the later years, it was difficult to tell at times whether or not Brezhnev had succumbed to the common fate of the long-term double agent, had forgotten who he was and *become* Brezhnev.

Harry brought him out of retirement for an afternoon because Brezhnev was tough. A good opponent, a nasty mouth, an unyielding son of a bitch. He was more like Brezhnev than Brezhnev, so Coolidge and the others would be impressed when Harry proceeded to destroy him. Harry believed in stamping out doubt wherever it surfaced.

Brezhnev seemed to move by individual acts of the will, putting one foot in front of the other. The conference table was so big, it was a major production for him just to get to his place, which was Burnish's customary seat, ninety degrees away from Harry, between Alex Hopkins and Leo Gardella. Burnish was in Eberhart's seat.

Harry was smiling weirdly, staring straight ahead, waiting for Brezhnev to negotiate the far turn and head down the home stretch to his chair. Harry had never liked the attention Brezhnev always got; the others couldn't take their eyes off him. Wearing all his medals, Brezhnev looked remarkably like his pictures. He was self-contained, inward-looking, and gave off the impression of possessing considerable skepticism about everything, even about the taking of his next breath. Yet he was still in there pitching, had not been defeated, was still putting one foot in front of the other.

Then it took a while to negotiate the sitting in the chair, which cost him his balance at least once and required a frantic grab at the table. Seated, the first thing he did was take out his electronic cigarette case and place it carefully in front of him. It was set to open at intervals of an hour and twenty-five minutes now, meaning that Brezhnev had lost ground of late; he had once had it up to three hours and thirteen minutes. It was impossible to tell what he was feeling; his face was hard Mongolian plain that did not yield easily to cultivation.

Brezhnev and Harry Dunn were old adversaries, dating back to distant days at CIA, where they had worked together, and formalities weren't expected or offered.

'Now that the President is comfortable,' Harry said, 'we can start. The subject is missiles, Mr. President. We think it would be beneficial to explore certain implications of missile strategy. We would like to start . . .'

Dunn stopped. From somewhere deep inside Brezhnev sounds were emerging that were a combination of repressed smoker's cough, catarrh, sob, and internal combustion engine starting up on a cold morning. It was Brezhnev's way of laughing. It was as though laughter was against the law to Brezhnev, or anyway improper, un-Bolshevik; the world was too serious for such behavior.

'I'm so witty,' Harry said, 'that sometimes I don't even understand my own jokes. Perhaps the President will deign to explain to us?'

Brezhnev swallowed his starved, nutritionless peasant's laugh, said, 'The mudsucker,' and made his laughing sounds again. Coolidge found himself leaning forward in his chair, not wanting to miss a word.

'The mudsucker,' Dunn said, nodding his head up and down, pretending to take it seriously.

'It's the reason you didn't get the racetrack system for your MX missile. It would have endangered the mudsucker.' Brezhnev sat back in his chair with great satisfaction, but then leaned forward to explain. 'That's a fish,' he said.

'We're making progress,' Harry replied. 'We've now decoded the President's idea of wit. Which I take to mean that certain conservationists in Nevada and Utah opposed the MX racetrack option in the interest of saving the' – it didn't come easy – 'uh, mudsucker, and therefore the nation has had its military security adversely affected. I can well understand the President's hilarity.'

'Suckers,' was all Brezhnev could manage to get out.

'Now if we can get back to the business at hand?' Harry said.

Brezhnev was looking at his cigarette case, waiting for it to go off.

'Is it in the strategic interest of the Soviet general staff to neutralize or eliminate the MX missile?' Harry asked.

'Of course.'

'How would you achieve that goal?'

'By means of socialist realism.'

Brezhnev looked around the table, straight-faced, although it wasn't clear if he was displaying military defiance or searching for an appreciation of his humor. There

271

was something different about the man this time. Had retirement changed him?

Harry was looking faintly nonplussed. 'Are you saying that the Soviet Union does indeed have the nerve, the strength of character in its leadership, to launch a mass missile attack on Minuteman?'

'Of course.'

'And it has the operational control necessary to do the job with a reasonable expectation of success?'

'Of course not.'

'Why not? What is lacking?'

'It is a matter of considerable gravity,' Brezhnev said, looking very grave.

'I would hope so,' Harry said, laying it thick. 'I would hope the Soviet general staff wouldn't be *flip* about a mass missile attack.'

'What does this *flip* mean?' Brezhnev whispered loudly to Hopkins, sitting next to him.

'Mr. Dunn is expressing the hope,' Hopkins replied dryly, 'that the Soviet government wouldn't destroy the planet on a whim. We would hope your government would give really serious and prolonged thought to it before wiping out mankind.'

'Ah,' Brezhnev said, gesturing that he understood.

Harry resumed the interrogation. 'Now would you mind explaining in particular what it is that oppresses the Soviet general staff about attacking the U.S.?'

'As I said, the gravity.'

'Yes, we heard you.'

'The polar route gravity.'

Harry closed his eyes in disgust at not having spotted it sooner.

'I see. All it takes is a little persistence. The Soviet general staff does not have the gravity calibrated over the polar route and therefore cannot be sure its missiles will travel in a precise path, the consequence being that counterforce accuracy would be degraded.'

'You don't understand the gravity either.'

'That would be a miscalculation. We have satellite plots of the gravity. So do you, for that matter.'

'A satellite is not a missile.'

272

'Corrections can be made for that,' Harry said.

'But they will not have been put to the test.'

'The mathematics are well known.'

'It is only theory. It has not been *tested*.'

'It's been tested over the Pacific. *And* Siberia.'

'But *not* over the polar route.'

Brezhnev put on his carefully constructed straight face, which was positively vibrant in comparison with his regular straight face, and signified that a demonstration of wit was forthcoming. 'In my country we call it Oblomov's Law: Anything that can go wrong will. Oblomov discovered it long before your Murphy.'

Giggles around the table, Dunn slumping back in his chair feigning exhaustion, Brezhnev sitting straight in his, indefatigable, the noble Indian at the council of the Western saddle tramps.

'You're quite high-spirited today, Mr. President,' Harry said, knowing that Brezhnev had won over the audience, and looking for a way to turn the tables on him. 'To what may we attribute this?'

'This is a very serious question,' Brezhnev said, looking around at all of them, sucking his cheeks in an apparent effort to keep from smiling. 'As you all know, I am dead,' he went on. 'And I am too old to start over. Such jobs are for younger men, the next generation. This is natural; the passing of the seasons, and so forth. It has liberated my spirit. I no longer have to worry about this one and that one, this consideration, that consideration. The life of a political leader, you understand. You do understand?'

'Yes, I think so,' Harry said.

It was unprecedented. Brezhnev showed his big Russian teeth and smiled broadly. He held his arms out wide. He looked like the posters they used to hang in Red Square on May Day. 'For the first time, I am in a position to tell you everything without fear of the consequences,' he said.

'That's really splendid,' Harry replied.

It was an odd, involuted notion – although reasonable when you thought about it – and Coolidge couldn't resist it: the idea that a surrogate who was paid to be a Russian politician would indeed be political about what he would say. Coolidge broke in.

'Are you saying that for your thirteen years as Brezhnev you were *not* reporting your true thoughts and feelings accurately?'

Brezhnev shrugged and waved a hand a few inches off the table. His eyes dulled with impatience for a moment, signifying that it was a childish question. 'American leaders only wish to hear what they wish to hear. Surely that is obvious. But now I am willing to be the bearer of bad tidings.'

'Then this is indeed a major opportunity,' Harry replied. It was hard to tell if he was annoyed or not, or if he believed Brezhnev or not, but he seemed to be tapping new resources in the man, so he resumed his questioning.

'In view of this liberation of yours, I am especially curious about what your answer will be to the following questions: Does the Soviet general staff . . .' Harry paused, trying to work his way out of the trap of his own rattled syntax. ' . . . or does not the Soviet general staff believe that the U.S. has the strength of character to attack over the polar route?'

Brezhnev nodded unequivocally. 'The United States has strength of character,' he said.

'Do you agree the MX missile is accurate enough?' Harry asked.

'Unquestionably.'

'Then where does socialist realism come to your rescue?'

It was almost as though the importance of the question had set up vibrations in Brezhnev's cigarette case; it went off, ringing loudly, because Brezhnev was hard of hearing. Missile theology came to an end while Brezhnev conducted his little ritual. He hadn't even smoked until he had become Brezhnev; now he was an addict. He pushed a catch at the side of the case, which stopped the ringing, and slowly took out a cigarette. The case was burnished silver with a red star in its center. It had belonged to the real Brezhnev; the CIA had stolen it from his daughter after his death. Brezhnev calmly lit the cigarette and drew on it, drew on it again, then spoke through the enormous clouds of the double drag. 'You'd be fucking yourselves,' he said, looking at Harry Dunn squarely for the first time.

274

'You would be hitting empty silos.'

'Launch on Warning?'

'Launch on Warning.'

'That's Russian bluster.'

'Try it. You will see.'

'You wouldn't dare delegate such authority. You wouldn't know how to. You've got to keep it all tight in your own hands. Launch on Warning is a Soviet fantasy.'

'Fire a missile at us, my friend, and it will come right back at you! Fire a thousand missiles and you will get back a thousand. But no interest, capitalist, only the principal!'

'I don't believe it,' Harry persisted.

'You will evoke that which you profess to fear. A mass missile attack on the United States of America.'

'Only profess to fear?'

'Sometimes I wonder.' Brezhnev was staring at his rapidly vanishing cigarette. 'A nation of suicides,' he mused. 'Suckers and suicides.'

It was probably a career first, but Harry was temporarily stymied. Coolidge took advantage of the silence. 'You say you would Launch on Warning. And yet if we don't believe you, it doesn't amount to a deterrent. That's vital. Convince us.'

Brezhnev stubbed out the microscopic remains of a cigarette. 'To try to convince you would look defensive to you. A sign of weakness, which you are always so diligently looking for in yourselves. Take your chances, Yankee.'

'But what about Oblomov's Law?' Coolidge said. 'Doesn't that apply to Launch on Warning? What about radar glitches? Errors in judgment? Errors in computers? Migrating birds?'

'Migrating birds,' Brezhnev repeated, eyes moving around the table with the glint that signified wit was approaching. 'What would the Pentagon do without migrating birds?' he asked them. 'Do you know what migrating birds are?'

'We're dying to know,' Harry said sarcastically.

'Birdshit.'

'Is that a fact?'

'We've spent *billions* on radar. What you people call the

Hen House in your satellite photos' – he looked at Vera – 'is not an antiballistic missile installation. It is the best search radar in the world. Believe me, we can tell the difference between a bird that is one foot long and a bird that is one hundred feet long. We will wait until we can! After which you will have achieved your deeply longed-for suicide.'

'You believe then that you could wait until the final few minutes – say ten, twelve, fifteen – by which time your radar would have informed you for sure that those birds were missiles, And then you would launch your devastating liquid-fuel missiles? Do I understand you, Mr. President?'

'You are mouthing the right words. Beyond that, who can say?'

Harry laughed appreciatively. 'The President is in exceptionally good form today. Now let's go to the headphones and see about this business of Launch on Warning.'

Burnish had a pair ready. He plugged them into a jack under the table at Brezhnev's position. Brezhnev was to hear it in the original Russian for believability purposes. Hopkins typed in a command on his keyboard. The loudspeakers mounted high on the walls immediately began to rush, and then a babble of voices, in the English version, was heard.

'This is Operation Freedom,' Harry told them. 'A practice alert at the missile base at Chelyabinsk.'

'What are those idiots waiting for?'

'Never mind. Give me a reading on fuel level.'

'What reading? It is the same as before. Maximum.'

'The same as before? It cannot be the same as before.'

'It is the same as before. It is maximum. Relax, it is all right.'

'It cannot be all right.'

'I tell you it is all right.'

'There should be evaporation, idiot. Switch to the fuel metering override detent. Quickly!'

'Oh my God.'

'Nothing. Nothing! We have had a malfunction!'

'Capsule Forty-three. Nature of incoming target has

now been definitely established. You are cleared to fire immediately.'

'*We are finished, Georgi, finished.*'

Brezhnev threw his headset on the table. Harry was smiling his fiendish smile.

'Peculiarly enough,' Harry said, 'the deputy commander for Chelyabinsk is Lieutenant General Sergei K. Oblomov.'

Brezhnev did not respond.

'Launch on Warning requires a high degree of operational control and efficiency. Along with some luck. *We* even have difficulties with it. But with liquid fuel missiles?'

'Enough will get off,' Brezhnev said softly. 'There will be enough to go around.'

'We wonder. We are not convinced.'

'There is only one way to convince you. I have already told you that.'

'I must say I am surprised by this feeling of security you have. Is this your vaunted socialist realism? A refusal to face the the facts?'

Brezhnev sat back in his chair, stone-faced.

'Tell me,' Harry continued, 'has the President picked up any word of our latest antisubmarine warfare program?'

'Your latest defector has said nothing of it,' Brezhnev replied.

'Oh, then, we must keep the President better informed. Leo.'

Gardella did input at his keyboard while Burnish turned the lights down to their normal low level and pulled back the drapes on one of the displays. The wall behind Brezhnev came to life. Harry could have shown it on the wall opposite the man, but that would have been too convenient for Brezhnev, who was now forced to swivel around painfully and awkwardly.

It was a Mercator projection of the world, centered on the United States. The Atlantic and Pacific oceans got the lion's share of the space.

'You are surely aware that we attempt to track every last Soviet missile submarine,' Harry said. 'We are now in a position to identify each and every one of them on station in the Atlantic and Pacific, all within range of the United States.'

'And more are coming,' Brezhnev said.

'Occasionally we succeed in identifying all twenty-three *simultaneously*. At such moments, we are capable of wiping out the entire Soviet submarine retaliatory force in minutes.'

Harry Dunn sat back and waited for a reaction.

They all watched Brezhnev slowly struggle to his feet, walk up close to the display, and put his glasses on. He was shaped like a rectangle. He had more black hair on his head than would be expected of a man his age. His head began to shake from side to side, and he turned back to the table with the grace of an elephant. 'Can an irrational policy come from rational men?' he asked. 'Your Herman Kahn said it was possible. He had an elaborate mathematical proof demonstrating it. And yet I cannot accept that. Irrational policy must come from irrational men.' He turned back to the map and studied it again. 'Clearly there is no lunacy gap,' he said.

'Is it lunacy to reach a winning position?' Harry said.

Brezhnev leaned on the table and retrieved his cigarette case. Then he was putting one foot in front of the other again, plodding back along the big table. The turning point in his life was when he could have been Khrushchev; he could have retired happily twenty years earlier, when Khrushchev was ousted. But no, someone else had gotten Khrushchev.

'It won't work,' he said, rounding the turn, heading toward the door. 'I take no responsibility. I wash my hands of it.'

Harry was sitting looking straight ahead, that odd smile still on his face. 'Why won't it work? Why? Why?'

'Goddamn fucking dollar. You couldn't do it without your fucking dollar; you will blow up the world with your fucking dollar.'

'Oh, *we'll* blow up the world!'

'But there is one thing your fucking dollar cannot buy. It cannot buy you a trial run. You will be shooting into the unknown. I wash my hands of it.' As Brezhnev reached the door, his cigarette alarm went off unexpectedly, ahead of time, taking him by surprise. His arms flew out in different directions, uncoordinated, like a puppet's. It was almost as though he had been shot. He went through the door cursing, finished, dead for the second time, and only one more to go.

As soon as the door closed on Brezhnev, Burnish went around pulling drapes and switching on displays. The computer, having stayed up and running, immediately began throwing out all kinds of stuff.

O.F.F. had climbed to 93.62 percent, a gain of 0.32 percent, in the last hour because Sergeant Ivan G. Krasnopolsky of the Strategic Rocket Force had been run over by a bus. Krasnopolsky was a maintenance genius in an important communications section and was known to be virtually irreplaceable.

Coolidge sat in the dimness, thinking, wondering, eyes wandering around the table, watching them. Vera, Harry, the others. There was a mood of confidence and optimism. It was beginning to look as though the Russians were indeed a pushover and O.F.F. was irresistible. Nothing had been overlooked. Harry, especially, seemed satisfied. He had taken on Brezhnev in close combat and beaten him.

'Well, Walter?' Harry said. 'What do you think?'

Coolidge nodded. 'You did it, Harry,' he said. 'I'm convinced.'

Names

It was the names that finally decided him. He had been close, but the names pushed him over. With every step he took, he passed hundreds of them. It was the bill for the Vietnam War, all the names inscribed on black marble.

As he walked past them, his mind was racing. He was a portable Library and he couldn't switch it off. His internal computer was up and running, flashing around the world. East Germany, West Germany, tanks, NATO, Czechoslovakia. How far an Abrams tank can go without having to change oil, which was important because you had to take the engine out to change the oil. What the Circular Error Probable of an MX is compared with the SS-18. Harry kept popping. And the Emersons, Vera, Charley Eberhart. All at the speed of light.

He must have passed fifteen thousand names when he remembered what the Vietnam Memorial reminded him of. The Grammatical Fiction.

Arthur Koestler had called Russia the place where the first person pronoun, 'I,' had become an empty shell, had lost its significance, was a fiction. 'I,' a universe, had been turned into '1' by the Bolsheviks; the individual had become nothing more than a number, sacrificed to other interests: the state, the party, Stalin, collectivization.

Twenty thousand names, twenty-five thousand. People touching them, photographing them, making rubbings of them.

What noble purpose had been served? There had never been a consistent or believable reason given. It had been an immense Light Brigade charging to its destruction without knowing the reason why, dying for the square root of minus one.

Thirty-five thousand of them. Forty-five thousand.

It was the end product of moral idiocy in high places. Fifty thousand. Each step a massacre. Fifty-five thousand. In comparison, the Nuclear Memorial would look like the Great Wall of China.

Fifty-eight thousand and twelve.

He kept walking, past Lincoln in his big chair looking out over the Reflecting Pool, and ambled alongside the water. Now, instead of names, he was checking an occasional tree. Even the trees were regimented in Washington; they had their own dog tags, tiny metal strips with a letter and a number stamped on them.

He was thinking about Charley Eberhart: *Coolidge has unconscious feelings of being above it all. . . . He doesn't know it, but he's a narrow technocrat. . . .* It was true that he couldn't remember ever having rooted for a baseball team. Score one for Charley. After checking a few more tags, he found the one he was looking for, tree number E-53. It marked a point far enough from the nearest microcam to constitute authentic privacy.

Coolidge sat down on the bench opposite E-53. The dried birdshit on one end reminded him of Brezhnev. A family of ducks glided by on the Reflecting Pool, all in a row, looking like targets in a shooting gallery. He looked around at the monuments. Lincoln at one end, Washington off in the distance. Winning really paid off in height of monument. Washington and Lincoln had been winners; Jeff Davis had been relegated to Statuary Hall on the second floor of the Capitol. He was lucky to get that; he had borne arms against his government. Benedict Arnold didn't have a statue in Statuary Hall. Of course, Benedict Arnold didn't have a constituency; an occasional furtive wreath was still placed on Jeff Davis's statue.

The path along the pool ran for a great distance, trees on both sides, a marvelous place for a constitutional. He knew they'd be along soon. He had Garvey's schedule for the day memorized. He could see them way off, marching along, Mutt and Jeff, Garvey looking like a British cabinet minister with his slow and serious walk and mien, as though always on the point of declaring war on the Boers, or deciding which regiment should go to India. Coolidge still found it strange that he would be involved with people like Garvey. Or Harry, for that matter, or Ives, or the President. Originally he had expected a much different career. He was interested in the daily lives of people, how they worked, how they played, how they got through the day. He had envisioned a quiet career studying them, perhaps getting a few good generalizations to his credit, maybe even a book or two.

The peculiar thing was that he'd grown up virtually apolitical, accepting the establishment's views on most things. He had never marched on the Pentagon. He was a college graduate who had allowed himself to be drafted and was lucky enough to spend his two war years at a desk in Mississippi, making corporal by the time he was discharged. Coolidge had been too wrapped up in anthropology to pay much attention to anything else: There was too much to read.

Even his six years at HEW hadn't changed him much. It wasn't until he'd found himself awash in data in the Library that he began to see how America worked. Americans weren't governed with the truth; Americans lived under government by cover story, cover stories which grew in time to have such reality that it was virtually impossible to penetrate or 'blow' them. Coolidge had accepted it at first. That was his 'realistic' phase. How could you hope to govern such a diverse country if you told the truth all the time? For a while, he accepted the fact that politics in America had been reduced to a few images and slogans – cover stories – behind which the real governing took place.

But the data banks of America were its collective unconscious. And as Coolidge searched through it, looking for the Doctor, he had at first resisted the notion that anything could be wrong. It was the Doctor who was wrong. It was the Doctor who was bad, evil, a betrayer – at best a megalomaniac assuming responsibilities that weren't his to assume.

But as he proceeded through data, his opinion of the Doctor had risen. He began to see the Doctor as a man struggling with problems of conscience and ethics and individual responsibility. The more intensely he searched for the Doctor, the closer he came to accepting a side of himself that was long repressed, now emerging almost against his will. He'd broken through his own detachment and indifference, and the Coolidge who had emerged was one who'd seen through the ultimate cover story, patriotism, and once you had seen that, it left you as nothing more than a hired killer, a defender of corporate profits, and employee of narrow, poorly educated, irresponsible fanatics doing business in a moral vacuum. They'd created a false reality with which they'd driven the rest of the country crazy for decades. With time it had turned into a fanatical, messianic vision, in the pursuit of which they had drained off a great part of the national treasure, the sweat of brows, as well as tens of thousands of young men – all a fake, a cover story, a business deduction. During his prowl through the collective unconscious, Coolidge's realistic phase had come to an end; he was back in favor of majority rule.

They were about a hundred feet away, and he could see Garvey gnawing at a jelly apple. So much for the British cabinet. Reed was doing the talking. They were about fifty feet away when they finally noticed him. They stopped simultaneously, in shock, and looked at each other. Then, without a word, they resumed walking. As they came abreast, they sat down on the bench, one on each side, Reed voluntarily taking the birdshit side.

'Davey,' the senator said, talking across Coolidge, 'what would you say the natural odds are for a meeting of this kind?'

Reed was leaning forward, elbows on knees, hands holding up face, thinking. 'In a normal American town, about twenty-eight thousand to one. In this town we are no longer accepting bets.'

'Washington cynicism, Walter,' Garvey said. 'Don't pay any attention to him. Funny thing – Davey here was just talking about you. Would you like to know what he was saying?'

'No.'

'Tell Walter what you were saying, Davey.'

'He's really putting me on the spot,' Reed said to Coolidge. 'But okay, it went something like this. I was telling the senator that I was getting worried about you. I thought you were in danger of becoming a bureaucrat. I thought that maybe you were becoming more interested in your job than in the public weal. I want you to know the senator disagreed with me.'

Garvey took a bite out of his jelly apple. 'Tell him everything, Davey. He'll find out, anyway.'

Reed grimaced and said, 'Tst,' as though really being put on the spot.

'I said that if you didn't tell us what O.F.F was, you were going to have a hard time living with yourself.'

Coolidge looked at him. Reed didn't know the half of it. Here it was, the end of the line, and Coolidge still didn't know why he was doing it, except, maybe, that there didn't seem to be any other volunteers.

'It's Opportunity For First-Strike,' the Doctor said.

'Of course, I could be wrong,' Reed went on, and then stopped. 'What?'

'That's right.'

'Did you just say something? Did he just say something?'

Garvey was nipping at his jelly apple like a piranha.

'I said that O.F.F. means Opportunity For First-Strike,' Coolidge said. 'We're going to off the Russians.'

Reed looked at Coolidge, and all the wryness and smart-guy attitudes dissipated, and the muscles in his face went slack. His mouth was hanging open. He had finally heard something that he could take seriously.

Garvey reared back and hurled his jelly apple out through the trees and into the Reflecting Pool. 'It's always the same in this business,' he said. 'There's good news and there's bad news.'

O.F.F.

Reed swore that he had gotten five hours sleep and was sober, or anyway within faking distance of being able to walk a straight line, so they'd let him drive the white American University van, which they were able to get because Garvey was a trustee.

Coolidge looked over at Garvey, sitting across from him in the rear. The senator was in his Sunday best, fat baby cheeks shaven smooth, black topcoat with velvet collar brushed spotless, soft black felt hat. It was his best British look; he was even carrying an umbrella. He was deep in thought, probably fantasizing about his political future.

Coolidge sat holding the black boxes on his lap. He didn't want them to bounce around and get out of alignment. He looked at Garvey's hooded eyes; he was probably taking the oath of office by now. You could almost hear 'Hail to the Chief.' It was time to strike. It was the reason he'd wanted Reed to do the driving, so there'd be a few minutes to talk.

'I know what you're doing with the Whip's wife,' Coolidge said.

Garvey came out of his reverie fast. He looked quickly toward Reed up front behind the wheel, and then back to Coolidge.

'You keep dropping these bombs.'

'I know where you do it. How often. I know where the Whip thinks she's supposed to be. I know that it's been going on for almost a year. It started at the cocktail party at the Aluminum Association. I know what her pet name for you is. It would look fantastic in a headline.'

Garvey's fat eyes were bulging. He had suddenly been

285

torn from dreams of the presidency to the realization that there was no aspect of his life that could be called private; Coolidge watched him running back through the last few years, recalling all his carnal sins.

'Speak lower. What else do you know?'

'The black hooker on K Street.'

Garvey closed his eyes.

'The secretaries you give an occasional thrill to.'

'Jesus God.'

'The promotions two of them got on the Appropriations Committee staff. Would you like me to continue?'

'I think I get the point.'

Coolidge pointed an index finger approximately between Garvey's eyes. 'Don't try to fuck me,' Coolidge said. 'I'm not going to warn you again.'

Garvey sat back and sighed, suddenly not worried about soiling his fancy topcoat against the wall of the van. 'To think that it's come to this,' he said.

'Don't give me that. You've stepped over plenty of bodies in your time. I'm not going to be the next one.'

'Why would I betray you, Walter?'

'We're blowing the lid off. Anything could happen. Who knows what's going to happen? And if you try to save your ass by giving me away, you're going to *lose* your ass. That's my personal deterrence policy.'

'Mutual Assured Destruction, eh, Walter? Okay, let it be as you say. I'm deterred. Permanently.'

They sat in silence for another twenty minutes, Reed doing an honest job of driving. The odds were with him; it was six o'clock on a Sunday morning, and there wasn't much else on the road. There would be virtually no one wandering around the campus either; they would all be sleeping off beer or sex or pot or, conceivably, study.

Reed found the radio station two minutes after driving onto the campus. It was easy – there was a tall radio tower standing next to it. He backed into the small unloading area at the side and kept on going as far as he could, stopping at the building line, the branches of a large tree scraping the roof of the van. With the rear door open, there was no way Coolidge could be seen going from the van into the rear entrance. He waited for Reed to

286

reconnoiter inside. He could hear the distant slap of tennis balls; otherwise it was totally quiet. When Reed came back and waved, Coolidge was inside the door in seconds, followed by a hustling Garvey carrying the coffee machine.

In the darkened studio Davey Reed seemed to know what he was doing; he found the light switch. Then, after about five minutes and twenty wrong guesses, he had the control panel fired up. It was something he'd picked up in his days as an advertising copywriter making radio commercials. Garvey got the coffee going and then went out to greet any early arrivals who would be drifting in through the front of the building like regular people. Reed was patching in one of the black boxes to the control panel while Coolidge was using the other one to sweep the place for bugs.

'Okay,' Reed said, after a lot of blundering around. 'I think we're in business. Try a listen.'

Coolidge went out into the studio and sat down on a high stool next to a lectern. It was where performers would normally stand. In the soundproof control booth, Reed was moving his lips but no sound was coming out. Coolidge shook his head. Reed looked thoughtfully at the control panel while chewing on a finger, and threw another switch.

'Can you hear me now?'

Coolidge nodded. Reed started to recite the Gettysburg Address. Coolidge listened with closed eyes. It wasn't bad. Reed's voice sounded as if it were coming from under water. It was about an octave lower than normal and none of his timbre or tone or personality was left in it. The black box had given him total anonymity. Coolidge made a circle with thumb and forefinger.

Wool ski mask on, Coolidge sat in the darkened control room and watched Garvey shepherd Emerson Foster into the studio, along with eight others who could roughly be described as the leadership of the Emersons.

The Emersons had slowly come together out of a shared fear. They were leaders of one kind or another in various walks of life who had one thing in common. They had lost faith, if they'd ever had any, in the arms race as a means of defending America.

The arms race had been going on for over forty years. It would take only 100 strategic nuclear warheads to destroy the Soviet Union, about 125 to destroy the U.S. Yet the U.S. had about 10,000 strategic warheads, and the Soviets about 7,500. Each year the totals climbed. They were making them as fast as they could produce U-235 and plutonium.

It seemed to make no sense. And now India had them. And Pakistan. China had them. France too. Israel was assumed to have them. South Africa was a probable. Argentina was close. The longer the technology was in existence and not banned by international agreement, the greater were the risks of atomic war, accidental or otherwise, not to mention the possibilities of nuclear terrorism. Even some bright high school students were believed capable of designing a bomb by now.

Would the U.S. and the U.S.S.R. never agree? Then the world was doomed. Wasn't it in both their national interests to curb nuclear weapons? Then why didn't they? As the Emersons talked together more and more, trying to find the answer to this atomic strangeness, they gradually realized that through their connections with one constituency or another they had come to represent, ad hoc, the American peace movement.

Emerson Foster was the logical leader. One of the biggest investment bankers in the country, he had more connections throughout the American establishment than anyone else. He could bring groups together. He could arrange for high-level briefings. Foster knew congressmen, senators, bureaucrats, presidents, businessmen, academics, journalists.

Yet the most they could learn was speculative. They had been unable to get an authoritative and convincing explanation of, or justification for, the arms race. Which was why they had come, at six o'clock on a chilly fall Sunday morning, to American University's radio station, to hear what the Doctor had to say.

They were all present. Admiral Dutch Anderson, retired; Bishop Patrick Hinds of the New York archdio-

288

cese; Joe Kiernan of the United Auto Workers; Sarah Weinstein, who was instrumental in developing the idea of the nuclear freeze; Purefoy; Ingalls; Rabbi Harold Mandelbaum of Washington, D.C., General Rudolph Witek, retired.

They were handling the situation rather well, Coolidge thought. They made a point of not looking at him. They were cool, chatting easily, pouring coffee, finding stools or folding chairs to sit on, draping expensive topcoats over music stands, on the piano, on a synthesizer.

They were all accomplished people who had done and seen a lot, but they were alive with anticipation. Coolidge could tell by the climate out in the studio that Garvey had kept his word: they didn't know what they were about to hear.

Feeling horrible, fearing a headache, the Garbageman sat before the control panel taking deep breaths, hoping the black box would disguise any quaver in his voice, waiting for the signal from Garvey to blow the whistle.

Emerson Foster was a short, slightly stocky, polite man of sixty-five. He had deep-blue eyes, lots of white hair, and teeth that were long in the caps. He was soft-spoken and considerate, and was known to be angered only by stupidity on the part of subordinates, at which time he became his opposite and turned into a corrosive, destructive critic. He regarded himself as a true conservative, as opposed to the bomb-throwing conservatives of the establishment, whom he considered to be on a par with anarchists. Foster's bank had investments everywhere; he wished to conserve them rather than see them blown up.

'Oliver, I assume you've done everything imaginable to protect this man's identity,' he said to Garvey.

'Indeed we have, Emerson. I think our security is one hundred percent so far.'

'Fine. Someday I hope we'll be in a position to do something for him. He rates it.'

'I don't envy him,' Joe Kiernan said. His beefy body looked precarious seated on a folding chair. 'There's no way he can feel good about doing this.'

'You've got it turned inside out, Joe,' said Bishop

Hinds, leaning on his walker even while seated. 'His moral perceptions being what they are, there is no way he could feel good *not* doing it.' Pause. 'Though I'll grant you, the cardinal might not agree.'

'Why don't we start, Oliver,' Emerson Foster said.

'Certainly.' Garvey was positively scintillating. It was his own big moment as well as Coolidge's; the people sitting around in the studio were in positions to give him a big push toward the White House.

'First, he's going to make a statement,' Garvey said, 'after which he'll take questions. Feel free to ask away, but in the interests of keeping the meeting short, he has requested that you stay very much to the point. Frankly, by the time he's finished, I don't think there's going to be much to talk about.'

With that, Oliver Garvey turned to the glass window of the control room and pointed a finger at Walter Coolidge.

'It is rapidly becoming possible to launch a preemptive first strike against the Soviet Union,' Coolidge said in his underwater voice, 'without the U.S. suffering a retaliatory counterblow. This ability is called exploitable nuclear superiority, and it has taken the atomic bomb down off the shelf.

'Why and how has this come about?

'An influential part of the American establishment has never been willing to coexist with a powerful Communist state like the Soviet Union. They are terrified of the appeal communism may have for the poor of all countries, including the United States. They do not believe they can compete peacefully with the Communists' selling proposition. This has led to a spiraling arms race, in the attempt to acquire a first-strike capability against the Soviets. This part of the establishment will never stop the arms race short of the military domination, if not the physical destruction of the Soviet Union.

'The U.S. has led the way through every escalation of the arms race, using periodic red scares to get the money out of the American public. We were first with the atomic bomb, the hydrogen bomb, the mass missile force (one thousand Minuteman missiles), the first ballistic missile submarines, the first MIRVed missiles, and the first MARVed missiles. In almost every case, the Soviets have trailed us by three to five years in deploying similar weapon systems.

'In some ways, they've never caught up. They have only one hundred fifty strategic bombers of which fifty are slow prop planes, as against about three hundred fifty American B-52 jets. Their submarines are fatally noisy. And their weapon, the SS-18 land-based missile, is liquid-fueled, which makes it difficult to keep on alert status and difficult to launch. The U.S. stopped making liquid-fuel missiles in the nineteen fifties.

'What is basic in all of this is that the arms race has not been the mindless acquisition of new weapons, as it appears to many. It has been the purposeful pursuit of superiority through accuracy.

'Missile accuracy is the key fact of the arms race. You do not need an accurate missile to destroy Moscow or any other Russian city. City-busting accuracy was achieved decades ago. A missile designed to destroy a city may sound inhumane, but in reality it is a peaceful missile because it is a *defensive* missile, a second-strike retaliatory missile. It is not a war-fighting missile; it is a deterrence missile. Its purpose is to frighten the Russians into refraining from a first strike on the U.S.

'Accurate missiles, on the other hand, are designed to be silo-killers. Accurate missiles are inherently offensive. Since there is no payoff to striking an empty silo, accurate missiles are, ipso facto, first-strike missiles.

'The MX, the Trident Two, and the Pershing Two are the most accurate missiles in the world. They are followed closely by Minuteman Three and a considerable number of the cruise missiles. Collectively these missiles give the U.S. the capability of destroying each and every Soviet ICBM.

'Since a number of the intermediate-range Soviet missiles are mobile, many of these may escape an American first strike. But these missiles can only hit Western Europe, except for those stationed in Eastern Siberia, which could reach parts of the western United States. The latter will be taken out with fast, depressed-trajectory

Trident Two missiles fired from Trident submarines stationed close to the Asian landmass.'

It was impossible for Coolidge to tell if they believed what he was saying. Except for Garvey, the faces were noncommittal. He was telling them something that contradicted American attitudes, values, beliefs. He was making a liar out of every American President from Harry Truman on. Was it too much to believe? Well, he would tell them; that was all he could do. He took a good breath, preparing to say the magic words.

'All of the operational capabilities required for the forcible disarming of the Soviet Union have been pulled together into a secret program called O.F.F., or Opportunity For First-Strike. It involves many weapon systems and procedures, and all three services. It is believed that Opportunity For First-Strike could bring the arms race to a successful conclusion in half an hour.

'It is deemed highly possible that because of O.F.F.'s overwhelming power, it would not actually have to be implemented; that the threat alone would force the Russians to do our bidding, a situation that has not existed since nineteen sixty-two, when President Kennedy ordered the Russian missiles out of Cuba. Toward this end, the U.S. has deliberately leaked the target navigational maps of the Pershing Two missiles to the Russians in order to show them how hopeless their position is.

'A third distinct possibility is that the Russians would spend themselves into dissolution trying to keep up with O.F.F., since their small GNP vis-à-vis the United States makes the arms race a far heavier burden on them than on us. They have tried to overcome their GNP disadvantage by stealing American technology instead of developing their own, but this hasn't made a substantial difference.

'Whether or not the Soviet Union fails economically, the temptation to actually use Opportunity For First-Strike would always be there as the "opportunity" recurred from time to time. The opportunity, as such, is a statistical one. It would not necessarily be a war that results from some immediate international tensions. It would be a war emanating from certain statistical events, some of which, like the weather, are not predictable and

292

have nothing whatsoever to do with the U.S.S.R.

'Opportunity For First-Strike is the sort of idea that the Pentagon itself refers to as counterintuitive. A counterintuitive idea is one that sounds crazy, offhand. Surely, one would think, the Soviets would be able to retaliate and destroy American society. Since it takes only 125 successful strategic warheads to destroy America, and the Soviets have over 7500, an American attack that is only 99 percent successful is a catastrophe; it would leave the Soviets with 1 percent – seventy-five warheads – and a vengeful frame of mind.

'Yet there is method to this counterintuitiveness.

'O.F.F. consists of three principal phases, all of which would be conducted approximately simultaneously. (*A*) Decapitation of Soviet Command and Control. (*B*) Destruction of the Soviet SS-18 ground-based ICBMs. (*C*) Destruction of the Soviet Union's submarine missile force.

'Curiously, the decapitation of Soviet Command and Control centers is a military act that has long been criticized by doves and arms controllers, since eliminating Soviet leadership and their communications would obviously eliminate any possibility of negotiation to end a nuclear war once it started. What the doves never seem to have understood is that negotiations are not desired; negotiations would interfere with victory.

'A specially modified Trident Two missile will be the first shot of the war. This missile is code-named Blanket Two. It will not contain the usual ten MIRVed warheads. It will consist of a single twenty-megaton warhead that will be fired from a Trident Two submarine positioned off Murmansk. The warhead will be detonated three hundred miles up, roughly over the center of the Soviet Union.

'The result (and purpose) of this explosion will be an intense burst of energy called the Electro-Magnetic Pulse, or EMP, which will propagate at the speed of light over the entire Soviet landmass. Metal objects everywhere will pick up a jolt of electricity of as much as fifty thousand volts. This will travel along telephone lines, power lines, and antennas, disrupting communications, power, radar, and computer processing. Airplanes will be unable to take off. Missiles will not be firable. (The EMP will also propagate outward in space and damage both high-orbit and low-orbit American satellites over Russia; replacement satellites will be on their launching pads, ready to go.)

'Initially, only this one missile will be on Soviet radar screens. It will not look like a mass attack to the Soviets. It may look like an accident or a mistake or an errant satellite. They will have only three minutes to think about it, after which their entire Command and Control will be fatally degraded.

'The moment Blanket Two is detonated, the Pershing Two missiles will be launched. These maneuverable or MARVed missiles are extremely fast, extremely accurate, and very close to the Soviet Union. They will have the job of physically knocking out the four alternative Soviet Command and Control centers. These are located in Moscow, Tyuratam, Kiev, and Chelyabinsk. Flight time to the Kiev center will be 4.67 minutes; to Tyuratam, 7.49 minutes; to Chelyabinsk, 7.52 minutes. Moscow, at 10.00 minutes, will be the longest flight.

'Thirteen minutes after the launch of Blanket Two, the Soviet Command and Control centers will be destroyed, and there will be military and political chaos in the Soviet Union. There is no response possible to these short-range attacks. So at most, there will now be only second-rate and slow backup channels for use by subsidiary commanders.

'To make their problems even tougher, it is desirable to destroy the Soviet early-warning satellites. The important Soviet satellites are all in low orbits and will be destroyed by F-15s flying to high altitudes and firing the Miniature Homing Intercept Vehicle. It is because of this mission that part of the American establishment will never agree to a treaty banning weapons in space.

'At this point, the U.S.S.R. will have only subsidiary commanders with catastrophically degraded input data to work with as a means of orchestrating a second-strike retaliatory blow against the U.S. They will have only twenty minutes in which to do it.

'The successful execution of Phase B, destruction of the SS-18 ground-based ICBMs, is helped by the fact that the SS-18 was obsolete the day it was designed. Lack of solid-fuel technology is a major Soviet blunder. They have 75 percent of their warheads installed in some eight-hundred SS-18s, and they are sitting ducks. There is no way these cumbersome liquid-fuel missiles can be made operational in the twenty minutes they will have available.

'A combination of Trident Two, Pershing Two, MX, and Minuteman Three will be launched against these eight-hundred missiles. Launch times will coincide with the launch of the Command and Control Pershing Two strikes, so that the SS-18s will be hit only twenty minutes after the longest Pershing Two strike – that is, Moscow center. The only point in debate has been whether to allocate two or three warheads to each SS-18. Some planners feel that with today's accuracies, three are hardly necessary and only add additonal fallout to the atmosphere. However, to ensure success and allow for failures, three warheads per SS-18 have been opted for. Furthermore, the SS-18s will be cross-targeted: each of the three warheads assigned to any SS-18 will come from a different missile. In this way, any one missile that's off course will not result in a "miss." '

Coolidge paused, mouth dry, pulse rate high, eczema starting up: a new patch above his left outside ankle. He swallowed what was left of his cold coffee for lubrication. He could see he had their attention. Most of them were staring into space, listening. Garvey was looking his way occasionally; Sarah Weinstein once or twice. Now and then one of the others would glance at him quickly, as though it were forbidden. He plunged ahead, getting in deeper.

'Phase C, destruction of the Soviet Union's submarine missile force, took longest to develop and is the most difficult part of the operation. It is made possible, in part, by the highly disadvantageous geographical situation of the Soviet Union. Because of geography, the Soviets require virtually four separate naval groups: the Northern Fleet, the Baltic Fleet, the Black Sea Fleet, and the Pacific Fleet.

'In addition, each fleet, should its vessels be ordered out to the high seas, must pass through a "choke point." The choke points are relatively narrow bodies of water through which the Soviet ships must pass to reach the open seas. They are easily monitorable. The four fleets and their choke points are as follows: Northern Fleet – between Greenland and Iceland and/or between Iceland and Norway. Baltic Fleet – entrance into North Baltic from Baltic Sea. Black Sea Fleet – the Dardanelles, connecting the Black Sea to the Mediterranean. Pacific Fleet – La Pérouse Strait into the Pacific.

'The U.S. Navy has been installing hydrophones in these choke points for over twenty years. It is impossible for a Soviet nuclear sub to reach open ocean without being detected. This effort is aided by the fact that Soviet subs are notoriously noisy. We always know how many there are in each ocean.

'Which is where SOSUS takes over. SOSUS – Sound Surveillance System – has been in operation for twenty-five years. By now, hydrophones have been planted on continental shelves all over the world. This constant listening has taught us a lot about the sounds that submarines make. As a technical reality, no two shafts, no two pumps, no two compressors are machined to precisely the same dimensions. Therefore they all make different sounds when operating. Consequently, every submarine produces a unique sound print. With SOSUS we have the capability to identify each and every Soviet sub by its sound print. (It is also possible to identify the characteristic tactics of individual submarine commanders, further adding to identification.)

'All of this data is fed into an enormous computer in California. Iliac Four is actually sixty-four huge computers ganged together. This colossal computing capacity can separate out the sounds of whales singing, shrimp biting, and all the rest of the cacophony of the seas. It can take the inputs from all the hydrophones, eliminate the noise, and pin down the location of each submarine to within a circle of thirty-two miles diameter.

'Thereafter the job is in the hands of aircraft, surface ships, and hunter-killer subs. With every week that goes by, more and more of the Soviet Union's submarines are being tracked *continuously*. At this moment, the Soviets have nine subs on patrol in the Pacific, eleven in the Atlantic. The continuous tracking of any one of these subs adds 3 percent to Opportunity For First-Strike. Since Soviet sub commanders are accustomed to being hounded relentlessly, they will attach no significance to the actual attack until it is too late.

'Soviet attempts to escape SOSUS by constructing titanium steel subs that can dive deeper and thus be harder to detect have failed. These expensive Alpha-class boats are *still* noisy.

'It should be noted that those Soviet subs *not* deployed when O.F.F. is launched will be destroyed as they attempt to pass through the choke points, all of which have been strewn with Captor mines. The Captor detection devices are capable of distinguishing between hostile and friendly submarines. Once activated by the sounds of a Soviet submarine, a Mark 48 torpedo emerges from the Captor housing. Should it miss the first time, it turns around and attacks again, at fifty miles per hour. It is armed with a nuclear warhead and can destroy a submarine within two miles of the point of detonation.'

It was too much for anybody to take in. He was overwhelming them with data. Technical data, implausible data. Its very complexity was why one administration after another had been able to hide behind one cover story or another. Listening to himself, Coolidge doubted whether even he would believe it were he on the other side of the soundproof glass. How had he gotten into this spot? He was complicating his life, with nothing to gain and a lot to lose. That's what a sucker did. A sucker and a suicide, as Brezhnev would put it.

'In order to prevent the premature implementation of O.F.F., all the elements that comprise the O.F.F. operation are assigned weighted percentage values in an extremely complex system for evaluating "opportunity." Successful tracking of all Soviet ballistic missile subs, for example, is worth 60 percent for each sub. But the "loss" of a sub previously tracked would subtract 7 percent. Since O.F.F. will not be implemented at less than 95 percent, the loss of a single sub will automatically deactivate the operation.

'Other percentages reflect on-line alert status for those

MX, Pershing Two, Trident Two, Minuteman Three, cruise missiles, B-52s, B-1s, and naval attack aircraft that are assigned to O.F.F. tasks. All of these missile systems are self-monitoring and report to a computer all malfunctions, or even slight deviations from tolerances.

'Weather is a factor included in total determination of "opportunity." O.F.F. depends upon accuracy; the warheads must land within about 150 yards of the silos. Should winds anywhere along the planned missile trajectories be high enough to degrade accuracy, 7 percent will be subtracted, thereby halting the operation. The aurora borealis and solar flaring are also accounted for, since these are capable of affecting sensors in missiles, satellites, and detection systems.

'Many other factors are taken into account – the maintenance readiness of the Soviet SS-18s, for example, or the availability of key personnel, from generals down to enlisted men in highly technical positions. Depending upon the time of day of the attack, some cruise missiles will have been programmed to take out the homes of these personnel, using high-explosive warheads rather than nuclear.

'When O.F.F. reaches 95 percent, the system is theoretically ready to go. A cautious President might wait for a higher figure. However, there is a time pressure to use O.F.F.

'The United States was close to a successful O.F.F. situation in the late nineteen fifties, based entirely on the B-52 bomber, but then the missile appeared and "opportunity" went away for a generation. It is now about to return, and this time it is going to be used as soon as possible.

'The freeze movement in the U.S. is exerting pressure. NATO populations are increasingly frightened and putting pressure on their leaders.

'The Russians are reinforcing the Kuril Islands. This is an attempt on their part to escape SOSUS. The Kuril Islands lie between the Sea of Okhotsk and the Pacific. If they can be made into a formidable barrier, Soviet ballistic missile subs might be able to operate in comparative safety inside the Sea of Okhotsk, using long-range missiles capable of reaching the United States. They are also trying to develop techniques for hiding under the Arctic ice, and even inside Swedish territorial waters.

'Sooner or later, space warfare will be an added dimension, a new complexity. It is conceivable that the Soviet Union might come up with a new technical development that would delay "opportunity" for yet another generation. So the sooner O.F.F. is implemented, the lower American casualties will be. No one expects 100 percent success; it is believed that a success rate of 99.8 percent, plus various civil defense measures to be taken, will limit American casualties to the range of twenty to twenty-five million dead. It is also believed that the post-O.F.F. savings in military budgets would easily cover the $250 billion (prorated over sixty-five years) for supplying life support and day care for the expected sixteen million cancer cases and mutant births that occur.

'It goes without saying that O.F.F. can't possibly work. Are there any questions?'

There was silence in the studio; they were all off in space except Garvey, who was glancing around, counting the votes.

'It's hard to believe,' Ingalls said after a full minute had gone by. 'Very hard. Don't misunderstand me, Oliver; I believe he's being sincere. But it's hard to absorb. Can the President be that foolish? The Joint Chiefs? Is this sanity? Are we talking about sane people?'

Joe Kiernan was sitting at the synthesizer, playing with the keys and switches. 'They can't all be crazy,' he said. 'That's impossible. That's too hard to take. These are big men. They wouldn't be where they are if they were crazy.'

'Well said,' Garvey replied. He paced around, drifting toward the glass booth. 'Perhaps the Doctor would give us a second opinion?'

The figure in the booth went to his microphone and the bubbling of his words floated through the room. 'I don't believe they're crazy either. They can put their shoes and socks on in the morning. They function. They're rational. One and one makes two. The difference, I believe, lies in their moral values. Twenty megadeaths seems an acceptable price to them to pay for the destruction of Soviet communism. That isn't insanity; it's moral idiocy.'

'A significant distinction,' Bishop Hinds said. 'I applaud it. The risk of becoming a moral idiot is the price one pays to be a leader.'

'What do you think, Herb?' Garvey said, going to the intelligence expert in the group. 'Does it ring true to you?'

Purefoy exhaled rather heavily. 'More or less,' he said. 'I have to say I'm not surprised at the ambition. Some part of the establishment has been thinking along those lines since nineteen eighteen, when we invaded Siberia. The technical details don't quite surprise me either. The vulnerability of the Soviet submarine force is the most dangerous fact on earth. What I do wonder about is the will to use O.F.F. I don't care whether you call it insanity or moral degeneracy. Does the will exist? That's the question.'

'Very well,' Garvey said. 'Rabbi?'

Rabbi Mandelbaum laughed grimly. He was seated on a folding chair, holding one knee up with two hands. 'I don't even trust my dishwasher,' he said. 'To believe in the success of this monstrous enterprise would require a greater leap of faith than I am capable of. I vote for moral idiocy too, and in my opinion moral idiots tend to be willful since they can't appreciate the consequences of their actions. They also seem to have forgotten John Kennedy's thought: "How could I have been so stupid as to listen to the experts?" I *am* surprised by one thing. Normally it's the liberals who accuse the conservatives of trying to turn back the clock. This seems to be the *sole* instance where the conservatives have accepted modernity and it is the liberals who are trying to turn back the clock.'

'Interesting point, Rabbi. What about you, Emerson?'

Foster was sitting on a high stool, legs crossed, arms crossed, staring at a crack in the floor. 'Oliver,' he said slowly, 'are you sure this man knows what the hell he's talking about?'

'This man is in a position to know. He's a Librarian, Emerson.'

Foster turned to the masked figure in the control room, taking a good look at him for the first time. 'As a practical matter, it is vital for us to know what makes you so certain

O.F.F. will fail. I ask this because there are many Americans who would approve of O.F.F. if they believed it was a guaranteed success. So this is basic: What are the obvious flaws?'

The masked figure hesitated, thinking. It was dim enough in the booth so that even the color of his eyes looking through holes in the mask was obscured.

'It's a fantasy,' the lugubrious underwater voice said finally. 'Nothing in engineering works the first time. Missiles are spaceships, difficult to launch, yet hundreds of them must be launched within seconds of each other. A sudden change in winds five thousand miles away could wreck the operation. That goes for every aspect of O.F.F. For example, no Soviet sub has ever actually been destroyed. It's elementary engineering practice. You must do it, perform it, make it happen, get the numbers down in the notebook. Until you have done that, you have not done it. The Pentagon does not have the test results on O.F.F. because it cannot be demonstrated, it cannot be tested in advance. O.F.F. is a crap shoot with, at a minimum, the lives of twenty-five million Americans riding on the roll.'

More seconds of quiet, allowing for cogitation.

'Then all nuclear scenarios are ridiculous,' the rabbi finally responded.

'I agree,' the man in the booth said. 'They are mind games. They are not reality. They are based on hopelessly optimistic assumptions. Garbage in, holocaust out. O.F.F. reminds me more than anything else of the most colossally stupid war of modern times, World War One. World War One, like World War Three, was meticulously planned for two generations. Thought through, games, pondered, games again, changes, adjusted, calculated, thought through again, over and over for two generations. Nothing was to be left to chance. The French had a mathematical equation which proved that French soldiers could capture any German position. The advance of the German right wing on Paris was calculated to the day. In the first thirty days of fighting, two generations of thinking were proved utterly, devastatingly worthless. In World War Three, it will be during the first thirty minutes.'

301

Emerson Foster played devil's advocate.

'Now wait a minute,' he said. 'Does the chairman of the Joint Chiefs know these are mind games? Does the President know? Do the Russians know?'

'So far I have given you facts. Now you are asking for intuition,' the voice said.

'I got where I am on intuition,' Foster replied. 'How does it feel in your gut?'

'They know and they don't know. They keep reassuring themselves. Nobody wants to be negative; it's bad for the career. Subordinates keep reassuring their superiors, and so on up the line. If you don't reassure your superiors about your area of responsibility, then you can't be doing a good job. Remember, this is a vast project. No one man or group feels responsible for the entire operation. At the lower levels, the feeling of moral responsibility is highly diluted. My guess is that most professionals would prefer to use O.F.F. only for threat value, but the higher up the line you go, the further you get away from the technical realities, and the less reluctance you encounter.'

'They know and they don't know, huh?' Joe Kiernan said. 'Stupid sons of bitches. Pardon my French, Bishop.'

'There is nothing sinful about precision of expression. They *are*, indisputably and beyond hope of redemption, stupid sons of bitches.'

'The problem is that they've got complexity working for them,' Purefoy said. 'The average hack politician doesn't even have to be sober to talk his way out of this stuff at a press conference. The public doesn't know which way is up.'

'We'll all have to think it through very carefully,' Emerson Foster said very carefully, looking at all of them.

Garvey took the cue. 'Sarah and gentlemen,' he announced, 'let's leave it at that for the moment. This meeting has gone on too long and we're jeopardizing the Doctor's security. May I suggest we file out at one-minute intervals?'

They were picking up their coats and turning for the door they had come in through when the gravelly voice took them by surprise. 'Don't think too long,' the Garbageman said. 'O.F.F. is 93.06 percent and climbing.'

Emerson Foster

Harry always found himself brooding about maintenance during takeoffs. It was the logical thing to brood about. He believed that Bernoulli's principle, which was what kept planes in the air, was inviolable. Bernoulli worked every time, but there could be slippage in maintenance.

Once the plane was in the air, he switched to brooding about having to leave Burnish behind in charge of the Library during a crisis while he had to fly to the Bahamas. It was possible the President was going through a regal phase, making everyone jump through hoops, enjoying the perquisites, getting Number One ego satisfaction. There was no sensible reason for the trip.

When he reached Miami, a Coast Guard amphibian was waiting for him. The water must have been too choppy or the wind marginal, or something: the pilot needed a few attempts to find the right angle and get into the air. It was turning out to be that kind of day.

After forty-five minutes, a lovely little island appeared down below, Cat Cay, a rich man's playground at the beginning of the tropics. Harry figured the President was getting a few days away from the pressure, which Presidents did in presidential fashion: they took the pressure with them.

Two F-14s materialized, one on each wing. There must be a carrier task force in the vicinity, the President's own little bodyguard. The F-14 pilots smiled, waved, vanished. Below, two destroyers were circling the island. It was autumn and the Caribbean wasn't quite glass, but it was close enough. The Coast Guard pilot set down neatly and then climbed the amphibian up on a concrete ramp to dry ground, where the Secret Service was swarming.

303

Harry was beginning to wonder if there was a big meeting going on. The island was getting plenty of attention. The Russians? Unthinkable. Besides, there weren't any reporters. Presidents never met with Russians without reporters. The nearest of the Secret Service looked Harry over, making sure he was Harry Dunn. He smiled; Dunn was unique. 'This way,' the man said.

There were no cars on the island; Harry had to squeeze into a golf cart. With Harry's bulk, it was slow going until the straining cart got up a small hill, leaving the beachfront behind. Then they rumbled easily along a wooden path that went the length of the small island past wealthy weekend homes, all of which were empty because it wasn't the season. They stopped at a clubhouse at the far end of the island. Ives was waiting for him on the porch of the weathered building, wearing his Hawaiian shirt but no smile. He looked grim.

What could it possibly be? Harry wondered. They were riding high. The Library was the covert hero of the administration. Ives just nodded and Harry followed him inside. It had to be serious; Ives didn't kid around like this. As they were going past an empty bar and dozens of tables and chairs, Harry could hear an unmistakable sound which frequently accompanied the presidential presence: the clicking of pool balls. They entered the game room just as the President dropped the fourteen ball in the corner pocket with a rifle shot.

'Hello, Harry. Thanks for coming,' the President said, chalking his cue. It had the presidential seal on it. He had also brought along his own bar, bartenders, waiters, and chef. The waiter appeared out of nowhere as the President began to think 'waiter.'

'Get Mr. Dunn one of those pink things,' the President said. 'You'll love it, Harry. It's a very pretty drink.' He drove the four ball out of sight and the cue ball spun back neatly to line up behind the next shot.

'Never get into the game with him for money,' Ives said. 'He's a hustler.'

The three ball lunged into a side pocket, but the cue didn't behave; the President was left without a shot. 'Balls,' he said.

Harry knew the President well enough to know that he was furious. He wasn't a ranter and raver; he toyed with you while the lava simmered. It had to be a beaut, whatever it was.

'Now this is nothing more than a run-of-the-mill problem in politics,' the President said, looking over the table with a strategic glint in his eye, as though counting the Senate for an important vote. 'Nothing but pure politics. Guess that's why I love this game so much.'

He circled the table, found his shot, bent low, the cue riding easily back and forth through his curled finger. 'There are all sorts of forces acting on a politician, pulling him every which way,' he said. 'He has to take them all into account. It's the physics of politics. Vector addition. Different forces of different strengths from different directions meeting at a point. Me.' He hit the cue ball gently and it coasted until it tapped the thirteen ball on the right shoulder. The thirteen ball obediently moved to a cluster of three balls having a little conversation together and tapped first one and then a second. Obediently, the nine ball began moving gracefully toward a side pocket in a direction 110 degrees reversed from the original motion of the cue ball. It dropped into the pocket, a masterpiece of political manipulation.

'That's what I mean, Harry. All the forces go to work to produce a resultant. Sometimes it's hard to understand why a politician does what he does. The subsequent action doesn't always resemble the forces that went to make it up. That's why people don't understand politicians. They don't understand the addition of vectors.'

'That's a wonderful two-minute course in politics, Mr. President,' Harry replied, leaving unstated the question: Why am I here? He glanced in Ives's direction, but Ives wasn't being helpful.

The President started cleaning up the rest of the table fast. In between shots, he complimented the Library. 'Walter and Vera, in particular, have been magnificent. I want to do something for them. I don't know what, offhand, but I want to show my appreciation to those two.'

When the table was empty the President laid his cue stick on it. 'Ah, here's your drink, Harry.'

The waiter had returned with an orange-colored drink. It had a pink smear of grenadine that was beginning to be dispersed by Brownian movement.

'By the way, Harry, here's a man I think you ought to know.' Harry looked at the waiter.

'Meet Emerson Foster,' the President said. Then added heavily, 'Of the Emersons.'

Foster and Dunn exchanged a clammy handshake. Then Harry stalled for time by taking a long swallow of whatever it was he was drinking. Foster and the President? What the hell was this? He had no data to work from. Nothing. He wouldn't have believed it possible that he could be taken by surprise like this.

The President was putting a gray sport jacket over his turtleneck sweater. 'You've been outfoxed, Harry. Worse than you realize. Worse than I ever dreamed possible. You've got a catastrophe on your hands and you're going to have to get the situation restored. Fast. Tell him, Emerson.'

Emerson Foster sat down in one of the red leather club chairs. He didn't relish doing it, but there were times when you had to swallow hard and do what was necessary for survival. He was exposed in Brazil; about a billion in bad loans. Only the President could help him. Was he to lose everything because of one error of judgment? It was this or jump out a window. He was only hoping that he could keep it from the others; he rather liked them and their crusade. They were doing the right thing; the weapons were crazy. But he could feel it in his gut right now, a strength, an urge, built into the nervous system from millennia spent in the jungle: the urge to survive. He had to get the President indebted to him. Deeply.

'I'm terribly sorry to have to tell you this, Harry, but have you ever heard of somebody called the Doctor?'

Harry was drifting slowly, randomly, along the beach, up to the high-tide mark, down to the low-tide mark. He was numb. He'd been betrayed by one of the people closest to him. A Librarian, a Judas, who had let out the single biggest secret. Human personality was indecipherable, the final great mystery never to be solved, more mysterious than God.

Conch shells lay here and there on the beach, incredibly beautiful, there for the taking, their job done. It was the lushness of the tropics, the warmth, the endless nutrients, that made them possible. They were mansions compared with the little studios northern shellfish had to live in.

How could it have happened at the moment of the Library's greatest triumph? Well, there it was. A fact, washed up on the beach. You had to pick up the fact and work with it. Pick up the pieces. What plans did the Emersons have? There had to be a way to contain them. What could buy Garvey off? There had to be something that old phony couldn't resist. But he would have to let the President worry about that end for now. His job was to find the Doctor, and be quick about it. Coolidge hadn't done his job; he should have spotted the leaker. Now Harry Dunn was stuck in his own conundrum, faced with the job of breaking into the feedback loop where all parties were suspect and all suspects knew everything. The President had said something that was trying to surface in his brain. What was it? 'Assuming you find out who it is, Harry, what do you do with him once you've got him?'

That was it. There was a way in. Dunn's Conundrum had a solution after all. It was so simple he must have been in a state of shock not to see it immediately.

He was beginning to feel better. He was beginning to deal with it. Damage-control parties were at work; the fire would be contained. He turned off the beach and went between two of the beach houses, back out to the path. The golf cart was waiting for him; the Secret Service had kept pace as he had drifted along the sand. He squeezed into it. There was going to be no nice way to handle the situation. There was only one thing you could do with a Librarian gone bad. The golf cart started rolling along the wooden path.

Gardella

Gardella looked around the room.

He saw interior space as a three-dimensional architectural drawing, a world of angles, radii, columns, beams, hidden dashed lines behind the façades. It was all a puzzle in space, the puzzle being how to get the most coverage of a given volume of space with the fewest number of microcams. Gardella could see with depth of field, with the fish-eye distortion of the microcam lens, with a portrait photographer's feel for lighting.

Sometimes Gardella stood there a moment after the job was done imagining the cavortings his microcams would pick up, the comings and goings, the immoralities, the amoralities, the cheating, the backstabbing. Documenting man's transgressions appealed to his Catholic sense of sin.

And this one was to be the ultimate violation of privacy, far more than any mere antic bedroom bouncings. This was going to be soul pornography, the ultimate exposure, and he would have to capture it in all positions. The soul was wily and could be elusive, but there was no doubt in his mind that he would get the shot.

Trash Report: #85-11-8

CASE NUMBER: 104759

ABANDONED PROPERTY DONOR: Senator Oliver Garvey (residence)

1. Two each empty beer bottles of the following brands: Amstel, Augustinerbräu, Bass Ale, Beck's, Grolsch, Guinness stout, Harp, Heineken, Kronenbourg, Watney's
2. Two dozen broken beer steins (approx.).
3. Pair of spectacles, broken.
4. Marked-up copy of *Mein Kampf* by A. Hitler.
5. Marked-up copy of *Capital* by K. Marx.
6. Marked-up copy of *Where's the Rest of Me?* by R. Reagan.
7. Pair ladies' panties, bikini style, torn.
8. Pair ladies' panty hose, torn.
9. Letter from Beer Institute.
10. Copy of speech intended for a convention of the National Rifle Association.

Trash Scenario

On Monday evening the senator and Davey Reed decided to learn firsthand what the attractions of imported beers are (item #1, empty bottles; item #9, letter from Beer Institute complaining about unfair foreign competition). Reed insisted on fresh steins for each brand so as not to contaminate any of the tastes.

While drinking, they discussed such topics as influential

thinkers of the Western world (items #4, 5, 6) and rejected their teachings.

At some point in the evening, Melanie Smith arrived (the eyeglasses are half a diopter too strong for Garvey and coincide with Ms. Smith's prescription).

What happened after she arrived is anyone's guess.

Notes

The use of Chinese laundry ink eliminates any possibility of determining who item #10 is about. One could hazard a guess – a well-known individual who always wins debates but always loses influence in the process – but it would be pointless speculation.

. . . but now that we've addressed the great issue of humankind's right to bear arms in a dangerous world, I would like to take a few moments to express my admiration for a gentleman by the name of [name obliterated]. (*Pause for cheers.*) What more daring, intrepid Defender of the Faith could there be? I fondly think of him as the courageous fellow who is given the difficult, even dangerous, task of receiving the kickoff in a football game.

This brave man is in the finest tradition as he stands there alone at the two-yard line. There is no backup, no safety net, no one behind him. It's all up to him. It's a quality that used to be called self-reliance. Our fellow waits coolly and confidently as the ball, the bone of contention, the argument as it were, sails through the air.

[Name obliterated] stands fast as eleven incontrovertible facts rush downfield straight at him.

[Name obliterated] catches the argument and presses it tightly to him. Amidst turmoil and impending disaster, he calmly assesses the situation. His discerning eye sees a possibility, a weakness in the constellation of facts, a vague statistical wisp of an outside chance, so slender that it would daunt an ordinary man. But not [name obliterated], who licks his lips, whose eyes brighten at the opportunity to show what he can do: *This* is his territory. A faint smile appears as [name obliterated] – war, famine, pestilence, and disease rolled into one – begins his run.

310

This man is crazy legs.

The facts are everywhere, swarming, enveloping, grim masks closing in from all sides; but the artful dodger is elusive. He weaves, he twists, he spins, he reverses. He rambles. He scrambles. He pirouettes! He goes to the inside, he goes to the outside, he leaps, he stiff-arms, he darts. The fact lie sprawled in his wake! In moments [name obliterated] is in the clear, eleven incontrovertible facts lumbering after him, falling farther behind with every passing moment.

Oh, it's a glorious fall day! Open country ahead, the goal line and vindication in the future, nothing to stop him now. [Name obliterated] has a great ravishing smile as he runs free. Free! The government is off his back! Individualism is triumphant! The free play of the market will cleanse the environment! Surgical bombing is officially approved by the American Medical Association! Nuclear war is winnable! Surgically!!

His legs pumping, [name obliterated]'s right arm sweeps outward to joyfully encompass all in the stadium. 'Do you see?' he seems to be saying 'Do you see? I've done it. I've done it again!'

Leaving panting facts behind forever, [name obliterated] sails over the goal line, spiking the ball: *That* for *them*. But alas, the touchdown is invariably called back.

Once again, [name obliterated] has stepped out of reality on the three-yard line.

Confessions of a Whistle Blower

He liked watching her drive. Vera always looked sexy driving. He had a good view; her dress always worked up accidentally on purpose. He was having hot thoughts about Vera again, which was why he agreed when she'd suggested a new restaurant in Maryland. The situation between them had to be handled, settled, resolved one way or another.

As they went up Massachusetts Avenue, he was trying to go about it logically, the way Harry would. What were his options? (1) He could forgive and forget her little indiscretion with Harry. Call it a mistake. Everyone made mistakes. Everyone had bad days, feeling sorry for themselves. She put on the brakes to stop at a light and her dress moved up another half inch. (2) Call it betrayal. She had betrayed him. Very simple classic case. He knew something about betrayal. He had just betrayed the inner core of the American establishment; to the outer core, granted, and for what he saw as a compelling reason. Was it possible Vera had a compelling reason? (3) Find a new woman. Who? (4) Regard it all as the price paid for total knowledge.

Total knowledge. They were going through Dupont Circle, not far from the Library at Connecticut. The house of total knowledge. Total knowledge was a dangerous thing. Worse. It was ruinous. Secrecy was a part of life. Who could stand up to total revelation?

(5) She had saved his life. That was worth something, weighed in the scales. How could you hate someone with luscious thighs who had saved your life?

'Something on your mind, Walter?' she said, switching off the radio, signaling that a conversation was coming.

'You've been murky lately. Unusually murky, that is.'

'The times are murky. I've got jet lag. I'm hungry. The eczema right above my inside right ankle is angry.'

'Balls.'

'It's possible that the fact that the world is close to nuclear war has me unduly upset.'

'I didn't say you were scared. I said you were murky. Why are you turned off?'

'I'm not turned off. My vitality is at a low ebb.'

Coolidge didn't know what to do about that one. He couldn't accuse her of infidelity without revealing the source of his knowledge. Vera and Harry were an item of data, *secret* data. That carnal act committed on Vera's living room couch was classified. For Your Eyes Only. Maybe the thing to do was forget it if he could and let nature take its course.

They were across the intersection with Wisconsin; she was going to be driving right past American University, where Coolidge had lost his bureaucratic virginity. That was another thing he wanted to forget. A headache had been hovering somewhere at the top of his skull for days, waiting to strike. What were the Emersons going to do with it? What would the reverberations be?

He watched the university out of the corner of his eye when Vera turned left and then left again; suddenly they were cruising slowly toward the campus entrance.

He was cool and disdainful. 'You're not taking me to the campus cafeteria, are you?'

'I have a chore to do,' she said. 'Won't take a minute.'

She turned onto the campus and was drifting along at three miles per hour, headed in the general direction of the radio station. Coolidge was trying to act bored, trying to see the expression on her face without looking at her. He was getting rattled. He didn't like coincidences. He was trying desperately to react to the scene with innocent eyes.

She pulled into the familiar driveway and eased the car all the way to the far end of the landing area, under the big tree, exactly where Reed had parked the van. 'Come in with me, Walter; this won't take long.'

He followed her through the station's rear door, down the corridor, and into the studio. She flipped on the light switch and strolled over to the stool Emerson Foster had sat on.

'Walter, we have a problem.'

'What's the problem? he said weakly.

'I know about the little talk you gave to the Emersons last Sunday.'

Coolidge stood looking at her. He thought he had heard it, but he wasn't sure. 'What?' he asked.

'I know about you and the Emersons meeting here.'

Her eyes were boring into him. He had never seen her look that way. She was suddenly another person, relentless, out to get him, out to ruin him. What was happening? His mouth was dry. He was going to have trouble talking. He wasn't even sure about his knees – or his sphincter, for that matter. He took a chance and moved to the nearest stool, trying to take a deep breath without showing it.

'Would you mind telling me what you're talking about?' he said.

She was looking him right in the eye. They weren't eyes of a lover, or even a friend. They were cop eyes.

'You told the Emersons about O.F.F.'

It was happening too fast. He was overwhelmed, out of his league. Why was she doing this? Harry had to have put her up to it. But how could Harry have known?

'Why are you saying these things to me?'

'Damn,' she said, her face beginning to relent. 'Oh, God damn it. God damn you, Walter.'

'Vera, listen to me.'

'I didn't think it would work out this way. I really didn't. I hope you can believe that.'

'You didn't think *what* would work out this way?' Coolidge's brain was beginning to work again. 'A test? Is that what this is? A test?'

'I don't think you passed.'

'You brought me here to trap me.'

'I brought you here to clear you.'

'Why am I a suspect?'

'It turns out, Walter, that one of the Emersons talked. The Doctor met them here last Sunday morning and told them all about O.F.F.' Vera still couldn't believe it. 'About *O.F.F.*, Walter.'

Coolidge finally understood it: the way out of the conundrum. One of the Emersons had ratted to Harry. Harry's Emerson had seen a man in a mask, without knowing who it was. But it was a *man*; the black box couldn't hide that fact. The Doctor was a man. Which meant that Harry had a sure thing in Vera. The conundrum fell. Vera would draw the job of testing Coolidge, because Coolidge saw the personal footage. Then Coolidge could be given the assignment of vetting everyone else by spending twenty-four hours a day on personal footage until he found a clue.

'I swear I didn't think it was you,' she said.

'Why are you so convinced it's me?'

'I saw the look on your face. You never were a good liar. Walter, I don't understand you. I don't understand this whole thing.'

'What are you going to do now? Tell Harry you think I'm the Doctor because of a look on my face?'

'That's what I'm supposed to do.'

'It'll be your word against mine.'

'That's right.' She stood up and started for the door.

'Well, it won't be the first time you'll have betrayed me with Harry.'

She paused, not turning around, and thought for a while about that one. 'Can I give you a lift?' she said finally, without looking at him.

'Thanks; that's okay.'

Coolidge sat there awhile, getting his wits back, cooling off, breathing. He could hear Vera's car backing out. He didn't know what to do with himself. A spy among the Emersons. At least it wasn't Garvey or Purefoy or Ingalls; there wouldn't have been any guesswork if it had been one of them. He left the radio station in a daze and walked slowly back along Massachusetts in the general direction of his apartment, trying to figure out what had happened to him.

It was circumstantial. Vera's opinion of his face. What kind of evidence was that? Woman's intuition. It was less than a smoking gun. How much did Vera's opinion count with Harry? Would she actually push the case? Vera?

He reached his apartment, miles later, without even

noticing that he had covered the ground. It was obvious. It didn't take any thinking. There was only one possible response. Go back to work in the morning, brazen it out, wait for Harry to pounce. Then deny everything. Suppose they gave him a lie detector test? The President loved lie detector tests. There was data on how to beat it. Plenty of bureaucrats knew how; he'd do some fast research. It was circumstantial only. He'd have to keep telling himself that; there was nothing else to do.

It took forever for morning to come.

Coolidge was walking down the corridor, putting one foot in front of the other. He was scared. His nerve endings were overloaded, jammed, rendered useless by unknown countermeasures. The clicking of her heels on the concrete floor sounded like jackboots. It was dark until she opened the door and switched on the light. She strolled over to the stool and sat down on it. There was a hard, unfamiliar expression on her face.

'Walter, we have a problem,' she said.

'What's the problem?' he said weakly.

'I know about the little talk you gave to the Emersons last Sunday.'

Coolidge froze the frame and looked at his face. He had spent half an hour looking at his face. It didn't even seem to be his face; he was looking at somebody else. The place must have been crawling with microcams. It was perfect, bringing him back there. Diabolical. Harry all over. Unnerving him, then springing it. He let the footage run and shot after shot of his face rolled by. It was a face taken by surprise – fearful, guilty, appalled. They had all the angles: left profile, left three-quarters, front, right three-quarters, right profile. Then high angle, all over again: right profile, right three-quarters, front, left three-quarters, left profile. Then low angle: right profile, right three-quarters, front, left three-quarters, left profile.

There were people who could conceal the most devastating of emotions, who were spiritual poker players, who didn't show it no matter how much was riding on the turn of a card. Coolidge wasn't one of them. Coolidge's countenance leaked. Coolidge's face looked like a typed signed

316

confession. Gardella must have done the job himself. Coolidge sat there looking at his exposed face, drained, not knowing what to do. He tried to force himself to think. What could he do? He was out of his element entirely. He was staff. He was dangerous. Once again Yeager had been proved right.

The word 'dangerous' started a thought. He began thinking. He'd violated the data. The data had been raped. He, Walter Coolidge, had done it. That meant only one thing. He was going to encounter the Protector of the Data. He entered Beebe's code.

There wasn't much to sort through that was recent; Beebe had been recovering from his war wounds. The computer went straight to a safe house in Prince Georges County.

Beebe's head was still bandaged. His legs were up on an ottoman and a cane was leaning against his chair. He was sucking on a Scotch and water. 'Glad you could make it,' he was saying.

The other man was sitting on a windowsill with his arms crossed in front of him. 'My wife's going to kill me,' he said. 'We've got reservations.'

Beebe giggled into his Scotch. 'Tell her there's a bonus.'

'Oh?'

'Double the usual.'

The man's eyebrows went up. He had an average face. Extremely average. He looked as though he could vanish into a crowd. There was nothing outstanding: no scars, no facial hair, moderate nose, moderate mouth. His clothes were self-effacing: tans and grays off the rack that almost fit. Coolidge thought of him immediately as John Doe.

'But it's got to be done right,' Beebe said, 'or you don't get the bonus. Execution, so to speak, is everything. I'm talking about an accident. A believable, plausible, demonstrable, irrefutable accident. Get it?'

John Doe was wandering around the room now. His height was average. 'Is he armed?'

'If he is, you're in luck. He'll shoot himself in the foot.'

'What kind of guy is he?'

'He's smart, but he's got no training, which means he's

dumb.' Beebe was delicately rubbing his bandaged skull. 'But he's liable to come up with some stupid, amateurish oddball tactic. Watch out for that. Don't look for a professional response.'

John Doe nodded.

'Here's his file.' Beebe handed over a thin folder with an accopress clip holding the pages in it. 'He thinks he knows it all. He doesn't.'

John Doe was flipping through the file. 'Is he right-handed or left-handed? It doesn't say. First thing I need to know.'

'I think he bats from both sides of the plate,' Beebe said contemptuously.

'I'll find out myself.'

'Do what you have to do. Just make it perfect.'

'I get the picture,' John Doe said.

Coolidge flipped off his monitor. No names or code names had been mentioned. He had brought the scene by entering 'Beebe,' not 'Doctor.' He tried to tell himself that they couldn't have been talking about him. It was too easy to get paranoid. Coolidge had been a hero up until the previous evening. Would Harry go that far? Why not? he thought. Harry was willing to risk twenty million; what was so special about the life of one man?

Harry hadn't shown up yet. No memos, no phone calls, no summonses, no Burnish.

They just might be willing to do it as an object lesson to the Emersons. The price of talking. He was going to need time to think it through.

He left his topcoat and strolled out to the elevators. He didn't even want to talk to Jake Shoemaker. The car took forever to show up. He went up to the main floor and strolled casually through the empty lobby. His car was in the Library parking lot. Harry Dunn would personally have to start the engine before he would ever get in it again.

Out on Connecticut Avenue, he slipped into a depression; everything was falling down around his ears. He had tampered with national power. High matters of state. He, Walter Coolidge, had tried to thwart the will of the

President. He had committed *the* worst crime in Washington, far worse than murder or rape. He had blown the whistle, which was a capital crime in the nation's capital.

He reached Lafayette Park at the end of Connecticut. It was more crowded than usual for this time of year. On the other side of the park a couple of dozen protesters were getting ready to picket the White House. Tourists wandered around, taking pictures, resting on benches. Coolidge found an empty bench near Pennsylvania Avenue and sat down heavily, wondering if the man in the house across the street actually wanted to kill him. He still didn't feel that important.

He thought through the timing again. He and Vera had gone to the radio station about 8 P.M. Bebee and John Doe had their nasty little chat at 11:30 P.M. Harry could have been watching the scene in the radio station in real time. It was possible, but was it probable?

Someone tapped him on the shoulder and he lifted off the seat an inch. A tourist, a woman of about thirty-five, thrust a Nikon into his hands. 'Do me a favor and take one of my husband and me, okay? It's all set. All you have to do is focus. This thing here.' She was already walking off to pose with her husband, the headquarters of the Western world in the background.

Coolidge stood up and looked into the camera, slowly bringing it into focus. The White House in the background, then the man and woman. Her husband was a classic: three-quarter-length jacket, map sticking out of a side pocket, light meter draped around his neck, big smile. Coolidge focused a hair more to bring in their faces and stiffened. It was John – *click* – Doe.

IV John Doe

Company

Coolidge tried to amble; it wasn't easy when your knees were quaking. Slow, unconcerned, no direction, relaxed, nothing on the mind. He was trying to preserve his one and only asset, which was that he knew John Doe and John Doe didn't know he knew. He'd put on the straightest face of his life, working hard at what he was worst at: acting. As he handed back the camera he'd looked at John Doe's eyes for a fraction of a second. They were uncomplicated, the expression blank, out to lunch, no communication. The man was a machine.

There was no plausible accident that could happen in Lafayette Park, unless a tree was struck by lightning, and probably even Harry couldn't arrange that, so Coolidge was able to resist the urge to look behind him. He left the park and crossed the street with guile and cunning, anticipating any imaginable vehicular onslaught, then continued his weak-kneed amble down Pennsylvania Avenue, past Blair House, turning right at Seventeenth Street.

Then he hustled up to H Street, where he caught a cab. He tried to be subtle about looking out the back window. When he got out in Georgetown, he watched the cab out of sight. The bar he was headed for was still four blocks away.

He sat at a small table sipping wine, trying to understand things. It couldn't have been a coincidence. As Reed had said, they weren't taking bets on coincidence anymore. Then why had he got away so easily? What was the reason behind the camera charade? That was puzzling until he remembered Doe's footage. Handedness. John Doe had been testing him for handedness. Doe was meticulous; Doe didn't move on incomplete information, even to knowing which hand Coolidge would be likely to react with, which suggested Doe had close-up work in mind. It was a terrifying thoroughness.

He had a second wine. There was an anxiety low in his intestines that wouldn't go away. Where could a fugitive from the Library go? Who could he get help from? Doe would undoubtedly be watching the Emersons, the telephone had been disinvented, and he no longer had the computer to tell him what was going on.

The television set behind the bar was on. He watched what passed for the news, feeling isolated, on the sidelines. The networks were still trying to figure out what had happened in the tank fight in Germany. The secretary of state, as usual, was giving the Russians hell for being trigger happy; the Russians were complaining about American provocations. The networks wouldn't get the story straight until it didn't matter. General Arlington C. Prager was looking good in interviews; maybe there was still a chance he could make major general. Then, as part of the same coverage, they cut to the Senator from Nowhere himself, and Coolidge heard the sanitized, sanctimonious voice of Oliver Garvey.

Garvey was on his way into a Democratic party lunch at the Palmer Hotel, doing his usual dance on the fence: The President was doing the right thing; the only thing the Russians understood was force; blah, blah, blah, blah; but we shouldn't ignore opportunities for negotiation; blah, blah, blah; and then slithering away into the hotel. Coolidge was beginning to understand why Davey Reed had to let off steam writing crazy speeches.

Coolidge was so used to seeing tape and film, it didn't get through to him for five minutes; it had been a live broadcast, plain old-fashioned real time. He knew where Garvey was. *There* was a step in the right direction. There were only the three he could trust: Garvey, Ingalls, Purefoy; the whistle blower was one of the others.

He took a cab to five blocks away from the hotel and then approached it on foot, neurotically, doubling back, going in the wrong direction, being random; no one was paying the least bit of attention to him. When he finally got there it was a mob scene, reporters all over the place, limos arriving and departing, people everywhere.

It wasn't a trash problem; he didn't know what to do with it. And there wasn't much time for on-the-job training: he was an accident waiting to happen. Was a crowd good or bad? Did it favor the tracked or the tracker? He could hide in it, but so could John Doe. It was the same inside the hotel, where there'd be crowds plus nooks and crannies for both sides to lurk in. Somehow he had to get close enough to Garvey to hug him, then stay within the perimeter of senatorial sanctity, like hiding from the king's soldiers in a church.

He tried to see it from John Doe's point of view. If Coolidge took the most elementary precautions, it would be hard for Mr. Doe to rig a really sincere, honest-looking accident. They would have to grab him first, then stage the accident. Which suggested the avoidance of enclosed spaces.

He stayed out of the hotel. He stalled around on the sidewalk across the street, keeping an eye on the entrance where the TV cameras were. That was the catnip, that's where Garvey would show up sooner or later. He spent the time window shopping, using the reflections in the store windows as radar, studying anybody who approached along the sidewalk, especially alert for that nothing form, that nothing walk, that invisible man, Mr. Doe.

It was disorienting. He'd spent his life crossing with the lights, playing the game. Now the everyday protections of society had been withdrawn from him. He'd become prey, an animal back in the jungle but with no evolutionary tricks of the trade going for him. He needed help. After two hours, the television people began to stir and he turned away from a shoe store window in time to see that unmistakable bowling pin moving out of the hotel entrance, gravitating toward the media.

Coolidge figured Garvey was good for thirty seconds of hot air for the evening news. He started across the street, pacing himself, watching the traffic, watching the people. Garvey, working the crowd, didn't even see him, but they got to the opposite sides of Garvey's limo at the same time.

Both doors on Coolidge's side were locked and the glass

was heavily tinted, so he couldn't see in. He hurried around to the curb side and made a grab for the door as it was closing on Garvey, but he felt his arms being pulled back. Two of the senator's aides had stopped him. The door closed and the car started off. Garvey, his best chance for survival, was getting away, getting smaller down Massachusetts Avenue.

He started to rehearse, mentally, while groveling to the two aides. They obviously weren't professional security types. 'I was only trying to get his autograph,' he told them, and kept talking until he sensed a slight slackening in their grip, still rehearsing, knowing full well whom he was imitating, who the role model was. When they were sufficiently lulled and human, he suddenly broke loose, gave them both a sharp rap in the stomach with his elbows, and ran like hell across the street, getting to a bus just as the doors were closing. Perversely, as he beat a middle-age woman to a window seat on the left side, he thought that Beebe would be proud of him; he'd learned at the feet of the master.

He couldn't get the window open and had to strain against the glass trying to spot Garvey's car. It was three blocks ahead. For a while it was almost a horse race; the bus was in sync with the traffic lights, loading on red, getting away on green, but it kept falling farther behind.

His head was still leaning against the glass, but he was no longer watching. He was musing on the absurdity of a garbageman defying a President. Of doing even worse than that: blowing the whistle. It was apparently the worst crime in a democratic society. It took him a few seconds to wake up to the fact that the bus had done something funny.

It had swung off Massachusetts Avenue and was racing down a side street. Coolidge slowly turned away from the window. There were only three passengers left in what had been a crowded bus. They were all men, and one of them was sitting down next to him.

'My name is Epps,' the man said. 'Please be calm, Walter.'

'Who are you? What is this?'

'Just be dignified about it,' Epps replied. 'It's the only

sensible way.' After two blocks the bus stopped and the driver got off without looking back. Another of the men got behind the wheel.

'Where are we going?'

'What difference does it make?'

Coolidge inspected his face. There was nothing threatening there at all: a friendly, chubby kind face. But distanced friendliness. A salesman helping you try on a jacket. Then he realized it was the same kind of professional indifference he'd seen in Mr. Doe. Everydayness. People doing their work. The indifference of the murderer, the untroubled extinguisher of universes. The bus stopped at a deserted street and Coolidge was hustled out the back door and into a long black car with tinted windows and jump seats. They were treating Coolidge like an object, something to be handled, processed, disposed of. They weren't reacting to him, or even seeing him. Epps reached inside Coolidge's jacket pocket and took out his wallet, removed the credit card and driver's license, returned the wallet. He handed the credit card and license to the man on Coolidge's right. 'Make sure it's a compact,' he said. The car stopped for a moment and the man got out. Epps shifted to take the empty seat next to Coolidge.

It was a safe house in Virginia. Small, middle-middle-class, anonymous. Surprisingly, the ordinary-looking garage was big enough to take the car, which was oversized. Coolidge was led into the house, past a kitchen, upstairs to a bedroom. They sat him on the bed with his wrists handcuffed in front of him. There was a magnum of white wine on a bureau across the room, sitting in a bucket of ice. The ice was a nice touch. Epps opened the bottle with one twist of his hand; it wasn't the kind that had a cork.

'We can pour this down you or you can enjoy yourself,' Epps said. 'Drink up.' He handed Coolidge a water glass full.

Coolidge looked at it. Driving under the influence; John Doe had opted for the obvious. He hoped he wasn't going to take any bystanders with him. How would they

327

actually work it? he wondered. He reached out with shaking hands – the rattling of the handcuffs was embarrassing – and grasped the glass. Seeing it as a painless way out, he took half of it in the first swallow. It went right to his eyes, tears forming. He burped, took a deep breath, swallowed the other half. It was getting to him fast. He was becoming dizzy. Though he could hear the glass being filled again, he couldn't see too well. The glass was put in his hands, but he wasn't ready yet. He needed to digest some of it.

'Drink,' Epps said, interested only in raising the alcohol level in Coolidge's blood.

He swallowed another half glass. His head was swimming. He had never realized how powerful wine could be; the stuff was poison. His head was beginning to pound, loudly, ominously. It was so loud even Epps heard it. No, it wasn't his head; it was someone with two wooden legs clomping up the stairs, sounding like doom. The pounding stopped and there was a rattling of the doorknob. The door opened arthritically and someone came into the room. Coolidge stared at him through an alcoholic haze and rejected the impression, tried again, squinting his eyes. It was Brezhnev.

He didn't have his medals on, but he was wearing his homburg and a stylish black topcoat. For a moment Coolidge had the crazy idea that he was a prisoner of the KGB. Brezhnev sat down on a chair near the night table and took out his cigarette case. 'Leave us,' he said.

Without a word, Epps and his friend filed out of the room. Epps was CIA; it wasn't even a John Doe operation. The President must have put the CIA on the case too. Brezhnev took out a tiny screwdriver, did some delicate prying at the cigarette case, and it swung open. 'One needn't be rigid about these things,' he said, lighting up. He blew out a ton of smoke, too old to worry about it, and held the cigarette with the tips of three fingers, thinking.

'These aren't great days,' he said.

Coolidge hiccuped. He was still holding the glass. He set it down on the night table.

'I used to meet with Schmidt of the Federal Republic, Gomulka of Poland, Kádár of Hungary, Tito, all of them. Keeping them in line, threatening, persuading, promising. There is nothing more complicated than politics; it's vastly more complicated than the highest mathematics.'

Coolidge was sweating now, from either fear or alcohol, Brezhnev was talking about other CIA surrogates or he was over the edge. Maybe it was both. Coolidge rubbed his eyes, trying to clear his head. What was Brezhnev doing here?

'Politics requires subtlety. Elegance. Canniness. Beauty. Insight. Today it is nothing but brute force. There is no more subtlety.'

'I'm inclined to agree with you,' Coolidge said.

'I talked them out of it,' Brezhnev said.

'You talked them out of it? Tell me. What did you talk them out of?'

'Your automobile accident,' Brezhnev said casually. He paused to take a monstrous double puff. 'I shouldn't exaggerate my influence. Not these days, anyway. But I speak for a segment of the Company. The Company is not monolithic, you understand. Many would be delighted to see the Library embarrassed. Why should the Company save the Library from embarrassment? The very idea of the Library is unsound and in the second place, they're going to get us all killed.'

'You're not going to kill me?'

Brezhnev was playing the favor down with an abrupt wave of a hand. 'It won't make any difference.'

'It will to me.'

'You're doomed. You're incompetent. I don't entirely disagree with what you have done, but that is neither here nor there. What do you know about escape and evasion? You didn't last two hours.'

'You wouldn't happen to have the key to these handcuffs, would you?' Coolidge said.

A massive Brezhnev eyebrow went up, then he reached into a vest pocket and took out the screwdriver. He stood ponderously and negotiated the few feet to the bed, one foot in front of the other, and bent to his work. He wasn't even looking; his eyes were way too old. He was picking it from memory.

'We would like you to last longer this time,' Brezhnev said, removing the handcuffs. 'It won't be long in any case, but you could do better.'

Coolidge was testing his ability to walk, pacing around the small room. He was ambulatory, but a straight line was iffy.

'You must stop being tight,' Brezhnev went on. 'You're doomed in any case, so have fun with it. Don't be trite; trite is death. Be creative. Do not use' – he leaned forward to emphasize the point – 'public transportation of any kind. Do not approach your friends. Anyone likely to help you will be watched. Beware of overestimating your opponent; it's paralysing. Take chances. You've got a curse on you, anyway; what have you got to lose?'

'Don't think I don't appreciate the advice, but how about helping me? You want to make a fool out of the Library? I'm your man. But how about a safe house and a car? And money.'

Brezhnev regretfully stubbed out the cigarette and stood up. 'Sorry, Vladimir. Bureaucratically speaking, it would be a nightmare. It's impossible. I'm sure you understand. Come.'

Brezhnev and Coolidge went back down the stairs together and Brezhnev told Epps to take him back where they had found him. In a few minutes, Coolidge was standing on Massachusetts Avenue, back at square one, feeling trapped, hopeless, nowhere to turn. The way Charley must have felt. Cursed.

He stopped, people brushing past him on the sidewalk. Something was finally coming through on the unconscious network. Dawn. Bingo. Light bulb going on. One plus one makes two. It had gone from the mysterious to the obvious in a flash: What Eberhart's curse was and why Charley had willed it to him.

Terminate the Doctor

Harry was 160 miles up and on a high, observing Poland. Vera's little observation platform had been built with a hefty safety factor, so Harry's weight wasn't an issue; it was his bulk that was oppressive in the small space. Harry was like a gas that expanded to fill the available volume. He hadn't waited for the latest satellite footage to be inserted into the computer, he was out on the platform with Vera as the film came up for the first time, fresh from enhancement processing.

'You're thirty miles south of Warsaw,' Vera said, watching him peer through the telescope. 'Note the convoy. Tanks, trucks, armored personnel carriers. Moving west.'

'They're not holding back,' Harry said, moving the telescope along the road with the vernier. 'They're committing themselves. They're walking straight into it.'

'Note the markings on the tanks,' Vera said. 'It's the Fifty-fourth Guards Tank Army. The man standing in the open car at the cross road is Major General Szymanski.'

'How do you know?' Harry said, looking the man over.

'I'd know that mustache anywhere.'

'It's classic, absolutely classic,' Harry said, still squinting through the telescope. 'The crack divisions. Wonderful. The bigger the commitment, the bigger the humiliation.' He was tasting it. All but one of the Soviet subs was being tracked now. Two hunter-killer groups had been assigned the task of finding the last one. Harry was tense, excited, almost exalted.

They were still hovering over Poland; Vera didn't want to go back yet. 'Harry, what about Walter?'

'What about Walter?'

'What's going to happen?'

'Why bother me with it? It's in the computer.'

'The computer has termination of employment, loss of accrued pay, vacation, pension, health plan, and insurance.'

'So?'

'Do you have anything else in mind for him?'

'We obviously can't indict him on violations of the Secrecy Act. He had us over a barrel. Hell, everyone working in intelligence does. You can just picture me testifying in court about how he leaked O.F.F., can't you?'

'No, I can't. That's the point.' She cruised up to Murmansk, where there was an especially heavy-duty ladder; her aerial platform shook violently as Harry delicately stepped off and onto the bottom rung. When he was safely on the catwalk, she said. 'Do you have anything else in mind for him, Harry?'

Nothing was to be held back from Librarians; it was All Eyes for everyone and everything. She was looking into his eyes now to see if he was sticking to All Eyes. Harry, who knew everything and always had the answer for you, was struggling with it, looking like a politician on the tube; the longer he took, the more frightened she was for Coolidge. 'If there's nothing in the computer, there's nothing,' he said at last.

The platform phone rang, but she kept looking at him for another second before picking it up. It was Burnish; the last Soviet sub had been picked up. Her voice shook when she said it. 'It's 98.00 percent,' she said. It was usable.

'Come on,' he said, holding out a hand to help her up the ladder. 'Let's go watch the fun.'

Opportunity had knocked. The Soviet submarines were all in range. The winds were beautiful, worldwide. The missiles were on line and ready. All the factors were right and there was jubilation in the Library. As the various status displays were updated, they were cheering. The bombers were 100 percent. The Pershings were 100 percent. The Tridents were 100 percent. Short of actual firing, it was a full-scale test of O.F.F

Vera was alone at the round table; the others were glued to the status displays, joking, cheering, admiring their own handiwork. There was nothing for them to do now, except wait for the Russians to accept the reality of the numbers and back down, as they'd done in Cuba decades before.

Vera entered Coolidge's name on her own keyboard and the display above it printed out the same old stuff. Discharged for cause, cancellation of pension rights, et cetera. If they had planned any actions against Walter it would have to be in the computer somewhere; you couldn't administer an organization from memory. Beebe, as Protector of the Data, would be involved, so she started with him.

After fifteen minutes everything looked normal, including Beebe's current assignments. Everything looked normal except for the expression on Harry's face when she asked him about Walter. She sat there wondering how to break through any layers of secrecy Harry might have created. There was always the common denominator. Money. You couldn't do anything without money. She tapped into the accounting department and looked at current expenditures. It took another fifteen minutes to find out.

'Emergency appropriation of $75,000 for Operation Prognosis. Freelance fee plus double bonus, $35,000. Remainder for nine freelance operatives, vehicle expenses, contingencies.'

She could hear the others in the background; the place sounded like an office Christmas party. What was Operation Prognosis? Beebe had got the money, but it wasn't on his assignment list. She looked over at them gathered around the displays at the other end of the room. Burnish was the butler, the least suspicious possibility, standing there in the middle of the state of the art of the late twentieth century, with his yellow legal pad in one hand and a pencil in the other. She entered his name and it came up.

'Operation Prognosis – Termination of the Doctor.'

She stared at it for five seconds to make sure she was actually seeing it and then hit the erase button. It was in the computer after all, but hidden. It was in the computer but it wasn't; Harry was trying to have it both ways. Harry himself was losing faith in All Eyes. She stared at her blank terminal. The Doctor needed a Doctor.

Orson Welles

Jake Shoemaker was sitting in one of his salvaged movie seats, moping, confused, troubled. He was having concentration problems; he couldn't keep his mind on the trash. Coolidge's office had been sealed by Beebe. Coolidge was becoming a nonperson; Jake couldn't find out what had happened. He was now reporting to Barber, who was a disaster; he knew nothing about trash but couldn't admit it, and was coming up with all kinds of crazy projects that were a waste of time. Jake was sitting there brooding when the phone rang.

It was Orson Welles. 'Hello, Welles here. Now listen carefully. I need Rosebud delivered to the art director's studio by nine P.M. tonight. Is that clear, old boy?'

'Who did you say this was?'

'Sorry, must have the wrong number.'

Shoemaker was staring into a dial tone. Orson Welles? Orson Welles looking for Rosebud? Who would waste the price of a telephone call with a lousy gag like that? It wasn't even a good imitation. He could do it better himself. He sat back in his chair, hands clasped behind his head, looking at the movie posters up on the walls. *Citizen Kane* was near the window. 'This is Orson Welles of the Mercury Theater,' he said aloud. It wasn't bad. Needed a little work. Not as good as his Laughton. 'To the art director's studio,' he thought. Literal translation: Take a sled to the art director's studio. He tried to think about it the way Coolidge would: intuitively, loosely, crazily, but soundly.

Coolidge was sitting at a small table in Shearer's Cocktail Lounge near Georgetown. It was ten-thirty and Jake hadn't shown up. Maybe Jake hadn't understood. Or

334

maybe he couldn't get Rosebud off the premises. But in that case he would at least have shown up to say so, or called and left word at the bar. He felt certain that Jake wouldn't be able to refuse the challenge; he'd have to prove that he'd figured it out.

It was asking a lot. Jake must know by now that Coolidge was an enemy of the people. He couldn't blame him if he decided to ignore it; a career could evaporate in two minutes in this business. Coolidge had brought Jake into the Library, but Jake didn't owe him this kind of favor. Nobody owed you this kind of favor. Coolidge poured the last inch of his fourth wine into the red globe that held the candle; the idea of drinking anything was odious, after that force feeding by Epps of the CIA. He signaled for a fifth wine. He had no idea what he was going to do if Jake didn't show up; Jake was his only possibility. It was getting to be eleven o'clock and the candleholder was getting kind of full when Shoemaker came hurrying in carrying an attaché case.

Shoemaker, a tense string bean, stood over him with a petulant expression on his face. 'I've been getting drunk for two hours at Gibbons Restaurant. *Cedric Gibbons* was an art director. Douglas Shearer was a *recording* director.'

Coolidge smiled broadly, relieved, grateful, happy. 'I always did get those two mixed up.'

'It just occurred to me that you always got those two mixed up. I thought I was going nuts!'

Jake slid the case under the table and sat down. It was a Rosemont smart terminal. You could connect into the Library computer over telephone lines with it, provided you had the code. Coolidge had it, thanks to the last will and testament of Charley Eberhart.

Jake leaned across the tiny table. 'Walter, what the hell is going on?' The waiter brought him a kir, blackberry liqueur and white wine.

'Don't ask.'

'Yeah, I figured it was something like that.'

'I had a hell of a nerve asking you to do this.'

'I'll say. It *is* a more or less generally speaking legitimate reason, isn't it, Walter?'

'I wouldn't exactly put it that way.'

'Walter, I've got to ask this. You're not going to turn up on Moscow television, are you?'

'No. Negative on Moscow.'

'It took me half the day to figure out what you were saying – that was a lousy imitation, by the way; you're out of practice – and the other half to decide what to do about it.'

Coolidge poured a sip of wine into the candleholder. Jake watched and said nothing. 'Why did you decide to do it?' Coolidge said.

'Walter, you put me on the spot with this. I mean, I had to think about it. This wasn't technique anymore. You know how I love technique; technique keeps you out of trouble. Doing things good, you know? Hell, you know – you're *all* technique.'

'I am?'

'Well, you used to be. That's when it was fun. This isn't fun.'

Coolidge shrugged. There was nothing to say. He had put Jake on the spot and there was nothing else to say about it. He'd thrown himself on Jake's mercy because there were no other choices.

'So I thought, what do you do in a case like this?' Jake went on. 'I mean, what the hell do I know? I don't know what you're up to. I don't know what they're up to either. I figured I know a lot more about you than I do about them, so I went with you. I figured whatever it is you're doing, it's probably the right thing. You've got to go by people.' Jake shrugged and took a healthy draft of kir. 'I'm gambling on you, Walter.'

Coolidge avoided the problem of saying thanks by staying with technique. 'Did you think about being followed when you came here?'

'I was devious as hell. I mean, they don't have anyone smart enough to have followed me. Believe it or not, I drove to Baltimore first.'

Coolidge giggled.

'You ever coming back?'

'Play your cards right and you could be the next Garbageman. Tell them you never did understand me.'

'Are you going to be all right? Anything else I can do? I

336

mean, of a reasonably discreet nature?'

'Got any cash on you?'

Shoemaker handed over eighty-two dollars.

'I'll need your car too.'

Jake took back eight for the cab home.

Coolidge shook his hand. 'You could pass a lie detector test, right?'

'You know, I think I could,' Jake said.

Coolidge was pretty sure the Wordsworth Hotel had never been microcammed; it was too tacky to bother with. But he checked it out. He dialed the computer, put the telephone on the modem, and typed in Eberhart's curse. READY appeared on his small screen, along with the blinking cursor. Eberhart's cursor, you might say; he was back in business. He felt at home having a keyboard in front of him again, and access, access to data, the world. He flexed his fingers with relish and started doing input like a starving man, starting with his own room at the Wordsworth. It was clean. Then he went looking for Senator Garvey.

Ives was being friendly, outgoing, manic, almost giggly. He'd come into the room like Santa Claus, carrying a mysterious and handsome blue box, which he had carefully set down on the low table in front of the couch where Davey Reed was sitting. Garvey's eyes flicked to the box now and then as Ives talked.

'The decision isn't final, of course,' Ives was saying. 'A few details to work out yet, as you can imagine. There's going to be a few dozen unhappy people in Congress to mollify, that sort of thing. But as of now, it looks like you're the big winner.' Ives had dragged it out long enough. He went over to the blue box, the top and sides of which were a lid. He lifted it off with a flourish. 'Dah dah!' Ives said. 'The Senator Oliver Garvey Particle Accelerator.'

It was a scale model. The surface buildings. Little typed cards describing their functions. A double white line running around the periphery, indicating the location of the thirty-mile-diameter particle acceleration tunnel.

Ives was going on like a chamber of commerce. 'Your state is going to be the world center for particle research for the next fifty years. Needless to say, billions will be spent. It's something like giving your entire constituency an annuity.'

Ives was beaming. 'Now I don't want to sound cynical. We don't mean it that way at all. We just hope that you'll keep helping us with defense matters as they come up the way you have been, but of course that's entirely your decision.' Then Ives stopped beaming. He was suddenly staring at the very backside of Garvey's eyeballs. 'The President sent me over here to tell you personally,' he said.

There was a moment of dead silence in the room, and then Ives reverted to charm. 'I know you're busy. Keep the model. Be good for showing off to the home folks when they visit, eh? We should be making a public announcement in a week or so; we'll arrange something with you. Photo opportunity in the Rose Garden, TV cameras, whatnot.' Ives turned up the smile another sixty watts, waved, was gone.

Garvey was thinking at ninety mph. So was Reed. They could read each other's minds. Garvey could no longer avoid looking at his speechwriter.

'What do you think?' he said.

'There's only one thing that could rate a bribe like that,' Reed said.

'Yeah.'

'They know.'

'Yeah.'

'They know we know.'

'Yeah.'

Garvey sat back in his swivel chair, staring out the window at the Capitol, but not seeing it. The President had just offered him the biggest piece of pork in history, asking nothing in return, except for the look on Ives's face that appeared for a millisecond and then flashed off.

'The question is,' Reed said, 'how does he know? How does the President know we know?'

'Yeah, I know.'

'The Doctor was careful,' Reed said. 'I mean, that's his business, he knows about that stuff. That radio station was not bugged. You know what that means?'

Garvey had gone to the model and was bent over it. There must be real possibilities if they were offering this much. He wouldn't be human if he didn't have greedy thoughts; it meant a safe seat for life. Was it too big a price to pay for a shot at eight years in the White House? You couldn't get the presidency without risking some losses.

'I said, do you know what that means?' Reed asked.

'What does what mean?'

'That they didn't have the radio station bugged.'

'Yeah, sure. They must have found out some other way.'

Reed looked at him.

'You can stop thinking it,' Garvey said. 'I didn't do it, Mr. Loyalty.'

'I'll admit the thought flashed through my brain, unbidden, for a fraction of a second. We ought to tell the Doctor. It could mean trouble for him.'

Garvey had the perfect excuse for inaction. 'How the hell do we contact him without compromising him?'

Coolidge froze the frame on Garvey's face. It wasn't encouraging. Adam Tempted by Satan: that's what he saw on the monitor. It was a lot to ask of a politician to turn down an offer like that. Coolidge had taken on none other than the President of the United States as an opponent, someone who had, among other things, the GNP to play with. What was going on with the others?

He went on a data binge for hours, searching for Emersons. It was the usual maelstrom of human events. Three insider swindles in the making on Wall Street, Ambassador Zhu tied to the bedpost, Ling-Ling saying, 'Please don't rape me,' to a tumescent Yeager, an under secretary at Agriculture arranging for a cushy job with a grain exporting company, the usual human inter-connections.

He spent forever tracking down Glenn Ingalls and found out that Ingalls was now the subject of an FBI investigation. They didn't even know about Reinhold Kunstner; they were looking into Ingalls's associations during the Vietnam days, when he'd formed a group against the war. It was a witch hunt. He went looking for Purefoy and found him at lunch with the attorney general; they were old friends and had a good time, during which the attorney general reminded Purefoy of the oath of secrecy he had signed when he was director of Central Intelligence and that it was still binding.

The President's strategy gradually emerged. It was a combination of arm twisting, jawboning, goodies out of the pork barrel, pressures, intimidations; the Emersons were *all* on thin ice, which was where the pursuit of peace in America left you.

The work had been exhausting and the news was bad. He switched the terminal off, put the phone back on its cradle, and sat down on the edge of the bed to think. He needed time, lots of time; he was running out of options fast.

The phone rang.

'You've been there for hours,' Vera said. 'Are you crazy? Get *out* of there *now*.' She hung up. There wasn't time to wonder. He folded the terminal back into the case, snapped it shut, and ran.

The World Is Round!

Vera had surprised herself. It was an impulse, without a lot of thought behind it. Mike Barber had told Beebe where Walter was hiding; Barber had spotted the telephone connection to Walter's computer terminal. She'd simply picked up the phone and called. But it was a sustained impulse; she had to call twenty times before Walter finally hung up the phone. It was unprofessional, stupid, dangerous. Worse, she'd run the risk of being called a woman.

She could justify it, if she had to. She hadn't been told that Walter was an enemy of the people; it wasn't in the computer. Not so's you'd notice. All Eyes seemed to have been altered to Mostly All Eyes. It was incredibly un-Library; Harry was violating his own rule.

She was wandering around the O.F.F. displays and tallies at the far end of the room. Everything was holding close to 100 percent. Over at the big table, Burnish was sitting with a bottle of Sambuca Romana and a pound of coffee beans. Gardella was sitting sprawled forward in Harry's chair, a hand holding up his chin, a glass in his other hand, a glassy look in his eyes. Gardella looked as though he were coming apart; his wife had left him for a retoucher.

She continued to follow the displays as they updated themselves, wondering why Walter had blown the whistle on it all. Walter had turned against O.F.F. Why? She knew him well enough to know that it couldn't have been for a stupid reason. It would have to be something big. Either Walter didn't want to kill sixty million Russians or he didn't believe we could do it and get away with it.

Vera went to her seat and fell in; Harry had wrung everyone dry.

'Is this thing going to work?' she said.

'Hell of a time to ask,' Gardella replied absently.

'Don't ask me,' Burnish said, chewing on an alcohol-soaked coffee bean. She'd never seen Burnish at the end of this rope before. 'I thought you people were the experts,' he said.

'Depends on what you mean by working,' Gardella said.

'What do *you* mean by working?' she said.

'Stop worrying about it; we won't have to use it.'

'Then why is Beatty home praying with his family?'

Gardella giggled. Then he slid over a glass of Sambuca with three coffee beans in it that Burnish had just poured. Beatty, the born-again Christian who was always gung ho to take on the reds, was having a failure of nerve, had fallen back on Jesus in place of Harry Dunn. It was the hot-line message that had done it.

The government of the United States cannot be responsible for the consequences if the government of the Soviet Union does not promptly withdraw four Soviet Armored divisions 100 miles in an easterly direction from the general area of Fulda Gap.

It was an ultimatum; face had been committed. The U.S. had gone to DefCon 2, one step away from war. The 'successors' had been alerted and were preparing to disappear into the Presidential Emergency Facilities without their wives. Barber, Farnsworth, and Hopkins had already left for the alternate Library site at Mount Weather. Harry was sleeping, Beatty was praying, Burnish and Gardella were drinking, and even the computer didn't know what Walter was doing.

Gardella was staring into his drink. When he spoke, it was very analytical and dry. 'How many will they be left with? That's the magic number. A dozen we could live with. Two dozen's getting rough. Three dozen means a political disaster for the President and probably the party. That's the equation.'

'I thought you said we wouldn't have to use it,' she said.

'Yeah,' Gardella replied. 'I'm saying in the worst case. It's all got to do with the Russian mental state.' He sipped the clear liquor, using it for fuel. 'They're a nation of chess players. They know about laying down your king. On the other hand, they know what it means to lay down your king.

It means you've taken a kick in the ego, deep down where it really hurts; you've surrendered to a better man. That's the toughest thing in life to do. I know what I'm talking about.'

It was impossible to tell if Gardella was more depressed about World War III or the retoucher who was now sleeping with his wife. Probably the latter; everyone had his priorities.

It brought to mind her own little accident with Harry. Harry *couldn't* have told Walter about it; he wasn't *that* insensitive. Although you could never be certain about men and sex. It was like a Super Bowl with some of them; what was the point of winning if nobody knew about it?

At first she'd just taken him home for a drink. Harry had seemed on the point of a nervous breakdown. It was when O.F.F. had broken 90 percent for the first time. Harry was practically babbling. The Library was his baby; so was the statistical analysis behind O.F.F., and now it was all on the line. Did those O.F.F. numbers mean anything in the real world, or didn't they? Or were they merely bureaucratic manipulations?

She'd had a tough time with him. Harry was trying to jump out of his skin, which would have been one of the natural wonders of the world. He kept saying that evolution might come to an end if he'd been wrong. All that evolving, that shaping, God's random sampling, three different *wings*, if you just considered flying. Independently invented! Birds, bees, and bats, he kept saying. The random invention of the flying machine, three goddamn times! All gone if he, Harry Dunn, was wrong.

The fact of the matter was that she hadn't considered it as sex at all; it was a patriotic act, doing the country a favor.

But how the hell had Walter found out? Did Walter have an inside track somehow? A special category of information? She'd been sensing something like that for weeks. The thought would have faded away – it was too un-Library – if she hadn't found Operation Prognosis hidden away in the computer. Were they checking up on everyone's personal life somehow? It was a monstrous idea; microcams in all their apartments. She felt revulsion, disgust, at the thought of it, at the total absence of privacy. What could justify that? Damn; it was so Harry, so ruthlessly logical.

'I'm sorry about Coolidge,' Gardella said, looking more and more maudlin. 'I'm sorry he did what he did. Had his reasons, I suppose. Hated to have been the one to catch him. Another casualty in the big war.'

There was that word again. Casualty. They were forever estimating casualties in the Library; it was almost like a currency. The body count. They were actually talking in terms of megabodies. Killing was the ultimate act of manipulation. Which was what they were doing more and more of. Manipulating, watching, judging. Christ, there was a lot of judging of other people, other countries. People we didn't even know much about. It reminded her of an old Olsen and Johnson skit, sorting strawberries over the telephone: that's good, that's bad, that's good. And old ineffectual Walter, the Garbageman nobody took seriously, was the one who'd blown the whistle on it.

She drained off her Sambuca and looked over at them. O.F.F. was 99.32 percent at the moment, which was about as close as you could edge up to Armageddon. It had to affect your outlook. Put a different coloration on things. Made you think about what was really important in your life. She stood up and started out.

'Stay cool, sweets,' Burnish said blankly.

She had an advantage. A big one. She knew Walter; Beebe didn't. She went downstairs to Russia and sailed her platform out over the great plains, east of the marshes, west of the Don, and hovered. She did input on the small keyboard; below, the Russian plains started to switch out, a few hundred acres at a time, to be replaced by satellite photos of the District of Columbia. The world was round; the same satellites that took shots of the Soviet Union photographed the U.S. on the return trip.

She knew; she just knew. There were some things that were constants in the world. She knew what he would be doing and approximately where he would be doing it. She did more input, pulled the relevant data out of the computer, and then bent over her funny telescope, looking for Walter Coolidge.

The Conspirators

Davey Reed had always been impressed by Emerson Foster. Foster was smart and smooth and knew who he was, and he stayed concentrated on things; he set goals, little goals and big goals, and he pursued them until he reached them, the little ones and the big ones. Which was how he'd become a centimillionaire, none of it inherited.

But no, Reed was thinking, there had to be something more. Reed could concentrate and he set goals all the time, but he didn't have a cent, much less a centimillion. Foster believed in himself; that was the difference; Foster had no doubts about what he was doing, whatever it was. He must have had a lot of bright ideas too, and energy, lots of energy. Drinking used up too much of Reed's energy. He made a delicate movement of an index finger and the waiter caught it right away. Reed and the waiter had good rapport; in a flash he was at Reed's side, pouring a rather astounding white wine into a rather astounding crystal goblet.

Emerson had everything. Emerson had rugs and wallpaper and chairs and end tables and chandeliers and his own waiters and a plush town house in Georgetown, all looking right out of an ad showing the rich at play. Reed had actually felt giddy the first time he'd stepped onto one of Foster's rugs, the nap was so thick. They were in the informal dining room, the small one, Emerson, Garvey, and Reed all but lost at the long table. The big dining room upstairs could probably hold the Senate and probably had.

Earlier, Foster had started things off by being ravishingly charming. 'I feel like Sam Adams conspiring against George the Third,' he'd said, leading them into the library for aperitifs before dinner. 'To victory over the King,' he'd toasted, winking, and Reed had actually felt a shiver, as though he were participating in a historic meeting, the consequences of which might go echoing on down time, ending up in elementary-school history primers; Reed let himself go off the deep end like that now and then.

But after dinner, dishes cleared, brandy, coffee, cigars, chocolate tidbits spread out, waiters dispatched for the evening, the tone began to change almost immediately.

'You'll be carrying the brunt of this thing,' Foster said. 'I must say I admire your courage.'

Reed glanced at the senator's face. Garvey didn't like the word 'courage'; courage meant you were taking risks.

'Have you read Davey's memorandum?' Garvey said.

'Read, memorized, shredded, and burned.'

'Any comments?'

'None. It's perfect.'

Reed nodded politely at Foster. He'd roughed it all out in two pages. The senator would call a meeting of his subcommittee and begin asking embarrassing questions of Harry Dunn and others; in public session if possible, in executive session if necessary. As revelations leaked out, the various constituent groups of the Emersons would react publicly, make statements, send letters to senators, representatives, editors, gradually build up a clamor from the grass roots that could not be ignored. The noise generated would be enough to get other senators interested, if only to cash in on it or, at the very least, stay ahead of it and not get run over by it.

'I think pacing is going to be basic,' Foster said. 'Our people are fairly conservative, after all. Most of them, anyway. They won't want to look foolish, unpatriotic, rash. It will have to be orchestrated very carefully. It won't be easy to get a consensus, to get them to move.'

'Yeah, right, the democratic process,' Garvey said glumly.

'For your own sake, you'll have to make sure they're all behind you, Oliver. You won't want to get too far out in front.'

'I'm worried about a few of them,' Garvey said. He

346

counted them off on his right hand. 'Kiernan, Purefoy, Ingalls, the bishop.'

'You think they're wavering?'

'Maybe, maybe not. They could go either way. They've got pressures to contend with.'

Foster nodded. He knew about pressures.

Now Garvey was counting on his left hand. 'I think we can count on Anderson, Witek, the rabbi, and Weinstein. They seem to be committed. But they aren't enough. I can't move without Kiernan. I can't move without the bishop. And Ingalls. And Purefoy. Those are all significant constituencies. This has to be broad-based or it'll fall on its face.'

Foster was toying with a silver coffee spoon; Reed figured it at seventy-five dollars minimum. Foster neither smoked nor drank. Could that be why he was a centimillionaire? How many millions had Reed poured down his gullet, he wondered.

'All in all, Oliver,' Foster said, 'I believe the thing to do is for you to count your losses now, before the fact. I insist that you be fair to yourself; there's a long, distinguished career here at stake.'

'He's always doing that,' Reed put in, hitting the brandy bottle. He was starting to tune out. Their faces were more interesting than their words. They had both been offered something juicy – he couldn't imagine the size of the plum it would take to get Foster's attention – and now were preparing possible lines of retreat. If they managed it well, they could get out with their winnings and still manage to look like nice guys. King George III could sleep safely in his bed.

'Go ahead, Emerson, count my losses.'

'One, the faucet gets turned off. You'll get what the President calls the Moslem treatment, a no-pork diet. That's to the end of a possible second term, Oliver.'

Garvey and Reed looked at each other. The Moslem treatment. The President had written a good line.

'Two, they'll try to make you out as an unwitting dupe of the KGB. You know the drill.'

'Three, it'll be a barrel of fun and maybe even save the planet,' Reed put in.

'Certainly,' Foster replied. 'But we're talking about the art of the possible. We have to at least consider the possibility that, as a group, we may decide not to move too quickly. At least for a while.'

'That is of course a possibility,' Garvey said.

'It certainly is,' Reed added. He halted the brandy glass in midair and put it back on the table, an improbable desire to be sober coming over him. The Oliver Garvey Memorial Particle Accelerator meant that the President knew there was a leak. Was there a chance the President had also figured out who the leaker was? He sat there trying it on for size. He didn't like the way Samuel Adams was talking at all. He was beginning to think that Walter Coolidge might need a friend.

Reed knew her car because he'd made the arrangements with Arthur St. Claire to buy it for her. It was in the small Library parking lot; there was only room for about a dozen cars and it was unguarded. He'd procured a pick from the guard at one of the Senate parking lots; they were forever leaving their keys in the ignition. The guard had given him a five-minute course of instruction. It took him ten minutes of blundering to get the door open. Then he waited, concealed in the shadows of the back seat, until whenever Vera decided the day was over. After two hours he could hear her heels on the asphalt. There was no way she wasn't going to be frightened, but he did it as nicely as possible.

'Now don't be alarmed,' he said, as she opened the door.

Vera jumped back two feet, started to scream, caught it, started to flare up angrily, caught it, then warily moved toward the car again.

'What are you doing here?' she said.

'Would you mind closing the door so the damn light goes out?'

She climbed in and slammed the door. 'What are you up to this time?'

'I'm looking for a friend of mine who's got a problem. I thought maybe you could help me.'

She lit a cigarette and, for three seconds, he could see a

lot in her face. A lot of contempt, for one thing. After all, Reed was one of the people who'd caused the problem in the first place. But it wasn't 100 percent; there was a little something to work with there, and he could also see that he was right. Coolidge *was* in trouble.

'Do you know where he is?' he said.

'Of course,' she replied.

Trash Tactics

Coolidge was trying to save his life the only way he knew how: by means of trash analysis. He'd spent hours at it – it was now three in the morning – working his way through garbage, looking for facts, connections, thoughts, juxtapositions. Having Jake's car, he was able to move around easily, but it took time approaching places from the rear, climbing fences, prowling through alleys. It was a precaution he took even though he knew John Doe's men were out tailing the Emersons, not the Emersons' garbage. He knew it because he had been stopping at public telephones all night, connecting into the computer, checking John Doe's calls to Beebe. As the night wore on, he took even more care in his approach moves; the Emersons would be coming home, wagging their tails behind them.

He'd started with kosher garbage at Rabbi Mandelbaum's synagogue and found what he called a 'binary.' In itself it meant nothing, a mimeographed schedule for the week showing that the rabbi was busy on the third, fourth, sixth, and seventh, but his assistants were handling everything on the fifth. Later, at union headquarters, he found that Joe Kiernan had canceled lunch with a congressman for the fifth; he got it off the back of a piece of carbon paper. It was the other half of the 'binary,' meaning that they added up to data. Confirmation: Admiral Anderson had tossed out a calendar page for the fifth with only one letter on it: E. Conclusion? There was an Emerson meeting set for the fifth, and it might even be starting in a few hours.

Coolidge had saved Emerson Foster's town house for last, and now he was in a narrow alley that ran alongside it, poking around in rich garbage; the remains of caviar, pheasant, great cigars. Along with a phone message slip that was provoking. None other than Eugene Ives had called Emerson Foster. The message, presumably written down by Emerson's secretary, read: 'Talk re Brazil?'

He put the lid back and sat down on top of the can, the computer terminal in his lap. Eugene Ives was talking to Emerson Foster. Wasn't that curious. And about the charming country of Brazil, where Emerson's bank had been shoveling petrodollars coming in from Arab countries, but without asking enough searching questions. It could be innocent; innocence showed up in the craziest places. On the other hand, when you had access to Gene Ives, you had access to the President. Access, hell; Ives had called *him*.

Coolidge sat there. Life was hard. He thought of the old cartoon: 'Now here's my plan.' All he had to do was get to the Emersons' meeting. Convince them their leader was a White House fink. Talk them out of quitting. Persuade Oliver Garvey to stick to his guns and be honest and take chances and do something constructive for the human race for a change. If he moved *real* fast, he might even be able to get there before John Doe did and thereby stay alive long enough to accomplish all those objectives. He'd hardly finished thinking the thought when even that remote prospect got remoter.

He heard the ominous sound of a garbage truck, ominous because it was three in the morning and because, when he looked down the long, dark alley and saw the truck coming to a stop, he saw that it wasn't a District of Columbia model. Beebe had finally realized it was the Emersons' garbage and not the Emersons that interested Coolidge.

He raced around to the rear of the building, but there was a wooden fence, about eight feet high. He stood there looking at it. He wasn't particularly athletic. He couldn't leave the terminal – he still needed it – and it was too delicate to toss over. He scrambled over the top holding on to the case, was clumsy and snapped off a foot of wooden board as he dropped down heavily on the other side. The noise got their attention. From the sounds they made running, he figured them for 225 pounds apiece. He sped down another alley and came out on the street. There was no traffic, no people, not even parked cars. It was O Street, N.W., looking like an archaeological dig; there were still stretches of trolley tracks left among the cobblestones. That's what he should have stuck with, *ancient* garbage.

He heard the truck engine revving up and started running. It was Germany all over again, being chased by a goliath. But how could you defeat a garbage truck? His only advantage was that they'd have to make it look like an accident; they'd have to be delicate about it. He could hear them swerving onto O Street. He was running full tilt along the sidewalk, not going in any particular direction; he was searching for an idea and he was fresh out. They pulled abreast of him; he could see the two men in the truck's cab, looking at him, estimating, planning, deciding. The obvious was to come up on the sidewalk and cut him off. He tried to think it through the way Harry would, looking for a garbage truck's weakness. Let's see now, what was the essential difference between a man and a garbage truck? Oh, right. *It* had to stay *out*side.

He was passing a basement apartment; he stopped and hurdled the guardrail over the entryway and came down flatfooted in front of a window. The truck's brakes were squealing as he smashed the window with the terminal and climbed into the apartment.

It was a bedroom and no one was in it. The door was open and there was a light coming from somewhere else in the apartment. He ran toward the light, coming out into a long foyer that went toward the rear of the house. As he ran down the hall, the place seemed familiar; there was probably a VIP living in it. He cantered past the parlor, where four couples were staring out at him, frozen, petrified. He almost tore the rear door off its hinges and was out, trampling a tiny garden, scrambling over another fence, and then turning left down an alley, out to the street again.

There was still nothing in the streets and he started for Wisconsin Avenue, which was the only chance of finding a cab; any halfway decent cabdriver ought to be able to lose

352

a garbage truck. But he was running out of everything; breathing had stopped being automatic, the terminal was getting heavy, his legs were getting heavy.

And Wisconsin was empty; there was never a cab when you needed one. He was standing on a street corner, winded, looking for a place to hide. There were only closed stores and restaurants and places of business. He stumbled across the street to get a different perspective. Nothing looked promising, but he started to run anyway, and then quit after ten feet. He had nothing left to work with.

He was leaning against the display window of a boutique, used up, when the garbage truck drove up, pinning him against the window with its headlights. He could hear two men get out of the truck and there was the sound of a car stopping. He watched the driver of the car step out and approach him. He had to get close before Coolidge could recognize him.

It was Mister Anonymous himself, the man in the street, John Doe.

Coolidge was going to be a minor accident case on a police blotter by morning. The three of them were standing there watching Coolidge breathe, waiting until he could walk again. They reminded Coolidge of Brezhnev's men; they were viewing him as an object. He was still reaching for big, deep breaths when two more cars drove up; all the fox hunters had arrived for the kill. The only thing audible in the street now was Coolidge's breathing.

Plus one other sound. It took a few seconds for Coolidge to recall where he'd heard it before; it was confusing in his rattled state, because the first time he'd ever heard it, it was terrifying: the sound of another man breathing.

'Uuuhhhh,' someone was saying.

Then Coolidge's favorite emphysema case moved into the headlights. He had an AK-47 in his hands this time. Last time they'd met, at the mansion, Coolidge had hit him on the head with *The Decline and Fall of the Roman Empire*. Coolidge didn't know what to expect.

'Lean on the truck,' Ned said to John Doe, advancing further into the light. There was another one with him, another old fool, sixty-five if he was a day. Two more came in from the left; they all looked as though they should have been using the AK-47s for canes. John Doe and friends were now leaning against a truck fender with their feet way out, being frisked.

'It isn't that I don't appreciate it,' Coolidge said to Ned, 'but would you mind telling me how you figured this out?'

Ned nodded at one of the cars. 'Uuuhhhh,' he said.

Coolidge picked up the terminal and walked over to John Doe, still spread-eagled on a fender. 'Tell Beebe for me that he sucks, will you?' Then he went over to the car. It was Vera's New Car II. He took one last deep breath, beginning to feel normal, or anyway what passed for normal in the life of a Garbageman. 'How the hell did you do it?'

'You're not the only one who knows everything,' Davey Reed replied. 'Get in.'

The Election

The hotel clerk was looking at him funny; it *was* six in the morning. The terminal was suspended between the shelf under the pay phone and his belt buckle, with the telephone receiver cradled in the modem, and he was awkwardly doing input on the keyboard trying not to drop the whole shooting match, knowing he must look like a freak from a computer salesmen's convention.

It didn't take a lot of nickels. Emerson Foster's bank was up to its ears in bad Brazilian loans; it was going to crash unless it got serious help, the kind that only Uncle Sam could provide. There was another tidbit. Emerson had chartered a plane to Cat Cay island, where the President had vacationed for a few days. Harry Dunn had come down a day later. It wasn't conclusive; you couldn't hang a man on evidence like that. But you could let him swing for a while.

He inputted Beebe and the terminal printed out the *bad* news. Beebe knew about the Emersons' meeting. John Doe had his orders. In spite of everything, Coolidge couldn't help smiling at the look on John Doe's face when Ned appeared with an AK-47, but there was no way Ned and his band of ancients could hold prisoners; they'd be in a safe house of their own by now.

He hung up the phone, folded everything back into the case, smiled wanly at the desk clerk, and went back outside the hotel to where Reed was parked at a taxi stand. He got into the car slowly.

'I think you better bail out of this,' he said. 'I'll drive myself.'

'I'm *sober*; it's all right.'

'They know where we're going. They'll be waiting along the way.'

'I've got a great idea. Let's not go there.'

'I've got to talk to the Emersons.'

Reed switched off the engine. 'Walter, we'll set up another meeting. You can hide somewhere in the meantime.'

'Where?'

'Where?'

'Where?'

'I don't know where. We'll think of something.'

'Forget it. There's no place to hide. Waiting is the bigger risk. And you can't get the Emersons together any day in the week. They're all busy people; some of them have to fly in from places. I'm going there now. Get out.'

'What do you expect to accomplish?'

'I need political power. That's what I want from them. We have government by cover story, but it's still a democracy. The Emersons represent people, lots of people. That's power. If they support me, *I'll* have power. I'll have a chance of surviving this thing. Bumping off an unknown intelligence worker is one thing. Doing it to someone who has grass roots support all across the country is something else; they wouldn't be able to cover it up. That's what I'm hoping for, anyway. Get out.'

Reed, sitting behind the wheel, was pulling the skin of both cheeks down toward his chin. 'I hate to be the one to tell you this,' he said. 'It's bigger than any of them figured on. They're wavering, Walter. Most of them. Especially the senator.'

'I know. He's got the hots for a particle accelerator.'

'It's like getting the whole pig. If he does it, I think I'm going back to writing dog food commercials.'

'He's not going to do it. *They're* not going to do it.'

Reed grinned at such simplicity. 'Look, Walter, it isn't going to be that easy. Do you know what it'll be like? It'll be like running for office. You don't know them; the Emersons are the public. You have to be a politician to handle that bunch. They go every which way on any issue. You know what I think? I say this sincerely, Walter. Go to Toronto.'

'I'm very disappointed in you, Davey,' Coolidge said quietly. 'You seem to be missing the point. There isn't going to be a Toronto either. Get out.'

Reed thought about it. 'It's hard for that to sink in,' he

said, turning the key, starting the engine. 'It's a funny thing, but I keep forgetting that.' He swung the car onto Eighteenth Street. 'It's the Emersons or bust,' he said. 'Right, Walter?'

Reed had spent 90 percent of his time peering into the rearview mirror, but nothing had happened until they were leaving the Beltway, a mile or so from the mansion on the hill. When it was too late, they saw John Doe's plan of battle laid out clearly. Doe was sticking with the cliché, the automobile accident, the norm in America. It was like seeing the diagram of an accident before the accident.

Four cars, hot rods riding high on muscular springs, were waiting near the bottom of the hill that led to the mansion. It would look like an early-morning drag race that went wrong. Minor court case, drunken driving perhaps, suspended license, nothing to it. The four cars, which were lined up abreast like cavalry preparing to charge, were now peeling off into line astern, like destroyers, roaring down the road at about one-hundred-foot intervals. Both sides of the road sloped up sharply; there was no way to run. Reed had taken his foot off the gas and they were down to doing about twenty; he was looking indecisive.

'May I make a suggestion?' Coolidge said.

'Give me the answer, Walter.'

It was an idea of Herman Kahn's, master strategist of everything: the way to play chicken was to show up drunk, wrench the steering wheel off the column, and toss it out the window.

'Floor it,' Coolidge said. 'Steady as she goes.'

The lead car was still half a mile off.

'You serious?'

'It's our motivation against their motivation. I doubt if they're getting paid enough for a head-on at ninety per. Besides, there's nothing else to do.'

Reed's foot slowly pushed the accelerator to the floor and Vera's New Car II shot ahead. Reed had a death lock on the steering wheel and there was a frozen look of fear and ecstasy on his face, as though he'd finally been given a chance at getting back at the bastards, any bastards.

Coolidge's eczema above the inside right ankle was flaring up and he decided to scratch it; it might be the last sensual pleasure he would ever experience.

Everyone was centered on the white line, a perfect game of chicken, harrowing, the world at stake, nerve endings jumping, egos riding, perceptions being tested, convictions being tested, the weighting of satisfaction versus reason. Coolidge could see the first driver's face. It was starting to go from smug professionalism and gung ho to an appreciation of man's frail grasp on existence. Coolidge had a weapon; it was the look on Davey Reed's face. The first driver took a good look at it and promptly chickened out, swerving over too far to the left, hitting the low railing at the side of the road, bouncing back, side-swiping Reed, bouncing off again, then disappearing behind them, making crashing sounds.

The force of the blow had shoved Reed off the white line. He pulled it back again; number two was coming up. Reed was doing ninety-five. The second driver looked like he was having a bowel movement. He swerved to the right but went too far, crashing through the steel rail and riding up the slope, but riding too far for his center of gravity; the car rolled over and came crashing back down on the road, catching fire.

Reed had the initiative now. There were two wrecks in the road behind him and number three, coming fast, had gotten an education, a look into the future. He tried getting around on the left, but Davey didn't allow him much room; Davey wasn't giving an inch, but it cost the two left-hand side doors, both torn off during the resulting sideswipe. Again Reed was forced over to the right by the blow and this time number four took advantage of the opening, like a halfback running for daylight, and disappeared past them.

Coolidge had to work up a little saliva before he could talk. 'Brake in a ladylike manner,' he managed to get out. Reed made a hair-raising turn to get on the hill, almost rolling over, but he had gravity working for him now, and recovered by turning into the roll at first, racing up the lawn, easing back onto the asphalt, then burning rubber all the way to a screeching halt in the midst of the

358

assembled cars of the Emersons, nicking one of them in the fender and scaring hell out of a gathering of chauffeurs.

Coolidge got out and looked at Vera's New Car II. It was rather rakish without any doors on the driver's side. He wondered who he could get to pay for it this time. Reed was still in the car; he couldn't seem to get his hands off the steering wheel. Coolidge crouched down on the gravel alongside. 'Davey, that was a nice piece of work. I talk a good line, but I don't think I could have done it.'

'Do you think it's too early in the morning for a little drinkie?'

'As the Doctor, I prescribe it.'

It was 7:30 A.M. and Coolidge and Reed both had a little drinkie in the kitchen, using the cooking Scotch. Then they went back out to the study near the front of the house, and for the second time Coolidge opened the door and caught the Emersons by surprise, this time all of them, seated at a long, narrow table having breakfast.

Reed went to the window to look for signs of enemy activity; Coolidge walked along the table studying faces. The bishop, Ingalls, Purefoy, the rabbi; General Witek and Admiral Anderson in civvies, Sarah Weinstein, Joe Kiernan. Foster was at one end of the table, Garvey at the other. It was the board of directors of peace on earth, hanging on to their beliefs by a fingernail.

'Why don't you introduce me, Senator?' Coolidge said.

Garvey had scrambled egg halfway to his mouth. 'Introduce you?' he said, incredulous.

'Of course. Where are your manners?'

Garvey shook his head nervously. 'I don't understand.' Garvey had become a raw nerve when talking to Coolidge. Coolidge's constant surprises had conditioned him. Garvey believed that Coolidge knew everything; no matter how crazy it might sound, Coolidge was always right; Coolidge had a data base second to none. 'What are you doing here?' he said, almost afraid of what the answer might be.

'You of course have realized that someone sitting at this table blew the whistle on the Doctor.'

Coolidge waited for various rustlings, stirrings, gasps, looks of shock to pass.

'Yes, I came to that conclusion,' Garvey said, careful not to look at anyone but Coolidge.

'Did anyone else come to that conclusion?' Coolidge asked the table.

'I considered the possibility,' Ingalls said. 'I'm being investigated by the FBI. Forty percent of my output is defense related. They've let me know it's in jeopardy.'

'Anyone else?'

'The cardinal has been unusually strong in his views of late.'

'Anyone else?'

'I'm getting it from all sides,' Purefoy said. 'They're even talking to me about some of the covert operations that ran when I was with the Company. Operations that now seem to be of dubious legality. Yeah, Coolidge, I thought of it.'

Coolidge was still moving slowly around the table. He had their undivided attention. 'I have to say I don't know what I would do under the same circumstances.'

Garvey was holding on to the arms of his chair; he looked as if he was bracing for an earthquake. 'Don't keep us in suspense. Who is it?'

Coolidge paused to frame the question. 'Shall we get through this in a dignified manner, Emerson?' he said.

Garvey's eyes slowly went from Coolidge down the length of the table to Foster. 'I can't let you talk to Emerson that way,' he said, but it was soft, no force, no outrage. The data base had spoken.

Foster was cool, composed, his own man with his own interests. He sat in silence for a long time, looking down at the tablecloth, and then he raised his eyes, looking back down the long table at Garvey. 'It was survival time for the bank, Oliver. I had to do it.'

'Ouch,' Garvey said.

No one spoke. They were embarrassed, for themselves and for Foster. 'You see, it's quixotic,' Foster said finally. 'It's too big. It can't be worked. Too many important people believe in and want O.F.F. Too many important people profit from O.F.F. They'll make us look like radicals, crazies. We'd lose our influence, our credibility.'

Coolidge had been leaning against a wall, trying to fig-

360

ure out how to launch his election campaign; he had his own credibility to worry about. He had to win big to win.

'Emerson is talking sense. Good political sense. There's no getting away from it.'

'You think you can break through?' Foster said to him. 'You won't make a dent.' Coolidge winced at Foster's next words. 'John Doe won't let you.'

'Yeah, you've got a point there,' Coolidge replied. 'He's a tough guy to handle.'

'John Doe trusts the generals,' Foster went on. 'He won't tolerate criticism of the generals. He thinks the generals know what they're doing.'

'Hell, even the generals think they know what they're doing.'

'That's slick,' Foster said. 'It's too easy; it rolls off the tongue.'

'The point is,' Coolidge replied, 'that generals are as fallible and self-deluding and neurotic as the rest of us, maybe more so. They spend their lives thinking about quick, violent solutions to difficult problems. That's one of the things we have to get across. My apologies, gentlemen,' he said in the direction of Anderson and Witek.

'Accepted,' one of them replied.

Foster shook his head. He was sticking to his place at the head of the table. 'You're trying to talk substance; this isn't a substantive issue. It's a political issue.' Foster seemed determined to justify his act of betrayal by demonstrating its inherent good sense. 'You know what it's like out there. John Doe has anticommunism in his gut; it's in the water he drinks, the food he eats. He's touched with fear and righteousness and fanaticism and hate. You're going to tell this man that the arms race is our fault?'

'It can be done.'

'You're off the wall, my friend. In the freest country in the world, it's impossible to have an open political debate on these matters. Not by anyone who wants to hold on to his political respectability. Oliver, yours is a conservative state. Call a subcommittee meeting on the question of O.F.F. and you'll be the messenger who gets killed. You know I'm right.'

Coolidge kept watching the faces as Foster talked. Why

walk into a buzz saw? That's what they had to be thinking about.

Coolidge dragged a chair up to the table and edged in between Sarah Weinstein and Bishop Hinds. 'What Emerson is telling you isn't news. It's what liberals have been telling each other for decades. It's impossible; don't fight it; you'll break your pick; pass on the problem to the next generation, let them handle it. That's what you're saying, isn't it, Emerson.'

'More or less. Crass as it may sound.'

'But it isn't crass, Emerson, it's stupid. *This* is the *last* generation. There isn't going to be another generation to hand it off *to*. The buck stops with this generation and there's nothing we can do about it.'

'Maybe yes, maybe no,' Foster replied. 'But you still refuse to deal with the problem that John Doe doesn't want to know. He enjoys his hate. It makes him feel superior. All any President has to do is go out to the country and rattle John Doe's cage every few years and he gets all the money he needs for the latest weapons systems. That's the politics of the situation; that's what we're up against.'

Coolidge resumed his campaign, talking to the electorate, working the hustings. 'That's only part of the politics of the situation,' he said, trying to look into as many eyes as he could catch. 'Everyone at this table is connected with groups all over the country. These are people who are not macho about nuclear war. They are asking questions. Their ears are open. They are at least willing to listen. We should be telling them something. It is true that there will be losses and you'll pay a price.'

'Nice words,' Foster said. 'And I can't deny it: in a noble cause.'

'The trouble with you, Emerson,' Coolidge replied, 'is that you're so realistic – that's in quotes, in case you miss my tone – you don't even understand what I'm talking about. This isn't a noble cause. It's a selfish cause. I'm talking about saving our lives, not to *mention* property, Emerson.'

Coolidge sat back in his chair, exhausted. It was Garvey's turn.

'What do you think, Glenn?' Garvey said, skittering away.

Glenn Ingalls thought about it, mashing his uneaten eggs with a fork. 'It seems to depend on your perception of the facts. The President has built a lot of first-strike missiles. They're not needed for defense. They're not needed to deter a Russian first strike. Their only use is war fighting or the threat of war fighting, which is almost as dangerous. If he isn't planning to fight a nuclear war or to threaten one, then the man is mad because he's spending all our money on missiles he's not going to have a use for. I personally am scared to death. I say call the subcommittee.'

'Herb?' Garvey said to Purefoy, starting to go around the table.

'I don't like this any more than Emerson does. I don't like kicking over garbage cans. Quite frankly, I'd just as soon John Doe stayed asleep. If he ever wakes up he's going to be trouble. But I don't think we have any choice. I think we're stuck. If we don't act, sooner or later there's going to be a nuclear war. So what are we risking? Call the subcommittee, Oliver.'

Garvey frowned. 'General?'

'Call the subcommittee tomorrow morning.'

'Admiral?'

'The subcommittee.'

'Bishop?'

'Subcommittee.'

'Sarah?'

'Subcommittee.'

'Rabbi?'

'Subcommittee.'

Garvey was drumming his fingers, thinking, weighing, calculating. The Oliver Garvey Memorial Particle Accelerator versus peace on earth, good will toward men, and maybe the presidency. If he called the subcommittee it would be the Moslem treatment: not *one* pork chop for as long as the President was in office. It came down to instinct, which was what politicians lived by. Maybe the time had come to make the move. It came in all careers, and if you didn't make the move when you had the chance, you'd regret it forever. The pieces all seemed to be in place; the auspices looked good. He looked at Coolidge, who was chewing ravenously on a piece of cold toast, his appetite having flared up when it began to look as though he had a chance at survival. 'Do you like little boys?' he said to Coolidge.

Coolidge barely heard him. He had the jam pot and he was looking around at everybody's plates, trying to find another piece of toast.

'Do you?' Garvey said.

'Do I what?'

'Like little boys. They'll try to get anything on you.'

Coolidge was spreading raspberry jam over the toast. 'I like girls,' he said. 'Big girls.'

'You're going to be on television for a month,' Garvey said. 'I will try to crucify you. Before the administration does. You're going to have to convince me on camera. I'm going to be tough.'

'I'll take my chances,' Coolidge replied, and then looked at Emerson Foster, the two whistle blowers tracking eyes for a few seconds over the heads of the others. Foster summoned up what dignity he could muster and went out quietly. As the door closed, Coolidge stood up, went down along the table, and took Foster's seat. 'There's one more point about John Doe we have to discuss,' he said.

The Bishop Goes to Lunch

Negotiating the walk to his limousine was always a major operation for the bishop, his walker supporting him, his chauffeur following close behind. There were the two steps down at the mansion's front door, miniature reverse Everests for him, each foot blindly reaching out for reassurance; then the few yards to the car drawn up close to the entrance, where the chauffeur was adept at holding up the bishop while getting the rear door open. And only then did the real work begin. First the bishop had to be rotated 180 degrees so that rather than climb into the car he would sit into it, then be rotated again, this time by 90 degrees, the chauffeur picking up the bishop's legs and swinging them inside the car.

'Thank God that's over,' Coolidge said, positioning the walker in front of him, resting both hands on top of it; it was the bishop's usual stance. Coolidge had spotted a glint of sunlight off to the west as he maneuvered down the steps. It might have been field glasses, gun metal, or nothing at all. But he intended to continue his little act all the way.

The chauffeur went down the hill slowly. The bishop didn't like speeding; they'd take it at thirty-five all the way. As they went along the approach road to the Beltway, Coolidge showed a concerned interest in the police cars and ambulances gathered around the wrecked hot rods. He was into the role; he crossed himself. It wasn't a bad idea, anyway. He'd found out where Harry and Ives were, using the portable terminal. He didn't like the idea, but he was going to have to have lunch with them.

When they pulled up to the 211 Club, Coolidge took a second look at the walker. It *was* a weapon. But he decided against it; if he needed a weapon at all, nothing would help.

365

He checked himself in the rearview mirror. Soft black felt hat, clerical collar, black suit; even his face had a pious look to it. It was fear, of course. 'Tell the bishop I'll send the suit back tomorrow,' he said to the chauffeur, and got out.

It was remarkable, the deference he got going into the club. There was no way he could keep his hat; the hatcheck girl wouldn't be discouraged. Fetching little thing too. As the maître d' threaded a path for him through the tables, Coolidge saw that Harry didn't recognize him for a few seconds. Then he did a classic eyes-popping vaudeville double take, nudging Ives sitting next to him, Ives's lower jaw actually falling before he could recover his cool and get it back up. There was a bonus: Beebe was with them, facing the wrong way; Coolidge took him completely by surprise.

'I understand you gentlemen are looking for me,' he said. He didn't bother to grope for the chair; the maître d' was certain to have it under him in time.

Empty Chairs

'Any old white wine will do,' Coolidge said to the maître d' as the latter was holding out his chair for him. Coolidge scanned the table. Ives was eating an anaemic salad. Beebe was having Scotch with a club sandwich chaser, his pager on the table in front of him, probably waiting for the call from John Doe that the Doctor had been eliminated. Coolidge could imagine the way the conversation would go: Too bad about Walter. Nice fellow once. Maybe we shouldn't have given him Eberhart's job. Damn good garbageman, all right. Oh well, no one was indispensable.

He looked at Harry. Harry, shocked, had spilled a pitcherful of béarnaise sauce on whatever it was he was eating; you couldn't tell what it was anymore. It wasn't often that anyone surprised Harry Dunn. Beebe had taken it rather well; not so much as a twitch. A slight smile conceded that he'd been surprised.

'I see you've got your pager out,' Coolidge said to Beebe. 'Any reports of my demise are premature. Your man is outside a mansion about twelve miles from here. He thinks I'm inside.' Coolidge had the decency to stop talking when the waiter brought his wine. He took a gulp-sized sip. 'Ahhhh. Restorative. Makes me feel like a young priest again.'

'Quit playing games, you son of a bitch,' Ives said quietly. 'What's on your mind?'

Coolidge stared into his glass for a while, thinking. Harry was spreading the spilled béarnaise as thinly as it would go. It was another election of sorts, campaigning to change people's minds. But these particular minds weren't easy to change. These were the hardest of nose. The only way to do it was to talk their language.

'You're going about this all wrong,' he said. 'I mean, as a piece of problem solving, it's not up to the usual Harry Dunn standard. Killing me doesn't make sense.'

'I don't know what you're talking about,' Ives responded quickly. 'We don't do things like that. You're obviously trying to spread bad rumors about this administration.'

'You're talking circumlocutously,' Coolidge said. 'That's not like you, Ives. Has this place been bugged recently? I thought it was a free-talk zone.'

'Make your point, Walter,' Harry said, chomping away.

'You're not going at the problem with any delicacy at all, Harry. I think maybe you don't have enough input. Garvey is calling his subcommittee. I'm going to be the star witness. The other, uh, Emersons – we're going to have to change that name – will back him up. He's going to get public support. It'll be orchestrated. Labor. Catholics. Lawyers. Physicians. Scientists. Businessmen. I'm talking about a sizable fraction of the country. So the solution to your problem, Harry, is to make me look bad. If you were really being objective about this you wouldn't kill me, you'd give me a bodyguard. Otherwise the smell will be colossal.'

'For what it's worth, Coolidge, you're kidding yourself,' Ives commented. 'You put your trust in that old whore?'

'You made your coffin, Coolidge. Go lie in it,' Beebe said.

'Walter,' Harry said, 'I suggest you leave quietly. You're out of the Library. Goodbye and good luck.'

'You're talking for the tape, Harry, I'm talking for ears. They're going to do it. I know it's hard to believe. But the Emersons all feel that things have gone about as far as they can go. This is a deeply held feeling that comes from all regions of the country. The price of destroying the U.S.S.R. is too high. They don't want to pay it. Nobody wants to pay it. Except for a few of you.'

'Okay, Walter, thanks for the information. See you.' Harry was still stuffing himself, but he was looking worried. Ives was 99 percent political, 1 percent reality.

He was capable of panic, if he was played the right way. For the moment, however, he was still gung ho, moving along the road at high speed playing his game of nuclear chicken.

'You were stupid, throwing your career away, Walter,' Ives said. 'You have no idea how stupid. The people of this country want a strong defense. The only subject for argument is the amount of the annual increase in the military budget. The Joint Chiefs have more credibility with the public than anyone else in government. That's the way it is.'

Harry jumped in, looking intently at Coolidge but working on Ives's psyche. 'It's even stronger than that, Walter. It's in the American character to frighten easily, to lash out. We all come from foreigners but we hate foreigners. So maybe it's self-hate, but that doesn't matter. You're going to fight hate with reason, sanity, logic, numbers?'

They were a think tank calmly discussing the demise of one of the thinkers.

'You can fool all of the people some of the time,' Coolidge replied. 'How long is "some of the time," I wonder? It's going on forty years now. You're pushing your luck.'

For the first time since he'd known him, Coolidge saw Beebe with glass to lips. The Scotch didn't fly through the air after all; Beebe moved the glass close to his chest as he brought it up to his mouth. It was camouflage. Then the wrist action unloaded it like a flash flood. Ives had pushed his salad away. He was rubbing his eyes. He didn't seem to like what he was hearing. Watergate was always the phantom. The cover-up that was worse than the crime. It was excruciating, trying to decide if it was worth the risk. Did you cut your losses or did you try to win it all?

'I'll say this once more,' Coolidge said. 'If you don't agree, fine. I'll go my way, you go yours, and let's see who gets hurt the most. Silkwood got it *on the way* to blowing the whistle. I've already blown it. Now that's fundamental, gentlemen. A lot of pretty sharp people know what I know. So even if I have a very persuasive automobile accident tomorrow, you'll be in the same place you are now, but you'll have an added scandal.'

Ives looked at Harry. He was rubbing the space over his upper lip. Harry looked back at him, not even pretending to

369

be talking to Coolidge anymore. 'You won't have first-person testimony,' he said to Ives. 'It'll be hearsay. We can deal with hearsay; it won't be persuasive.'

'Bishop Hinds won't be persuasive?' Coolidge said. 'Rabbi Mandelbaum? Herb Purefoy?'

'Do you seriously think Bishop Hinds would go before a Senate subcommittee with this kind of stuff? It's preposterous.'

'Harry, don't you see what I'm wearing for God's sake? I got the bishop's *pants*.'

Ives slapped the table. 'Wait a minute, Harry,' he said. 'Let's talk about this.'

'We have talked about it. We gave it a lot of discussion. Let's not panic.'

'Things have happened, Harry.' He nodded at Beebe. 'Your men couldn't keep Coolidge from the Emersons. That's a new development.' The muscles in his face were turning to steel. Ives was alarmed; when the political mind was alarmed, there was no talking to it. Actions in the real world came to an end. 'Call him off, Harry.'

'You can't be serious.'

'We need more information. We've got to find out about Garvey. I'm going to talk to the President right now.' He started to go, then stopped. He pointed a finger at Dunn. He wasn't kidding. 'Call him off, Harry.'

Coolidge took a rather large sip of restorative in the silence that followed; it hit bottom with a wonderfully warm feeling that spread throughout his body. Harry looked as though, at long last, he'd lost his appetite. Coolidge turned to the mean mien sitting next to him. 'You heard what the man said, didn't you?'

Beebe gazed into Coolidge's face for an eternity. He was in good control of his face. Nothing moved. His eyes were indecipherable. You might guess what he was thinking about, but there was no solid data to work on. After a long time, a smile began to grow in that desert, getting wider and wider. 'Your life depends on a politician, huh, kid?' he said; then he picked up his pager and left, chuckling.

'Good job, Walter,' Harry said after a while. 'That's a magnificent detachment you have. You were like a doctor, operating on himself. A doctor. Heh. I hate to lose you, but I'll never understand you, not if I live to be a thousand.'

'Two thousand,' Coolidge said, thinking: Harry would never understand because it wasn't a problem that could be solved. As it turned out, he, Coolidge, was the conundrum, the ultimate conundrum. The human being who somehow manages to absorb new conflicting data, data that dissolves old connections, old ways of thinking, and forms the basis for change. There was nothing Harry or anyone else could do about it.

'You're smart, Harry,' he said. 'Even brilliant. You have imagination, you have fantastic work habits, you have energy, you have it all. But with all the data you have coming in, you're never going to understand the world. Know why? Because you're ignoring everything that doesn't fit. You might just as well not have a Library; you're one of the most uninformed human beings I have ever known.'

Harry's driver took him back to the Library. He was feeling fat; one of these days, when the pressures eased, he was going on a diet; he was carrying 120 extra pounds around, like a soldier with two full packs on his back. He avoided the Reference Room – the three empty chairs in there unnerved him – and went to his private screening room. One of these days, he was going to have to do some serious recruitment.

He scaled the steeply raked steps of the screening room and was home, back behind his console, the world at his fingertips. He called up NATO and it was ravishing. The Russians were over a barrel. The 27th Shock Army was pulling back deep into East Germany; the 54th Guards Tank Army had stopped dead in its tracks; the magnetometer readings were going down.

The Navy was still chasing every last deployed Soviet sub, but there was rotten luck at the North Pole: bad winds had subtracted 7 percent from O.F.F., pushing it back down to 91.00 percent. But that was all right; soon, soon. The Russians had eaten shit; that was the important point. They'd better get used to it; it was going to be a steady diet.

He switched to the *Worries* program to get a fast sample of the world's neuroses. Pictures and statistics started flying past. It was a phantasmagoria of conflict, proof that Homo sapiens was unable to live with himself; they were all on the warpath.

The Shining Path Maoist guerrillas in Peru. The Sikh political party, Akali Dal, in the Punjab. The Maximilian Hernández Anti-Communist Brigade in El Salvador. The Sindhi, Pathan, and Baluch minorities in Pakistan, the National Union for the Total Independence of Angola, the Tamil guerrillas in Sri Lanka, the Moro National Liberation Front in the Philippines, the Committee for the Struggle for Northern Epirus in Greece.

It was endless. Mauritius was demanding the return of Diego Garcia, America's most important strategic base in the Indian Ocean. Six separate armies in various combinations were clashing in Lebanon: the Israelis, the Syrians, the Phalangist Christian militias, various PLO factions, and the Lebanese army. There was a five-way dispute over the Spratly Islands in the South China Sea, involving Vietnam, the Philippines, Taiwan, China, and Malaysia. There was fighting in Chad, fighting in Iraq, fighting in Ethiopia. The Ethiopian army had taken it from two directions at once. The Somali army had beaten it in the Galgadud region and the Ethiopian Liberation Front had beaten it near Halhal. And there was another coup attempt in Ouagadougou, capital of Borkina Fasso, which was what they did when they weren't fighting border wars with Mali.

Harry switched it off. Enough. Instability was epidemic. But once the Russian hash was settled, things would go easier, the planet would settle down. He sat there watching a blank screen. But he began to see nightmarish visions on it: Garvey making headlines, Coolidge becoming a TV star on the evening news, ghastly performances by the President at news conferences, the Russians laughing up their sleeves.

He couldn't stand it; he did input. He was going to have to handle the True Garbage himself for a while, until he could find someone who could bear to watch that stuff without flipping out. At the least, it would distract him from his own problems.

*   *   *

372

The sexiest part of a woman was the face, Coolidge was thinking. That's where it showed. They couldn't help revealing it there; it came from inside, exposed, uncon-cealable, the face doing a cooch dance while the body was dusting the mantelpiece. 'Take your skirt off,' he said. He hadn't felt this turned on in ages.

'You look provoking in a collar, Father.'

'The blouse. Off.'

'If we lived together,' she said, unbuttoning, 'we could save on rent.'

'Your place or mine?'

'The plumbing's better here.'

He looked her over. 'I'll say it is. Off.'

She worked her slip up over her head.

'Which closet can I have?'

'The one opposite the small bathroom.'

'I'll take it.'

Pause.

'Uh, I know about you and Harry.'

'I got the message the first time. How the hell did you find out about that?'

'The Garbageman knows all. I want you to remember that. I'm not liberated. Bed check every night, lady.'

'Deal.'

'Why?' he said. 'That's what I'd like to know.'

'It was an aberration, a relapse. I think we were both deranged by East Germany. Were you very jealous?'

'I got the migraine of a lifetime. Off the bra.'

'By the way, Walter, how are you going to support me?'

'You've got it backwards. You're going to support me. While I finish my thesis. I never did get to Part Two of *Inner City Trash*. I'll become a doctor with a small *d*. Want to play doctor? Off the pants.'

She was standing there in heels and earrings, waiting while he defrocked himself.

'Why did you help me?' he said. 'What changed your mind?'

'I'll tell you the truth, Walter: It had nothing to do with love.'

'Wonderful. I'm extremely pleased that you were intel-lectually rigorous about it.'

'I decided I was more frightened of Harry than I was of the Russians.'

He planned to go through the apartment later, when she wasn't there, and pry out the microcams. No sense making it easy on Harry. He stood next to her, caressing, staying above the shoulders for a while; that always drove her crazy. There was no doubt in his mind that he'd be able to do it on camera; let Harry watch this time. It would be yet another conundrum for him: How do you watch people's personal lives without watching your former flame making it with your worst enemy?

'What's going to happen?' she said.

'I don't know. It's a crap shoot.'

'Then how about some Chinese, baby?'

'Let's leave the lights on,' he said.

THE CHILLING NOVEL OF THE
ULTIMATE *PSYCHO*-LOGICAL CRIME

from the award winning
WILLIAM BAYER

The two murder victims had little in common – one was a lonely call-girl, the other a prim schoolteacher.

But there was one brutally tantalising connection – their killer had decapitated them both and then switched their heads . . .

"Riveting. It is a novel in which the grit and madness of New York are palpable. It does high honour to the grand tradition of the American psychological thriller." Thomas Keneally

"Very exciting. The plot is impeccable. I recommend it highly." *The Spectator*

0 7221 14958   CRIME   £2.50

NOCTURNE FOR THE GENERAL

JOHN TRENHAILE

Stepan Ilyich Povin, the KGB general who featured in Trenhaile's
highly acclaimed first two novels, has been betrayed by his deputy
and is now cruelly entombed in an Arctic concentration camp.

He has suffered two years of beatings and interrogation and fears for
his life. But the Kremlin have been secretly keeping him alive.

For Povin unwittingly retains the final link in a chain whose
completion would be very useful indeed to his oppressors – and
equally revealing to British Intelligence who draw ever closer to the
deadly prison camp . . .

ADVENTURE THRILLER   0 7221 86479   £2.50

Also by John Trenhaile in Sphere:
A MAN CALLED KYRIL
A VIEW FROM THE SQUARE

WILLIAM DIEHL

IS BACK WITH AN EXPLOSIVE NEW THRILLER

HOOLIGANS

Jake Kilmer wasn't in Dunetown for the sightseeing –
nor to play the slot machines. He was there on racket
squad business, checking out a nice bunch of *cosa
nostra* boys called the Cincinnati Triad who were
taking the town for every cent they could get. Now, it
seemed, someone was taking the law into their own
hands to try and clear Dunetown of the mobsters –
someone who, like Kilmer, was trained to kill in
Vietnam . . .

ADVENTURE THRILLER   0 7221 30074   £2.75

ALSO BY WILLIAM DIEHL IN SPHERE BOOKS:
CHAMELEON
SHARKY'S MACHINE

A selection of bestsellers from SPHERE

FICTION

HUSBANDS AND LOVERS	Ruth Harris	£2.95 ☐
SWITCH	William Bayer	£2.50 ☐
VITAL SIGNS	Barbara Wood	£2.95 ☐
THE ZURICH NUMBERS	Bill Granger	£2.75 ☐

FILM & TV TIE-INS

BOON	Anthony Masters	£2.50 ☐
LADY JANE	Anthony Smith	£1.95 ☐

NON-FICTION

LET'S FACE IT	Christine Piff	£2.50 ☐
A QUIET YEAR	Derek Tangye	£2.50 ☐
THE 1986 FAMILY WELCOME GUIDE	Jill Foster & Malcolm Hamer	£4.95 ☐
THE ABSOLUTELY ESSENTIAL GUIDE TO LONDON	David Benedictus	£4.95 ☐

All Sphere books are available at your local bookshop or newsagent, or can be ordered direct from the publisher. Just tick the titles you want and fill in the form below.

Name _____

Address _____

_____

Write to Sphere Books, Cash Sales Department, P.O. Box 11, Falmouth, Cornwall TR10 9EN

Please enclose a cheque or postal order to the value of the cover price plus:

UK: 55p for the first book, 22p for the second book and 14p for each additional book ordered to a maximum charge of £1.75.

OVERSEAS: £1.00 for the first book plus 25p per copy for each additional book.

BFPO & EIRE: 55p for the first book, 22p for the second book plus 14p per copy for the next 7 books, thereafter 8p per book.

Sphere Books reserve the right to show new retail prices on covers which may differ from those previously advertised in the text or elsewhere, and to increase postal rates in accordance with the PO.